The Gates of Midnight

Jessica Stirling was born in Glasgow, and has enjoyed a successful career as a writer. Her previous novels include those in the Stalker trilogy, *The Spoiled Earth*, *The Hiring Fair* and *The Dark Pasture*. In this Beckman trilogy, the first two novels are *The Deep Well at Noon* and *The Blue Evening Gone*.

Jessica Stirling lives in Scotland.

Jessica Stirling

The Gates of Midnight

Pan Books London, Sydney and Auckland

First published 1983 by Hodder and Stoughton Ltd
This edition published 1984 by Pan Books Ltd,
Cavaye Place, London SW10 9PG
9 8 7 6 5 4
© Jessica Stirling 1983
ISBN 0 330 28167 4
Photoset by Parker Typesetting Service, Leicester
Printed in Great Britain by
Richard Clay Ltd, Bungay, Suffolk

For Rosemary

Contents

1 Worlds Apart 6
2 Soft Options 62
3 Seller's Market 91
4 Falling Leaf 145
5 Desperate Women 199
6 Calling the Roll 242
7 Postscript: 1947 276

1 Worlds Apart

Standing squarely before the little Queen Anne mirror, melon-breasted Mrs. Butterfield lifted the steel helmet from its candy-striped box and placed it reverently on her brassy curls. She adjusted the webbing strap under her chin, fished a lipstick from her cardigan pocket and touched up her mouth, precisely redefining the orchid bow. She pursed her lips, wetted them with the tip of her tongue, popped the Tattoo back into her pocket and hands on hips, swung round to show herself to her employer.

"What d'you think then, Hol?"

There was no formality in the relationship, one of the benefits of the war.

"Delightful," Holly answered.

Mrs. Butterfield peeped at her profile in the glass.

"Mad little face-framer, just right for those warm summer nights on the tiles. Think a topknot of Javanese cotton would go with black paint?"

"I rather doubt it."

"Well, hell," Mrs. Butterfield tipped the tin hat back from her brow, "Deanna Durbin ain't got much to worry about, I'll nob."

"Perhaps not," said Holly, "but you're bound to knock the wardens off their perches, Norma, which is, unless I'm much mistaken, the whole idea."

"Got to keep my hand in for when 'is Nibs gets home." One hand on the lid, the other extended, Mrs Norma Butterfield performed a swinging rumba which made the floor of the old shop creak and the array of Staffordshire figurines on the shelves dance in harmony. "Anyhow, a girl's entitled to a bit of fun—provided it's innocent."

Innocence was not a quality one would readily associate with the twenty-eight-year-old blonde. Holly smiled. Ten years ago she would have joined the younger woman in the impromptu dance and shared the moment of gaiety, but now a smile was the most that she could manage. Even that token would have pleased her elder brother, Maury, who, concerned for her health, had insisted on Norma Butterfield being "taken on" as assistant manageress in Holly Beckman King's "new" antique shop in the Fulham Road.

As usual, Maury had been absolutely right and Norma Butterfield's company had proved the tonic Holly needed to draw her out of depression after her husband's death.

Everything seemed to have happened at once in the autumn of 1939, Europe's woes and Holly's becoming, in the woman's mind, woven together. In August of that year Kennedy King had died of lung congestion, after a short illness. Eleven days later, Holly's son, Christopher, graduated from Cranwell and became a fledged and active pilot officer with the Royal Air Force.

Five weeks later, forty-eight divisions of the German army and sixteen hundred Luftwaffe aeroplanes attacked Poland, East Prussia and Slovakia, seizing Danzig and the Polish Corridor.

Holly, in mourning, listened to the news on her wireless in the downstairs parlour of her home in Chelsea, a house that, without Kennedy, seemed as cheerless as a tomb. On that same afternoon, the French mobilised and on the following day, Saturday, September 2nd, the RAF flew an Advanced Air Striking Force to France. Though Christopher hastened to London to reassure his mother that his squadron, based at West Horsfall in Kent, was not yet under "marching orders", Holly, vulnerable and desperately afraid, for a period lost her touch with reality.

It was not that she fell into fits or that grief stole away her reasoning, she simply could not unite with the nation in its tempered enthusiasm for war, for girding its loins, for "bashing Hitler", for putting the promise of a Golden Age aside to take up the sword of freedom, justice and honour. She abjured the platitudes of propaganda, recoiled from the manly talk that her son and brother, with the best will in the world, substituted for solace and reassurance. She remembered far too well the last war and the long wake of its aftermath, the so-called years of peace and fulfilment. She recalled her youth without that roseate glow which fell fancifully over the century's second and third decades. She had learned to live without illusion, and her capacity to absorb pain had been diminished by it. No cynic, Holly now expected only the worst.

Life, as Maury pointed out, had damned well better go on and, sensing his sister's lack of volition, he had taken it upon himself to see her right.

There was, of course, no problem at all about money.

Thanks to Holly's acumen and dedication—a dedication that had almost cost her her marriage to Kennedy—King's Fine Arts and Antiques had many thousands of pounds tied up in realisable assets. Apart from small legacies to his close friends, Simon Black and Emma Chubb, Kennedy willed the entire fortune to his wife and his stepson, Christopher Deems. But Holly had little use for the money, no desire to travel to escape the rigours of the brand-new war, to head for Canada or America where she might be able to indulge her selfish passion for things of the past. She had all but given up "the high life" and international trading. Even before Kennedy's last illness, she had been inclined more and more to small-scale dealing which, as Maury remarked, was just as well, considering the way the market was going. The vast barn-like shop in the Chalfont Arcade was sold up. General stock and special collections of antiques and pictures were sold *en bloc* to an American-based shipper who whisked them out of England before a U-boat blockade could close the Atlantic. The cherished items which Holly wished to retain, mostly porcelain and china, were stored in the basement apartments of her Chelsea home. It seemed as if Mrs. King, like so many business people, intended to put herself in mothballs for the duration.

War and collecting were ill bedfellows. In due course, Maury predicted, it might even come to the stage where you would be delighted to swop a Hepplewhite-Sheraton sideboard for something yellow to put on the cheeseboard. Even so, he was not content to see his sister languish. Condoning Holly's "selfish" lack of interest in the war effort, in not enlisting as a nursing assistant or a mother's aide or in re-training to become something in a factory, Maury fired ahead and secured her a little shop in Fulham, not too far from the spot in Pimlico where her career had begun and where, Maury assumed, she had once been happy.

As autumn dragged into winter the immediate impetus of the struggle in Europe and the threat to England waned. Boredom redressed the balance. Patriotism yielded to bravado and self-concern. Trade in London was not as bad as all that. The search for and purchase of "trinkets", which included antiques ancient and modern, was approximately categorised with poetry readings, underground concerts, people's art shows and the like, with "carrying on regardless" in a city that had been drained, in part at least, of its children and young men.

The shop was situated on the corner of the Fulham Road and Lyndhurst Grove, a quarter-hour's brisk walk from Holly's home in Chelsea. Maury had purchased the property from a leather-goods' retailer but at one point in its history it had been a public house—Manthorpe's Vaults—and had an ideal cellar, deep, well bricked and dry. Sandbagged and timbered now, the cellar had become a vault of another kind. Each and every morning, each and every evening, Holly and Mrs. Butterfield packed and unpacked the choicest items of stock—fragile glasses, dainty figures and silverware—and lugged them to and from the cellar in specially joinered trays.

Air raids, which had been particularly an obsession in the autumn of 1939, had not materialised. Certain bright-eyed optimists, the nation's ostriches, declared that Hitler knew better than to drop bombs on the British, an opinion that Maury did not share. A redoubtable realist, Maury had also had installed two big shutters of sheet iron which were ugly but terribly reassuring, hung on oiled hinges inside the windows. The plate glass itself was given a Tudor look by an inevitable lattice of sticky tape. Through its interstices, potential customers peeped as at a penny-show, to catch the glint, glimmer and subtle shine of the precious treasures within.

In the morning, now that spring was here, the sun cleft the rooftops across the narrow highway. Its rays shaped the spire of the Inverness Church and the paddle of grass in the private garden of Lyndhurst House, and lit up the frontage of King's Antiques very nicely, together with the clean sandbags and painted board frontage of the coffee house next door, Fracelli's Fine Foods and the narrow slot of the Home Defence Recruiting Office with its windowful of posters. In spite of changes to its surfaces, and the altered preoccupations of its people, London was still London. Holly's arctic hurts thawed out a little with the coming of spring. Nurtured and protected, she could almost hold to the belief that, come what may, she would be "all right" for the duration, and that Maury's gloomy prophecies that the war would last a long time might be, after all, an exaggeration. She could see herself mellowing into contented decline in the Fulham Road, ambition behind her, the achievements of her prime quite satisfying enough to sustain her through the next twenty-five or thirty years.

It might have been a different story if she had desperately needed to juggle a profit from the business. But that sort of pressure had been removed. Astonishingly quickly, she settled into routines that had seemed irksome at first: hoisting and barring the windows, shifting small stock, doling out her petrol ration to cover collections and deliveries of larger pieces, blackout, fire drills and all the other general civilian regulations with which a shopkeeper had to comply. In this area, Mrs. Norma Butterfield was of enormous help. In addition, the fact that Mrs. Butterfield spent most of her spare time engaged in training for night work as a member of the Fulham Branch of the Auxiliary Fire Service convinced Holly that she was justified in continuing to operate such a trivial concern as an antique shop. The wage she paid was generous and kept Mrs. B's body and soul together. But Holly's conscience did not tweak her into joining Norma Butterfield in fire-spotting sorties or in recruiting into one of the many volunteer services that abounded in the city. And it was April, winter past, business ticking over, novel aspects of trading in wartime showing up to stimulate the widow, that constant biting fear for Chris easing to occasional bouts of apprehension. And Mrs. Butterfield had been given her brand-new, black-painted tin helmet with her number and AFS stencilled in yellow on the bowl. And Holly felt, for the first time since Kennedy's death, that life might have a little purpose after all, even if that purpose was merely to survive decently and defiantly.

"Have you heard from Les lately?" Holly asked.

Norma Butterfield continued to dance.

"Nope. Not much of a letter-writer, neither of us. Thank God we ain't got no kids. Think," she changed the rhythm to a foxtrot, "I'd be in fits if we had kids."

Leslie Butterfield had been one of Maury's messengers before the war. He had enlisted with the first wave of ardent recruits in October, 1939, and was currently serving with the BEF as a Military Policeman "somewhere in France". Holly had met Les Butterfield only once, during embarkation leave. Three or four years Norma's junior, he was a tall, fresh-faced young man who radiated strength and self-confidence. He reminded Holly, just a little, of the way Maury had looked thirty years ago, before the Kaiser's war.

"Les loves being a copper. He always was a bossy boots. Do this, do that. Fond of spit and polish." Norma displayed an unflagging, almost religious faith in her husband's ability not only to endure military service but to enjoy it. "He'll have picked up some little French piece by now, I'll nob. Les ain't going to go without a nibble of the old currant bun for very long."

Initially, Holly found Mrs. Butterfield's confidences somewhat dismaying but she soon grew used to them. There were, it seemed, regulations governing the Butterfield marriage, an unaccustomed freedom which Les and Norma had worked out in principle, prior to his departure for training depot number one.

"Sex," said Norma Butterfield, "is what brought us together, like. Lack of it ain't going to drive us apart. Of course, when the war's over it'll be different. Then it'll be up to me to keep 'is Nibs happy, like. And him, me."

Such candour disarmed Holly. She was tempted to pry, not out of salacious curiosity but in an attempt to relate the younger woman's attitudes to her own experiences, to discover where essential differences lay. More than one kind of war was being fought. A more subtle conflict had shifted into the bedrooms of England, a conflict from which Holly believed herself excluded—until that April morning.

Mrs. Butterfield stopped dancing. She whipped off the tin hat with alacrity and a degree of embarrassment and, tugging down her salmon-pink jumper, sailed past Holly into the gloom of the main shop.

"Good morning, sir. Interested in anything in particular, like?" Norma Butterfield's enquiry invariably sounded like an invitation to sin. "Brassware, silver, pottery, perhaps? Nice trinket for the girl-friend or the wife?"

The hard sell was not to Holly's taste but she hadn't the heart to "have words" with Norma about it. Before the war, Les and Norma had operated a market stall in their spare time and had made a good thing out of it too. Butterfield Senior, as Norma called her father-in-law, had been a street dealer all his life and was still at it in the wilds of Portsmouth where he sold souvenirs to naval ratings. Mrs.

Butterfield's knowledge of bric-à-brac was bred in the bone, and her efficiency, learned at Daddy's heels on the cobbles of street markets, was robust.

Hoping that the poor customer would not be frightened off, Holly left Norma to it. She stepped behind the hessian curtain which partitioned off the sales and display area from the tiny office.

On the desk was a cardboard carton filled with twists of newspaper which protected four stained pottery figures that Holly had purchased from a very elderly gentleman in a handsome flat in South Kensington. The old gent had no real idea what the figures were worth; been in the family for years, he said. Ingrained with dirt though they were, the four figures were unchipped and showed no signs of hairline cracks. Holly had paid well for them, backing her belief that they were valuable late eighteenth century pieces by the Staffordshire potter, Neale. She had just put her hand into the box, lifted out the portrait figure of a girl with roses on her apron, and held it up to the single shaded bulb hanging over the bench, when a voice at her shoulder said, "Holly?"

She glanced round.

The man was in his middle forties. He sported a neat beard. His eyes were grey and his hair, clipped short, was grizzled grey and brown. With beard and tanned complexion, he might have been a high-ranking naval officer, though he wore a roomy, lightweight herring-bone topcoat and carried his hat in his hand.

"Holly, don't you recognise me?"

"I—I'm sorry."

He came forward, close to her, into the fall of pale yellow light from the bulb.

"Says he knows you, Hol," said Mrs. Butterfield from the curtain's edge.

"A long time ago," the stranger said. "Twenty years, in fact."

She had seen him last in St. James's Park in the golden October of 1920, with the Palace caught in the rays of the afternoon sun and the Mall carpeted in red and yellow leaves. She had been there with Emma Chubb, who had been as breezy and assertive as Norma was now, with Christopher tucked into a high-wheeled Swann baby-carriage. She had been married to Captain Deems for only a few months. But the meeting that long-ago afternoon had been etched into her memory, given poignancy by the fact that the child in the baby-carriage had not been fathered by her husband but by the man who had come to say goodbye, by the stranger who confronted her now.

"David," she said. "David Aspinall."

She held the rose-dress figurine in her fingers and stood motionless, staring, as the man stooped and, without otherwise touching her, kissed her brow. Flustered, Holly stepped to one side, saying, 'An old friend, Norma. Here, take this." She stuck out the stained pottery portrait, which Norma Butterfield accepted. "Give it . . . give it a wash, please. At the downstairs tap."

Mrs. Butterfield could not suppress a grin. She was being given the brush-off, dismissed. Saying nothing she went out and down the wooden staircase to the basement cellar, leaving Mrs. King and the stranger alone.

"How did you find me?" asked Holly. "I mean, how did you find the shop?"

"Mumford gave me the address. I was astonished to discover the old fellow still in the land of the living."

"He retired from legal practice four years ago."

"Yes, I know. Andrea kept me in touch with—with that sort of thing."

Andrea was David's sister, a snobbish, selfish woman with whom Holly had had a great deal of unpleasantness in the 1920s, soon after she had inherited a share in Aspinall's Antique Shop.

Seeing David before her now, much altered by the years, suave and charming but no longer raffish, Holly was possessed by an awareness of how fleeting life can be.

All that had happened to her—Christopher Deems' death, her affair with the American, all the dealing and double-dealing, her marriage to Kennedy—became as wispy as ground mist. She was carried back out of the secure uncertainty of the war, back to her days as a girl just out of the Lambeth slums, struggling against prejudice and burning with ambition and passion, a romantic who had squandered her youth in learning that romance was not a thing that could be tracked down, acquired and preserved, like a piece of Spode or Worcester. Now, at forty, Holly realised only too well that first loves and first lovers were figments of another world and, in the pearl-grey reality of one's middle years, not to be trusted.

"I'm afraid," said Holly, stiffly, "that you have the advantage of me. I haven't kept in touch at all."

"I'm not surprised," said David Aspinall.

"Meaning?"

If he sensed her wariness, her hostility, David gave no sign of it. He certainly was not deterred. The old-fashioned charm was still in evidence but tinctured now with bluntness, a directness that Holly had never associated with the weak, vacillating young man with whom she had once been madly in love.

"Meaning that I treated you shabbily, Holly, and you've every right to harbour a grudge."

"It isn't that. I've been too busy."

"I understand."

God, he was patronising her. She was the slum kid again, nineteen again. He was patronising her as he had done in the shop days; the handsome, dissolute young army officer, son of the owner, willing, out of the goodness of his heart, to give the plain little slum kid her chance. Some chance it had turned out to be. The ugly duckling from across the Thames had developed into a beauty, had acquired a degree of social poise that had given her an entrée into the finest homes in Europe and allowed her to mingle easily with millionaires and aristocrats. For the first time in several years Holly Beckman King felt a welling of genuine anger. Whatever news Andrea had had of her and had imparted by way of letter across the seas to Hong Kong, it could not begin to depict how difficult life had been and what she had really achieved.

She said, "I doubt if you do, David."

"I'm free until two o'clock. May I take you to lunch?"

"Why?"

"Because I'd like to. I've been out of England for twenty years, Holly, and I don't feel terribly at home here."

Girl struggled against woman, romantic against realist. "Why *are* you in England?"

"My term of contract finally expired," said David. "Besides, the country's at war, need I remind you? And I was a serving officer."

"Are you back in the army?"

"Believe it or not," said David, "I'm an officer in the Royal Navy."

"The navy?"

"Yes."

"Will you have command of a ship?"

"No chance of that," said David. "Besides, I wouldn't know what to do with one. Naval Intelligence. Very hush-hush. I'm one of a team, with an office in the Admiralty. In actual fact, Holly, I've been with the navy for seven years. Overseas Volunteer Reserve."

"But what do you *do*—or shouldn't I ask?"

"At the moment," said David, "not much. My experiences in Hong Kong weren't wasted, however. Apart from learning a very great deal about the movements of shipping and the like, I also made many friends in high places. Such expertise is rather valuable now. Thus, when I offered my services, through appropriate channels, my offer was promptly accepted."

Another sinecure, thought Holly. David had spent the Kaiser's war behind a desk, safe in Whitehall.

"But we're not fighting in the Far East," she said.

"Not yet," David answered.

"Oh, you don't suppose—"

David put his finger to his lips and imitated the furtive, hunch-shouldered spy figure that had recently become popular from Ministry of Information leaflets.

"It won't imperil the security of the nation, however, if I talk to a lady over lunch. Lassister's still do something rather decent in spite of rationing. Fish?"

Holly was curious. She had heard nothing of the Aspinalls for years.

Seventeen years ago, Maury had told her quietly one evening that David's wife, an invalid, had died. Beyond that she knew nothing of the family with whom she had once been so closely linked. Though she had hated them—hate was too strong a word—at the time, she felt unwonted wistfulness, a transient bubble of nostalgic regret. Chris was safe now, safe from hurt from the knowledge of the bargain that she had struck with Captain Deems.

The "deal" had been done to protect her unborn son, to prevent him from being born a bastard. As far as Chris was concerned,

Deems was his father—Captain Christopher Deems, poet and war hero, warrior and martyr. It was a relationship that Kennedy had never tried to usurp. Nobody now alive knew the truth, except Maury, and she trusted her elder brother with the secret as she trusted him with everything else. It had taken a war to delineate the wavering circle of circumstance, a mark as fine as a pencil line, to bring it to that April morning in the Fulham Road, to the little shop which was not so different from Aspinall's, in spite of sandbags and taped windows, a small, tick-over, cosy sort of establishment of just the right size and scope to contain her aspirations.

"All right," she said. "But I must be back without fail by two-thirty."

"A sale?"

"My assistant has a fire drill at three.".

"A shade different from the old days, Holly, what?"

"More than a shade," said Holly Beckman King.

The triangulation of sector airfields dotted across the county had convinced Maury Beckman that his country place at Applehurst was as safe as anywhere.

The village could hardly be classified as the industrial heartland of South-East England. Any bombs that fell there would surely be strays, ejected cargo from returning bombers, or dribblings from damaged Stukas. Standing on the uneven lawn in front of the large, rambling cottage, one could not imagine an intrusion of death and disaster.

Limes sheltered the house, no ruled avenue of trees but a casual collection of the blessed things beneath whose soaring branches humbler vegetation flourished, a rough girdle of growth that Maury had forbidden his gardener to tame. The protective hedges would have gladdened the heart of the Jutish landowner in the distant days before the foundation of the Kingdom of Kent. Maury saw his *sulung* ploughed with unsentimental awareness of its significance, though the job was done with a tiny, coughing tractor and not eight oxen yoked in a team. Behind the limes, in a spur of old forest, was a *denn* for pigs. Maury had acquired the glossy, black and white Wessex saddlebacks along with many other agricultural items in the late summer of 1939, conscientiously forestalling the commands of the Ministry of Food.

The Beckman town house in Richmond was not what you would call vulnerable but it was, more or less, within the confines of the capital and Ruth Beckman had taken to spending more and more time at Applehurst.

"It's either that or join the WVS, which I don't flamin' fancy," Ruth declared. "If Maury wants it, I'll take my shot at the war effort by being a goddamned Earth Mother."

Property magnate Maury had put his personal interests into cold storage. He had lost the best of his young managers and agents and had experienced some qualms of conscience—the Socialist in him had died hard—about making another fortune out of the war's victims.

Now he headed a War Department sub-committee of Acquisition and Adaptation, which meant that he had some call on the labour pool and a great deal of influence and responsibility.

Farm land, mansion houses, schools, church properties and any other oddments, vertical or horizontal, that the powers in Whitehall took a fancy to, Maury acquired. He had a legal department of seven aged lawyers and twelve aged clerks. Four land-brokers and a multitude of sub-contracted estate agents were answerable to Mr. Beckman, as well as building contractors, glaziers, slaters, joiners and every sort of Tom, Harry and Dick in the building trades. What Maury got out of it was the thrill of the power of it all, rekindled zest for the trade he had rooked since young manhood, plus an annual petrol allocation that would have kept a division of tanks on the road.

Here, there and everywhere, Maury seemed able to do the impossible at the mere whisk of a handkerchief, to pull not rabbits but houses and office blocks out of thin air. He had had his "rest", the throttled-back years between his wedding to Ruth and the outbreak of hostilities. Now he was ready to roar again, to take off like a Hurricane.

Over the years, Holly had leaned heavily on Maury's competence. In the present circumstances, however, she was shy of directly summoning his aid. She had travelled down to Applehurst after lunch on Saturday afternoon in the hope of "bumping into"

Maury, accidentally. Mrs. Butterfield was left in charge of the shop. Holly needed no special invitation to spend the weekend in Kent and Ruth was only too pleased to see her. The day was fine, the sky clear and, in cardigans, the two women took tea upon the lawn. The ceremony was much less grand than it sounded. Informality suited Ruth a treat, particularly as the lawn was the province of the children of the house, her own pair plus seven evacuees whom Maury had fostered and for whom he had made special provision.

A wing had appeared behind the cottage—more Maury magic. The prefabricated structure, an oblong of wood and glass, looked like a barrack block, but was furnished with nice little beds, bathrooms and toilets and other mod. cons. Originally Maury had "contracted" for twelve children but five had returned home to London shortly after Christmas when the expected air raids had not occurred. The seven that remained had formed their own community, Maury becoming their provider, Ruth their surrogate mother along with Mrs. Akers—Wilf Akers' mum—who had been employed as cook and general factotum.

All had not been smooth, of course. There had been problems of adjustment for some of the children but, being sharp little Londoners, the majority soon realised that they were on to a good thing and had written home begging to be allowed to stay. The village school had been increased by three teachers to cope with the influx—Maury wasn't the only property owner to take in evacuees in that part of Kent—and a horse-bus stopped at the bottom of the lane each weekday, to collect the Beckman mob.

In its midst, almost if not quite indistinguishable from it, were Maury and Ruth's treasures, Holly's nephew Charles, and her niece Laura. Laura was too young for school but Charles went off with the others to learn his sums. He was far happier participating in the rough and tumble of the village school than he was at home in Richmond where he attended an establishment more in keeping with Maury's income and status.

Milk and orange juice flowed freely. Big, fist-sized buns which rolled steaming from the kitchen ovens were dispensed, and the games and squabbles went noisily on while Holly and Ruth strolled like Titans among the Minnows, sipping from tea-mugs, the inevitable cigarette in Ruth's lips

"Yeah, I see the problem," said Ruth, to whom Holly had confided the latest strange event. "Did he ask you out again?"

"He did."

"And you accepted?"

"I—yes, I did."

"Rather a cheek, blowing in from Hong Kong after all these years," said Ruth, "an' expecting just to pick up where he left off."

"I'm not sure that he does."

"What then?" said Ruth. "He's a sailor, isn't he?"

"Hardly," said Holly. "He's a commissioned adviser to the Admiralty, whatever that means."

"Handsome?"

"He's put on a little weight," Holly answered, obliquely.

"Who hasn't?" said Ruth. "Except you."

The bountiful years had filled Ruth out. In her mid-thirties now, she was no longer quite as petite and feline as she had been when Maury had fallen in love with her. At that period she had been Ritchie Beckman's wife, a prisoner of the brother's obsessive jealousy, kept captive in Paris and various parts of America and, latterly, in London, where she had been born. She was dark and still vivacious and could be very seductive. Holly was as slender as she had always been, weighed hardly a pound more than at twenty, and had not shed her poise in the stressful times. She dressed smartly, was exceedingly well-groomed and except for the sprinkling of silver in her black hair, might have passed for thirty-two or three.

"It's that Maldano egg-flip you scoff," said Holly. "It'll blow you up like a barrage balloon eventually."

Ruth chuckled. "There isn't much of it left. I asked Maury to put down a stock of it but he blew me a raspberry, said you didn't 'put down' egg-flip, unless in the veterinary sense. I expect he'll show up with a dozen bottles, though. You know how he spoils me."

"Only too well," said Holly.

Ruth glanced ruefully at the battling children. "Who else but Maury'd go find a ready-made family just to keep his wife happy?"

"I—I had hoped to have a word with Maury," said Holly.

"About this sailor guy, the old flame?"

"Yes."

"What's it got to do with Maury?"

"Oh, not much. I just—Maury may know about him."

Ruth put her hand on Holly's arm and looked at her closely. "This David, he hasn't got anything to do with Ritchie, has he?"

"Of course not."

Ruth was still apprehensive in case her former husband, Maury's brother, would reappear and seek revenge upon her for her desertion.

It was years since any member of the Beckman family had had word of Ritchie. He had taken refuge from the law by lying low in Paris. Though his name was never mentioned, Ritchie had been in Holly's thoughts of late. Unwitting anxiety toned down her fear for Ritchie since the German occupation of Poland and the declaration of war against France. Flippantly, Maury suggested that Ritchie would fall on his feet, would wind up selling the Eiffel Tower to a German armoured corps or, more seriously, would scarper off to America or Canada with his young French wife, at the first sign of trouble. There was sense in what Maury said. It would be typical of Ritchie to run. He was after all Jewish, a fact that kept a dark undertone of concern in Holly's mind.

Ruth had no such concern for Ritchie's welfare. Her only worry was that he would suddenly reappear and in some manner damage the happiness she had found.

"You sure?" Ruth persisted.

"Cross my heart."

"Crazy to worry about him," said Ruth. "But I can't help it. It's this war, like a big pot, everything stirred up in it so you never know what's goin' to come out in the spoon. Like this guy from your past."

"I almost married David Aspinall."

"Really? What happened?"

"He married somebody else instead."

"Stood you up?"

"Pretty well."

Ruth dropped her cigarette to the ground and crushed it with her Wellington boot. "Steer clear, darling, that's my advice. Once bitten, twice shy."

"It's a little more complicated than that."

"You don't want to be bitten again?"

"He's changed—I think."

"Leopards don't change their spots, even when they get old. Did you *really* love him?"

"I thought I did—twenty years ago."

"You were only a kid, like me when I met Ritchie," said Ruth. "None of us knew *what* we wanted when we were that age. I certainly didn't. And look where it landed me. There's an excuse for stupidity when you're twenty but not when you've grown up."

The conversation was interrupted by the sound of a car engine. The children heard it first. Whooping and shrieking, they streamed away through the trees towards the elbow of the lane that linked the front of the cottage to the village road.

"Maury," said Ruth. "He promised he'd try to look in. I don't see much of him, these days."

Car tyres squeaked and in a minute or so Maury strode round the side of the cottage, preceded by the children. He carried Laura, the youngest, in his arms while Charles clung possessively to the hem of his topcoat. The evacuees followed on, glad to see the father-figure, also eager to find out what gifts he had brought this Saturday afternoon.

Maury was big and broad-shouldered. Even the best hand-cut tailoring could not disguise his alderman's girth. He was still nippy on his feet, however, still a stalker, a strider, always on the move. His round-brim, fur-felt soft hat rode upon the head of Beryl Minns, the tribe's totem-pole, a lanky Lambeth lass of thirteen. His suede gloves flopped on the paws of Alfie White, ten, while the Bedwell twins, Eddie and Albert, fought for the privilege of bearing the royal umbrella, English twill-silk regalia much battered by tender loving care.

"Get back, you savages," Maury shouted heartily, then, spying Holly, cried, "And why wasn't I informed that Mrs. King was here, tell me that, you lot?" He cuddled Laura against his cheek. "Didn't tell me Auntie Holly was here, did you, Dewdrop?"

Still surrounded by the children, Maury came over to the garden chairs where Ruth and Holly had seated themselves. He kissed Ruth on the lips and Holly on the cheek, and gently divested himself of his offspring.

The bulge in the breast pocket of Maury's overcoat was now the object of all eyes and the clamour had died. If Maury's fosterlings had learned anything, it was that manners tended to be favoured more than demands and that the biblical principle—the First Shall be Last, etc.—was strictly applied when it came to dishing out the weekend's loot.

"Gloves here. Hat there. Brolly on the bench," said Maury. "Tallers onna right, shorters onna left, in single rank, *size*."

The children lined up on Beryl, jostling, measuring haircuts, standing on toe-tip, until a pecking order had been established, not with Laura on the end but a poor seven-year-old runt named Muriel Pople who, the Beckmans feared, would never grow much taller than three-feet-six because of illnesses in infancy.

As usual, Maury started at the short end, with Muriel.

The brown paper bag was enormous. How Mr. Beckman managed to keep it inside his coat was more than the children could imagine, not even Beryl. He unfolded it from the flaps of his topcoat and shook it by its brown paper ears like a rabbit. The gesture obtained rapt silence and had a goggling effect on nine pairs of eyeballs.

It was the third time that Holly had witnessed the ritual. Not for Maury just a plain old poke of sweets and fruit. Within the paper bag were nine little parcels, done up with tinsel string, like Christmas, each with a label which Maury's secretary, Mrs. Percy Kent, had hand-printed that forenoon.

Maury bowed and extended his large hand.

"For you, mamsell."

The parcel was triangular. The label said it was for Muriel. The child picked it delicately from the man's palm and obediently stepped away.

"And you, young miss."

Laura tucked her head between her shoulders, tongue between her teeth and, with a wondering glance up at Daddy, took the pill-box-shaped parcel and retired.

"Master Edward Bedwell."

"Fanks, Mister Beckman."

"No thanks necessary, a quick salute will do."

Salutes became the order of the day for the rest of the rank. Even Beryl, who felt herself a bit too old to indulge in juvenile games, snapped one off and retired with her tiny, intriguing trophy.

When everyone had been to the bag, Maury said, "Ten paces step back, *march*."

Nine pairs of legs counted ten paces.

"Parcels will be opened on the count of three. Ready?"

"*Ready*."

"Three."

Chuckling, Maury sank on to the garden seat between his sister and his wife and accepted with gratitude the cigarette that Ruth had lighted for him.

"Hope I've got it right." Maury nodded towards the parcel-openers. "You can tell by the amount of trade and barter that goes on. Gobstoppers, liquorice roll, chewing gum, rock, orange-leaf chocs—God, what must their insides be like! Anyhow," he patted Holly's hand, "it's good to see you. How did you come down?"

"By train. I walked from the station. Such a lovely day."

"Didn't you call the office?" said Maury.

"No. I thought you'd be away."

"I was. Over at Walton. I'm tracking down a site for a new Ciphers' Training School."

"Did you find one, darling?" Ruth enquired.

"After a fashion. The lads'll give me no thanks, though. Know what? It's a monastery. The monks are willing to share. I have to square it with some cardinal or other, on Monday. Shouldn't be a problem."

"With that Shylock hooter of yours," said Ruth, "the old cardinal'll probably kick you straight out."

"RCs seldom give problems," said Maury. "I regret to say that the most trouble I have is with the Samuels and the Solomons. They're convinced I'm trying to screw them. Besides, some of them don't seem to think it's their war at all. There's a few—I can't hardly believe it—who say they'd rather see Russia on the premises than an Imperialist lackey army."

Abruptly, he switched off the topic. Ruth did not like him to bring the pettiness of war administration home with him. He said, "Staying overnight, Holly?"

"No, it's a flying visit. I'm expecting Chris tomorrow. He said he'd try to get home for the day."

Maury frowned, hesitated, squeezed her arm. "I wouldn't count on seeing him this Sunday, love. Not with what's going on. Didn't you hear the news this morning?"

"What now?"

"There's another battle on at Narvik and an air raid on Scapa Flow. Now, now, that doesn't mean Chris will be involved. The Air Ministry won't send their best fighter squadrons into this scrap. But I don't imagine there will be too many passes floating about the stations and 'dromes."

"Norway, then Denmark, in one week," said Ruth. "'Where's the little bastard going to strike next?"

Maury could have given his wife an informed guess by way of answer but he let that subject lapse too. He had no desire to distress Holly, particularly as she seemed to be getting over Kennedy's death and settling into the shop. God knows how long that phase would last, though, with hairy tales of a German invasion going the rounds in Whitehall.

"Tea, dear," he said. "I could use a nice hot cuppa, Ruth, if you'd be so kind as to rustle one up."

Ruth Beckman needed no further hint.

"Something to eat, Maury?"

"No, I managed to grab a bit of lunch today, believe it or not."

Summoning the brood, Ruth led the children out of that part of the garden to give her husband and sister-in-law a few minutes of privacy.

Maury wasted no time. "What's the problem, Holly?"

"You always know when something's wrong."

"Perhaps because something's usually wrong these days. Is it the shop? Don't you like the shop?"

"Oh, no, the shop's marvellous." Holly hesitated, then slowly and warily told Maury of David's visit.

"David bleedin' Aspinall! Well, I'll be damned!" said Maury, when his sister had finished her account of the unexpected meeting.

"Did you know he was back in England?" Holly asked.

"How could I have known, love?"

"I thought, perhaps, you'd bumped into Miles Walshott."

"Haven't seen Walshott in four or five years. Our paths don't seem to cross any more. David Aspinall. How damned inopportune."

"Inopportune?" said Holly. "That's an odd word to use, Maury."

"I mean, with—with Kennedy, an' all."

"Coincidence," said Holly. "I'm sure."

"With Aspinall you can never be certain."

"He's changed, Maury."

"After twenty years, I should hope so. Does he still sport that fancy moustache?"

"No," said Holly, with a slight smile. "A full beard."

"Admiral of the damned Fleet."

"Commissioned advisor to the Admiralty; very hush-hush."

"And the band played 'Believe it if You Like'."

"Maury, he's asked me to dinner."

"What did you tell him?"

"I haven't given him an answer. I put him off. He said he would telephone tomorrow."

"Is that why you can't stay for the weekend?"

"No, Maury, I *do* expect Chris home."

Maury stared at the dun-coloured grass between his shoes. "What do you want me to say, Holly? I reckon you've already decided what you're going to do about Aspinall. You're going to encourage him, aren't you?"

"Not that, Maury."

"Well—see him again."

"I need company, Maury."

"You're welcome here any time, or at Richmond. You know that."

"It isn't the same."

"You mean you need a man?"

"Maury, that's a detestable thing to say."

Maury got to his feet suddenly. He was irked by Holly's resistance, by the very strength of character he had tried to rekindle. "You should join the WVS or something, if it's company you want."

Holly sighed. She understood why Maury was so down on her.

"A lunch and, perhaps, a dinner," Holly said, "hardly hurls me into bed with him."

"Knowing you, it's only a matter of time."

Holly, too, rose from the bench. "I think I'll catch the early train back to London, Maury."

Maury relented, took her arm. "No, look, I'm sorry. That remark was out of order. I'm weary, old girl, tired of trotting about. Most of the time it's fun but every so often it catches up with me. You understand? When I hear about Narvik or Copenhagen and I begin to think—"

"You don't have to explain to me," said Holly. "I had the feeling you'd think me all kinds of fool. But David's here and I admit I'm glad to see him."

"You didn't really trot down here for advice, did you?"

"I thought I'd tell you in person, before one of your London cronies spreads rumours."

Maury sighed too. "Did you tell Ruth?"

"Of course, she doesn't know David," Holly replied, "but she advised caution."

"How times—and people—change with shifts in the wind," said Maury. "Ruth advising you to be cautious; what a turnabout."

"Ruth's quite right," said Holly. "What's more, I *intend* to be cautious. In any case, David may not wish to resurrect our old relationship."

"If you thought that, Holly, you wouldn't have come rushing down here."

Holly glanced at her brother. "You know me too well, Maury."

"I don't know you at all, half the time."

"Here's Ruth and the children, bearing tea."

Maury raised his hand in greeting as the procession emerged from the kitchen yard at the side of the cottage, weaving between the gable of the oblong dormitory and the fuel shed.

"What time's your train back to town?" he asked.

"Half past nine."

"We'll eat dinner with the kids, then I'll drive you to the station, if that suits."

"Fine," said Holly.

There were still traces of light in the western sky, a silken feeling to the young spring night. Afterglow delineated the budding apple trees in the orchards which flanked the road between Applehurst and the market town of Hillfrome. Cooling air had summoned wisps of ground mist from the ponds and tillage of small Kent farms. It lingered across the hedgerows, obliging Maury to drive at somewhat less than his usual crisp pace. It was warm in the old Humber and smelled of scuffed leather and cigar smoke. The little bronze glow of the dash lights made it cosy.

Outside, however, there was still that desolation which the blackout had brought, as if the countryside of England had slid back into an era before man had colonised the land, and the looming, unlighted shapes of cottages and occasional bungalows that the car passed were not dwellings at all but burial mounds or barrows where no glim was needed, no lamp or lattern required to guide and comfort the inhabitants.

The station at Hillfrome was deserted. A coal fire in the waiting-room cast a reddish whorl on the windows. A gas lamp, dimmer than a candle, whispered behind the boards of the ticket office.

Maury parked the Humber, lifted his hand, peered at his wrist-watch. "Five minutes, if it's on time. It usually isn't, unless it's carrying troops or airmen on a movement."

"Thank you."

"For what, love?"

"For everything you've done for me."

"My God, you make it sound like the sailor's farewell. Don't tell me you're turning into one of those women who must dramatise everything."

"I don't know what I'm turning into; what I've turned into, for that matter," said Holly.

"I'll be staying over in Richmond most of this week. We're leaving the children where they are for the rest of the summer. It isn't fair to shunt them about like parcels. Give me a call at home and we'll dine in. The Deanes are looking after the house. Mrs. D's a pretty fair cook. Will you call me?"

"Of course, Maury."

Outside, in the cobbled square before the station, a farm cart rumbled into view out of the darkness. Three giggling girls scrambled from the flatbed and waved to the driver, who made no response.

"You'll have some company on the train," said Maury.

"Who are they?"

"Land workers going up to the city for a night on the tiles."

"But they're girls."

"The barriers are down, Holly."

"They seem so young."

"Young folk today are worlds apart from us, love," said Maury. "Worlds apart."

"It's the war, I suppose."

"And other things. Good things."

"You approve?"

"With reservations, yes."

"Utopia is just a war away?" said Holly, as she opened tne passenger door and prepared to get out of the car.

The girls shouted raucously as the farm cart trundled off into darkness again. The farmer or farm-hand made no acknowledgment. He probably didn't approve of girls, certainly not of their "wild goings-on".

"A long war away," Maury murmured.

He took his sister's arm and escorted her across the cobbles ana into the little station. The train was visible on the half-mile straight that drove through Hillfrome and curved up towards Maidstone.

"Got your ticket?"

"Yes."

"Take a cab at the other end. Don't risk walking in the blackout."

"Yes, Maury."

The train squealed, hissed and braked alongside the platform. An elderly porter had appeared, like a troll, from nowhere. He wagged a bull's-eye lantern vigorously as he called out the name of the station in a dialect only a native could understand.

"Be careful, Holly."

"Careful? Of what?"

"Aspinall."

"Oh, Maury, he isn't an ogre, you know. And I'm not a child any longer."

Maury kissed his sister and gave her a hug.

Leaning from the compartment window, the land-girls spotted the kiss and chirped and whistled in ribald good-humour.

Maury pulled back, opened the door for Holly and helped her

up into the empty first-class compartment. He slammed the door behind her.

She stood by the open window. Already the city seemed to have repossessed her. She looked far too smart, too fashionable for the casual country station and the shabby steam train which would toil its age-old route through the bumpkin villages and towns of rural Kent.

Hands in pockets, shoulders raised, Maury told her, "Remember, love, it's Chris who could be hurt."

"Maury, that's a cruel thing to say."

"True, though. He knows nothing of David Aspinall. It would wound him now to find out that his father wasn't Deems."

"Why should Chris be involved at all?" said Holly.

"These things have a way—" Maury's remark was obliterated by the shrilling steam, whistle and deafening grumble of the train. The guard bawled another mysterious chant and the carriage shuddered and lurched forward.

"Call me," Maury shouted, "at the office. Monday."

Holly gave no sign that she had heard.

She had already retreated into the compartment and closed the window with a snap.

South of Trondheim, that very afternoon, British troops had trekked through fretted snow to link with Norwegian forces fighting near Oslo. U-boat activity was considerable in the fjords, and German war-planes were making it hot for destroyers. Logs from the *Cossack* and the *Altmark* and other line ships which had relentlessly pursued the enemy up the nine-mile stretch of the Rombacks Fjord in the second attack on Narvik had reached appropriate departments in the Admiralty; David had spent the day with Commodore Haynes and four commanders, poring over reports of the on-going combat.

Lieutenant-Commander Aspinall had no role to play in the debates. He took no sides in "assessment" squabbles, or the recriminations which were bandied about the big chart-table in Room 111 in the old Admiralty building. At this time he was present as an observer, to "be informed", to learn the ropes. He had no specialist knowledge of North Sea and Baltic trade routes and was not so gauche as to try to impress himself upon his superiors.

After hours of silent observation, he grew bored with the emphatic, petulant voices touting traditional answers to ultra-modern questions born out of a situation which nobody in that room seemed quite to comprehend. He was relieved when the meeting broke up shortly after seven and he was able to hurry off to Fulham to pick up Holly at the shop, and head for the civilised amenities of Houssard's Grill Room.

David did not brag to Holly that he had spent the day in the company of high-ranking officers of the naval staff. The woman suspected that he had donned dress uniform to impress her which, without doubt, would have been true of the old David. Of all uniforms in all armed services, that of an officer of the British navy was most designed to give a man presence, to imbue him with a dignity less assertive than army and less tailored than Royal Air Force. Naval dress smacked of functionalism and lent, in colour and cut, a certain sort of arrogance, a quality which David Aspinall, complete with beard and the weathered features of a veteran traveller, emanated in no small measure.

Holly Beckman King, however, had changed too. She was no longer related, outwardly at least, to the plain brown town-mouse shop servant whom David had seduced. She was barely second cousin to the young woman he had deserted, out of guilt and shame, in his gambling days. Latent style was latent no longer; nor was her beauty. Both had flowered in the intervening years. She was all, and more, that David had dreamed of and dwelled on during his long exile among the islands of the China Seas.

Two of many images that composed the memory of Holly Beckman were juxtaposed in their meeting; the tidy, dim-lit cave of the shop with its clutter of trade items, the woman within it, keys in hand, dark-eyed, dark-haired, accoutred in the undemonstrative fashion of a respectable widow, yet one who is not ashamed of her figure or her wealth; the turban-style hat in jet satin, the silver-fox collar to the slim coat, beneath which she wore a simple, black evening dress, advantaged by a relaxed line to the décolletage. A wedding ring and a single dulled opal spoke of their life apart.

He wondered what his sister Andrea would have to say when he cruised in with Holly Beckman on his arm. Andrea had always detested Holly but now would be repaid for her meanness, surely, when she saw how unfair the years had been; Andrea had run to fat and had never quite achieved the status that her fond ambitions had once demanded.

In the taxi-cab David began conversation. He had always been garrulous. The difference between the new lieutenant-commander and the old khaki captain was that he now knew just when to keep his trap shut and when to make himself heard. Stern lessons had been learned in the social enclaves of Hong Kong where British officials, sea-trading Taipans and mercantile assistants raised snobbery to heights undreamed of by his bourgeois sister; one had had to learn to play very subtle games indeed if one hoped to get ahead in any of the cliques.

Sensibly, David neglected the progress of the war as a topic of conversation. Narvik, Rombacks Fjord, Lillehammer and Oslo, which had occupied him all day long, might not have existed as far as the couple were concerned. Nor did David raise the name of any serving man, Chris included, during the course of the extravagant dinner, a meal in which austerity was obscured by culinary ingenuity.

The restaurant was packed. Houssard's was a byword in many a London mess, the Mecca for many an officer stumbling off the train from Portsmouth. In his day, old Houssard had been the captain of a French frigate and had retained his sense of poop-deck efficiency in the running of a West End eating house. Delays between courses were regarded as hanging offences, for few sailors had ever had the chance to acquire the military habit of the partaking of leisurely dinners, and much preferred food to come at them thick and fast.

David was aware that he had no real right to regard himself as a fledged sailor. For all that, he was not coy about his experiences. He probably knew more about ships, shipping and sea routes than any man in the room. He had risen to the august position of senior manager in a firm of shipping agents, Gilson, McDougall & Grant, whose activities were, to say the least of it, rather octopodous and, here and there, very slightly nefarious. His original four-year contract had somehow spun itself out into sixteen. He had not returned to England on leave, not even to bury his wife Linsey, or his mother. All the bits and pieces of business that were necessary in respect of wills and properties were done through the executive offices of Mr. Mumford and Miles Walshott.

So David had missed his son's growing-up and had lost the woman he had once loved. But he had never quite given up hope. When war clouds gathered over Europe, and British Intelligence services began serious recruiting in the ports of the free world, David seized the opportunity, pulled every string available to wangle a commission that would bring him home.

It was not, however, desire that drove him to be blunt with Holly, to plunge into a courtship which, a year or two back, would have been considered scandalous. In early middle-age, in common with all men, David had taken to glancing apprehensively over his shoulder and doing little sums in his head. With luck, he had twenty good years left; thirty if he cut down on cigarettes and whisky, and Mr. Hitler didn't drop a bomb on his head. At the best of times, it was not a situation that lent itself to patience.

"I've talked enough about myself," said David. "What about you? Have you been happy, Holly?"

"Very happy."

"King—your husband—he was a dealer, wasn't he?"

"Yes."

"Chalfont Arcade?"

"Yes."

"I heard you were successful in paintings, selling works of fine art."

"Where did you hear that?"

"I believe Andrea mentioned it in one of her letters."

It wouldn't have been difficult for Andrea to obtain information about her career. There had been articles in journals and newspapers about her more successful coups. She wondered if Andrea had also sent David clippings from the papers which had linked her name with that of the Broadway star, the now-famous Peter Freeman. She thought also of all the things that David did not know about her, that nobody knew—the falling in and out of love, the uncertainties and disillusionments.

David said, "Whatever became of your brother Ritchie?"

"He went abroad," said Holly, "back in 1933. I really have no idea where he is."

"You never did get on well, did you?"

"No."

"And your son, in the air force, isn't he?"

"A pilot."

David pursed his lips and nodded his approval. "I can't really believe it, you know. The last time I saw him—your son—he was an infant in a tiny wool bonnet."

On occasions Holly wished that time might have stood still, that Chris was still an infant whom she could coddle and defend against the sword-bearers and spears. But she had never drawn the rein on Chris. She had shared him with Kennedy and the memory of Christopher Deems, had acknowledged that he was a man's man, whose boyish pastimes had hardened into obsessions, whose games had become real life, and whose passion for flying could not be denied. How could Chris be anything other than happy with his lot, protected by youth and immortality? When she looked at her son, she saw Christopher Deems, not David Aspinall. She even fancied that he resembled the gallant hero of Bullecourt and the Somme, not—as he did—the raffish, reckless lover of her youth.

Holly said, "Fighter Command. He enjoys it."

David said, "Enamoured by the glamour, I suppose."

"Lord, no! He's always wanted to fly, ever since he was an infant in an angora bonnet."

"In the blood."

"What?"

"His father—the war poet. Death and glory, all that."

Holly studied the familiar stranger across the table. Suddenly there was panic in her breast. She remembered Maury's warning; Chris will be hurt. Would Chris be hurt? Was he too old now, too sensible? And when David looked on the face of his son, would there be instant recognition, would that which had been only suspicion suddenly flare into surety?

"I'd like to meet him," David said. "Soon."

"No, I—"

"When?"

"David, please don't."

"Don't what? Surely, Holly, you don't hold a grudge against me now? What happened between us is long buried. Oh, it might have

36

been different if the war hadn't come along, if—"

"You would have stayed in Hong Kong then, wouldn't you?"

"Possibly," David answered. "Probably not."

"Weren't you on to a 'good thing' there?"

"I had a very good position in the firm, if that's what you mean."

"Parties, girls, horses and cards?"

"Holly, Hong Kong society doesn't accommodate those capers, at least not in its more responsible citizens. And I was a very responsible citizen, I assure you. After what happened—not just between us, but to poor Linsey—I wanted no more of the high life. You may find it hard to believe, Holly, but I didn't have a girl in every port."

"I can't imagine that you remained celibate."

David laughed. "Hardly that, at least not at first. Later—it would have been too risky."

"But you didn't marry?"

"I never found anyone I liked very much."

"Fortunately, I did."

David did not accept the challenge. He offered the bottle of Château Grillet. "More wine?"

"No, thank you."

"Holly, I understand your reluctance to accept me as I am, to believe that I'm sincere—"

"Sincere? One doesn't have to be sincere to eat dinner."

"I want to be friends with you, to see you again."

Holly hesitated.

She was not hypocritical. She was drawn to him, caught in the gossamer of the past, lightly entrapped by sentiment and sentimental feelings. When she thought of it, she found that her resentment was a fallacy. She did not resent him in the slightest. Yet she remained afraid of him, of what he might do to her through Chris. Her secret had been safe for almost twenty years. Only one man in the world could challenge it, and here he was, seated across the dinner-table from her, sipping wine in the candlelight.

How stupid to be concerned about such trivial matters when men were dying in the snows of Norway and the cold seas of the Skagerrak, when tanks were crushing the life out of the defenceless regions of France.

"I would like to meet Chris," David said.

"I don't see much of him. He leads his own life in the RAF," said Holly, quickly. "I'm never sure when he'll be home."

"Sunday?" said David.

"Sunday? I—"

"Let's make it Sunday. Usually no training flights are made on Sunday, this still being a God-fearing nation. I'm sure Chris can arrange an evening in town. Will you ask him, Holly?"

It had happened so very suddenly. Holly was caught totally off guard. David was rushing her, thrusting his way swiftly into her life.

"Please," he said.

"I—I can't promise," Holly said.

"I'll call about seven."

"David, I—"

"Take you both to dinner."

"David, why are you doing this?"

"Doing what?" said David. "I'm just anxious to meet your son, that's all. Put it down tó the fact that I have no children of my own."

He did not meet her eye, looked instead at the waiter and signalled for coffee as he spoke; Holly could not read the inflexion, decide whether he had told her by it that he knew about Chris, had always known about Chris. On the other hand, the remark might have been perfectly casual and his desire to meet her son no more than a small part of the process of becoming, for convenience, her lover, taking up where he had left off so many years ago.

Holly had been wooed by many men, flirted with, even pursued. But she had no need now of flattery, of seeking a relationship to prove that she was capable of allure. According to the latest cranky textbooks on femininity, she had fulfilled her role in nature. If it hadn't been for the war, she would have been content to tend her little shop and patiently await the day when Chris would find a girl to marry and, in due course, present her with grandchildren, set the seal, as it were, on her identity. But, in the context of the future, the war could not be ignored.

It was fortuitous elements that had brought her most happiness—and most pain. One part of her still clung to the past, afraid to take chances. But the other part, dormant these several years, embraced risk, impelled her into a jaunty state of confidence in the face of the monstrous threats that crouched across the Channel. She had noticed how the coming of the war had wakened Maury from bear-like slumber, had refreshed him, given him energy in middle life, an excuse to act with purpose. Why should she not take risks also, not with her profession but with her heart?

There in Houssard's, with its pack of uniforms and yellow candlelight, Holly became conscious of her life as a continuous process of growth, a process which she could not halt, could not put into store like a fragile china figurine. Christopher was dead, Kennedy too. But she was still alive and not yet old.

In David she glimpsed the singular expression of her son; in the mature man, bearded and stalky, a melding of past and future which, if she permitted it, could easily become irresistible, an anodyne to external dangers.

She smiled at him with warmth and, reaching across the table, touched his hand. It was a gesture made without wholehearted conviction on her part, masked by the situation. But David accepted it with such ineffable delight that she responded to calculation.

"Sunday," she said. "I'll bring Chris along, if I can."

In the face of unloving enemies, defiance took many strange forms in the spring of the year of 1940.

As a Parisienne, Madelaine Cazotte was not impressed by the second-rate treasures that the Swiss classed as grand art, nor by the pile of painted Gothic, the *Schipfe*, that stared blandly back at her from across the Limmat.

There had been rain in the high Alps, so the hotelier had informed her with that air of frowning gravity with which the Swiss, like the English, discuss the vagaries of weather.

In the city of Zurich, however, there was no sign of rain. Pavements were dry and the sun shone on the breakfast balcony of the St. Regula, though a fresh, April breeze licked feathers of foam from the strong, brown flood of the river, swollen with snow-melt. Awnings were up, scarlet-striped pleasure boats were moored by the tourist quays, shops stocked with the many fine goods that the exporting countries of Europe still had to offer and, as in Paris these last eight months, one would hardly have thought that, on the face of it, there was a war on at all.

The journey across France, of course, had been fraught with difficulties and inordinate delays. But Madelaine's documentation, including visa and travel dispensation, all in order in the name of Natalie de Polignac, had cleared her through the checkpoints of the warzone and across the border into Switzerland. What turned the trick was an open letter of introduction from the *Banque Nationale Suisse*. It smoothed her passage across all frontiers, for her countrymen, even the Communists, had an inherent respect for money; next to hard cash, credit currency was considered to be the key to all doors, a handmaiden of commerce. Nobody, not even a hard-bitten and harassed douanier at Dijon, had failed to treat the woman with an efficiency that came very close to deference.

The fact that Madelaine was beautiful, young, mysterious and obviously very rich also helped.

She had no problems once she reached Zurich. She was known in the St. Regula, quite a regular visitor, Madame de Polignac, over the years. She was "interested" in art, not politics, and shared with her host, the innkeeper, a healthy perspective on neutrality, favouring no race or creed above another when it came to doing business, though her clients did tend to include a high proportion of Germans of late.

Herr Oberisch was such a gentleman. Young, charming, though rather flabby, he was reputed to represent a committee of the German National Art Fund. Of German origin—his parents had migrated from Konstanz on the Boden-See in 1915—the hotelier and his staff were sympathetic towards Herr Oberisch who, sighing almost tearfully, would explain that his professional duties had become most difficult since the unfortunate misunderstanding between the Fatherland and La Belle France had sown doubt and suspicion even between friends and the friends of fine art.

Blond, moon-faced, blue-eyed, Herr Oberisch was so saddened by the events in Europe and so vulnerable to slight that the German-speaking staff of the St. Regula rejoiced at his good fortune in having such a nice, steadfast lady-friend as Madame de Polignac to comfort him and, with the utmost discretion, to share love with him in the small hours of the night in her bedroom on the fourth

40

floor. One night, every six months or so, they would have a romantic dinner, a walk by the river, a covert rendezvous in the Madame's room, a breakfast—and *au revoir* until the next time. Even the dourest Protestants among the chambermaids and waiters were touched by the lovers' predicament. None but the most hardened sophisticates on the staff of the St. Regula, however, and there were few of those in Zurich, could have imagined what went on in the dark hours in Room 9 on the fourth floor, or have realised that love had nothing to do with it.

Madelaine Cazotte—alias Madame de Polignac—did not suffer by the perversities that Wili Oberisch inflicted upon her. On the contrary, she was roused by them, a willing party to the decadent acts. She had even taught Wili a few tricks that had not previously been in his repertoire. She was not disgusted, certainly not bored, by the Austrian's demands, the more so as she cared not a fig for the man. Both understood that love-making was only a minor part of their cynical relationship, which had to do with money, not sex, and least of all with love in any recognisable frame of reference. For all that, in public Madelaine played the romantic heroine to the hilt. Wili Oberisch was amused by it, did his bit by slipping a little bunch of snowdrops or freesia on to her breakfast plate, by kissing her, with tender shyness, behind the neck when waiters were looking: a nonsense, a fabrication, a forged romance, as neat as any of Madelaine's other deceits, spiced by the fact that her body still ached from his athletic attentions and that she was weary and sated and anxious now to conclude their business and be on her way back to Paris and her undemanding husband.

That morning in April, 1940, Madelaine had chosen a Matita *bon voyage* wool dress, cream with a filigree chocolate stripe. She wore the matching coat about her shoulders, since the season was spring. Wili's plump fingers touched the collar, brushed the hair on the nape of her neck. She put down her coffee-cup and turned her head slightly as his lips touched her below the ear.

"Whore," he whispered, in French, then, bashful as a boy, sat down opposite her, his back to the river. He kept a weather-eye on the glass door which connected the breakfast room to the balcony upon which there were no other guests.

Madelaine had already finished breakfast. A hearty eater, she had done full justice to the lavish meal served up by the hospitable Swiss.

Oberisch contented himself with a little liver pâté scraped on to hot buttered toast, washed down with a bowl of strong black coffee. He pecked up the food quickly, then lit a cigarette and, when the waiter returned indoors, slid a slender notebook from his waistcoat pocket.

Madelaine took a similar book from her purse.

No unframed masterpieces reposed in the luggage of either dealer. No fistfuls of marks or francs would surreptitiously change hands. Credit and trust, mutual interdependence, were the seals of the contract. Such was the volume of "trade" that the Cazottes and Herr Oberisch had been called upon to handle this past four years, that elaborate systems for the transportation of canvases involved crates and trucks, not merely kid-skin cases and cabin trunks.

Purged by madmen in the offices of the Third Reich, Germany's National Socialist regime had been in process of ridding itself officially of all forms of "degenerate" art. The Bible of Nazi aesthetics was *Cleansing the Art Temple*. Lists of State-approved painters included only those artists who were willing to prostitute their technical ability to the cause of the State. All artists of merit had either fled or gone into hiding. To unscrupulous dealers, however, the fate of contemporary artists mattered not a damn.

The Oberisch-Cazotte partnership, and others like it, had devised ingenious ways of exploiting the bizarre and farcical vandalism of the House of German Art and its administrative lick-spittles. Not all Germans were philistines. Even dedicated Party members adhered in secret to a love of fine painting and culture. Men and women of taste, education and discernment survived in the upper echelons of the Third Reich; some of them even enjoyed the underground privileges that went with rank.

The children of successful self-made men were particularly prone to be bitten by the art bug, to come down with severe and incurable cases of acquisition. The confiscation and burning of thousands of paintings and drawings deterred the ardent collectors not one whit. It saddened them, made them gnash their teeth impotently, angered many and caused a few to turn yearning into plotting, with that methodical cunning which is the hallmark of the breed of collector with whom Oberisch-Cazotte did business.

The number of "private collections" of decadent art increased dramatically in German towns and cities, and "little cellar galleries" in country houses and large farms were legion. Traffic in paintings of all periods flourished. Picasso and Matisse were now in as much demand as works by Cranach and Dürer. Taste and politics could not be bound together by order of the Führer. Agents and clever dealers had a field-day. Certain officials in government, however, understood the value of a pfennig and even the redoubtable Goering was not above auctioning off confiscated "degenerate" masterpieces to obtain funds and foreign currency for the Reich. Herr Oberisch and Madame de Polignac had had their fingers in that little pie, too, and had cleared from it a more than tidy sum.

Now, with Europe collapsing and the smell of smoke drifting over everything, collectomania had reached fever pitch in certain high places. The short but profitable hey-day of the forger and confidence trickster moved towards its zenith.

Thanks to the genius of Madelaine's father, Claude Cazotte, and the experience of her husband in such matters, upwards of three hundred of the masterpieces which had been burned in the court-yard of the Berlin fire brigade in 1939 had not been masterpieces at all but forgeries from the Cazottes' "fake factory" in Paris. Gauguins and Van Goghs, Cezanne landscapes and Braque still lifes, Pisarros, Utrillos and Toulouse-Lautrecs had all been saved from the flames, whisked away, masked by replacements, from the apocalyptic servants of philistinism and found nice safe homes, out of the light of day, on the walls of wealthy patrons, in Germany and Italy as well as in France.

During their previous bi-annual meetings in Zurich, the couple had exchanged and correlated the works which Oberisch required with those which the Cazottes could guarantee to supply. Since the outbreak of war, the Cazottes' task had become easier. Quality forgeries were no longer required in many cases; "approximations" were quite suitable for the transfers that Oberisch had arranged. Usually the notebooks contained details of sizes and subjects, indexed to specific painters, dictated not only by demand but by the raw materials that Madelaine's husband had acquired, the aged canvases and dated frames, even the rarity, now and then, of inferior work by an artist in demand which could be titivated up by Claude and turned into a masterpiece, complete with an "authentic" history.

Unknown to either Madelaine or Wili Oberisch, however, each had come to Zurich to tell the other that the situation had changed, that things could no longer be as they were. For this reason the pair were slightly less direct than usual.

Oberisch did not meet the woman's gaze as he riffled through the pages of his notebook. "Impressionists?" he said, speaking now in German, now in French.

Madelaine, too, flicked over the pages of her memorandum.

"Renoir, a small canvas, study of a bather, in oils, with an attribution giving the Cagnes period, 1907. Pink and red, as you would expect."

"No, not Renoir," said Wili Oberisch.

"Dufy, a broad panoramic landscape in gouache."

"Dufy is far too risky, sweetheart, as I have told you before."

"He sells in Paris."

"He *works* in Paris, does he not?"

Madelaine did not answer. Raoul Dufy had once authenticated as his own work a small, early sub-Impressionist painting which her father had done as an exercise in style. The artist's mistake had pleased her father very much.

She read again from her notes. "A Greco?"

"Religion!" said Oberisch, with a trace of derision.

"What *do* you want, Wili?"

"Italians and Dutch."

"Italians are large. Obtaining decent grounds is difficult. Dutch masters take much, much time."

"To paint, yes," said Wili Oberisch. "To buy, no."

"Buy?" said Madelaine.

Oberisch had closed his little book and puffed on his cigarette while staring past the woman, at the glass door.

"Acquire," said the German. "In Paris."

"I do not understand you."

"In three months, six at the most, sweetheart, traffic will be very difficult and exchanges between us will be sadly hampered."

Madelaine felt a certain hollow apprehension in her midriff.

"We have been at war, your country and mine, for months and it has made—" she said.

"But soon," said Wili Oberisch, "soon it will."

"Paris?"

"Would you not like me to come to Paris, to be a partner in your business? Free trade between Berlin and Paris, between my clients and your shop?"

"Wili," said Madelaine, "there will be no more forgeries."

It was Oberisch's turn to be surprised.

His blue eyes whipped to her face. "What do you say?"

"My father has gone, Wili, gone to Canada to live in retirement with his brother in Toronto."

Oberisch nodded. He did not seem unduly dismayed by the news. "He is not young, of course. Disturbances are not to the taste of old men. No matter, sweetheart, no matter."

"I'm glad that you understand. I did not make much effort to stop him. He is not a kindred spirit. To be candid, he has never worked happily, knowing that his paintings are being sold to you, to German clients."

"But what of you, Madelaine?" said Oberisch.

"I will stay in Paris. Nothing will ever make me leave."

"Not even the Germans?"

Madelaine smiled, eyes shining. "I would welcome the Germans. France is administrated by old men. There is no longer enough money about and the Socialists are waiting in the wings. For all their peculiar tastes," she smiled more warmly, "I feel that the Germans would do well for France. But I would not like to see Paris razed to the ground; that worries me."

"Paris will not be bombed, Madelaine," said Oberisch, as solemnly as if he was delivering a vow on behalf of the military high command. "We are not barbarians. Ach, the things I could do if—when we are in Paris. You and I together, we could make such a wonderful killing."

Madelaine leaned forward, elbows on the table. "Wili, what do you have in that head of yours?"

"Not in my head, sweetheart. In my notebook. Orders. Orders for so many expensive things."

"Already you are taking orders for the treasures of France?" said Madelaine. "Is it not premature?"

Smugly, Herr Oberisch shook his head. "Not *too* premature.'

"Tell me what you have in mind."

"When is your connection to Dijon, Madelaine?"

"At a quarter to twelve."

"Then I will tell you briefly what is afoot."

The German dealer lit another cigarette, poured himself a second bowl of coffee and discharged himself of all that he felt Madelaine must know to prepare herself for Nazi occupation, to lay the foundation of the new business venture which he and she would undertake, hopefully before autumn tinted the chestnut trees on the banks of the Seine.

In conclusion, Oberisch said, "Can you do this for me?'

"With ease," said Madelaine.

"You will need the help of your husband, however," said Oberisch, "and I cannot believe that he is sympathetic to our cause."

"Ritchie," said Madelaine, "will do as I wish, provided there is a fat profit in it for him."

"Are you sure he will co-operate with us, sweetheart?" the German asked.

"Quite sure," said Madelaine.

Tennis on the station's bumpy tarmacadam court, and participation in Warrant Officer Worsley's programme of steeplechases and cross-country marathons, had brought Chris to such a peak of fitness that he seemed to vibrate with energy and well-being. His skin was clear and sun-dusted, his eyes bright, his body muscular. He moved with a panther-like restlessness about the room in the dusty old Victorian mansion in Tite Street. Beneath the glow of health, though, there was tautness, a faint, ever-present suggestion of nervousness, like an athlete before a contest, the feeling that Chris was impatient to be on with something else.

The young man accepted the sherry that his mother poured but did not carry the glass to one of the room's comfortable armchairs. Instead, he paced the length of the carpet, and back again, glancing up at the antiques on the mantelshelf as if he had never seen them before. He lifted a little cream-coloured clay cradle with red slip decoration, and examined it closely for a moment.

"Staffordshire?"

"Yes, a christening gift."

"Eighteenth century?"

"Very early eighteenth. Pretty, isn't it?"

"Awfully well-preserved."

Chris's interest in antiques was peripheral, though, over the years, he had gleaned a smattering of knowledge on the subject. To Holly's disappointment, he had shown no inclination to follow her into the trade.

Chris gently replaced the cradle on its cork mat on the mantelshelf and lifted instead a tiny pug-dog ornament decorated under glaze in blue and brown.

The young man grinned. "Lord, Mother, what a hoarder you are. I remember when you bought this Longton Hall item. In that junk shop in Torquay. When? 1933, wasn't it?"

"Yes."

"It hasn't grown any more handsome. That was rather a decent holiday. I was alone with Dad most of the time. You came down for the weekends. Stayed in the Royal Devon, and I had a whole day's sailing with a friend of Dad's."

"So you did. I'd forgotten," said Holly.

"I really enjoyed myself. It was better than being abroad."

"You're like your—like Kennedy; not much of a one for too much sun."

Putting the pug back in place, Chris sipped his sherry and paced the carpet once more.

"What time did he say he was coming?"

"Seven."

"It's that now."

"I expect he'll be here at any moment."

"Aspinall," said Chris. "Son of the old man who first took you in?"

"You make me sound like a waif," said Holly, "or a pint of milk."

Chris laughed. "I can't imagine you as a girl."

"Thank you very much."

"You know what I mean."

"Of course. I used to try to imagine my grandfather as a young man, in Russia, but never could. To me he was part of Lambeth, never young." Holly watched her son with a certain caution. "I never burdened you much with reminiscences, did I?"

"Lord, no! Told me hardly anything. I learned more about your early years from Uncle Maury than I ever did from you. And lots about my real father, mostly from Kennedy. Strange, that."

Holly remained silent, hearing the loud tick of the French pedestal clock, and the soft, friendly sigh of the wind from the river, which nuzzled the garden's solitary lilac beyond the tall windows.

"Who is he?" said Chris, touring the area by the window. "Aspinall?"

"I told you, the son of the man who left me an interest in my first shop."

"Did you know him well?"

"Quite well. He was a—rather an ally."

"Ally. What an odd expression."

"The other members of the family resented me. David stood up to them on my behalf."

Chris came round by the rear of the sofa on which his mother was seated and, with a silly swiftness which startled her, leaned over the cushions so that his face was close to hers. "In love with him, Mother, were you?"

"Don't be ridiculous!" said Holly. "I was hardly more than a child. He was an officer in the army."

"Where did he fight?"

"He didn't. He worked in Whitehall."

"But, I suppose, he cut a dashing figure."

"He doesn't now."

"Be rather difficult at his age," said Chris, without malice.

"He isn't that much older than I am."

"What did he do, professionally?"

"He was a gambler."

"Pardon?"

"For two or three years he supported himself by gambling."

"Speculating, you mean?"

"I mean gambling, as in roulette."

"Good Lord, how unusual. Did he go bust?"

"He decided to give up the fast life. Went abroad, to Hong Kong, as a shipping agent's right-hand man."

48

"Fascinating!" said Chris. "I'd no idea you knew such exotic chaps when you were young, Mother."

Holly rose and poured herself another sherry.

She was exceedingly nervous of the meeting, unsure of how Chris would react to David. Chris had always been "a man's man", however, and David emanated a kind of masculinity that the young officer might find magnetic, in addition to any rapport there might be along the bloodline, in the connection between a son and his father.

Chris glanced at his wrist-watch. "Exotic—but not punctual."

It was four minutes past seven o'clock.

As if in response to Chris's reprimand, the doorbell rang and Holly's house-servant, Dolly, an acerbic sixty-year-old spinster, padded from her cubbyhole below stairs to answer it.

Flustered, Holly rose and went to the drawing-room door, opened it wide and waited there, looking across the mansion's echoing front hall, while David was admitted.

To her surprise, David wore naval uniform. She had expected him to be attired in a comfortable three-piece suit, not to flaunt his warrior caste, an attitude that Holly—out of touch with patriotism—still found gauche. She expected it from Chris, who was youthful and ardent and a genuine fighting man, but not from David who, in her eyes, was little more than a glorified office worker. The uniform, however, had not been put on for her benefit. It was to impress Chris, to put David on an even footing with her—with their—son.

David kissed her on the cheek by way of greeting. It was an over-familiar gesture for the state of their relationship, yet Holly did not resent it. She allowed David to take her hand as she led him into the drawing-room and introduced him to Chris.

The men shook hands warmly, without stiffness or hesitation.

"I've heard a lot about you, sir," said Chris, as he poured David a whisky.

David followed the young man to the drinks trolley. "Just a whisper, please, and lots of soda water. I've no stomach for liquor."

"There's beer, if you'd prefer it."

"Not before dinner," said David. "Whisky will be fine."

Chris made two identical glasses of whisky and soda, and poured another small sherry for his mother. It was an occasion, perhaps, for a toast, but none of the three quite knew which aspect of the meeting deserved blessing.

David raised his tumbler. "Cheers!" he said, lamely.

"Cheers!" Chris echoed, while Holly said nothing at all.

Now that she saw them together, it was a revelation. There were so many similarities between the men; too many. She feared that they, too, would become aware of it. It was in the eyes, on the brow and the firmness of the mouth. Son and father. Everything seemed to shout it aloud. Why had she been such a fool as to bring them together? All the years of secrecy had been swept away in an instant. Chris's infancy, boyhood and young manhood had, somehow, been negated, Christopher Deems and Kennedy imperiously wiped away, their influence upon her son negated by a kinship that could not be denied.

Neither David nor Chris seemed at all aware of the remarkable likeness between them, and drank whisky-soda and chatted like a couple of casual acquaintances who had met through a third party in a Service club. Within minutes, they were deep into discussion of the progress of the war.

Shakily, Holly went out of the drawing-room to find her coat and hat, to hurry them away into the warmth of a restaurant, to the three-cornered intimacy of a dinner-table where she could not be ignored.

The car at the kerb was a little BSA Scout, a soft-top which somehow seemed too frivolous for somebody of David's age and rank. Chris was immediately taken with it, as he was by any machine with a raked-back bonnet and a rasping throttle sound. Courteously, Chris shoe-horned himself into the narrow back seat, and Holly took her place beside David in front.

"Half a damned knot's about all I can manage in the blackout," said David. "My eyesight's not what it was, I'm afraid."

There was light in the sky, however, and the promise of moon-light later. The pleasant airs of spring growth from Chelsea gardens, and the faint, salt tang from the flood-tide on the Thames, were soon lost in the reek of exhaust and petrol fumes.

Hugging the steering-wheel, David nosed the Scout along Tite

Street and into Waverley Place, away from the river, following the route that Holly took each morning on her way to the shop. There was little traffic on the road but the pavements had more than their fair share of Sunday-evening pedestrians, couples and families heading down for a sniff of the Thames and a stroll along the Embankment before supper.

David's uncertainty as a driver made Holly relax a little. If he had been dashing and careless, she would have suspected him of awful masculine competence, or of showing off. But, at forty-five, David had no need to prove himself master of all abilities and was content to nurse the vehicle through the streets, regardless of the poor impression he might be making on the young daredevil at his shoulder.

"What'll she do on the open road, in daylight?" Chris asked.

"I've no idea," said David. "I only have the thing on loan for the evening."

"Oh!" Chris sank back and readjusted his cramped legs, while Holly, to whom driving a motor car was almost second nature, restrained a twitching left foot and tried not to clutch David's arm as he weaved erratically through Brompton and on to the section of Knightsbridge by Hyde Park. He followed the road left, headed out along the Edgware Road and around the north end of Regents Park. David's concentration was devoted to the ribbon of kerb, to the painted lines of junctions, and white-gloved policemen who attended the major crossings. He did not indulge in conversation and, when Chris put an occasional question to him, only grunted in reply.

At length, however, Holly could not restrain her curiosity.

"David, where are we going?"

"Hampstead."

"It's a long drive for dinner."

"I'll bring you home, never fear."

"Going to Surtees', are we?" Chris asked.

"No," said David. "To my sister's."

"Andrea's?" said Holly.

"Yes."

"I—does Andrea know we're coming?"

"Of course. She's looking forward to meeting you again."

"I wish you'd told me, David," said Holly.

"Why?"

"I—"

"You wouldn't have agreed to come."

"That's true. Andrea and I could never stand each other."

"As a matter of fact," said David, "I couldn't stand Andrea either."

"Why, then, are we going there for dinner?"

"To rub it in," said David.

The reply was mischievous but not without an undertow of seriousness.

In the rear seat of the Scout, Chris chuckled as if he understood the nature of the game that David Aspinall was playing, and reckoned that participation might, after all, be fun.

Time had not been at all kind to Andrea. She had grown both stout and haggard in unequal proportion. Her waist, bosom and bottom had waxed large, while her equine features had caved in so that she had become a woman of daunting ugliness.

Tall and autocratic, however, she carried off her plainness with an authority that was so regal that the big family house in Hampstead seemed but a poor substitute for Windsor Castle or Sandringham. A silk crêpe evening dress in claret showed too much bust and bare shoulder for such a hefty woman, and a careless dusting of peach powder on the arms had smudged the material. A bead-and-chain hair-band piled her crowning glory even higher on her head, the locks lacquered with artificial ebony to disguise the grey.

Andrea, it appeared, was absolutely determined not to grow old gracefully.

The woman was backed—there was no other word for it—by Miles Walshott, her stockbroker husband, whose passivity hid the sort of subtle diplomacy which would have been the envy of foreign ambassadors; also by her children. At seventeen, Mark was a beanpole youth with his mother's elongated facial characteristics, but a much more cheerful disposition.

Stephanie, nineteen, had apparently been visited by a legion of good fairies at birth and bore no resemblance to either her mother or her father. Miles called her, without exaggeration, his true English rose. She was slender, blue-eyed and ash-blonde. Just at first, her innocence seemed almost like vacuity, as if lack of brain had been the price she had had to pay for beauty. This impression, though, was quite false. Steve, as she was called, had her father's gentle wit and acuity, unblemished by adult cynicism. She had chosen an evening dress of navy blue and silver, with tiered overskirt and tight-fitting bodice which enhanced the impression that here was a girl who had blossomed into womanhood that very afternoon.

The maids carried away the coats and hats while Andrea, who knew how to make an entrance without moving a foot, remained with her family within the confines of the library whose massive, carved-oak doors opened inward, revealing the room and the group like curtain-up on *Dear Octopus*.

"David, my dear!" Andrea called, utilising the sonorous acoustics to the full. "How wonderful to see you!"

Now the hostess advanced, halting at the threshold until the guests were ready for audience. Andrea spread powdered arms and offered her bosom to her brother, who hugged her warily as if she was a gigantic Etruscan pot which might prove to be cracked.

"And this is your new lady-friend," Andrea cooed. "Do come, my dear, and let me look at you."

Mischief on David's part now hovered on the verge of malice. Holly experienced a moment of angry resentment. David, however, was determined to extract the last droplet of satisfaction from the meeting and did not announce Holly's name, allowing his formidable sister to go through her effusive routines, grinding away at making an impression on this stranger who knew her only too well.

Andrea hauled off and, taking Holly by the arm, trooped her towards the passive husband and children.

Miles Walshott's recognition was instant: a flicker of surprise suppressed behind a wry smile. He met Holly's eye and gave what might have been a wink. Miles had aged well, his hair silver, his smoothly-shaven cheeks rubicund with health. He shook Holly's hand and murmured, "Welcome to our humble home," and gave a tiny chuckling cough to show that he at least appreciated David's little joke.

"What a fine character," said Andrea, dragging Chris out of obscurity. "What is your name, young man?"

"Christopher, Mrs. Walshott."

"And what do these funny things on your pocket mean?"

"I'm a pilot, ma'am."

"A pilot; do you hear that, Mark? He's a pilot. I'm sure if you ask him he'll tell you how dreadfully dangerous flyin' can be."

Leaving Chris stranded awkwardly in front of her son, Andrea swooped once more on Holly, while gesturing to her husband to do the needful with the liquor trolley.

Holly saw now that Andrea was being paid back for her ridiculous assumption that any woman with whom David struck up a relationship must be at best *déclassé*, and at worst not much more than a tart. Pilot sons and Paris gowns had scotched that old-hat prejudice. Now Andrea was roving in search of some other convenient prejudice, a hook upon which to hang vehement disapproval of any female rash enough to strike up a friendship with her brother.

Foolishly, Andrea imagined that David, too, had been preserved in moral aspic for the past twenty years. She saw him as no more than a heavier version of the raffish young officer who had led the family such a devilish dance all those years ago, and recalled with horror David's wife, the corrupt Linsey Leigh-Jennings, who had created scandals galore, but who had eventually substantiated Andrea's naïve belief in divine retribution by dying in a nursing home in 1932, abandoned by her husband, and virtually friendless.

Andrea had expected a wartime version of Linsey Leigh-Jennings, some brash, baubled widow, out to sink her hooks in "Aspinall" money, a vampire all set to take advantage of a lonely, middle-aged man—and of the blackout regulations—to lure him into trouble. It was endemic to Andrea's character to look at the surface of people. For this reason there was still no recognition; nor did it occur to her that she did not yet know the woman's name.

Sailing from port to port, Andrea marshalled the guests through cocktails and, tugging on a bell-sash that might have been attached to Old Tom, signalled to the harassed and complaining maids in the cavernous kitchen that, ready or not, dinner was about to be served.

To David, Holly whispered, "Why didn't you tell her it was me?"

"She wouldn't listen."

"You could have made her listen."

"Please, Holly, let's see how long it takes for your identity to dawn on her."

"Miles will tell her."

"Not him."

Drinks tucked away, the party moved through the grand old house and into the dining-room. It smelled aromatically of pine logs and Scottish peat, several tons of which Miles had possessed the foresight to have transported down from Perthshire, "in case the miners decide to strike in sympathy with Russia."

It was, in fact, halfway through dinner before it dawned on Andrea who her guests really were. In conversation with Mark and Stephanie, Chris inadvertently made some passing reference to his father, "the poet, Deems", which though not picked up at once by Andrea, stuck in her mind and struck chords of memory.

She peered at Holly across the remains of the ragout of lamb, frowning. Her son Mark was going on about war poetry and an English master at Harrow who thought Deems the finest of all the trench poets, with the exception of Owen. By instinct, Andrea ignored ninety per cent of all that her son ever said; she hardly ever absorbed irrelevant information, data that did not pertain to her domestic regime or her social aspirations. War poets lay far from her ken. And yet the name Deems rang a very loud bell. She peered at Holly curiously, while the maids fussed at clearing the meat and vegetable dishes and prepared to bring in the puddings.

Rising, Miles did the round with the wine bottle.

"Madam?" he said to Holly.

"Thank you." Holly pushed forward her glass.

By now, Andrea was sitting bolt upright, chin tucked in, all eyes. The frown had become a scowl.

"Madam?" she said. "Madam what?"

Feigning surprise at this breach of good manners, Miles and David looked quickly in Andrea's direction, while Chris broke off his talk with the Walshott children and, with interest, watched too.

"Miles? What is Madam's name?"

"Come to think of it, I really have no idea."

Andrea wagged her finger, head cocked. "You *do* look familiar, you know. All evening I've had the oddest feeling that we've met before."

"Oh, yes," said Holly. "We've met before."

Much to everybody's astonishment, Andrea shot to her feet. The wagging finger pointed in accusation. "You're the Beckman gal, aren't you?"

"Why, so it is. So she is," said Miles.

"*What* is he doin' with you?"

"Enjoying my dinner, Andrea. Do sit down," said David.

"Holly Beckman, at my table."

"Mrs. King," put in David. "Holly King."

"You knew. You all knew. It's another damnable joke at Mother's expense, isn't it? We'll all have a laugh at Mother again; what does she matter, after all?"

"That's not true, dear." Miles set down the wine bottle and patted his wife's powdered shoulder. "It was only a bit of a joke."

Seating herself, Andrea rounded on David.

"It was *your* idea, of course. As if I didn't have *enough* to put up with, you have to *humiliate* me too."

Andrea Walshott's anger was so tinged with hurt that Holly reached across the table and clasped her hand, a gesture intended to assure Andrea that no malice had been intended. Holly felt very guilty now at being a party to David's silly jape.

"It . . . it was supposed to be a surprise, Andrea," said Holly lamely.

"I'm . . . I'm . . . I'm *sick* of surprises."

And then, incredibly, Andrea shed her authoritarian manner, put her face into her hands, and began to cry.

She wept without histrionics, shaken by deep sobs.

Instantly, Holly realised that it was not merely David's ill-timed and misconceived game that had so affected the woman, that the little conspiracy had opened other wounds. In Andrea she recognised vulnerability, understood instinctively what lay behind the sudden flood of tears. While Miles, Stephanie and David fussed around the weeping woman, Holly got up, took Andrea's elbow and, with a solicitude that almost amounted to tenderness, led her from the room.

Much to everybody's bewilderment, Andrea went meekly with her arch-enemy, cleaving to Holly as if to her one and only friend.

Once outside the dining-room, Holly closed the door and put an arm around the big woman, comfortingly.

"Oh, God! What a fool I've made of myself," Andrea sobbed.

"It's the children, isn't it?" said Holly softly. "The children and the war."

"Yes, yes. I'm sick with worry about them," Andrea confessed. "And nobody understands."

"I do," said Holly, and guided her hostess gently towards the drawing-room where they might find peace to talk a while, without interruption.

The beaver-fur quilt was something of an heirloom. It was one of the few things that Ritchie Beckman had managed to hang on to during his years as a rover. The quilt had cost him a fortune ten years back, and had come to symbolise warmth, wealth and sexuality. In spite of Maddy's peevish complaints that it was moth-eaten and beginning to niff, Ritchie would not part with it. It covered the big double bed in the Cazotte house in the Rue Flavine most adequately and Ritchie spent a lot of time in that bed.

Since the outbreak of the war, he had lost a deal of weight and consequently felt the cold much more than his young wife. Maddy, it was hard to realise, was a mere twenty-six years old; he seemed to have known her for ever.

Snuggled down under the beaver-skin quilt, Ritchie watched his wife undress by the light of the shaded lamp. If Maddy was at all aware that Ritchie was still awake and squinting at her through slitted eyes, she gave no sign of it. A little bit of voyeurism did nobody any harm, after all; it was one of the milder indulgences that shored up their relationship and secured for Ritchie the illusion that he still possessed the girl's heart as well as her body.

Long ago he had given up meeting her at railway stations and airports, given up the hope that she might keep him informed of where she was, what she was doing and when she would return to Paris. She was his runner, she said. She couldn't be expected to cable or telephone every time she wanted to use the powder-room, could she?

The truth was that Ritchie had not only lost his wanderlust but had sunk into a state of apathy, spiced with anxiety, which kept him, mainly, indoors. He would hardly leave the house without Madelaine, did business through her or by telephone, and, when she was away, doodled listlessly about the studio and living apartments, counting the hours until she returned.

He knew, of course, that she gave the German a "good time".

It excited him to think of the fat-bellied kraut teased and tormented by the lithe young woman. He imagined Oberisch—and others too—as extensions of himself, middle-aged, out-of-breath and appreciatively passive in the acts of love.

It excited him to think of what Maddy had been up to and what she would tell him when she returned, how she would react when he asked her the rote questions, "Did he do this? Did he do that? He wasn't as good as me, was he?" But even his excitement was low-pitched and dull, and only those first few minutes after her return roused Ritchie and restored in him a sad awareness of how far down he had sunk from the pinnacles of success in the Twenties and early Thirties, when he had been married to Ruth and was the sharpest art dealer in the Western hemisphere.

Maddy knew that he was watching her.

Studiously, she ignored the motionless mound under the fur, remained in profile as she placed one dainty shoe on the chair and unworked the tiny pearly buttons of her dark green silk camiknickers, slipped off the wide shoulder straps to let her beautiful breasts fall free.

Ritchie did not move.

She slid off the filmy garment like a snake shedding its skin and, quite naked, seated herself at the dressing-table in the corner and, with quick dexterity, combed her hair and removed her make-up.

Without preliminary, she said, "The Germans will be in Paris by August."

On his side, Ritchie did not stir. "Who says?"

"Oberisch."

"I'll believe it when I see it."

"Oh, darling, how blind you are."

"The French won't let Paris fall."

"The French will be only too delighted to hand over the keys of the city to Herr Hitler, provided he guarantees to protect it—and us."

"Is that what Oberisch told you?"

"I believe it, *chéri*. Business will boom under the Nazis, mark my words."

"C'mon to bed, love."

"Coming, coming."

"Tell me what else Oberisch says—later."

"What's been happening?"

Madelaine rose and turned, facing her husband. In one hand she held a perfume spray and in the other a hairbrush. She atomised the fine perfume in three whispers across her body and touched up her hair with the brush before tossing it aside on to the dressing-table.

"*Voilà*," she said.

Ritchie propped himself up against the huge, flop-eared pillows stuffed with finest goose-down, and sheathed in silk. "Nothin's been happenin'."

"Did you go out?"

"Only to the *tabac*, for a newspaper. You just back? God, the train must've been hours late."

"It was." Madelaine walked to the bed. "Travelling is becoming so tedious, *chéri*. Be thankful that it's me and not you who has to do it."

She leaned to kiss his brow and Ritchie put both hands upon her breasts. "Oberisch wouldn't like it, if it was me showed up in Zurich."

"*Chéri*, Herr Oberisch is all business."

"I'll bet he bloody is."

Madelaine stripped back the beaver-skin and sheets and kneeled across her husband, straddling his legs. "All you men of the world are the same."

"Only some of us are better, right?"

"How I have wanted this. All day, riding in those trains, I have wanted this," Madelaine crooned.

Ritchie braced his hands upon her shoulders.

"Do the krauts really expect to be in Paris soon?"

"*Si, si*. Aug-gust. Aug-gust."

Ritchie ignored the feline caress of her body. He held her, studying her beautiful face, searching her expression for some sign that this was not gossip or boast but that Oberisch had inside information which he had passed on to Maddy. Ritchie felt the eroticism that had been with him for three days diminish, flicker out.

"An' you reckon it'll be good for us, for the picture business?"

"*Si*," said Madelaine, intently. "*Si-si, monsieur.*"

Using all his strength, and no tenderness, Ritchie heaved her away from him and pushed her on to the beaver-skin. She tumbled into a provocative pose, surprised but not displeased at the rough handling.

"Listen." Ritchie pinned his wife with his hands. "Did you tell him that your old man had gone off to Canada?"

"Naturally." Madelaine concentrated on business, switching from one profession to another as easily as she breathed. "I told him Papa had gone and there would be no more paintings to order."

"How'd he take it?"

"He has other ideas for making money. When Paris is a German city, Wili Oberisch intends to come in with us, to expand with us into a partnership."

"With you?"

"With both of us, darling. Oberisch knows how clever you are. It may be me that he deals with in Zurich, but he is aware that I am only your puppet."

"Don't give me a soap job, Maddy, for Chrissake," said Ritchie.

His animation caught the woman off guard. She squirmed into a sitting position, hugging her knees with her arms, and frowned at him. He had hauled himself up against the headboard, no part of him touching her now. His face was suffused with blood, like anger or passion, and he looked coarse, like a peasant. They had that in common, still; they were both peasants and, in periods of stress and high emotion, their reactions could not be predicted.

Madelaine said, "Wili Oberisch is just a dealer like us, only interested in making some money out of the war. That's all. He will look out for us."

Ritchie said, "Maybe he'll look out for you, Maddy, but he don't give spit for me."

"He doesn't approve of Hitler, of the things the Nazis are doing to Europe."

"The hell he doesn't," said Ritchie. "He's German, and all Germans are Nazis under the skin. Anyhow, he knows too much about me for it to be healthy."

"Ritchie, I tell you—"

"For starters, he knows who I am."

Even in bureaucratic France, Ritchie had forged an iron-clad identity for himself. Officially, he was the French Canadian second cousin of Mme. Cazotte, son of Claude Cazotte's elder brother's son, according to all documents. He had come from Quebec to Paris in 1933 and had married, by arrangement, within the family. His name was Cazotte, too, and he was now a citizen of France, having waited long enough for the honour to be bestowed upon him by the French authorities.

The picture shop in the Boulevard St. Germain was a perfectly respectable front, Madelaine a perfectly respectable wife. Ritchie's oddly-accented French was attributed to his North American origins. The handful of dealers and clients in France who knew him as Ritchie Beckman, in the pre-1933 era, were hardly the sort to shop him, and considered false papers as run-of-the-mill, new identities as matter of course. More than sixty per cent of those shysters had fled to America, anyhow. Madelaine was his front, his protection, disciple and mentor in one. He had put himself in her hands in more ways than one, back in the old days. He hoped he wasn't going to have trouble with her now.

The art business was shifty, and Maddy and he had learned to live with it, to revel in it, but now it had all the fragility, the precariousness, of a house of cards.

Once before, long ago, Ritchie had had to flee for his life from guys who were bigger and more ruthless than he was; he had the uncomfortable presentiment that he might soon have to take wing again, with or without his lovely young wife.

Madelaine said, "Many people know who you are."

"Yeah." Ritchie pushed himself further up in the bed. "But they ain't krauts. Listen, kid, don't you realise I'm English?"

"I have not forgotten."

"Bad enough bein' English right now, with just the Frogs to contend with, but when the Nazis get here—"

"I will look after you, *chéri*."

"Maddy . . ." Ritchie hesitated; the admission burned like mustard on his tongue. "Maddy, don't you realise I'm not only English, I'm also a bloody Jew?"

"I know, I know—but you don't look it."

"Come again?"

"You don't look like a Jew."

He was suddenly shocked still. His eyes flared with surprise. "And what," he asked quietly, "does a Jew look like?"

"Big nose, large head—"

Ritchie leapt from the bed. "You've been sucked in by that Nazi crap. You *believe* it, don't you? Jesus, Maddy, you're halfway to being a bleedin' Nazi yourself."

"How can you say that? *You* don't like Jews either. You told me so, many times. You told me you *hate* to do deals with them. Is that a *Jew* speaking?"

"I don't practise the religion. Never have. Never."

"Why do you worry, in that case? Who will ever think—?"

"Somebody will."

Sympathetically, she put her arms about his waist and drew him to her. There was no hint of sensuality in the gesture. It was motherly, protective, perhaps possessive.

Ritchie's outburst of rage was short-lived. He allowed himself to yield to her and knelt on the floor by her side while she stroked and petted him, both of them naked but devoid of physical desire.

"What is it, *chéri*? Are you afraid I will leave you? I will never leave you, no matter what. Madelaine will look after you." She stroked his neck, massaging it with strong, slender fingers, coaxing his head down on to her knees. "There's nothing to fear. Nobody will ever know the truth, Ritchie."

"Somebody will," he said.

2 Soft Options

Magic wands had no place in Stephanie Walshott's scheme of things. More of a pragmatist than her mother, she did not expect that circumstances would automatically bend to accommodate her will or that her merest whims would be instantly gratified. She did not even take it for granted that her father would make the sun to shine upon her, though Miles had the happy knack of appearing with a brolly when needed. Steve thus enjoyed a sense of security hand-in-glove with self-reliance. By the time she reached nineteen, she was more than capable of making up her own mind and of making her own mistakes. After one meeting with Chris Deems, though, young Steve was confused.

Frustration with the humble role that Andrea had picked out for her swelled in Steve. Until the outbreak of war, she had been content to put up with a genteel education, one which would fit her for a respectable job and eventually attract the right kind of husband. Andrea had already drawn up a shortlist of "eligibles" and had coyly tested out her daughter's magnetism by thrusting her in the direction of these titled younger sons. Titled younger sons, however, were too preoccupied, just at that period, to give an English rose more than a passing glance. Wedding bells had been drowned out by the chatter of ack-ack and to lascivious eyes Steve Walshott was not a good bet for a night on the town.

For eight months Andrea had left Steve much to her own devices. Mother's concern had gravitated to her son, a dreamer who was growing too fast and, Andrea feared, might complete his journey from cradle to grave with heartbreaking rapidity. To Andrea, the world was a black and white affair and the mere donning of a uniform would immediately condemn Mark to death. She could not overtly express her fears in a society apparently dedicated to heroics, and concentrated on trying to persuade Mark to duck away from joining up. This was a demanding obsession—Steve was merely a girl—and Mama was neglectful of her daughter's needs, imagining her to be immune to the lure of war and patriotism.

Whether falling in love with Chris was an excuse for shaking herself out of idleness, or *vice versa*, was a moot point. Steve had already been three-quarters inclined to join the war effort before the young pilot stepped into her ken. In her pink and white bedroom, with her Priory Close school uniform still hanging in her wardrobe, she dreamed about bouquets and horseshoes, a first kiss under the willows, moonlight on Honeymoon lake, a little home for two, et cetera, but also applied herself to studying the sheaves of pamphlets and leaflets which government departments disgorged to entice the unwary into war work.

Steve was a practical, level-headed girl, not without a certain condonable vanity. Her first rebellious impulses were soon put to flight. Heavy industry, airframe-fitting, spot-welding, polishing searchlight glasses, folding parachutes, and a host of similar conveyor-belt operations might have seemed glamorous in terms of defiance of Mama and convention, but a few hours of careful consideration convinced Steve that a handsome RAF pilot would hardly be attracted to a girl with calloused palms and dirty finger-nails, one who turned up for dates smelling of Woodbines and soot. Nursing, at first, seemed to be the answer. But in 1940 the nursing professions were still suffering restrictions imposed by a tight labour market; entry was jealously guarded by the establishment.

One by one, Steve eliminated all civilian employments open to a girl of her age and education: after that—the Services. To cut a short story even shorter, Miss Stephanie Rose Walshott did the rounds of the recruiting offices and succumbed to the forthright blandishments of Mrs. (Junior Commander) Harriet Smythe in an upper office in a red-brick block in Sorrell Street, Westminster.

Junior Commander Smythe was seated behind a desk, on which rested a bowl of red carnations and a framed photograph of her twin daughters.

Junior Commander Smythe was a no-nonsense type who gave it to Steve straight from the shoulder.

"Why do you wish to enlist?"

"To serve—to serve the country."

"Trouble at home?"

"Oh, no!"

"Not pregnant, are you?"

Steve was shocked by the impertinence, the audacity—

"I should say not."

Mrs. Harriet Smythe smiled and offered a cigarette from a plain teak box. Steve, who had only smoked in secret until then, took one of the cork-tipped Churchmans and allowed the officer to light it for her.

"If you do join the ATS, it won't take you long to learn to call a spade a spade." Junior Commander Smythe blew out a plume of smoke. "I can see you're not the hard-bitten type and that, Stephanie, is very important. The idea of service with the Auxiliary Territorial Service often appeals in principle to a gal from a mimsy background. Mimsy; you do understand?"

Steve nodded and tried to appear bold with the Churchman.

"Boy-friend or brother in the army?" enquired the junior commander.

"A young man—"

"Officer?"

"Pilot."

"Engaged to be married?"

"Oh, no. Nothing like that."

"Did he talk you into coming here?"

"No."

"One must always bear in mind that there are great differences between women and men; I do not mean the very obvious ones. Your contribution to the war effort, if you choose to make it through the ATS, will be quite separate from that of your man friend. You won't find yourself walking side by side with him, Stephanie. Enlistment, the donning of a uniform, will not make you his equal. I do not believe in that sort of purpose; nor, indeed, in that sort of equality. In an ideal world, women must be able to look up to men."

Steve regretted now that she had even mentioned "her young man"; Mrs. Smythe had been side-tracked.

Steve had misjudged the woman, however; sharpness and experience pushed the interview in unexpected directions. Later there would be more orthodox meetings. Mrs. (Junior Commander) Harriet Smythe was a fisher of women, *par excellence*, more anxious to protect and improve the quality of the Auxiliary Training Service than to appease the tender feelings of potential recruits.

She glanced at the form that the woman sergeant downstairs had invited Steve to complete, details of age and schooling, health and family background. It was not an application, as such, the sergeant had explained; it was no formality signing on in the ATS. You had to be vetted to see if you were "the right sort". At that moment, Steve wanted to be "the right sort". The rest of her list of possible offices was forgotten, and the girl in her supplanted the woman.

Oddly, too, the initial impulse—Chris—which had got her going, was not in her thoughts at all.

Junior Commander Smythe laid the cigarette in an ashtray. She had a long face, a little like Mama's in contour if not in expression. "Stephanie, let me ask you—do you *want* to join our service?"

"Yes. Yes, I do."

"You see, it's essential for you to be emotionally committed. We are an emotional sex, there's no denying it. But there's no reason why one should not turn emotion towards one's work. Without an emotional impulse, something's missing." Junior Commander Smythe lifted her cigarette and took one long puff, then dabbed it out in the ashtray. "Discipline, for a woman, is not as it is for men, not a rote-thing. We aren't sheep. We must understand, must love what we are doing and believe with our hearts in the reason for it."

It was difficult to imagine Mrs. (Junior Commander) Harriet Smythe delivering her recruiting speech umpteen times a day, day after day. It seemed utterly sincere and fresh, a revelation from the heart.

"Now, Miss Walshott, are you still firmly of a mind to become a trainee in the Auxiliary Training Service?"

"Yes, I am."

"As you have not yet reached your majority—twenty-one—the written approval of a parent or legal guardian is required. Will that pose a problem?"

Thinking of Papa, not Mama, Steve answered, "Not in the slightest."

"Good." Junior Commander Smythe got to her feet. She offered her hand, which Steve shook. "Sergeant Manners will provide you with the appropriate forms. Have them filled in and delivered, by post will do, to this office. You will be summoned to a further interview and, depending on that and the result of a medical examination, you will be considered for service."

"How long will all this take?"

"About a fortnight."

"Thank you, Mrs.—I mean—ma'am.'

"I hope," said the junior commander, "that I haven't given you the impression that the ATS is a soft option."

"Oh, no," said Steve.

"I fear there will be no soft options in this war, for men or women."

Mrs. Smythe accompanied the girl to the door where, in the narrow corridor, the sergeant waited to take charge of her again.

"By the way," said Mrs. Smythe, "do you have any special skills? Nursing training, typewriting, aptitude in foreign languages, that sort of thing?"

"I have French," said Steve.

"Do you speak it like a native?"

"I speak it like a sixth-form schoolgirl," said Steve, then added, "I can drive a motor car."

Junior Commander Smythe's expression lit with surprised pleasure. "Can you, indeed? What do you drive?"

"BSA Scout, an Allard and, sometimes, when Daddy's with me, the Bentley."

"Three litre?"

"Four and a half."

"It's not too much for you?"

"Goodness, no," said Stephanie Walshott. "It's really rather easy."

Three-tonner, thought Mrs. (Junior Commander) Harriet Smythe, as she delivered the girl into the sergeant's tender keeping. Convoy drivers were much in demand. She hoped that the Walshott parents would not prove sticky; the ATS could use a girl like Stephanie.

Returning to her desk, Mrs. Smythe lit another Churchman and penned her recommendations on to the single sheet of official government paper which would, in due course, become the basis of Steve Walshott's service record.

Apart from the discreet replacement of inkwells with typewriters, and the bullet-shaped brass dockets with glass-domed tickertape inlets, Miles Walshott's panelled chambers in Lower Lombard Street had hardly changed at all in twenty years of commodity trading. The polished walnut desk and the cabinet of special share folios, bound in chestnut leather, were just as Steve remembered them from her "treats" as a child. It was three or four years since last she had been here, her first unaccompanied visit.

Miles was delighted to see his daughter, though his first reaction when Mrs. Coombes ushered her in was one of anxiety.

"Nothing wrong at home?"

"Everything's perfectly fine, Daddy."

"Does your mother know you're here?"

"She thinks I've gone on an outing to Kew, with Barbara Brown."

"Lying to Mama; whatever next?" said Miles, mildly chiding. "Would you like coffee?"

"Please."

Miles had been a coffee-addict all his life. Through the intercommunicator, he sent for a pot, and drew out the client chair for his daughter. Gracefully, she folded her long legs and raised her chin with a trace of her mother's authoritarianism. Steve had never been a deceitful person; she must have a good reason for fibbing to Andrea, though there had been numerous occasions in the past when he had fabricated a "wee white one" just to keep the peace.

Mrs. Coombes brought coffee on the stained wooden tray that had been a gift from Miles' Aunt Cordelia, now deceased. It was half past three in the afternoon and the day's trading was still warm if not piping hot. Nonetheless, Miles instructed his secretary to hold all telephone calls and to delay his appointment with Lady Lumley with due *politesse*.

"Just passing, dear, were you?" Miles asked, over the rim of his cup.

"Daddy," said Steve, without preamble, "I want to join the army."

"Girls don't join the army."

"The women's army; the ATS."

"Why?"

"To *do* something, to get out of the house. To serve, Daddy. I want to serve."

"But the army—"

"I've had an interview, just come from it. I need your approval." Steve produced the form. "Here."

Miles finished his coffee. He seated himself, put on his spectacles, and read the form that his daughter pushed across the desk at him.

Plain, straightforward. Term of Service—he read—Duration of Hostilities.

Without any hesitation, he took his fountain-pen from his waistcoat pocket and signed his name in the appropriate space. He folded his hands, laid them on the form, and looked wistfully at his English rose.

She appeared so exquisite, so young and fragile.

Miles was no fool; he knew perfectly well what "service" implied. No safe billet behind sandbags, no funkhole in the deep country for Steve. Whether it was whim or fashion, or whether she truly felt impelled to serve Britain in this practical manner, hardly mattered. He would not question her motives. He would accept them at face value. Chances are, he told himself, Steve herself doesn't quite know why she has taken this momentous step. He remembered the Deems boy, Holly Beckman's son, only a year or so older than Steve and just as innocent in appearance; he flew fighter aeroplanes every day. How did Holly feel about it? Miles asked no favours, no privileges. Persuaded by clinging aunts, he had ducked service in the last war, but he could not shirk responsibility in this one, nor abrogate his responsibility to Steve.

"Mama," he sighed, "will go up like a barrage balloon."

"Do you mind, Daddy, what I've done?"

"Of course I mind. I don't want you marching to war. But I'm not going to try to stop you, Steve. I'd be a fool to do that."

"I know—at least, I think I know—what I'm letting myself in for."

"Eyes wide open?"

"Wide open, Daddy."

Miles pushed the form across the desk.

"Leave your mother to me," he said.

Benares brassware, even in wartime, was hardly a drug on the market. The collection which Holly purchased from a colonel's widow in Ipswich was of prime quality. The leathery old woman had parted with her treasure reluctantly. Inflation had pumped the bellows of the national economy and all sorts of vulgar dispositions were hanging in the air. The widow had decided to sell her prized possessions and buy herself a modicum of safety and comfort in a

Lakeland hotel. Holly had given her a very fair price for the goods.

That particular afternoon, Holly and Norma were engaged in taking an inventory of the brassware. None of the items had been lacquered, so that the dappled lustre and chased and embossed figments were almost clean and sharp. Holly's problem now was to decide whether to sell the items singly or turn to the Client Book and endeavour to find a buyer for the lot.

A couple of years ago, the question would not have arisen. A telephone call, a letter of quotation—somebody would have snapped the brassware up *in toto*. But the Client Book was almost obsolete. Even the most ardent collectors were hampered by lack of ready cash and the sneaky feeling that the pursuit of such an excellent but useless pastime as collecting *objets d'art* was unpatriotic. Safe premises in London were rare. Insurance was expensive, and poor, harmless collectors were vulnerable to bomb blast, as well as moth and rust.

Holly unpacked the straw-stuffed cartons, held each item to the light, and dictated a brief description to Mrs. Butterfield who noted it down in a large notebook in an appropriately round hand.

The women had been at the task for an hour that Monday afternoon before Andrea Walshott pushed through the shop door and, with a face like fizz—Norma's graphic description—glared into the gloom.

"Where are you? I know you're here," Andrea cried, as if Holly had deliberately hidden from sight behind the Victorian screen at the rear of the shop. "Come out at once."

"Who the hell's she?" murmured Norma.

"Mr. Aspinall's sister."

"The sailorboy's sister?"

"Yes."

"Looks like he unbolted her from the bow of a frigate," said Norma Butterfield. "What's she shoutin' about?"

Though the day was fine, Andrea toted a stubby little gamp which, with belted trenchcoat and gas-mask case, gave her the aggressive appearance of an invader.

She poked the gamp towards Holly. "You put him up to it, did you?"

"Andrea," said Holly, "what on earth are you talking about?"

"Your precious son . . . he corrupted her. In ten days . . . corrupted her."

Soft answers, Holly realised, would cut no ice.

It was ten days since the strange dinner party in Hampstead. She had seen David on two occasions since then, when he dropped into the shop casually and had taken her out to lunch. Holly supposed that the weary old animosities which had existed between her and the Aspinalls had been buried once and for all, that Andrea and she had established some sort of rapport; yet this was the Andrea of yore, loud and peevish and irrational.

"Andrea, shut up," Holly snapped.

Brolly wilting, Andrea obeyed. Few of her acquaintances—she had no real friends—were willing to abandon good manners even under provocation, and it was thus that she got away with incivility.

"Norma, bring a chair for Mrs. Walshott."

Sizing up the situation at once, Norma Butterfield strode out with a solid, wooden nursing-chair, dusted the seat with her sleeve, and thrust it at Andrea who, momentarily silenced, plumped herself down.

"Who is this woman?" Andrea found her tongue again.

"Name's Butterfield."

"My partner," said Holly.

Neither appeased nor pacified, Andrea placed the brolly across her knees like a rifle. "Your son and my daughter are having an affair."

"Nonsense!" said Holly.

"What's more," Andrea shot on, "he's so turned her stupid little head that she's joined up, mobilised herself."

Norma Butterfield, who had somehow become caught up in the conversation, put her hands on her hips and nodded. "Good for her."

"Andrea, I—"

"Signed her life away," said Andrea.

"What mob?" asked Norma.

Andrea did not seem to realise that the big-breasted woman had no part in a private discussion. They were of a size, both large, both assertive; reason enough for them to relate to each other in the heat of the moment.

"ATS," said Andrea. "Auxiliary Training Service. Uniforms and rifles."

"Nope, no rifles," said Norma. "Ack-ack batteries, the servicing thereof, but no guns for the girls yet."

"What do you know about it? You're not one of them, are you?"

"One of what?" said Norma.

For the moment, Holly was content to let the conversation run. She was not unduly upset by Andrea's sudden appearance, though she found the linking of Chris's name with Stephanie Walshott's disquieting. How could it be? They had met only once, in company, and Chris had been engaged in a full training flight programme all week. It might be the age of the whirlwind romance, but it was patently obvious that Andrea had grasped the wrong end of the stick.

"An ATS woman?" said Andrea.

"No, I ain't," said Norma. "I help fight fires."

"Oh, you're all the same," said Andrea, dismissively, but Holly felt that it was time to try to make sense out of the angry accusations.

She said, "Chris and your daughter hardly know each other."

"He came for her last night, to the house, without so much as a by-your-leave, not a word to her mother, he just *turned up* on my doorstep. The pair of them went sailing off, bold as you wish, to some drinking establishment, arm-in-arm. I never thought I would see the day—"

"None of us did," put in Norma, shrugging.

"What's more," Andrea rushed on, "they didn't return until well after midnight and they had the audacity to stay together in my drawing-room, eating fish and chips—eating *fried* fish and chips—until after two."

Holly said, "Why didn't you ask Chris to leave?"

It was exactly the right question, posed at the right time.

Andrea's mouth opened, then closed again.

"Well?" said Norma Butterfield.

"My . . . my . . . Mr. Walshott wouldn't let me."

Holly said, "I don't see, Andrea, what Chris has to do with Steve's decision to join the ATS. She must have made up her mind long before Sunday."

"At dinner, while you and I were having our chat, he persuaded her then. I thought he'd go for Mark—"

"Go for Mark?" said Holly. "I hope, Andrea, that you're not accusing Chris of being some sort of one-man press gang."

"His very presence—"

"Strewth!" Norma was flabbergasted by Andrea's wilful stupidity.

"If Chris and Steve . . . if they *have* been out together," said Holly, with more assertion than she felt, "I see no harm in it."

"Nor me," said Norma Butterfield.

"I don't see what it has to do with you," said Andrea.

"I'll make some tea," said Norma, prudently.

"Do," said Andrea. "With lemon."

Holly moved the shabby screen and seated herself at her desk chair, swivelled to face her adversary.

She was nervous again. Chris had telephoned from West Horsfall on Thursday but had not mentioned his intention to call on Stephanie Walshott, had said nothing at all about the girl. What had happened? Where had the relationship seeded? Why had it blossomed with such rapidity? Was there, in the young couple, an instant attraction, magnified by the fact that they were cousins?

Holly put her apprehension to one side, controlling herself admirably.

"How did they contact each other?" she asked.

"Letter, telephone. How do I know what young people get up to, how they do it? In my day—"

"When did your daughter enlist?"

"Last week, last Friday."

"Who signed her parental release form?" called Mrs. Butterfield, from the depths of the kitchenette.

Holly pressed that sensible question. "Well, Andrea?"

"Her father."

"I see. Your husband knew of Stephanie's intention."

"But nobody told me. Nobody thought to consult me."

"Perhaps because you'd have made a fuss," said Holly. "And nobody has time for fussing, these days."

"What *do* you mean?"

In spite of herself, Holly was being forced to side with the

73

impetuous youngsters. Defending their actions to Andrea, however, did not alter her attitudes or quell her fears.

She said, "You've heard the wireless, Andrea, read the newspapers. You know the war's going to get worse."

"Oh, that! I've been hearing nothing but war, war, war, until I'm sick of it. The war's no excuse."

"That's not what you told me ten days ago," Holly said. "You've no cause to blame Chris for your daughter's enlistment."

"It was only after she met him—"

"Might as well blame Hitler," said Norma Butterfield, as she brought in the tea.

"I don't know what I'm going to do. Stephanie. Mark next."

"All you can do, Mrs. Walshott," said Norma, "is keep your pecker up, like the rest of us."

"I'll talk with Chris," said Holly. "Have you told David?"

Andrea shook her head. "Should I?"

"If the friendship's going to last, yes," said Holly.

Andrea seemed to have run out of argument, out of anger. Her shoulders were slumped and she sipped her tea with the air of a woman to whom the herb is the only comfort.

Andrea's ability to cope by dominance had been washed away by the enormity of events. Her lifelong frustrations had proved to be shallow, silly things, now that they were shown in the vivid illumination of conflict. Her stability was fundamentally threatened. The war had come at a bad time for her. There was no pleasure in it for women, no drop of satisfaction to be obtained, as there was for Maury, no intensification of the force which made Chris glow when he talked of aerial combat and which had probably impelled Steve Walshott into the ATS.

Andrea was faced with her first real loss; the possibility of it terrified her. Though nothing in the "phoney war" of the past months excited, let alone justified, this sense of dread, the long-laid ghosts of twenty years ago rose up once more.

When the tea had been drunk, and Andrea had wept a little and been comforted not only by Holly but by Norma Butterfield, Holly said, "How did you come, Andrea?"

"By taxi-cab."

"Norma, pop out and find Mrs. Walshott a cab."

"Right," said Norma, and went out into the Fulham Road to try to flag down a cruiser which, at that hour of the afternoon, was a rare visitor.

Andrea and Holly stood by the shop door.

"I hope," said Andrea, "that you took no offence. I didn't mean to suggest that your son wasn't—wasn't decent."

"Quite!" said Holly. "I'll talk with him."

"It won't last," said Andrea. "Not in these troubled times. Nothing lasts."

"I'll do what I can to make sure it doesn't," said Holly.

Perversely, Andrea was nonplussed by Holly's sentiment.

"What do you mean?"

"I mean, I don't want Chris to have a relationship with your daughter."

"But—but—"

"Isn't that why you came here today? To put a stop to it?"

"Well, yes, I suppose it is," said Andrea. "But—you agree with me?"

"Completely," said Holly.

"But why?"

"Chris and your daughter aren't right for each other."

"Oh!"

"And here's your cab," said Holly.

The telephone in the drawing-room was ringing when Holly reached home that night. The drawing-room was hardly ever used. Holly preferred the compact lounge to the rear of the house, with its view of the narrow garden trembling, at this season, with spring leaves.

On entering the half-darkened room, the presence of Kennedy was everywhere. Here, on the gigantic, limed-oak table, he had done most of his cataloguing and accounts. Favourite pieces still decorated the mantelshelf and board chests; Georgian silverware, fluted candlesticks and mustards, coasters, tumbler cups and porringers. His morocco-bound *Dictionary of Hallmarks* was open on the table, together with a scrolled folder containing his notes. On the winged armchair, his spectacles still lay exactly as he had left them on the day before his death.

Holly reached the telephone before the housekeeper could toil upstairs. She lifted the receiver.

"Mother?"

"Chris, where are you?"

"On station."

"Are you all right?"

"Absolutely fine."

"Chris—"

"Look, Mother, I can't say too much but there's the devil of a flap on. No doubt you'll hear about it on the wireless. I don't want you to worry."

"A flap? Chris, what's happening?"

"Now, *please* don't worry. There's no need to worry. Do you comprehend?"

"Yes," said Holly, her heart thudding. "Yes. I understand."

"*Sincerely*, don't worry."

"Yes, yes."

"I'm not packing my bathing suit yet."

The phrase meant that the squadron were not being sent abroad. Without effort, Holly found that she was able to put the possibilities into a corner of her mind. There was nothing she could do about this latest "flap", whatever it might be. The BBC would inform her in due course. She would listen to the radio over dinner and far into the night, leaving it on while she worked at her portable typewriter, or knitted. Chris had told her not to worry; she would obey him as best she could.

"Might be a week or so before I get home," the young man said.

"That's all right, darling."

"This line isn't so hot, is it?"

"Chris, have you been seeing the Walshott girl?"

"What?"

"Stephanie Walshott—"

"Steve? Yes. On Sunday. Quite surprising, really."

"When did you—did you ask her out?"

"I didn't ask her, she asked me."

"Girls don't—"

"Sent me a letter, out of the blue, inviting me to meet her on Sunday. Not as bold as it sounds. She enlisted in the ATS and she wanted to talk about service life and all that sort of griff. I managed time off, a late pass. Sorry I didn't let you know. Bit of a surprise, actually."

"*She* asked *you*?"

"She'll be off to a basic-training camp in a week or so. Brave little thing, considering her upbringing. It won't be much fun for her at first, I'll bet."

"Will you see her again?"

"Hope so."

"Chris—"

"Listen, Mother, there's a queue a mile long for this blower. I must dash. Remember, don't worry. I'll tell you when to start worrying. All right? You're all right?"

"Chris, will you—do you like her?"

"Who? Oh, you mean Steve. Of course I like her. She's a peach."

"Chris—"

"Look after yourself, Mum. Goodnight."

And he was gone.

Holly replaced the receiver. She had had no chance to reprimand or reproach him; no cause either. He had come and gone in that whirl of sound, like the noise of one of the fast planes he flew, speeding on to "his business", to duties and tasks that she knew nothing about. Had he called Stephanie Walshott too? Had he, perhaps, called Stephanie first?

Holly stood before the empty fireplace, looking up at a huge landscape in its gilded frame. The painting was handsome, sombre, realistic to the last flake of bark and blade of grass—the stamp of a true Hobbema, the seventeenth-century Dutch master—down to four cheerful peasants, not cowed by the sober, woodland setting, in the corner. The painting, however, was a forgery, a brilliant fake; too brilliant to languish in the cellar of King's emporium for long, not to be shown and enjoyed. What matter if the hand of Meindert Hobbema had never touched brush to that canvas?

The painting was a memento of failure, of Holly's brother Ritchie, her one and only reminder of his scoundrel existence. It was Kennedy who had insisted on hanging it here in the Chelsea drawing-room, who eventually saw humour in that whole involvement with crooks and rogues, who said, "If it isn't by Hobbema, it should be." Holly had agreed.

In the waning light of the spring day, the painting seemed almost vibrant.

When the door opened, Holly turned.

"When will you be wanting dinner, ma'am?"

"Half an hour, if that's suitable."

"Quite suitable. Shall I set a place in the dining-room?"

"No, on the small tray in the lounge, as usual," said Holly. "Oh, and put on the wireless, please. I believe there's important news coming on the air."

"Indeed there is, Mrs. King," the housekeeper said, with inappropriate relish. "The Huns have invaded Holland."

Paris-Soir and the little bakelite radio plugged into a lamp socket by the bed, had given Ritchie some, if not all, of the news. He knew only too well how to interpret it, plus the rumours that Madelaine brought in from posh cafés and restaurants, guff, most of it, which Ritchie processed with due cynicism. In the course of the day, though, the wireless service had gone *phut*, and no amount of twiddling rang change from it.

Madelaine insisted that all was normal on the café scene, though there seemed to be a shortage of fresh butcher-meat and, for some reason, of vermouth. The Belgians hadn't managed to repulse the German advance, the line at the Albert Canal had already begun to fall to pieces, and the Belgian government was *plutôt affolé* and making hasty plans to evacuate Brussels. The next line of defence was on the Belgian frontier. Patriots talked of it as a Siegfried Line in miniature, an analogy which made Madelaine chuckle.

"They take victory for granted," Madelaine said. "They are all so complacent."

Ritchie was slumped in a Minty chair, with his feet on an alabaster table, sipping a very dry martini.

"There's always the Maginot Line. Papers say it's impregnable."

Madelaine said, "It is not the fortifications that will buckle, it is French morale." She gave that gleeful, malicious chuckle again. "Ah, no, *chéri*, Reynaud and Daladier will squabble us into capitulation. There will be no *blitzkrieg* in Paris."

With the radio more or less out, Ritchie had to rely on newspapers, full of optimistic crap, and on Maddy for his reports—the Battle of the Meuse on Monday; the destruction of Rotterdam by a hundred Heinkels, with thirty thousand dead, so it was claimed, in raging fires from the margarine stores, burning still and spreading, Tuesday; on Wednesday the surrender of the Dutch army and the first frantic stirrings of panic in the City of Light. No panic for Ritchie-boy, though. He had the lovely Maddy to look out for his interests. Thursday, the buses went off the streets, to ferry troops to the expanding fronts and haul in refugees from Reims. And Madelaine came home from her day-long promenade and told him that the Maginot system was a wash-out, and that the politicos were tearing out each other's guts in the Chamber.

Ritchie was standing by the window in his dressing-robe, unshaven, a slim American cigarette stuck in his face.

"Bleedin' quick, wasn't it?" he said, in English.

Madelaine flung her hands explosively into the air, fingers fluttering, a child's expressive gesture, stripping ten years from her age. "*Boof! Boof*! We prepared for a standstill sort of war; the Germans would not play. They are moving, moving all the time, as they did when they took Poland. *L'invasion est en marche*."

"Better iron your swastika, Maddy," said Ritchie, smiling too.

"They say the Paris railway stations will be bombed tonight. But I do not believe it."

"Because of Herr Osterisch's promise?"

"I will see that we have papers—just in case."

"Papers?"

"Documents, passports and visas. Fargeau is doing a roaring trade, as you can imagine." Fargeau was the best forger in Paris. "But he has promised he will make us two perfect sets by this evening. I am having dinner with him. Will you come?"

"And spoil the fun?" Ritchie smiled. "No, no, love. I'll have an early night."

"As you wish."

No, love, as Fargeau wishes, Ritchie thought. Fargeau was reputed to be the richest "artist" in France, after Picasso started paying income taxes. A peasant with the instincts of a jackal, he would surely make Maddy pay for favours, with her skirts raised. Did Madelaine know what she was in for? She was a big girl and could look out for herself. Maybe she would threaten Fargeau with "the Germans", warn him what would happen when the Nazis commanded the *bureaux*.

Madelaine made herself pretty and went out about nine p.m.

Ritchie was asleep when she returned home. This time the woman did not waken him.

In the morning, very early, Ritchie found her sleeping like a corpse in the handsome single bed which had belonged to her father and which they kept in linen and aired in the "guest room" behind the studio. She would sleep, Ritchie knew, until noon or after.

He checked her purse, found two sets of faked passports, complete with photographs and blind-stamps, pre-dated back to 1938. Husband and wife, Franco-Italian, name of Gozzoli. The second set, innocently enough, were in the name of M. and Mme. Chable.

So many identities did he have now that at times Ritchie could barely remember who he was. The thought of travel, of *being* that other person, daunted him.

From the window of the upstairs room, he looked down into the cobbled street. Not a soul was in sight, not a fruitman or flower-seller or a baker's boy, not even one of the bicyclists collecting his sack of journals from the depot on the north corner. Today—ironically—Ritchie had intended to venture out with his wife to visit the annual Trade Fair at the Porte de Versailles which had opened on May 11th and had continued for the sake of prestige, though its aisles were almost deserted. Maybe, Ritchie thought, the Fifth Column will try to keep the fair going until the Führer drives in triumph along the Champs-Elysées, an event which, to hear Maddy rabbit on, won't be so long.

The apartment, the building, the street, were all silent, the morning light calm and pastel. In the Luxembourg, the rhododendrons would be in bloom.

Ritchie had no idea what casual impulse nudged him into the streets. He was well-stocked with ciggies and could wait for the newspapers. Whatever it was, it wasn't a desire to sniff the flowers in the *jardins*; he had never been that kind of guy. Dressed in one of his London-cut suits and wearing a light, black-wool topcoat and soft "Chicago" hat, he emerged from the doorway of his shady *atelier* and set off, at no great pace, towards his favourite quarter—the Marais.

Many tourists, even some sensitive Parisians, found the Marais sinister and oppressive, haunted by memories of the Revolution, bloodshed, the slaughter of aristocrats in the Rue du Roi de Sicile below which, in the Rue d' Archives, lurked the oldest closes in Paris, reeking with the musty odour of Middle Age barbarities. Much of the ancient stuff was gone. Small bustling manufactories were tucked into the cul-de-sacs, tiny cheerful *bistros* supported the bases of the old, old, tenement-like buildings which, in spite of florid iron grilles and painted wooden shutters, had that same air of secretiveness which Ritchie recalled in parts of old Lambeth and the lodgeries of Waterloo and which summoned him fondly from time to time.

It was not then circumstances which led Ritchie to the artisans' *bistro* on the corner of Rue des Rosiers and Rue de Vallon, on the outskirts of the Hebrew ghetto, but desultory habit, and appetite wakened by the air of the May morning. The *bistro* just happened to be there. He had never been in it before but the name, stippled in rust-red paint across the plate-glass window, appealed to him, the Americanised influence patent in it—Zack's—though, as it happened, the place was run by a couple from the Artois.

Zinc bar, a dozen round marbled tables, beer kettles stacked by a striped curtain, tall oak taps, many bottles on the shelves and a slate "menu" propped against a big, brown wireless set which sizzled louder than the cooking pans; there were few customers, though it was no longer early morning. Two lorry-drivers crammed in food from coarse plates and a disconsolate old codger in the canvas apron of a slaughterman dipped a black-crust bread roll into his bowl of *chocolat*.

From behind the bar the burly, surly proprietor took Ritchie's order for bacon and scrambled eggs. The man squinted at the smartly-dressed stranger. "English?"

"*Non.*"

"You are about early today."

"*Café noir, s'il vous plaît*," said Ritchie.

In the arch of the servery, the man's elephantine wife appeared, sizing up the stranger too.

Ritchie lit a cigarette while he waited for his food. The barman's curiosity did not upset him, did not fire his paranoid tendencies. He had nothing to fear from Zack. He could be out of here and away, vanishing into the depths of the Marais before they could threaten him. Perhaps that was why he felt so comfortable in the narrow-streeted quarter.

Food was put before him. Perched on a bar stool, Ritchie scoffed it quickly and with relish. The lorry-drivers left. The slaughterman took a long time filling a briar pipe. In three or four minutes Ritchie would be up too and away, safe out of it. He need not have answered the proprietor's question, need not have acknowledged the faint purpose—an inclination, no more—which had brought him here.

The man placed a muscular elbow on the zinc.

"What do you want, monsieur?"

Ritchie finished the strong coffee and put down the cup.

He looked straight into the peasant eyes, filled with mean doubts.

"I'm looking for a room," he said in French.

"A room? You?"

"For two," said Ritchie.

The gigantic wife gave a snort of laughter. Even in the shadow of invasion and occupation there were those who looked out for their own pleasure. *For two*; like a password, totally convincing and comprehensible to the owners of the *bistro*.

"Show him the board," boomed the wife from the kitchen.

From beneath the bar, the man drew out a large oblong of plywood, much frayed and stained with grease. Drawing-pinned to the front surface were twenty or more plain postcards, each with a hand-printed message, ill-spelt inducements to buy or sell; a Ford motor-car engine, a baby's cradle-cot, the services of a house-painter, two African palms in green tubs.

Ritchie's eye travelled up and down the columns. He saw nothing pathetic in the advertisements. Suddenly he was engaged on business again, business that had nothing to do with Madelaine.

Had he had this in mind all along?

Room. One clean chamber. One year to lease.

He hardly noticed the price, his eye dropping to the address.

Apply, 17 Rue de Vallon.

Minutes away, seconds away; convenient for eating in this place where he had already begun to establish cover. They would not think it strange, these peasants, if the "mistress" was never seen.

Ritchie didn't even know why he wanted a roof of his own, let alone a "clean chamber" in the Rue de Vallon. Instinct moved him, the wily fox, the born deceiver. He had had a string of bolt-holes in several different cities, including London. They had always proved useful. Always.

He did not write down the address.

"You have what you wish?" asked the proprietor.

"Thank you."

Ritchie did not tip. Not yet. He did not want to be jeered at or to be thought "peculiar".

The old codger watched him through pipe smoke, and Zack, with something close to a leer, growled, "See you again, perhaps."

"Perhaps," said Ritchie, as he went out.

It was waiting for him, secretive, nondescript, secure—Number 17 Rue de Vallon, a hundred yards from the corner of the Rue des Rosiers, a self-imposed Hebrew ghetto.

There was no concierge in the cubby in the hall. Ritchie did not ring the handbell. He preferred to be alone to make his reconnaissance. The place smelled of cooking, not unpleasant, and of coal-smoke. By the bottom of the stairwell was a dim corridor with an apartment door, and at the rear another locked door which, he assumed, led out into a yard. The stairs were protected by a banister which looped and curved upwards, five storeys, lit by a glass dome the colour of a lemon lollipop.

Soundlessly, Ritchie went up, floor by floor, listening at each door. Brass plates told him who lived there, then the plates were replaced by cards until, on the fifth floor, the banister gave way to a shaky iron hand-rail and a landing on which, face to face, were two varnished doors.

Slowly, stealthily, Ritchie ascended to the landing. He peered down the stairwell, down and down, then looked up at the skylight.

When the door clicked, Ritchie stepped back and involuntarily braced himself, hand in the pocket where, in his Chicago days, he had kept a gun.

Five or six years old at most, slim and tidy in the way of French children, the boy stared at Ritchie with dark, solemn eyes.

Ritchie smiled and bent his knees. Sitting on his heels, on a level with the child, he said, "Hey, what's your name?"

"I am called Alois."

"Well, Alois, this is a nice place to live, uh?"

"*Oui, M'sieur.*"

"Do you stay with Mama and Papa?"

"Papa is a soldier."

"Hey, now; a soldier."

"He has gone to Heaven."

Momentarily nonplussed, Ritchie did not know whether he was being invited to share a fantasy or if the child's father really had been an early victim of the war.

When the woman spoke, Ritchie shot to his feet.

The woman said, "It is true. My husband was killed."

She stood against the half-closed door of her apartment. It was not the grief but the loneliness in her face which struck an immediate chord in Ritchie. She was sallow and drawn, handsome rather than pretty, and patently Jewish.

Ritchie wondered if her confidence had been made to a fellow Jew, if she saw him at once as that. Impossible! Then he thought how ridiculous it was for the woman to be a war-widow. Only a handful of fighting men had died. Their names had been blazoned in the newspapers.

"Where?" he asked.

"At Vosges, in January."

"I didn't know that there had been fighting at Vosges, madame."

"An attack by two German patrols. A major came to tell me the news. He said, though I do not believe him, that Chaim was the first French Jew to die in uniform. I have heard other things since."

"You have my—my sympathy, madame."

Behind the woman was another child, two or three years older than Alois. He did not cling to his mother's skirt, but stood back in the umber shadow of the hallway watching with fierce concentration and, Ritchie imagined, suspicion.

Ritchie said, "I am in search of the concierge—about a room to let in this building."

"It is that room." The woman nodded at the door behind him. "It is my room and I wish to lease it for one year and two months."

"Papa's room. He works there," said Alois.

"It has been cleaned, and I have put furniture there now. It is no longer a workshop. You wouldn't know it had been one."

"What did your husband do?"

"He made shoes, m'sieur," said the boy in the shadows.

"If you are interested in the room, m'sieur . . ." said the woman.

"I should like to see it," said Ritchie, with that air of polite indifference with which he automatically commenced all transactions.

The elder boy fetched the key and the little family, sticking together, showed Ritchie into the apartment. To his surprise, it was spotlessly clean and contained not a trace of the husband's work trade, not so much as a few crumbs of leather. Obviously the woman had applied herself, with a practicality which Ritchie appreciated, to making the apartment habitable. The floor had been newly varnished, a faded rug was by the bed, flowers in a bowl on the miniature dining-table by the window. There was even a rocking-chair with a print cushion on it, and the gas fire had been fitted with two brand-new pipe-clay sockets. In a cupboard there was a small sink and a two-burner gas stove with a grill oven.

"The water-closet," said the woman, "is on the lower floor."

"Shared?"

"With one family, a wife and husband."

The ceiling was low. The small window gave a view of the Rue de Vallon.

Secure. Very secure.

"Why," said Ritchie, "is the lease for fourteen months?"

"Payable by the month," said the woman. "To answer your question, m'sieur, Chaim—my late husband—paid rental on the rooms for eighteen months, before he enlisted. He was a volunteer, you see, but he did not think that the war would last too long, or that it would come to Paris."

"Papa is a gunner. He has killed many of the Bosches."

"Hush, Alois," the woman said.

"He has gone to Heaven with the other soldiers."

"Shut up, Alois," said the elder boy.

"Does the concierge have to approve the lease?" asked Ritchie.

"She will want to meet you," said the woman, "but she will not make any trouble. You are not a tradesman?"

"No."

"You will live here—with your wife, perhaps?"

"No," said Ritchie. "I am in Paris only from time to time but I no longer wish to put up in hotels. The hotels are not what they were." He paused, then added, without inflexion, "For the likes of us."

"I understand," said the woman.

Ritchie made a show of looking round. But his mind was already made up. The atmosphere of the place appealed to him; its decent shabbiness, its anonymity.

"I'll take it." He extracted his wallet and fingered from it a sheaf of one-hundred-franc notes, counted them swiftly on to the table by the flower-bowl. The woman and elder son observed with awe. "If convenient, I prefer to pay quarterly, in advance."

"It is very convenient, m'sieur," said the woman. "I will write you a receipt."

"No need," said Ritchie. "If you insist, though, you may leave it on the table and I'll collect it tomorrow when I come round with my luggage."

They went out on to the landing. The woman locked the door and gave Ritchie the key.

"Thank you, madame." Ritchie glanced down at the child who clung still to his mother's hand; he stooped and offered the boy his hand. "And you too, M'sieur Alois. You have been most helpful."

Ritchie turned to go downstairs.

"Sir," the woman said. "May I ask your name? For the receipt."

Ritchie opened his mouth, a lie deft on his tongue. But for some reason he told the truth.

"Beckman," he said. "Richard Beckman."

"Until tomorrow, then," said the woman, "M'sieur Beckman."

"Until tomorrow," said Ritchie.

The main purpose of an air force, Chris had been taught, was to hunt and attack an enemy wherever he might be. In consequence, it followed that attack was the fundamental of all air strategy. Attack was the best method of defence in the air as in other elements of combat. At which point in his relationship with Stephanie

Walshott, Chris found the entrenched principles of his profession colouring his approach to love, he could not be sure. Certainly the girl had made first contact, flown the first sortie. Though Chris had been aware of her as a desirable piece from the first instant of meeting, he had not permitted himself to consider Stephanie as a possible objective and had contented himself, to continue the metaphor, with "flipping his wings" at her during the course of dinner at the Walshotts'.

By their third date, however, Chris was in a flat spin over Steve and, he imagined, very much at a disadvantage.

Trouble was, he wanted her so badly, wanted her in strictly barrack-room terms. A raw and guilty response to her rose-like beauty was all mixed up and confused with noble sentiments and knightly romanticism and the underlying suspicion that he was behaving like a perfect swine even to think of her in such a context.

As yet Chris was without sexual experience. He had necked with the cousin of a schoolmate at a parents day once, and got very hot under the collar. He had enjoyed half a dozen nights at the pictures with one girl or another, including a WAAF trainee officer who—in Chris's priggish opinion—had no moral scruples at all and whose "forwardness" had immediately turned off the tap. With Steve it was different, so totally, completely, heart-stoppingly different that Chris spent his days in dreamland. He could not shake off his fantasies even when he was performing split-second manoeuvres in a Hawker Hurricane at 300 m.p.h., thirty thousand feet above the English Channel. He became agitated and defensive, inattentive at briefings and moony about the mess.

"What's wrong with Deems?"

"He's in love."

"Good God, is that all? Snap out of it, Deems!"

"He can't, poor sod. He's got it bad."

"Tell him to bed her quick then, and get his mind back on the job."

"Deems, old boy, love is like malaria: quite shattering at the time but soon over. Liable to recur, though, without warning. As Wally will tell you. Isn't that right, Wally?"

"Spot on, old chappie. Play the field. Safety in numbers."

"Don't look so glum, Deems."

"Bed her, my son, that's an order."

"Bed her or wed her, or both."

"That'll cure you. Guaranteed."

The most infuriating thing about it was that it had happened so rapidly. Whirlwind romances were for typists and spotty LACs, not Cranwell-trained pilot officers. He was behaving like one of the cardboard heroes in *My Confession*. He'd be lagging brilliantine on his hair and growing a handlebar moustache next. He was so far gone that even ragging didn't sting him.

What made matters even worse was that Adolf wasn't standing still. A blind parrot could see that the RAF would have its hands full in a matter of weeks. Steve would be off to training-camp with the ATS and he would be lucky if they managed to contrive passes together.

With his sort of luck, the powers-that-be would probably post Steve to North Wales or the Outer Hebrides and he wouldn't see her at all for months and months.

Pressed, Chris spent most of his evenings out of the mess.

For the first time he was conscious of being "rather well off" financially. Not for him tailored uniforms with red silk linings, nifty sports cars parked behind the armoury, and champagne suppers at The Tadpole or The Spring Onion. He had never felt inclined to pursue the sweet life, to indulge himself to the limit of his income. But in courtship, his inheritance became enormously useful. After that first alfresco fish-and-chip supper in Mrs. Walshott's elegant parlour, his rendezvous with Steve were made in more hectic places, in The Piccadilly, in the '39 and Ponts, to be precise, where he could treat her to oysters and entrecôte steaks and they could dance to the velvet saxophones of Chester Berry's American dance band—anywhere he could hold her in his arms, without actually risking being alone with her.

Due to a sudden influx of recruits, Steve's call for training in the ATS was delayed. She received a nice little stencilled letter telling her so, and professed to be disappointed at the delay. Was she informing him, Chris wondered, that she had had enough of his company and that diving off to "square-bash" would be a decent excuse for dropping him? As he couldn't spend all his time with his arms around her, and her blonde head resting on his chest, the couple exchanged vast amounts of information about their past lives and their opinions of everything under the sun.

Both Chris and Steve were intrigued by the odd relationship between the Aspinalls and the Beckmans.

"My grandfather's still alive. He married again, to an ex-professional Salvationist. He's Jewish. Did you know that my mother's side of the family were Jewish?"

"Yes. Mother made it plain."

"Is your mother against people of Jewish extraction?"

"My mother is against most things, Chris. Go on, tell me about your grandfather. He sounds nice."

"Lord, no, he's anything but nice. Tough, selfish, what a certain patronising type of social student might dub as a 'character', but he isn't terribly likeable. Beer and betting-shops."

"Why did the Salvationist marry him?"

"I really have no idea," said Chris, whose private opinion was that Cissie had found Leo sexually irresistible, for some obscure reason. "They live in Hastings now. My Uncle Maury bought a house for them, and my mother chips in to help keep them in style."

"What else?"

"My great-grandfather was Russian. He was killed in a fire—the same fire that killed my father—when I was only a few months old. Mother has a photograph of him. He looks like Leo Tolstoy on an off-day."

"It's all so rich, Chris, compared with our lot," said Steve, "though Papa had a string of aunts with names from Shakespeare, umpteen of them. He lived with them on a rotation basis after his parents were drowned."

"Drowned?"

"In a boating accident. Papa was really very fortunate not to be with them. Boating made him sick and he was left on the bank. He doesn't talk about it. I only vaguely remember one of the aunts, Cordelia, a fearful-looking woman with piercing eyes and a really mad cackle. She died about ten years ago."

They spoke of the Aspinalls' shop, speculated on why Steve's maternal grandfather had employed Chris's mother in the first place, on whether Uncle David and Holly had actually been in love for a bit.

"She was probably too young for him."

"Do you think so? Attitudes were very different in those days, remember."

"Yes, I suppose they were."

And so on; school, teachers loved and hated, holidays at home and abroad, all the intense inconsequentialities upon which close relationships are founded and which enrich the repressed desire for intimate sexual knowledge, for the touching and the loving and the midnight sharing, to be wanted, to be satisfied, the sterling love of young people in pure confusion.

At night, on their third date, Chris stood with Steve in the shadow of the huge laurel hedge outside the Walshott home and they kissed, kissed desperately and with breathless passion, and parted, exhausted and exhilarated.

At length, on the very day that the Dutch army surrendered and the BEF's retreat to the beaches of Dunkirk began, Steve's letter of induction into the Auxiliary Territorial Service came through.

And Chris cried, "*Where?* Where are you being sent?"

"Rhys Park."

"*Wales? Wales, my God!*"

"Kent, actually."

"*Kent?*"

"It's some rambling old manor, apparently, about fifteen miles from a place called Horsfall."

"*Horsfall?*"

"Not far from an RAF station, so I believe."

"You're pulling my leg."

"I'm not, Chris, honestly."

"Darling, darling, how wonderful!"

That night, in the shadow of the Walshotts' laurel hedge, Chris touched the girl's breasts, and Steve pressed her quivering body against his thighs. For an hour they kissed and caressed, and Steve cried into his shoulder and together they cursed the war which would separate them. With delicious feelings of doom to temper their hunger, they parted for a fortnight or so, to do duty for King and Country and sip the cup of honour manfully.

And across the murmurous strip of the Channel, at that same hour, RAF bombers were blitzing Dinant, Namur and Aachen, and Von

Rundstedt's Panzer corps were roaring on towards Calais, impervious to the existence of Chris and Stephanie, combatants not destined for glory until the second wave.

3 Seller's Market

Christie's, the famous London auction house, plunged into the war effort by undertaking the management of a series of art sales on behalf of the Red Cross. Not to be outdone, Partington's followed suit. Young Mr. Trevor, who was impatiently awaiting call-up into the Royal Navy, stirred up a string of sales in aid of the Combined Services Benevolent Fund, a charity which received much publicity and support in the days immediately following the British Expeditionary Force's dramatic retreat from the sands of Dunkirk. For the first time, the British people really felt that they were in a war, a real war, not the brass-farthing affair tinkled out by the newspapers and the wireless but, at last, the genuine article. In one odd corner of English life, in the environs of aesthetes and moneyed speculators as well as small-time collectors, the response to the pictures of dunned and weary troops streaming back from the trains, of the dead about the beaches and the wounded on their stretchers, and the new PM's cock-pheasant voice telling everyone what a triumph Dunkirk had been, the response was amazing. Mr. Trevor, with a staff of wizened old men and young girls, could not cope with the deluge of donations, and drummed up the assistance of several well-known dealers, Holly King among them. Holly was not put out by Mr. Trevor's invitation. Mr. Trevor always had been an honest bully.

"What's more," he had told her, "I'll expect something decent from your stock. I know you, Mrs. King, you're not in any danger of being on the dole queue. Think of what it will mean to the poor wounded soldiers lying there in agony to realise that somebody cares, that their wives and little ones will not go hungry because—"

"Trevor, for Pete's sake," said Norma Butterfield, "who do you think you are? Mr. Churchill?"

Holly said, "Who's going to buy all this stuff you've got?"

"Everybody will buy. Buying's part of the fun, and a nice salve to conscience. The same folk who cleared their attics and cellars will trot round to the rooms with the express purpose of filling up the shelves again. What will you give me?"

In the end it was the Benares brassware; to be sold as a single lot.

At the sale, Holly sat in the high desk beside Mr. Trevor, while Norma Butterfield did a stint on the floor as an unpaid porter.

The collection of Indian brassware went to a devilishly-handsome, dark-skinned gentleman, elder brother of a serving officer in the Gurkhas. He presented it, along with a rather grisly Landseer, and a grotesque, silver-chased ram's-head snuff mull, to the brother's regimental mess. He paid exorbitantly for the trophies in crisp Bank of England five-pound notes.

The first Partington sale realised the best part of four thousand pounds, all of it profit for the Benevolent Fund from whose offices in Shaftesbury Avenue Holly duly received an official letter of thanks. But such sales, the daily duties of the shop, and peripheral engagements with the "war effort" did not satisfy Holly or lessen her sense of unreality. The nagging anxiety she had experienced the previous autumn had altered into a kind of bewilderment, heightened by Andrea's intrusion into her life and by her contacts with David.

Though extremely busy in the dark days of the Dunkirk evacuation, David managed to find time to drop in at the shop or, late at night, to Tite Street where, he seemed to believe, he was sure of a welcome. In all conscience, Holly could not deny him her company. He asked little enough of her, a glass of whisky, more often a bite to eat, a chance to sit down and chat before, in half an hour or so, he had to drag himself back to the secrecy of the room in the Admiralty.

The relationships which blossomed around Holly King were like the products of an eccentric gardener working in a hot-house: Chris falling in love with Steve; Andrea using her as a confidante; David treating her less as a woman with whom he wanted to have an affair than as a favourite younger sister. There was never so much as a whisper of impropriety in his conversation. His kisses were delivered fraternally on cheek or brow.

While many citizens were finding the experience of war enriching, Holly felt that it had soured and rendered arid the opportunities of the Thirties. She craved stability, peace, and suffered guilt because of that selfish craving. Maury, the Requisition Committee's factotum, whirled happily, and Ruth remained in the wilds of the Kentish countryside, tending her brood. May bridged into June, the high-summer months spanned by the magnitude of events in France, growing rumours of imminent German invasion, and the sudden scarcity of basic commodities in British shops.

Holly was without the consolation of Norma Butterfield's company for several days. Ferried home from France, Norma's husband was granted a short leave before being regrouped as part of a "special unit" up in the north of Scotland, a post for which he had applied immediately upon returning from the Normandy coast. When she returned to the shop, Norma was much less ebullient than before, more concerned for Les and his welfare, and thoroughly disillusioned with the news which poured out of the wireless which was only a quarter of the truth, according to Les who'd been there and seen it.

Norma would not be drawn, however, except to declare with some heat, "Too many mugs in charge of this war, I'll nob, just like the last 'un. Things don't change, do they, Hol?"

"They say three hundred thousand men were ferried away from the beaches," said Holly. "That really is a tremendous achievement."

"They only got away 'cause Adolf's got mugs on his staff too."

David had a different tale to tell.

"The whole army," he said, with quiet satisfaction. "It may have been a bit of a muddle, but we managed to save the army virtually intact. Believe me, Germany will rue that mistake."

"So it was a German mistake?"

"A very serious tactical error. God knows why, but the Panzers failed to push their advantage. If they had, all the small craft in the world wouldn't have saved the BEF. There wouldn't have been a man left to bring home."

"Norma's husband says it was a shambles."

"It probably seemed that way to a participant," David told her. "Dunkirk may not have been a victory, but it was anything but a disaster."

"The Germans will overrun France now, won't they?"

"The French will make peace of sorts," said David, "but yes, I'm afraid we'll have to stand alone for a while."

"You make it sound—I don't know—grand?"

"Grand? No, hardly that. Desperate would be a better word for it."

"David, is there a danger that we will be occupied?"

He looked at her, gauging her ability to understand the implications of that question, the horrendous import of the answer.

"A danger, yes. But we *do* have an army, redeemed from France. I fancy Hitler won't be too hasty in rushing across the Channel. And the longer he waits, the better it suits us."

"How long will he wait?"

"First he'll secure France, then he'll begin a process of softening up, a sort of blockade. Already the U-boats are wreaking havoc with our colonial routes. There will be a big job for the Luftwaffe too, I imagine."

"Aeroplanes?"

"Hm!" said David, tactfully switching off the subject. "But not for a while, Holly, if at all. Personally I'm much more concerned with the German navy, it's strong, very strong."

"Will Chris have to fight?"

The steady gaze again; David rubbed his hand softly over his beard. "Yes, Chris will have to fight."

"When?"

"Very soon."

Dry-mouthed, Holly said, "He'll enjoy that."

"Of course he will," said David.

The little parade-ground had been laid that spring, an extension of the sweeping driveway which led up to the country mansion of the Lofting family who, having sacrificed their seat, had wandered like lost sheep for a while then embarked for Connecticut where a distant cousin had promised sanctuary. As a sacrifice, the baronet and his lady had left behind three sons and one of their two daughters, plus the only decent pack of fox-hounds in the county of Kent. Long before Steve Walshott arrived at Rhys Park, the dogs had been hived off to sundry homes, and the domestic staff, one elderly caretaker excepted, had been re-allocated to cottages on the outskirts of the village of Colebourne. Gardeners came every day to tend the vegetable rows and fruit bushes and to plough and prepare spare acres of ground behind the stables, grumbling to any ATS girl who would listen that it was the wrong season for breaking into the earth. Though the coast was distant, the great sweep of sky which could be seen from the parade-ground seemed like a seascape and there was the hot, salt smell of dunes in the air, an illusion to which city-bred girls like Steve never quite adjusted, and which led to day-dreaming of silver sands and blue waves and bathing costumes while they marched and sweated in their unfamiliar uniforms, feeling remote from themselves and strange.

Background and upbringing did not seem to matter in the ATS after the first week of traumatic adjustment. Barmaids rubbed shoulders with debutantes—well, one genuine debutante—and the daughters of dockers conferred openly with the pampered children of vicars and public school headmasters on how to soften the leather of issue shoes, or get away with a dab or two of make-up of just the right shade to fool Sergeant Sims, who was never fooled at all. Steve chummed up with Cecily Bywaters, daughter of Sir Garrard Bywaters, the infamous "hanging" judge, and Cecily's erstwhile chamber-maid, Mary Hibbert, a formidable team now that they had been relieved of the burden of class divisions.

In addition to drill, the programme of training included lectures on army matters, civic affairs, health, dietetics and simple first aid, during the course of which the forty recruits were assessed for the trade training which would follow three exhausting weeks of "square-bashing". Billets were dry and warm, beds hard, food plain but satisfying enough to appetites made hearty by a hard day's labour in the open air. Only in the late evenings did Steve enjoy the luxury of "a little weep". Andrea would not have been gratified to learn that her darling did not miss home at all but pined for Christopher rather than Hampstead.

In the evenings Steve dreamed of him. West Horsfall was only twenty miles away. Planes frequently roared over Rhys Park, and Steve would lift her eyes from the sticky tarmac as the Hurricanes swept past, imagining Chris looking down on her with pride and affection. She wrote to him every day, garrulous letters full of details with which he must already be familiar.

After twelve days of uninterrupted training, which seemed like months, the trainees were granted a leave pass from ten a.m. to ten p.m. on Sunday. They shot off in all directions in taxi-cabs, buses and trains. A few even went home.

Chris contrived to be free for eight hours and tooled up to Rhys Park at a quarter past eleven at the wheel of a pale-blue Railton sports car which he had borrowed for the afternoon. Steve wore her dress uniform, in which she still felt clumsy and unfeminine, though Chris assured her that she looked wonderful, more womanly than girlish and that he had always had "a thing" about ladies in tunics.

"Where are we going? London?" Steve asked, as she climbed into the sports car, enviously observed by the handful of poor souls who were obliged to spend the day moping about the post.

"No, not London. It's a Christopher Deems Mystery Tour."

"In that case," said Steve, "I want to see the sea. Oh, God, do I want to see the sea!"

"Your wish," said Chris, "is my command."

Through leafy lanes, through tiny villages, out on to the broader roads that wended through Etchingham and Robertsbridge, past the brushy Darwell woods, the Railton whisked the couple, leading them, appropriately, to Battle. There was no hold-up at the Mountfield level crossing, and soon the car was whizzing up the long, easy hill and into Battle High Street.

Chris had booked luncheon at The George, a good hotel near the Abbey. Close by, Chris said, were the fields of war where, nine centuries ago, Harold's Saxon ranks had buckled, and William the Norman had surged down from the heights to claim victory and the kingdom.

The young man and his woman, in air-force blue and green khaki, ate a cold buffet and drank beer in the panelled dining-room, with the window open to the drone of bees and birdsong and the scent of roses budding on the borders of the Abbey lawns. And Steve talked, talked and talked, like a chatterbox, amusing Chris by this change in her character, the loss of the shy and reticent maid he had left by the laurel hedge in Hampstead a mere two weeks ago. He understood the syndrome; he too had changed during his first weeks at Cranwell, before individual traits had righted him and to some degree steadied the keel.

"It's almost decided," Steve went on, helping herself to a second dish of cold rice and pears—an economy dessert—"that I'm to be posted to a motorised unit for on-the-spot training."

"To do what?"

"To drive, of course."

"Officers, or what?"

"Officers?"

"High rankers always have their own drivers, don't you know?"

"Oh, God, I never thought of that. I assumed it would be convoy work. Lorries."

"It probably will be," said Chris. "Unless a general takes a shine to you."

"What if some general does?"

"I will personally drop a tiny bomb on his tin helmet, that's what," said Chris.

"I didn't think you were the jealous type."

"Indeed I am, where you're concerned," said Chris. "You're mine, Private Walshott."

"Am I?"

"Aren't you?"

"I suppose I am, if you want me to be."

"As soon as the war's over—"

"I just knew you were going to say that," interrupted Steve.

"Or before, perhaps," Chris went on, "you really will be mine."

"Am I to be given a choice?"

"When the time comes—of course."

"When the time comes I might say no."

Levity, the spurious lightness, went out of the exchange. Chris reached across the luncheon table and took her hands in his. "Are you inclined to say no?"

"I—Chris, I hardly know you."

"I feel as if I'd known you all my life, as if I'd been only half-alive until we met."

Steve was oblivious to the cliché. The young man had spoken words that mirrored exactly what she felt in her heart. She too had succumbed to this weird affinity, the feeling that her meeting with

Chris Deems had been inevitable, a process as inexorable as growing up, that she had somehow been "saved" to fall in love with him and that now she was whole and complete. The astonishing thing about it was that he was with her and part of her *all* the time. She wondered if he shared this experience, but did not know how properly to ask him.

She answered him softly, "Yes."

"Do you know what I mean?"

Again she answered, "Yes."

"Perhaps," said Chris, "you'll change your mind."

"I doubt it," the girl said.

Chris drew in a deep breath and released her hands, sat back. "Well, I have one black sheep in the family. My grandfather. If you're willing, I thought we might drop in on him this afternoon and get it over with. And see the sea while we're at it."

"Your grandfather?"

"Old Leo. My mother's dad. I told you about him. He lives in Hastings."

"Is he expecting us?"

"No. I thought we'd just arrive," said Chris, "and surprise him. We don't have to stay long. But I'd like you to meet him."

"What's he really like?" asked Steve.

"Really awful," Chris answered.

Each year, about the end of winter, about the time when little grass seeds and slumbering weeds in the Beckmans' patch of garden flexed and stirred and contemplated heading for the surface, old Leo raked in the bathroom closet and produced his magic bottle of Fynnon Salts, a big, brown, economy-size jar from Boots, which indicated to Cissie that spring could not be far off now.

When the cold east winds had relented and there had been warm rain and some sunshine and April had dovetailed with May and the growth was too obvious to ignore, Leo would rattle in the kitchen drawer and bring out a large teaspoon, would draw a tumbler of plain water from the tap and, in Cissie's presence, and with all the showmanship of the Great Marvo about to transform *aqua* into vintage port, would mix and imbibe a daily dose of salts, and rabbit on pitifully about his rheumatics and how any sort of effort pained him, like, and wasn't age a bleedin' curse.

Cissie, not in the least deceived, would nod stoically, root out her gardening gloves and canvas pinafore and green galoshes and waddle down to the shed and oil the Qualcast and hone the shears and, in due course, would roll the mower down the path and set about the estate. And Leo would emerge from hiding and risk injury to his vertebrae by lugging the deckchair on to the narrow flagstones above the border and would sit there and oversee the operation, with a cigar in one hand and a beer mug in the other, the very image of capitalism and male domination.

Not, it must be said, that Cissie minded doing the lawn. She was nearly twenty years younger than her husband, a hefty, muscular dwarf of a woman who oozed competence and energy and regarded the garden as an extension of the front hall which, with Ewbank and feather duster, was unarguably her domain. Leo's performance amused her, though she gave no hint of it and feigned sympathy. In fact, the old bloke was getting on in years, had used up the biblical promise of three score and ten, and she was just glad that he had to fake ailments and still felt strong enough to go to such lengths to avoid work.

Cissie had loved Leo, warts and all, since first he'd wooed her out of her bloomers and into his bed. The past decade had been the happiest in her life, what with everything neat and secure and the house their own—thanks to Maurice—and regular monthly allowances arriving direct to the bank in the Queen's Road from the investments Maury had made on their behalf and from Leo's daughter, Holly King, whom Cissie didn't much like, but hardly ever saw.

Naturally the war had made many changes to the sedate façade of Hastings, but the Beckmans' comfortable life-style had not been seriously affected as yet. They still shopped and went round to the Court Hotel bar of an evening for a drink and a chat with the regulars, to the Rex Cinema and, once in a while, to the Gaiety Theatre when there was a variety act Leo fancied, which meant, really, some lady songbird who showed her legs. Leo bragged about his grandson, who was an RAF pilot, and about Maury who was something with the government, and peppered his conversation with every banal phrase that went the rounds and that he picked up from the wireless and the *Daily Mirror*. In the past few weeks he had taken to shaking his head and muttering, "Gawd 'elp poor little Belgium," a country he frequently confused with Norway. "Better the Bosche than the Bolshies, though, eh?" A rhetorical question to which there was no sane reply. Leo had also gone out and bought a dartboard with Adolf's face painted on it and would hurl a curse at it, in lieu of arrows, as he passed the kitchen door where it hung, or stand with hands on his buttocks and threaten the caricature with all kinds of horrors on behalf of the British Harmy and "Our Mr. Churchill, Gawd Bless 'im".

Defences along the coastline, searchlight batteries on the cliffs, barbed wire closing off the beaches, brick and corrugated-iron shelters built into the gardens like Saxon burial mounds, many naval boats in the vicinity of the pier, and lots of servicemen in the pubs, these were but the stage-trappings of war to Leo; propaganda and wireless and newspapers' reports, a kind of serial which Leo did not in his heart take seriously. There was still a flat-race season, a football card, brewers' drays to be seen on the streets, cigars and cigarettes to be had from Mr. Sternoaks' corner kiosk, and Cissie to make sure he got the best of the meat. There was still sunshine to warm his old bones, and hedges to be trimmed and a lawn to be cut. And his missus to do it all.

Leo was asleep under the *News of the World* when the Railton rolled up the avenue of self-contained bungalows and stopped at the sunburst gate.

Cissie had finished the lawn and had brushed the grass clippings from the path and taken an oily rag to the mower blades. Now she was toying with the shears along the outside of the flimsy privet hedge. Before she recognised the young man, she had had the thought that the couple looked handsome and well-suited to each other. Both were slim and tall in their respective uniforms, the blue of the Royal Air Force and the green-brown of the ATS. The motor car wasn't the sort one saw often in St. Clement's Avenue, amid the brick, Tudor-windowed bungalows.

The couple wandered towards the garden gate, hand-in-hand and, seemingly, unsure of themselves.

"Cissie?"

It was only then that she recognised Leo's grandson, Holly's boy.

"Christopher?" the woman said. "What are you doin' here?"

"We were passing," said Chris, rather shyly, "and I thought I'd drop in and introduce you to—to Steve."

"Steve?"

"Short for Stephanie, actually," said the girl.

"Come in, come along."

Cissie stabbed the hedge clippers into the lawn and stepped across to the gate, opening it in welcome. Somehow she felt favoured by the young man's unexpected call, by the fact that he had brought his lady-friend here, without reluctance, to show her off to Leo.

The three had a brief flutter of conversation, in low voices, at the gate, then Cissie led the couple up the flagged path to the deckchair where, beneath the newspaper, Leo snored.

They stood around watching as Cissie shook her husband's shoulder. "Leo, see who's come."

Grunting, snorting. The paper slid away. Leo peered blearily up at them. He had never been subtle, never able to disguise his expression. First there was fear, a scowling sort of suspicion as if they were rozzers come to quiz him about some long-forgotten misdemeanour. Guilts rose out of the silt of sleep. Then there was calculation, an instant switching to self-interest, threaded through with pompous pride.

"Whossit, whossit?"

"Chris," said Cissie. "Your grandson—and his lady-friend."

Steve glanced at Chris, who squeezed her hand.

Leo struggled to extricate himself from the sag of the deckchair. Nobody offered to help and for a moment the old man was totally without poise or dignity, short legs waving, cheeks puffed out, until he found purchase and sufficient strength to heave himself on to his feet. He thrust away the paper and covered his fly-buttons with his hand, and patted down his crumpled shirt.

"Just havin' a forty winks, like. Caught me unawares, like. 'Scuse me, miss."

It was, Chris knew, the uniforms that Leo first responded to with excessive respect.

The old man looked well enough. Gone was all trace of the Lambeth pallor, of simian ferocity. Spruced up, he might have passed for a retired colonel, with plump, rubicund cheeks and brush-cut, snow-white hair around a balding crown. He still had the red-eyed glare of one who expected to be obeyed, however. Ten years of marriage to Cissie hadn't quite robbed him of that, and age never would.

"Been doin' the lawn, like," said Leo, before proper introductions were made; he waved expansively at the mown square. "Want ter sit on the grass?"

"Leo," said Cissie, "fetch the camp-chairs." She turned to Chris. "Unless you'd prefer to go inside."

"Not 'im," said Leo. "He's been stuck in an airyplane all week. Needs a breath of clean air. Right, son?"

"Right, Grandpa," said Chris with a perfectly straight face.

"Fetch the chairs, then," said Cissie.

"I'll give you a hand," said Chris.

The old man and the pilot officer went into the house by the front door and through the hall to a cupboard under the attic stairs. Puffing, Leo unlocked the door and handed out three canvas folding chairs.

He straightened. "Who's she, then?"

"Oh, a girl I know."

Leo grinned lasciviously. "Camp follower?"

"What?"

"I mean, your bit on the airyplane station. What's she do? Used t' be batmen in my day. Heard about you RAF blokes, how you get all the girls what's goin'."

"Have you been at the brown ale?" said Chris.

"Eh?"

"Steve's not in the air force. She's in the ATS."

"Steve?"

"That's her name."

"Gawd Strewth! Only Steve what I ever knew were a lightweight, fought up the Lincoln Halls Sat'day nights. He was Steve."

"It's short for Stephanie."

"Steve," said Leo, and laughed.

Chris carried the three chairs out to the garden while Leo, still chuckling at the manner in which he had disadvantaged his grandson, followed on.

The lush shadows of the trees gave a feeling of twilight, though, in the span of British Summertime, it was hardly yet evening and dusk was a long way off. In an hour's time, Chris was due to report through the gate at West Horsfall and, without delay, collect his equipment and make his way out to the dispersal hut by the runways.

He said nothing of what lay ahead to Steve.

Five or six miles out of Rhys Park, in a leafy lane he had noticed earlier that day, Chris stopped the Railton. He checked his wrist-watch, lit two cigarettes and gave one to her.

She looked sleepy, sated with sunshine and replete with the grand high tea that Cissie had insisted on serving them at half past five.

"What do you think of them?" Chris asked.

"They're funny."

"Peculiar or ha-ha?"

"A little of both."

"Well, now you've seen my grandfather," said Chris. "The family are all rather odd, I suppose, and on a windy night you can hear skeletons rattling in all the cupboards. But, basically, old Leo is the only blood relative by whom you might be offended."

"Why should I be offended?"

"He isn't like you lot, like anyone you've been used to."

"It's terribly difficult to associated him with you, Chris."

"I suppose it is."

"Do you think he approved of me?" asked Steve.

"Of course. He's always been putty in the hands of a beautiful woman."

"Not like you."

"It's the one failing I inherited from him."

"Do you want to touch me?"

'Yes."

She unbuttoned the jacket of the tunic, looking down at her fingers and not at Chris.

Beneath the white shirt blouse, her flesh was pale, her breasts showing against the material. She had removed her slip and brass-ière, quite calculatingly, in the bathroom before leaving Hastings. She had felt stubborn and defiant, wicked and sensual, but had thrust probity aside.

Dimly, Steve realised that she was behaving against all that she had been taught to believe about modesty and decency. These were virtues, however, that she could scorn only in the pretence that morality had been changed by desperate circumstances. By putting on a uniform she felt that she had attained freedom. Yet she was afraid of this new-found liberty and the strength of emotions released by it. But fear was tempered by a kind of nobility, as if she was making a sacrifice to some great cause when, in fact, she was only yielding to her instincts.

She lay back against the leather seat and let Chris caress her with fingers and mouth. Need for him built in her with astonishing rapidity; also sadness. This romance was so raw, nerve-quickened gestures hastened by the threat of a future so obscure that she could make no proper provision for it. Chris kissed and fondled her for two or three minutes, bringing a wave of intimate responses. She attributed to Chris a less naïve approach to sexual matters. As it happened, Chris too was riding a wave of purely instinctive responses, checked and reined by protectiveness, a masculine discipline which caused him to draw back from her almost angrily.

"No." Chris pulled away from her. "No. I don't want to—to—not rushed, not here in a car."

There were sudden tears in Steve's blue eyes.

"Don't you—?"

Chris did not comfort her, did not dare touch her, draw her into his arms. He put his hands on the steering wheel of the Railton. "Don't I want you? Damn it, darling, of course I do. You're so—so beautiful. Yes, I want you. But it isn't right. You know it, and I know it. I won't allow it to be— well, spoiled."

Steve drew in a deep breath.

He was being sensible. English. Decent. In his way he had restored romance, given her back stability. She felt the need in her wane and spread outwards into a grateful, gentle panic.

Chris started the car.

"We mustn't play around," he said. "Not us."

"How long will we have to wait?"

"Lord knows."

'Chris, I don't want to wait for you. In case—in case we wait too long."

"I know," he said. "I know."

He backed the car out of the lane and on to the road that would carry them to Rhys Park. He worked on the wheel with vigorous determination, his lean, handsome young face set in an expression of frowning urgency, as if time had abruptly run out for him.

Steve buttoned her shirt and tunic carefully. She was not ashamed. She put on her hat and held it with one hand and looked at Chris, not at the roadway, as he dashed the little car along.

Evening shadows were palpable now. In the high, enamelled vault of the sky, two silvery barrage balloons floated like moons.

"Chris, you aren't angry with me?"

"Steve, I love you." ·

"Is that true?"

"I don't tell lies."

"I know," she said.

"Would you marry me?" he said.

"Yes."

It seemed as if the car had floated off the ground, rising like a silent aeroplane to skim the hedges. But Chris hadn't stopped driving, hadn't slowed. The question, the proposal, was as pressed as her seduction of him had been.

"When all this is over," he added.

"Yes, darling." Reassuringly, she put her hand on his arm.

"You know I love you, don't you?" Chris said.

Statements of fact; he spoke as he would to a rigger, with politeness, no emphasis. It was the way they were, Steve realised; in character, together.

"I'll wait," she said. "I'll wait for ever, if I have to."

"Are you sure?"

"Yes."

"Shall we tell anyone?" he asked.

"Not yet."

He nodded.

Ten minutes later he weaved the Railton carefully up the drive-way to the manor at Rhys Park, past the parade-ground and the camouflaged three-tonner and the groups of girls who strolled in the warm twilight upon the lawns and pathways, exchanging gossip and confidences.

Quite openly he kissed and hugged her for two or three seconds, then, holding her arms, stared into her face. "Did you mean it, Steve?"

"Every word of it.'

To her surprise, he gave a little whoop of delight and spun the wheel. She stepped back as he reversed again and, turning to wave to her, headed off into the darkness of the shrubs that lined the driveway.

She stood quite still.

She was no longer buoyant, though. She felt horribly alone. Like a sinister echo, she recalled the conversation, the momentous dialogue of which every girl was supposed to dream. She had given her promise as matter-of-factly as she had offered her love. Knowing Chris, he would make it stick. But she had told him "for ever" and for ever might not last very long.

"*Steve? Stevie?*"

The girls, her friends, were seated by the wide-open window of the ground-floor canteen.

"What a corker, Steve!"

"Are there any more at home like him?"

She felt tears well up, but fought them, smothered them with her will and, straightening her shoulders, walked across the paving to the window.

Two hours and thirty-eight minutes later, Pilot Officer Deems, having been rushed out to the aircraft dispersal post at West Horsfall, to a Hurricane fighter already warmed and throttled, cracked off into the moonlit sky to intercept any one of the thirty Heinkel bombers which were trolling at intervals up the estuary of the Thames.

At that moment, and for the next fifty minutes, Chris did not belong to Stephanie Walshott, to his mother, or to anyone else. He was alone in the hands of God.

Leo Beckman rolled over, looking for a kiss and a cuddle, hopeful that his nap might have given him the strength to impose something more than mere rough-hewn affection on his stout wife. He had no idea what time it was or what had wakened him. He did not think that he had been asleep for more than a quarter of an hour or so, for he never managed to sleep long on his back.

The ceiling had a big dart of pallid moonlight on it and he saw shadows shift and, haunted by an old man's fear of the dark, and with a pagan dread of unexplained things, sat bolt upright, still groping at the empty place on the mattress where Cissie's hip should have been.

"Ciss? Cissie? What's happenin'? Where are you? Is it a bleedin' air raid?"

He thought—imagined—he could hear the sounds of whistling bombs and the drone of engines and the grumble of ack-ack batteries, the audible paraphernalia of threat stamping along the Sussex coast in search of little Leo Beckman. He stiffened, mouth open, head cocked.

"Cissie?" he wailed. "Cissie?"

Her voice was laconic. "Leo, shut up."

"What's happenin', Cissie?"

"Nothin'."

Leo listened again. She was right. There *were* no sounds. It was so bleedin' quiet outside he could hear the rustle of his wife's long, cotton nightgown and, up close, the thud of his heart, the gurgle of his stomach and a little phlegmy wheeze in his throat.

"Where are yer?"

"Go t'sleep, Leo."

"I want yer in bed with me."

"In a minute, in a minute."

Now he could see her.

Cissie was seated at the dressing-table. A stab of moonlight reflected from the ceiling into the glass. Her stolid, squat shape was outlined against it. Above, a swag in the blackout curtains admitted the moonlight like a searchlight beam.

Leo had no notion what his wife was doing there. She never wore muck on her biscuit and had no need to lard on cold cream before bed.

Frightened by the unusual, the unexplained, in a weak, tremulous voice he enquired, "Ciss, what yer doin'?"

"Sayin' my prayers, if y'must know."

Prayers! Gawd, was that all?

In spite of superficial cynicism, Leo Beckman was relieved, even grateful to his wife who, though she seldom cast it about, was an ex-Salvationist and had some expertise in commandeering the ear of the Almighty.

Leo sank back and stared at the ceiling.

After a minute, he said, "Put in a word for our Chris, eh?"

"What d'yer think I'm doin'?"

"An' a word for our Ritchie too."

Cissie was taken aback. It was years since they had heard from Leo's favourite son, months since the old man had even mentioned Ritchie's name.

"Why him?" said Cissie.

"'Cause the poor bugger lives in France, don't he? Go on, ask God ter look out for me boy too."

"Course I will, luv," said Cissie, and returned, unabashed, to her prayers.

Armed guards protected government buildings and metro stations. Restaurants, cinemas, cafés and theatres closed at half past ten. By night and day the streets were crammed with Citroëns and Renaults, and a Noah's Ark parade of trucks, vans and horse-carts piled high with luggage toiled over the bridges, making for Switzerland or the south before the Panzer flood engulfed them. The Battle of France was four days old. The Germans were on the Marne and, in the west, had pushed almost as far as Pontoise. The growl of heavy artillery was audible in all parts of the city. A pungent odour of pitch pine wafted from the burning forests to the north and west which, as the day cooled towards evening and the breeze dropped, became sweet and not unpleasant. Paris, for all its harried air, was beautiful still in the early days of June, and the citizens who had no fear of German occupation had difficulty hiding their cheerfulness.

In the warehouse adjacent to the shop in the Boulevard St. Germain, and in the basement beneath its stone floors, one such citizen prowled, purring with pleasure at the hoard of stock she had acquired in the past month, stock which would be re-sold to wealthy officers of the Reich at a very fat profit indeed. The citizen's husband was less pleased than he should have been, however, given his character and history; Ritchie Beckman, alias M. Claude Cazotte, was not happy.

"Why are you so solemn, darling?"

"There's so damned much of it."

"Of the finest quality, however."

There were paintings by Cleef and Claude Lorrain, Ostade and Le Brun, Vivarini and Gericault; a folio of four superb cartoons in chalk by Asmus Carstens—for which Maddy already had a buyer—two paintings from an altar-piece by Hans Multscher, a single small Rembrandt which had come dew-wet with the owner's tears as he parted with the family treasure to obtain money to keep him alive in Switzerland and buy passage to America in course of time; a listed landscape by Phillipp Otto Runge which, Madelaine said, would sell like a shot to the Federal Purchase Office in Hamburg. There were, too, some excellent canvases by Impressionists and Post-Impressionists. The "famous French"—Corot, Millet, Poussin—were represented by quality works, as well as satchels of drawings and engravings.

"Also," Madelaine reminded him, "they cost us next to nothing."

"Yeah."

"The Jewish merchants are so full of fear. What is a painting to them when their lives are at stake?"

"Yeah."

"You do not approve?"

"It's no skin off my nose."

"No skin . . .?"

Ritchie did not translate the English phrase. He said, "Money's money, kid. I just hope *we* never have to swop a Rembrandt for two tickets to Menton, or a couple of *bifteck* sandwiches."

"No, no, *mon cher*. We will be rich."

She would be rich, not him.

Over the last couple of weeks, Ritchie had stirred himself. The bolt-hole in the Marais wasn't the only arrangement he had made. He had been probing into the exact state of the business, into bank statements, deeds of stock and details of the partnership which he had left to Maddy over the past five or six years. He had to admit she'd bought well. In addition to paintings, there were sculptures and silks, porcelain and glassware, some silver, even a Lucien Falize gold cup in the Renaissance manner, as beautiful and rare as the one in the Paris Musée. An Aladdin's cave, no doubt about it.

Maybe the best piecemeal trove in Paris right now, since "square-dealers", like old man Lenormant, had been running down their stock for the past half year on the unspoken assumption that Europe would not be much interested in things of beauty for some time to come. But some German collectors were not willing to toe the official party line, to settle for "approved" art, the sickly junk which Hitler venerated. Billets in Paris would soon be decorated with the nice little numbers which packed the Cazottes' warehouse and, if the terms of the Armistice were reasonable, German high flyers wouldn't baulk at paying high prices.

For all that, Ritchie Beckman did not enjoy the circumstances which drove clients to the shop, buyers turned sellers now. Their arrogance and pride was diminished and anxious humility fitted them ill as they unwrapped a painting or dragged in a crated sculpture from a taxi-cab.

Still smiling, still charming, still sexy and suave, Madelaine would greet them as if all was well. They would show her the goods. She would make them an offer.

"Madame, what is this you tell me?"

"It is, regretfully, a price for the times, sir."

"It is robbery, theft."

"It is all we can afford, sir."

"I cannot part with it for such a sum."

"Then I suggest you try elsewhere."

Some would leave—only to return later. Most accepted the paltry sum that Madelaine dolefully offered them.

"It is a buyers' market, as I'm sure you will understand. But, if it is of assistance, I can pay you in cash and in any one of several currencies. Francs, if you wish, or United States dollars. Lire, perhaps? Even—" she would shrug and put on her most lugubrious expression, "—even Deutschmarks."

A surprising number jumped at the chance of a fistful of Deutschmarks, gentlemen who were *au fait* with each point shift in rates of exchange, prim elderly women as sharp as embroidery needles in financial matters.

Now and again Madelaine would consult Ritchie.

"Would you drop into the shop today, *chéri*?"

And she would show him a drawing or a painting and ask him if it was genuine. And he would say that it was—even if he had his doubts. And Maddy would thank him and dismiss him, return to her telephone and account books, to the big, brown safe in which she kept the cash. Most of the clients were Jewish; some were not rich. Sown with class prejudices, and grandson of a Russian Jew, Ritchie Beckman found a thin fluid seam of pity in him which had somehow thawed out these last few weeks. He detested the long-snouted autocrats, the French Catholics, and most of the others, but those who came most furtively of all, ashamed not just of the need to scratch up capital, but of their race and creed, those he pitied.

Not a lot, true—but enough.

God knows, he had problems of his own. His wife-partner practically owned him. Lock, stock, barrel, soul and body. He had been a willing party to the possession and could not condemn her for looking out for herself. She was young, energetic and ambitious, qualities which had drawn him to her in the first place. In a world at peace she had been a perfect wife for him.

"I could do with some money, Maddy."

"What for?"

"This and that."

"I will bring you some from the shop."

"Can't I use the shop account?"

"It is not advisable."

"Why the hell not?"

"We need all our capital. It is raining opportunity, Ritchie. How much do you need?"

"A few bucks, that's all."

He would not squeeze her, did not dare. She was smarter than he was, always had been. But she had work for him to do, serious business, the big, fat deal that bloody Herr Oberisch had handed her six weeks back, in Zurich.

Oberisch's clique wanted the Italian Collection, the seventeen paintings which hung in the private gallery of the house of Comtesse Dubriel.

"You must get them, Ritchie," said Madelaine. "Wili has a market for them."

"Germans?"

"A consortium of army officers, I think. What does that matter? Wili is extremely anxious that the collection should not be sold to somebody else or, as is more likely, spirited out of Paris before he can get here."

"Why doesn't he stick a spy on the house and just grab the gear as soon as the tanks roll into Paris?"

Madelaine took the question seriously. "It is not in the nature of Germans to be thieves. Besides, there will be much else to occupy army officers at first. In addition, there is the danger that the collection will be removed."

"Yeah, okay," said Ritchie. "I see the sense in it. But what do you expect me to do about it? The old bird hates my guts since I cheated her out of those Dutch paintings back in Thirty-three. She ain't going to let me past the front door."

"Since the Comte died, she has no money."

"How do you know?"

Maddy tapped the side of her little nose, a ridiculously inappropriate gesture. "Trust Madelaine."

"Do I tell her we're buying for a gang of krauts?"

"Richard, it is important to me."

"How about me?"

"It will be extremely useful to have Wili Oberisch for a friend, to have good relations with those military clients of his. The soldiers will govern Paris, and our destinies, after France falls."

Ritchie did not disagree, but Madelaine's grandiose phrases seemed so at odds with the light-hearted tone in which she pronounced them that he began to wonder just exactly what bleedin' Wili *had* promised her during those trips to Zurich, and what the cow was keeping back. Once the German dealer had what he wanted, chances were strong that he wouldn't give a curse about the "destiny" of Maddy Cazotte, and would shop her husband for a few extra cookies. Ritchie knew Oberisch's type only too well. Loyalty wasn't a word in their vocabulary.

"Please, Ritchie. It is vital. Do you not see?"

"Yeah, sure," said Ritchie. "You want me to buy the Dubriels' Italian masterpieces for an old song. We bung them into the vault against the day when Wili comes marching up the boulevard with a fistful of Deutschmarks and an Iron Cross apiece as a reward for being great little collaborationists."

"Half of France is collaborationist."

"I ain't a Frog," said Ritchie. "No more are you, kid. You're Canadian, remember."

"I *want* the Dubriel collection."

"So—why don't you get it yourself?"

"Only you can do this thing, *chéri*. You are so very, very good at it. No other person can do it so well."

She kissed him on the mouth.

Ritchie did not flinch.

He said, "Okay."

"Pardon?"

"I said, okay. Hell, what've I got to lose!"

A handful of days before Paris was declared an "open city", in the midst of all the confusion, Ritchie Beckman swung into action once more.

Fear brought M. Lenormant of the old-established Galerie Voltaire to the house in the depths of the Marais at the invitation of Ritchie Beckman. M. Lenormant, a party to Ritchie's dirty deals back in the early Thirties, had been, and still was, a friend and colleague of Holly Beckman King, a perfectly respectable art dealer of the tradition. But fear, and boredom too, made the old fellow jump in response to Ritchie's telephone call and a conversation which, by its brevity, implied threat.

M. Auguste Lenormant was bored because business had never been worse. Months ago he had sold off the best of his stock in anticipation of disaster, had moved his wife and unmarried daughter to a cottage in the hills above Montpellier. He had remained in Paris, in the big apartment in the Rue du Faubourg, unconsoled even by a mistress; M. Lenormant was *that* respectable. He was bound to the city and *galerie* more by resignation than necessity. But the boredom almost drove him mad. He had squared everything away far too early. He had nothing to do, nothing to worry about, really, since he had nothing of value left to be destroyed by the Bosche, nothing to lose except his life, and he didn't put much of a price on that, considering he was seventy years old and stiff in the joints.

Stork-like, a pillar of rectitude, M. Auguste Lenormant arrived in the Marais by taxi-cab and had himself unloaded, by chance, at the corner on which Zack's café stood. He had the Parisian's instinct for direction and, without appearing to check the numbers, tick-tocked down the Rue de Vallon to the doorway of Number 17, where he paused to finish his cigarette and brace himself for whatever astonishments might lurk within.

The concierge, Madame Tutois, had already been won over by Ritchie's charm and generosity. With more politeness than she had shown in years, she directed M. Lenormant to the top floor. Madame Tutois' suspicions that the wealthy M. Beckman might be connected with a Fifth Column were partly dispelled by the arrival of the second visitor, who was even more respectable than the first. Unless M. Beckman was resurrecting the Musketeers, the snowy-haired gentleman did not seem to represent a threat to the security of France or, indeed, to anyone.

M. Lenormant climbed the staircase slowly. No smell of burning trees here in the Marais, no sound of distant gunfire. The district was quiet. Artisans and colonial *immigrés* had gone to ground. He climbed to the top floor where, standing on the little *carré*, silently watching his ascent, was Beckman, plumper, thickened, in fact, and coarse, but Beckman nonetheless.

"I thought it better to meet here than at your gallery or mine," Ritchie began, without preliminary. "In case we're being watched."

M. Lenormant did not respond to the spur. He did not enquire as to why he, and/or Beckman, might be under surveillance.

Ritchie ushered him into an apartment on the left of the landing, a shabby place suitable only for a workman, not for somebody of Beckman's calibre.

There were two armchairs of scuffed moquette, and a table upon which somebody had laid a new, white lace tablecloth, on which stood a salver with glasses and a bottle of cognac. A box of cigars and another of cigarettes stood on the table too. The signs of hospitality worried Lenormant more than the threat had done; he distrusted Greeks bearing gifts.

He was not the only guest.

In one of the armchairs, rosy-cheeked and wispy, sat the

legendary *Fantôme*, the biggest rogue in European art, M. Hugues de Rais.

De Rais had outlived his own reputation and, these past half-dozen years, had kept himself so invisible that many believed him to be dead, or gone to America, the two being, in M. Lenormant's opinion, somewhat akin.

"Lenormant." De Rais got to his feet, quick as a fox cub in spite of his years. "How are you, my old friend?"

"I am well," M. Lenormant answered, formally.

"We are in the grip of hard times, are we not?" said de Rais, as if the German tanks had been ordered to run over art dealers and nothing else. "Who can do business to the sound of guns? It is bad for you too, no?"

"It is bad for France," said Lenormant.

"We do what we can," said de Rais with a brave, almost simpering smile. "Will you be seated? Will you take cognac?"

"No," said Lenormant.

In a dark blue hopsack suit and knitted tie, Beckman leaned against the edge of the table. Outside—abruptly— there was a sound like the bark of a machine-gun. All three men started. Motor cycle. The din was offensive to the nerves, even after its source was identified.

"I will have a cognac after all," said Lenormant.

Ritchie Beckman served him, gave him, too, a cigarette, American brand. M. Lenormant tried to relax. He was sorry he had ventured here, put himself at the mercy of these men. Beckman was bad enough, God knows, but in partnership with Hugues de Rais . . .

"What do you want of me?" M. Lenormant asked.

"Help," said Ritchie.

"How can I help you?"

"I have a proposition," said Ritchie. "Will you listen to it?"

"I will listen."

"It concerns the collection of masterpieces in the Dubriels' house in the Boulevard de Sebastopol. Mainly the Italian stuff."

"I see," said Lenormant, sibilantly. "What, may I ask, does the Comtesse Dubriel's collection have to do with me?"

Beckman explained.

It did not take him long to put his proposition to the elderly dealer. It was obvious that de Rais had heard the plan before; they had probably cooked it up between them. As Ritchie Beckman went on talking, M. Lenormant's face fell, and his glaucous eyes lit with utter disbelief.

When Ritchie had finished, Lenormant said, "You cannot be serious, Monsieur Beckman?"

"Oh, I'm serious all right. Never more serious in my life."

"What," said Lenormant, "what is your price?"

Ritchie shrugged. "For me and de Rais, twenty per cent."

"Twenty per cent of what, though?" Lenormant asked.

Ritchie hesitated.

"God knows!" he said.

For the first time in months, M. Auguste Lenormant laughed out loud.

West Horsfall's dispersal hut stood in solitary splendour in the midst of several hundred acres of open plain. Ash trees and tragic willows which had graced the ditch line for centuries had been hewn down, exposing a tiny cottage with a red-tile roof which crouched, with gables hunched, a half-mile south of the runway's end.

Blaze Cottage provided a convenient landmark for the squadron's raw recruits, chaps who found Kent as featureless as a nursery quilt, a flattened patchwork of fields and string roads, and who flew mainly by instruments and wireless. Chris Deems was no longer regarded as one of "the lost boys", though once, out of carelessness, he had brought his Hurricane down at Morton Hackett and been very surprised to find a bunch of jeering strangers on the turf.

Forty feet long, the hut contained a coke stove, a ping-pong table, three folding card tables, a dozen iron cots, assorted chairs, a large dustbin and, by the door, two benches. One was graced by a notice tacked to the wall above it—*Office*—and the other with a telephone. Arm's-length from the telephone, night and day, sat an officer or sergeant, sprawled in a club lounger, feet propped on the dustbin lid. For twenty-four hours, turn and turn about, the West Horsfall squadrons manned the post, ready to respond at a moment's notice to the muster alarm. On the turf outside, the planes waited, their engines warmed up every three hours so that they could take to the air instantly. Meals, and countless "tea-breaks", were ferried over from the NAAFI, a mile away, eaten *alfresco* on the beds or off the ping-pong table by the young men who remained clad in complete flying kit, boots and all, throughout the whole of the hot June day.

But now it was night. Most of the pilots slept, drowsing in the chairs, propped like corpses on the unsheeted beds, sticky and a little odorous after fourteen hours of duty. Naked light bulbs shone wanly on them. Planes warmed up outside. Some, a few, stirred and fretted in their sleep, and others wakened and reached for their cigarettes, or rubbed their eyes like children roused from a dream.

Chris never slept. He might occasionally close his eyes to screen out the dismal light, but his senses remained alert, his body poised to run at the first shattering noise of the telephone, the clang of the bin lid as it hit the worn linoleum.

He was not alone in this habit of tension; a dozen or so in the squadron, three in the flight, were possessed by it. It was not often discussed among them, save with the embarrassed secrecy usually reserved for sexual problems. Yet each knew of the others' "weakness" and each envied unimaginative lumps like Gustave the Pole, Billy Dryden or Jock Abercrombie, lads who could nod off anywhere, any time, and who snored abominably and unrepentantly.

On the handful of nights when the phone did not ring, and the flight was not on regular patrol duty, Chris would pull his chair close by the open window, smell the cool, dew-moist country air seeping through the blackout curtain. He would take out his notepaper wallet and would scribble letters to Stephanie, rambling, loving, unstyled letters, not works of which his father, the poet, would have been proud, but which served the purpose and brought from Steve letters in a similar vein, though not quite as long.

Steve now was a fledged ATS woman, "on job training" at a transport depot in Chipton Road in far-off Wanstead. She was billeted in a commercial hotel in Leytonstone and missed Chris more now than she had done amid the companionship of training camp. Her life had settled very quickly into a drab routine, enlivened only by training stints as a provisional driver of heavy vehicles, three-ton trucks and rackety old lorries, around the London army camps. Later—quite soon, in fact—she would be sent out on "long hauls", delivering new trucks from a railhead at

Leyton to units spread all over the South of England. The changes in her life had been so rapid and dramatic that she felt like Alice stepped through the looking-glass.

Chris, however, had long settled into his vocation. With years of training behind him, the difficulties and vicissitudes of RAF life accepted and acceptable, he found vividness now only in the air—and in the hours he spent with Steve.

Later, Chris could not separate that night from many others, could not put an exact date to it. He knew only that the moon was not full but waxing, and the night too clear to be really warm. He was glad of the fleece flying jacket which kept chill draughts from his neck and ears as he lay in a lounger, the letter wallet on his knee. He composed sentences haphazardly in his mind, his muscles, as always, tense, keyed to respond to the jangle of the telephone.

Chris Deems, therefore, was first out of his chair.

Sergeant Todd snatched the telephone from its cradle and swung towards the waking pilots.

"Yellow section. Yellow section. Take off. Take off."

Chris had already plucked up his helmet and oxygen mask, hefted his parachute from the dump by the door and was first out, sprinting, into the shiny-sixpence light of the field.

Night fighting was a comparatively new art to the command, and techniques were by no means perfected. Eye-masks for the pilots in waiting had not come into general use, though Chris thought they made the devil of a difference in the first ten minutes after dispersal. The "patrol system" out of West Horsfall was, at best, tentative. When a section was scrambled, however, weeks of training and the competitive enthusiasm of ground crews made take-off a swift and simple procedure.

Guided by radio telephone to visual contact with enemy bombers, the pilot had only a split second to plan and execute his attack, to hold visual contact long enough to thumb the gun button and deliver a killing burst from the Hurricane's eight machine-guns. So far only a handful of RAF pilots had made successful "kills" after dark, and they were spoken of with a certain awe.

Rigger and fitter had started up Chris's Hurricane, and an anonymous LAC—a new bod—helped Chris into the cockpit and his harnesses, tapping him on the helmet when all was ready.

The cockpit was as familiar to Chris as his room in the mess. Though burdened with over sixty pounds of equipment, he felt comfortable and, at last, relaxed.

The voice of the controller crackled and hissed through the radio earphones.

Seven enemy bombers were picked up by the searchlights. Formation flying across Ashford, heading, apparently, for targets in the Gillingham area. How the controllers deduced this fact was more than Chris could imagine. The ultimate targets of the Nazi aircraft did not matter. He would be directed to an interception point, along with his two companions in the piece of Yellow section which had been allotted to the job. He had no option but to trust the voice on the R/T just as he trusted the men who fuelled the tanks and checked the engines, and the girls who packed the parachutes. He was at the centre of a complex web of mutual dependence, and accepted that point without concern.

Cleared, he signalled for the chocks to be yanked away and, with two floating lights to guide him, cracked the Hawker Hurricane off over Blaze Cottage into the silvery sky.

Unlike some of his companions in the West Horsfall squadron, Chris loved the old Hawker Hurricane. He had no desire to be transferred to the larger, faster Spitfires. The Hurricane had virtues that Chris valued highly, ease of handling and stability chief among them. He believed that a good pilot could utilise these qualities to make up for the machine's patience in reaching altitude.

"Benjy?" Chris asked.

"Yes. Do you hear me?" the controller answered.

"Loud and clear."

The voice was distorted but it was nice to have the image of a friendly face to hold on to.

Listening posts across the Home Counties would be fussing with their sound locators, trying to plot the course and altitude of the seven raiders, to give threatened areas as much advance warning as possible. Strung by the R/T to the ground controller, Chris had no need to contact his two flying mates, Peter Greaves and Gustave, the snoring Pole. He was conscious of them though, shapes in the sky like anchovies in blackberry aspic. Pierced by searchlights and the flak spurts of ack-ack guns, the sky seemed like a reflection of the

Kentish landscape—passing rapidly away—like a trick mirror he had once seen in his parents' gallery, with a spectral series of images painted on glass leaves behind the silver-nitrate, so that one looked at oneself floating in and out of focus like a phantom. The plane was Chris's whole reality; the vibrations, the hot oil smell, the roar of the prop, the patches of heat and cold on the skin of his body as if he too was constructed of metal and fabric, a component plugged in by a fitter, wired to operate efficiently to a prescribed stress limit.

Climbing steadily, Chris flew the Hawker Hurricane east, in touch with base all the time. It was cold at higher altitudes and he liked that, felt sharpened by it, making slight alterations in direction with particular precision and rapidity in response to Benjy's whisperings.

Time was a zero factor: to airmen minutes were hours.

Benjy told him that the enemy was near.

Chris lifted the plane another five hundred feet and began to weave, high but not excessively so, out of contact with his two companions and concentrating on the glass of the cockpit, burningly eager for his first sight of his first night bomber, his first real chance at a kill.

Gillingham, Chatham, Gravesend and the Tilbury docks; all natural targets for a staggered bombing run by the ever-bold Luftwaffe. Chris "sat in" along that line at 20,000 feet and, twenty-one minutes after taking off, glimpsed the enemy.

One plane, not seven, presented itself, a laggard or a straggler perhaps, or just some unlucky sausage-eater lying at the rear of a spear formation. But the glimpse was all Chris had, and then the aeroplane was gone again.

Fleeting though the glimpse had been, Chris identified the Nazi machine immediately; a Dornier "flying pencil", a prototype of which had won the Alps Circuit race back in 1937 and had been the wonder of the Cranwell "first form". Recent bomber conversions were heavier but still elegant and slippery. Dorniers carried a crew of four, were armed with six machine-guns and had a gun position in the nose projection which gave cover to attack from below and behind, a recent innovation and a dangerous one for unwary British pilots.

Still expecting to find seven planes, Chris gave the Hurricane full boost in order to overtake the laggard and find the rest of the formation. Seconds later, he picked up the Dornier again and instantly realised his error. The Dornier was lost; it had dropped its load and was wending back towards the coast. A single plane was very suitable prey for a young pilot keen to make his first night kill. It was a game still, a noble exercise of the nerves and the will, as trench fighting had been for his father for a month or two in Flanders two decades ago. But the rate of progress was due to catch up with Chris, to catch him out in minutes, not weeks, in the shiny night sky above the Medway trough. He did not have to wait for winter and the mud, death in foxholes, and the rats, the bloody grind of clawing for possession of nameless seams of earth. He even had Benjy with him, whispering on the radio phone, though he heard not a word from the second sighting to the death.

The Dornier was "light", its belly empty, and it climbed to avoid detection.

Chris climbed too, chasing to 30,000 feet, then, closing, throttled back and swung out to strike. He thumbed the button.

Ammunition bolted outwards. He squeezed the button on the control column once again. The eight Brownings blazed. Tracers chalked the route of the shells, a ten-second burst flinging close to 2,000 rounds into the Nazi's body.

Oil smeared the Hurricane's hatch. Chris jammed the stick forward to avoid collision, drove down then and gave left rudder, yawing erratically. The plane came up, the tea-brown slick of oil stroked away enough to let him see again, see enough.

The Dornier had ceased to climb. Belly above him, Chris took the angle offered, closed and fired again, the target caught perfectly in the centre of his reflector sight, hovering, spitted on the intermittent tracers—and firing back. Shivering naked white bullets flickered past Chris and the Hurricane was out and clear, and in a steep diving turn once more.

Chris knew he had made a strike, a great strike. He cheered into his mask and chased the sinking Dornier down, following the trail of white smoke which poured from its motors.

When the parachute burst open just ahead of him, Chris leapt in his seat with fear, straps and harnesses tightening against his body.

It was all over in a flash.

Gunner or navigator, Chris never knew which, only that the young German's face was actually visible, twenty feet from his own, the enemy suddenly materialised, given features, substance. Snug leather helmet and swaddling black jacket made no difference, served only as a frame for the face, mouth agape, eyes white as eggs, hands raised as if to push the plane's wing away. The parachute, arrested, billowed down around the body like gigantic wings.

The thump of contact jarred through the Hurricane's cockpit. The plane sawed. Gaze still fixed upon the apparition spiked to the wing, Chris's fists closed on the control, and his foot squared the rudder bar.

The face was gone—head, body, even the great pale canopy of the 'chute.

Horror stayed deep in Chris, like a glass dagger, staunching its own wound, a smooth, hard hurt. He applied his intellect, like a salve, by scanning the wing for damage, and testing flight stability. There appeared to be no serious damage. The parachutist had sliced into the wing between the front spar and the landing light; the leading edge of the wing was metal.

Chris checked the function of the ailerons and fired a five-second burst from the Brownings, then banked the plane and brought it round again. He was badly shaken but, like the Hurricane itself, undamaged. He searched the sky for signs of the wounded Dornier, to take up the hunt once more. Another 'chute, quite beautiful in the moonlight, floated far below him. And there was the Nazi bomber, one engine squirting out white smoke, a signature of dark brown smoke scrawled after it too. The enemy. The boys, scared, in the cockpit, sick and sinking, fighting as he would to save the plane, caught and identified in the moment of their dying.

Thrusting aside revulsion, Chris closed his teeth on his under lip and tensed his trembling hands. He weaved the Hurricane and picked up the Dornier from the side. It was diving but not, he thought, out of control as yet, not completely

Both of the raider's motors were smoking now and it was down to 8,000 feet. Chris jabbed the button and, out of the corner of his eye, saw the guns blaze. He winged away, returned, sent another burst into the stricken German plane, snarling again to himself as he did so, sticking grimly to his prey.

Seven thousand, six thousand, five: it seemed inevitable that the Dornier would plunge into the earth. Blackout prevented Chris from seeing if dwellings lay below. No town, no village, he was sure. But an unsuspecting family, cottagers who might be wiped out? Did they twig at all that death might descend from the sky? Hanging close on the Dornier's tail, Chris pumped out the last of his ammo.

A couple of thousand feet above ground, the Nazi plane sprouted tendrils of yellow flame and, a second later, exploded.

Debris clattered against the skin of the Hurricane.

Chris banked the plane away. He felt the fighter sit down on itself.

Dizzy scarlet clouded his senses as he swooped out of the dive, nosing upwards to the heavens. He used the throttle and cut boost and sailed round in a spiral like a buzzard, sailed over the splash of smoke and spill of flames which smeared the ground below. He felt sick, not at downing the plane but with the memory of the young German airman hung on the wing.

Benjy's voice whispered in his ear.

Benjy had been with him all along: Jiminy Cricket.

Chris breathed deeply, swallowed, rapped out his report.

Benjy told him to come on home, gave him the bearing. Congratulated him. Gustave, unseen, had confirmed the kill. Piece of luck, really, Gustave the snoring Pole being in the vicinity. Not the big bomber formation, of course. Blue section had finally tracked it down. But a Nazi was a Nazi. Good man, Deems. Good man.

Chris flew the fighter back to West Horsfall and landed cleanly.

He had been in the air for forty-seven minutes and had killed at least three men.

There was something decidedly peculiar about Miss Coates. The skinny Scottish spinster owned and operated the Edinburgh House Residential Private and Commercial Hotel in Armville Road, Leytonstone, where Steve lodged. Miss Coates was very attentive to her girls, kindliness itself, in fact, but she had a creepy interest in their personal habits and private lives which was extremely disconcerting, and tainted the shabby billet with an atmosphere that could only be described as sleazy.

After a heavy day behind the wheel of a Leyland lorry, or a stuffy afternoon learning to read OS maps standing on one's head, Steve and her two ATS companions returned grudgingly to Armville Road. They regarded it not as a haven and a sanctuary but as a place where they had to be constantly on guard against the prying Miss Coates, with her simpering smile and unctuous manner.

There was nothing outside the hotel to warn Steve what she would find within; no Railton sports car, no unusual transport.

But Miss Coates, with a sly leer, greeted Steve at the doorway, where she had clearly been lurking for some time. It was a fine night but sunshine did not suit that part of Leytonstone, nor Miss Coates who, with wee dabs of powder and rouge, looked in the evening light grotesquely like a madame.

She took Steve by the arm and drew her out of the protection of the group as they filed into the hallway. Lightly holding the young ATS girl, Miss Coates made a large eye in the direction of the smoking room—a downstairs parlour where the wireless was kept—and said, "You've got a visitor."

Steve was surprised.

"A *man*," said Miss Coates. "Came in a taxi-cab."

"Who? Did he say?"

"Didn't tell me his name. One of our lads in blue, y'know. One of *them*. He's been waiting all the afternoon. In there. Wouldn't even tak' tea. He's been asleep on the sofa. *Lying down.*"

"Yes, I know who it is. Thank you, Miss Coates."

Steve tried to disengage herself. Miss Coates' grip tightened.

The painted features crimped in an expression of seriousness.

"You'll be wanting to be left alone with him?"

"For a few minutes, at least," said Steve.

"I'll see to it, lass. But you must give me your assurance that you'll tak' precautions."

"I beg your pardon?" Steve was genuinely puzzled.

"A nice girl like yourself. Precautions. Perhaps the chap'll have something."

"Miss Coates, I really don't think—"

"After all your training, it wouldn't be fair to the country, would it?" said the Scots woman then, patting Steve's arm. "But nobody can blame you for havin' a wee bit of fun."

"Miss Coates, that's quite enough." Steve's tone echoed Andrea at her most indignant.

She brushed past the woman and went into the smoking room.

Chris was seated on the sofa; half lying, really, for his head and shoulders were slumped against the floral-patterned cushions. His hair was rumpled and he looked white with exhaustion. Steve's mind was still buzzing with outrage at the audacity of Miss Coates and her perverted insinuations.

Blinking, Chris sat up.

Steve leaned over the back of the sofa and kissed him on the cheek. She was still dressed in her ATS uniform and felt untidy and unfeminine.

Chris massaged his eyes with his fingers, yawning, then managed a bleak smile. "I had to come, darling. I hope you don't mind. I felt I had to see you."

Instinct told Steve that the horrible Miss Coates was listening at the door. She took Chris's hand and drew him to her, kissed him properly, hugging him, then whispered, "Take me out of here, please."

"I only have a couple of hours, Steve."

"For a walk in the park, anywhere. Out of here. I hate this place."

"Of course."

Chris put on his cap and, taking her hand, led her to the door.

Miss Coates had sidled away but hovered by the cubbyhole under the stairs. Sweetly she called out, "Will you not be wantin' your dinner, then, Miss Walshott?"

Steve hesitated. "No, thank you."

"Will you be back before mornin'?"

"Yes, Miss Coates, long before morning."

"So long as we know," said the woman, then, with a ghastly smile at Chris, added, "Have a good time, and tak' care."

Hand in hand, the young couple walked quickly up Armville Road, hastening away from the Edinburgh House Hotel and the unpleasant Scotswoman.

There was no romance in the atmosphere of Leytonstone; a row of shops, a hairdresser, greengrocer, clothing store, the School of

Commerce by the bowling club pavilion. Overhead floated a single soft barrage balloon, its thick cable looped to an unseen anchor behind a railway shedding.

"I feel like a prisoner," said Steve. "I don't see why the War Department won't let me stay at home and travel to the depot by car every morning, or by bus for that matter."

Chris said, "You're not a civilian now. It's all part of the discipline."

She had expected sympathy, not argument. Though they had left Armville Road, they were still walking briskly. She said, "It would save the War Department a great deal of money."

"Don't talk rot," said Chris. "You'll be here for a month, then sent elsewhere. Wherever you're needed. It's—"

"Chris, I've had an exceedingly trying day."

"*Damn it, haven't I?*"

She realised how selfish she had been. She recalled the fatigue in him as he lay upon the sofa in the seedy parlour, and the fact that he had travelled, somehow, from Kent just to spend a few hours with her. She felt tears start, suppressed them, drew him closer and made him halt.

The setting was astonishing; no intimate café, no rustic lane, only the sprawling anonymity of the outer London suburbs where neither of them felt at home; and the time too, the tea-hour on a fine young summer night.

Steve said, "Why *are* you here, darling? Why did you come?"

"I wanted to see you."

"Is that all?"

He said, "I—I killed three men last night."

On the pavement, by the rectangle of allotments, backed by a frieze of sprouting cabbages, a trellis of peas and skeletal glass greenhouses, a detail of landscape with the figures of old men in it, the young couple drew closer still.

The girl put her arm about him. All she had to offer was herself, her touch. *Piffle*, her mother would have shouted, *they were only Germans*. But Steve understood, in part, the nature of his grieving.

She said, "But—but it isn't the first time, Chris."

"First time I've seen one. Not just a 'chute, but a man, a face. A human being."

"Do you—can you tell me?"

He had come here to tell her, to share the experience. He could not go home to his mother; she would read too much into it, would make it much more complex and symbolic than it really was. He could not go to anyone else, because there was nobody else, only casual friends and acquaintances who would consider him a weakling for hating what he had done, for the suffering that the death of an enemy caused him. If only Kennedy had been alive; Kennedy would have understood.

Chris looked at the girl. Nineteen. How could he expect her to understand?

Standing together on the pavement by the paling of the suburban gardens, he told her tersely what had occurred. He did not embellish the account, did not plead with her or bore her with an explanation of his desperate need to see her, touch her and, most of all, to talk with her. If only it hadn't started so awfully badly. If only he hadn't come at all, had coped with it on his own, as so many others had learned to do.

Then Steve put her arms about him and hugged him.

She wept for him. She shed the tears that he couldn't shed for himself, became the surrogate, displaying the pity that he could not express, the sensitivity that was despised in fighting men, in all men, except poets, who had gone out of fashion, and damned pacifists and conchies and cowards. She held him close. No English rose now, fragrant with bath salts and Paris perfume, but giving off a dull whiff of tobacco smoke and the motor exhaust which still clung to her clothing.

She said, "Do you want to go somewhere, Chris? Take me to—to—somewhere?"

"There's no place to go."

"Back to—to the hotel?"

"God, no!"

"Do you want to—to make love to me?"

And he did; that was the most dreadful thing about it. He had wanted to make love to her since the moment the Hurricane's wheels had touched the turf at West Horsfall. He had been exhausted and nauseated and excited all at once. He wanted so badly to lie with Steve against him, to feel the softness of her naked body, to hold her tightly against him, to love her. He wanted to gain from the death of the German parachutist, the blood on the wing, but he had not yet acquired the knack of unscrupulousness. Perhaps he never would.

"I want to marry you," he said.

"We can't; you told me that we can't."

"I want to know that you're mine."

"We won't be together. They won't let us be together."

"Some of the time. Enough of the time, Steve. Isn't it better than nothing?"

"How can we?"

"Other ATS girls manage it, don't they?"

"But my parents, your mother . . ." Steve protested.

"In a couple of months, you and I might be kneeling in a trench on Brighton beach fighting off a horde of German Panzers. In six months we might be under the heel of the jackboot; and yet we fret and worry about what Mama will say to a marriage. Steve, I haven't time for that sort of thing. We haven't time."

"Yes," she said. "You're right."

"Do you love me?"

"Yes."

"How long will it take?"

"I don't quite know."

"Two weeks," Chris said, answering his own question. "Three, at most, should see the paperwork through."

"Are you sure?"

"No."

"Chris—"

"Don't you want to marry?"

"What will happen?"

"We'll have as long as we're given."

"How long will that be?"

"Lord knows."

Steve said, "If the parachutist had fallen into your propeller —"

Chris looked startled. Perhaps the thought had not occurred to him, so guilty had he been at causing the death of another man.

Perhaps he had put it down into his sub-conscious.

"I'd have baled out," he said quickly. "Yes, I'd have had time to bale out."

The girl said nothing for a moment. She disengaged her arms from him and wiped her eyes with a handkerchief, a square of plain khaki cotton marked with smears of diesel oil.

Marriage in the middle of a war, marriage to a young man she had known for six weeks and from whom she would be parted almost at once, marriage to a young man who might be killed at any time? Did she dare lay herself open to the risk of a broken heart? Had she that much courage, that much desire?

"Yes," Steve said. "We must marry as soon as we can."

At least it would get her away from Miss Coates.

It seemed late to Holly, though, a mere eight years ago, the night would have hardly begun, and the sparkling excitements of London, after theatres were out and nightclubs winding into full swing, would have sustained her energy after a full day's work. But now, at ten-thirty, it seemed much later, and the unexpected visitor, in consequence, seemed threatening, like a telegram at dawn.

Holly wore one of Kennedy's cardigans, a cable-knit pattern with leather buttons and elbow patches, thrown over her shoulders to keep her warm. Though it was summer and the air warm, the old house in Tite Street struck her as perpetually damp. Tiny coal fires in the library grate spoke of frugality rather than cheerfulness and warmth. The cocoa mug, biscuit plate, cigarettes, all emblems of Kennedy too, gave the woman an androgynous quality, added in subtle ways to the feeling that she was not so much isolated as self-contained, divided by experience rather than years from the young girl who, with a certain bravado, had invaded her privacy at that hour of the evening.

It did not take Stephanie Walshott long to come to the point.

There was in her a brusqueness that reminded Holly of Andrea, though there was no weight, no annoyance behind it.

Holly lit a cigarette. Seated in the wing-chair by the grate, she heard the girl out.

"When was this decision made?" Holly asked.

"This evening."

"And where's Chris now?"

"He had to go back to the station. He's on night flying."

"I see. Did he tell you to come here?"

"No. He doesn't know."

"Wouldn't it have been more prudent to let Chris tell me?" said Holly. "I presume that you are telling me, rather than asking?"

"Chris wouldn't want you to be offended."

"But you don't care?"

"I beg your pardon?" said Stephanie.

"You really don't care whether I'm offended or not, whether I object or not."

"Of course I do, Mrs. King."

"If I asked you—if I begged with you—to wait a while—"

"We'd rather not."

Holly held the cigarette in finger and thumb, hands folded in her lap. Smoke rose in a stream against the rays of the lamp, and the girl was partly obscured by it, softened.

In the ATS uniform she looked authoritative, bossy; Andrea with official status. What, Holly thought, did this girl know of her, of the fullness of the life she had led, its density and richness? Did Miss Walshott, for instance, realise that she had been unfaithful to Kennedy, to her husband, and had, for a time, come close to abandoning Chris for ever? Did that give the girl a right to treat her so disdainfully? Did the girl know, could she possibly know, what anguish had been suffered when Chris was an infant, what the history of his twenty-one years added up to?

The echo of the voice of the man who had married her, when she was full of another man's child, rang softly in her memory, usurping Kennedy. *We are all other men's children, Holly, all strangers in spirit to ourselves.* She hadn't been old enough to understand what Christopher had meant. Now she saw proof and truth in the girl's determination. Holly did not want to lose her son to somebody so immature—yet that was inevitable. The young were their own masters, in war or out of it.

Cousin marrying cousin? Maury was right; it was an outmoded taboo. Medically and legally there was nothing to prevent it. For

130

all that, Holly felt sympathy for Stephanie shrivel, and a degree of bitterness take its place.

She had lived her life too quickly and too soon. All that was left to her, thanks to the war, was uncertainty and doubt, anxiety and loneliness. Now—for different reasons—this girl, this child, was about to tug Chris from her, draw her son into the same whirling error, a marriage made too soon.

Holly said, "The wireless predicts an invasion within the next couple of months; a German invasion. Is this a good time to marry?"

Steve answered, "It's the only time we have, Mrs. King."

Holly said, "You've only just joined up, put on a uniform, signed an oath of loyalty to the King—isn't that enough novelty for one year?"

Steve answered, "I'm in love with Chris."

Holly said, "And you're afraid that he may not survive the fighting, is that it?"

"I want to know that I'm his wife, even if it's only for a few months."

"And if you survive the war, if the marriage is intact in two or three years, however long it takes to defeat the Nazis—what then, Stephanie? Do you not think you might wind up married to a man you hardly know?"

"I'm older now than you were when you married Chris's father."

"Who told you that? Chris?"

"Uncle David."

"How did the subject come up?"

"I asked him about you."

"Did you, indeed?"

"He told me that he wanted to marry you, but that you turned him down. Is that true?"

"He married somebody else."

"If you—if it hadn't been for Chris, would you have married Uncle David?"

"If it hadn't been for Chris? What do you—?"

"Being pregnant."

So, from this unexpected source, this innocent, Holly had

finally learned the truth; David had known all along that her marriage to Christopher had been a forced one. Did he also know that he, not Christopher, had fathered her son?

She had lost much more than the initiative now. She had lost the assurance that she was right, that Chris and Steve should wait, should "be sensible", that she, Holly Beckman Deems King, had gained even one tiny grain of wisdom in the course of her existence or had ever made a decision ruled by the head and not the heart. What, after all, did the future hold for them? Only the promise of hardship, fighting, a hellish catalogue of uncertainties, far greater than any she had ever encompassed in the selfish days of her girlhood.

"I think Uncle David would still like to marry you," said Steve Walshott.

"That," said Holly, curtly, "is beside the point. Chris is of age to marry without anyone's permission, least of all mine. He must take the matter up with the RAF authorities, see what they have to say about it. And you—you must have your parents' permission. Have you thought of that, Stephanie?"

"We have," said the girl. "It's for that reason I'm here. To settle things."

"I won't interfere, not between you and your mother. Besides, she wouldn't listen to me."

"But may I tell her that you won't stand in our way?"

Holly said, "Is that all you require?"

"That," said the girl, "and a room in your house."

"A room? Here, do you mean?"

"Yes, please."

"Whose idea is this? Did Chris suggest it?"

"No. It's my idea," Steve admitted. "But it's a sensible one, Mrs. King. You have so much room here, and Chris and I will not be much together. Even so, we will need a place to call our own and I wouldn't want to begin married life in a series of nasty little flats."

"Chris may not want it."

"I'm sure he'd prefer it to staying with my mother in Hampstead."

Holly managed a faint smile. "I'm the lesser of two evils, am I?"

"I'm due for posting soon. If I'm married and have a convenient address I'll be given permission to billet out of barracks. That's the procedure. I'll still be in the ATS and liable for transfer posting and all the rest of it, but the War Department's fairly protective of its ladies."

"How do you know all this?"

"I've made enquiries."

"That's very calculating of you."

"I'm just trying to be practical, Mrs. King."

"Tell me, Stephanie, are you, perhaps, just trying to—what's the phrase?—to 'work your ticket'?"

"Oh, no, Mrs. King. I don't want to leave the ATS. But I love Chris and I want him as well as a career in the service. I see no valid reason why I can't have both."

Holly stubbed out her cigarette and immediately lit another. It did not occur to her to offer one to the girl. Even in uniform, Steve Walshott seemed far too young to encourage in the tobacco habit, too young and too delicate. There was nothing delicate in the girl's approach to the future, however.

Steve said, "Will you give us house-room, Mrs. King?"

"I'll—I'll consider it."

"You see, if my mother believes that we have a decent place to live—"

Holly interrupted. "What if you have a baby?"

"I don't intend to have a child until the war's over."

"Easy to say."

"I'll be very careful."

"Stephanie, it isn't that I'd object to having you here."

"Say that you will, then, please."

"The upper floor's virtually empty. In rather a mess, but—"

"Chris and I will sort it out. Please."

The expediency and convenience of the request was undeniable. It was just the sort of suggestion she might have come up with when she was Steve's age if she hadn't been so intent on being independent. More materially, it was the kind of thing that might have been expected to come from a mother, a means of keeping her son close to her for a few more precious years. But Holly had always given Chris his head, his freedom. She had never molly-coddled him. Indeed, she had been so afraid of being thought a "smother" that she had never been as demonstrative as she would have wished.

Now, ironically, Chris, the man's man, had fallen for a very astute and possessive young woman.

What was she to do? How could she deny the girl her entitlement, her shot at happiness in a world falling apart at the seams? Holly's first marriage, to Christopher Deems, had been part and parcel of a process of national rebuilding. Steve's marriage would be a flouting of processes of destruction. There was daftness in it, but also decency, a precipitate sort of honesty.

Holly said, "I'm making no final promises, Steve. I'll want to talk to Chris first. But—"

"Oh, thank you, Mrs. King."

"If Chris is of the same mind, yes, you may live here for as long as you wish."

Gone the woman, the disciplined soldier; suddenly Steve was on her knees by Holly's chair, her arms about the older woman.

Unbidden, Holly thought of Steve's grandfather, the long-dead Mr. Aspinall who had treated her so well, with kindness, affection and more respect than she was due so many years ago. Surely Mr. A. would have approved of these latest developments and read into them, perhaps, a nice little twisting of fate, like the stem of a Venetian goblet, subtle yet perfect.

The girl was weeping. Her apprehension, her fears flooded out without inhibition and Holly, who was not used to it, awkwardly stroked her soft ash-blonde hair and comforted her as best she could.

"I love him so much, so very much," Steve sobbed. "You can't imagine how much I love him."

And Holly, smiling, murmured, "Perhaps I can, Stephanie. Perhaps I can."

The downfall of the House of Dubriel, bankers and landowners since long before the Revolution, had begun with the machinations of Count von Bismarck and Kaiser Wilhelm and ended, effectively, with the appearance of an unscrupulous *socialiste* from Lambeth, Ritchie Beckman. That, at least, was how the Comtesse Kati Dubriel chose to interpret her personal history which, since the death of her five fine sons in the Great War, had been a tale of pride and poverty and stupid involvement with unscrupulous art dealers who had pillaged the best of the pictures for profit. Beckman, so the Comte had declared, was a force that would not be denied; yet the Comte had entered into criminal transactions with the Englishman willingly.

Now, however, her dear husband was dead, and she lacked his fatalistic strength. The Germans were at the gates of Paris, and Beckman and his gang were once more within the confines of her house, intent, without doubt, on robbing her of all that remained of her past, of the grandeur and richness that lingered in the private galleries and, in particular, in the Italian Room.

Kati Dubriel had no protector, no defender, nobody whom she could trust to make decisions for her. She was entirely at the mercy of Beckman, Lenormant and the one they called de Rais.

There was no time, no possibility of begging for delay.

Beckman knew it and would take advantage of it.

She hardly listened to his harangue. She knew that he was robbing her and she was powerless now to prevent him. She would have been better in the hands of the Gestapo than left to the mercy of this English Jew and his suave French cohorts.

Dumpy, dowdy, owl-like, clad in a nineteenth-century ankle-length mourning dress of rusty black and with her scant white hair untidily pinned, the Comtesse Dubriel had been roused from her hermitage in the sprawling apartment on the third floor. The draughty chamber contained her bed, her wardrobes and an incongruously ugly bakelite table upon which her meals were served. Running the house this past couple of years was a slatternly cook-cum-maid, the only servant who would work for the pittance that the Comtesse would pay.

The Comtesse truly believed herself to be poor. While the upkeep of the great mansion lapsed, and its many treasures grew dusty, the careful investments that the Comte had made, shortly before his death, would have kept the widow comfortable in the normal circumstances. But the income had withered and the see-saw fortunes of the international money market had blown the bunting off the tree. The Comtesse Dubriel was in a worse state now than in the period when the Comte did his shady deal with Ritchie Beckman and put himself, and his honour, in the Englishman's pocket.

Many of the antiques had been sold; even some of the paintings. But the Italian Room's contents remained intact, a monument to the great days of the Dubriel family, when collecting masterpieces was considered a hobby and not a means of investment for return. All that was left, really, of past glories was the collection, and the Comtesse was comforted by it, though, in truth, she hardly ever entered the long gallery now or gazed on the works.

It was directly to the Italian Room that Ritchie Beckman dragged her, however. His manner was forceful, almost brutal. The Comtesse imagined that this was but a foretaste of the sort of thing an undefended woman might expect when the Nazis invaded the city. She made little or no differentiation between one foreigner and another, had no wireless, took no newspapers, and acquired her news from the malicious lips of Peta Brichard, the servant, who brought it from the market-place and distorted it to suit her sadistic disposition.

Now the Comtesse sat with her shrivelled little hands folded in her lap like claws, her chin tucked in and her eyes glaring, while Beckman, dressed like a gangster, paraded about the long, mote-filled gallery, haranguing her, telling her some fable about Germans, when all he meant to do was thieve her paintings and justify himself in the process.

The presence of M. Lenormant did not incline Kati Dubriel to credulity. Lenormant had always been self-seeking and shifty, though he had a few shreds of honesty clinging to him. The other one, de Rais, clearly thought it all a huge joke and sat, legs crossed, on the frail *papier mâché* sofa of pearl and painted gilt, grinning, shaking his head and crying out softly from time to time, "Oyez, hear-hear, oyez," in the English tongue, as if to spur Beckman on to more intricate lies.

"You're right, Comtesse," Beckman was saying. "It's the next best thing to a robbery." He spoke in a mixture of smooth French and idiomatic English which Kati Dubriel, if she had cared to open her ears, would have had no difficulty in understanding. "I don't figure you'll trust me as far as you could throw the Eiffel Tower—but what the hell! Listen, do you hear what I'm saying?"

"Comtesse, it is to your advantage, I assure you," put in Lenormant.

The Comtesse glared at him, silent as a mute.

Beckman went on. "You had better listen, old lady, because I'm only going through it once. Remember, I'm not asking for permission, for agreement; I'm telling you. Why am I telling you? Because you don't have the ghost of an idea what's going on outside. Hear the guns? Smell the smoke? That's the Bosche. Do you reckon you're safe enough behind your big wooden doors? It ain't so, old lady. There's a little guy called Oberisch with your address in his notebook, and he's coming right here with his van to haul off every goddamned painting you've got."

Fra Angelico, Veronese, Tiepolo, Titian, Canaletto, and one superb Botticelli, a work which even a few experts believed to be lost, hung on the faded cream walls like evidence.

"Oberisch is a kraut dealer with a commission from a bunch of Nazi big-shots to seize your Italian paintings," said Ritchie. "How do I know? Simple, Comtesse. My wife—yeah, my wife—is Wili Oberisch's Paris agent. I'm to persuade you to part with the seventeen Italians, plus anything else I think is worth having, and to pay you peanuts—a pittance—for them. The idea is, you'll be so desperate to sell right now, you'll take the offer and clear out."

"I will not leave Paris," said the Comtesse. "You will not make me leave Paris."

"That," said Ritchie, "is what I figured."

The woman closed her lips again, pressing them together like a little beak.

Ritchie said, "The idea is that I buy your collection—all nice and legal and legitimate—and sell it to Oberisch, who auctions the stuff among his Nazi clients. It isn't, that way, like stealing. But if I *don't* get your paintings then Oberisch is going to find another way of laying his mitts on them, of 'claiming them' for the German State, for the Party. Have you got me so far, Comtesse?"

The Comtesse Dubriel did not deign to reply.

"Suit yourself," said Ritchie.

"I beg you to try to understand, madame," said Lenormant.

Hugues de Rais said, "You have imparted the bad news, Ricardo. Now tell the lady the good news."

"The good news is that we've no intention of letting the Dubriel collection fall into the hands of the Nazis," said Ritchie. "Sure, I'm a bastard. But the krauts are an even bigger bunch of bastards and I'm not going to be pissed on by them or anybody else."

"To the point," said M. Lenormant.

"By tomorrow, the day after at the latest," Ritchie Beckman continued, addressing himself directly to the Comtesse, "the German army will march into Paris. With it will come all the grafters and hustlers and leeches of the day. Collaborationists will come crawling out of their holes. Getting in and out of the city will not be easy. That's why I'm not giving you time to make up your mind."

"Concerning what?" Kati Dubriel found her voice.

"Concerning the seventeen paintings in this room plus, maybe, eight or nine from the gallery next door. Concerning getting them safely out of Paris and out of France, into cold store for the duration of the war."

"You will take them, I suppose?" the Comtesse sneered.

"Nope. Monsieur Hugues de Rais will take them."

"Do you imagine that I am foolish enough to let you do this? I will call for the prefecture first."

"For all we know," said Ritchie, "the préfet is a goddamned Nazi sympathiser. He'll stop us taking the paintings only to secure them for himself, for the krauts. Listen, I'm not *stealing* the things. I knew you'd think that. I'm going to pay for them."

"Hah! Conscience money. Ten francs each, eh?"

"Not francs," said Ritchie. "Dollars. United States dollars. Three hundred *thousand* United States dollars, Comtesse."

The Comtesse's expression changed; her eyelids, like tiny brocade flaps, flung up and she had to struggle to hide her astonishment.

"Cash?" she said.

Beckman and de Rais exchanged glances, amused.

Hugues de Rais said, "We could not raise that much in dollars, cash, Madame; not in the present climate. It would be impossible."

"Hah!" said the Comtesse scornfully. "I thought as much. I will refuse your 'kind' offer, monsieur. I will keep my paintings, thank you."

It was M. Lenormant who spoke now. "I have in my pocket the equivalent of fifty thousand US dollars in francs and marks. Both currencies will be honoured by the banks during the early months of the occupation, I am sure. The remaining sum of two hundred and fifty thousand dollars will be transferred to an account in your name in the Bank of Zurich and I will personally present you with a letter giving the account number. This can be done within twenty-four hours, in spite of difficulties."

"I do not like American dollars."

"Christ!" shouted Ritchie. "You're a dumb old bag, so you are."

"Ricardo, please," said de Rais. "Comtesse, dollars will be the most stable currency in the months or years ahead. Dollars will be the most likely safeguard against deflation. The franc, the German mark," de Rais shrugged, "even the pound sterling—how do we know what will happen to these countries? But the Americans are materialists, and they are not at war. The Swiss will look after your money best if it is in dollars."

The Comtesse had retained much if not all of her acumen in matters directly relating to money. She put up no further argument on this point. Secretly she had been intrigued with the deal and the care that had gone into its spinning. Of course she did not believe that she would ever see the quarter of a million dollars, or that she would ever see her paintings again. But she was selfish and greedy enough to appreciate the security that such a large cash sum as fifty thousand would give her, advantage over her fellow citizens if—when—the Germans ruled France.

She said. "What of the paintings?"

Hugues de Rais answered, "I will personally take them to a safe place, madame. They will not be sold or offered for sale, not even one of them. The collection will be preserved intact in a vault in Switzerland until this devilish war is over—then the collection will be returned to you."

"What of the money then?"

"It will be transferred back into our account, Comtesse," said Lenormant.

"To whom does this money belong? Where did it come from, such a grand fortune?"

"From me, mostly," said Ritchie. "It's my buying fund. But I didn't have enough, so I brought in Lenormant and de Rais. Right, gentlemen?"

The Frenchmen nodded.

"You will, I give you my word, have the right to the money," said Lenormant to the old woman. "You have my word too that the collection will be completely safe."

"I do not believe it," said Kati Dubriel. "He—" she darted a finger at Ritchie, "he will sell my paintings as soon as he has them."

"Not to the Nazis," said Ritchie Beckman. 'Not to anybody. See, I'm not going to be in a position to trade with the krauts. I'm English, I'm Jewish, and they'll take me for all they can get."

"Your wife, she will protect—"

"The hell she will," said Ritchie Beckman.

"It is your intention to run away with my paintings and to sell them in Switzerland," the old woman said.

"I'm not *going* anywhere," said Ritchie. "How can I *go* anywhere when you've got all my money tied up in the Bank of Zurich? Did you think I was kidding? I can't touch that account, Comtesse, not without your written instruction."

"What if I die before the war is over?"

"We'll sell the paintings. But it won't matter to you then, will it?"

Kati Dubriel sniffed. Her claw-like hands moved agitatedly, fingers drumming together soundlessly and rapidly.

"Who will look after the collection?" she snapped.

"I will," said Hugues de Rais. "I will drive the lorry myself. I will see to it that the paintings are properly stored."

"Are you not from Marseilles?"

"I am, madame, but I doubt if Marseilles will remain in French possession for very long, no matter what sort of 'arrangement' Pétain may choose to make with the Bosche. I do not trust the Bosche to keep promises. After consideration, Switzerland is the best place for us."

"You, Beckman, what of your sister in England? I would, to a degree, trust her," said the Comtesse Dubriel.

"England? What possible value would there be in going there?" said Ritchie Beckman. "England will probably be German territory too, before the summer's out. I told you, Comtesse, I want to keep your paintings *out* of German hands. This Wili Oberisch, he's a bloodhound—a determined little swine."

"Believe me, Comtesse, it is a breed we understand well," put in de Rais with a self-deprecating smile. "In metaphor, Herr Oberisch is our German cousin. He won't rest until he has what he and his clients want, namely the Italian Collection of the House of Dubriel."

Now, suddenly, the old woman believed these men. She did not trust them one centimetre, not even the stork-like Lenormant. But she believed them. They were, by the nature of their profession, as devious as foxes; and yet they had been so direct. Force was not in their natures; and yet they had been forceful. They were telling the truth about the Germans. There had been approaches made in the past, discreet, avaricious enquiries; some of them, now that she thought of it, from Germans. The Comte would have nothing to do with these men, would not even permit them to enter the house, to view the treasures in the long gallery.

Kati Dubriel felt a great fear engulf her. The paintings were all that remained of the great days of the Dubriel family, her husband's family. His last wish was that she would cherish the seventeen canvases, the nub of the collection, cherish them as she would have cherished her children, if they had survived the last German war, her grandchildren if ever they had managed to get born. If there was even a grain of truth in what the three dealers told her, then she must risk everything to keep the paintings out of German hands. She, too, hated the Germans. Denying one German his wish was satisfaction enough. Denying them possession of the Dubriel collection was something that would warm her cold old heart in the bleak days to come. And, she thought, the fifty thousand American dollars would come in very handy too.

She said, "How will it be done?"

Beckman said, "Do you have many servants?"

"One; a female."

"Do you trust her?"

"Hah!"

"In that case," said Ritchie Beckman, "we'll come around tomorrow morning, lock you and the servant in a bedroom—and rob you."

"In case she is a collaborator?" said Kati Dubriel.

"Right," said Beckman.

"What of my money, my fifty thousand dollars?"

"I have it right here," said Hugues de Rais.

"What if the Germans come, looking for my paintings?"

"Tell them," said Ritchie, "you were robbed by a Jew."

"They will believe that, madame," said M. Lenormant.

"Because it will be true," said Kati, Comtesse Dubriel.

The fingers on her shoulder had become exceedingly strong all of a sudden. She winced a little and tried to slip from the chair, from his grasp, but Ritchie would not allow it. The grip tightened. She experienced a fleeting awe of him, an emotion she had not felt in relation to Ritchie since the first days of their meeting, when she was little more than a child and he was rich and arrogant and demanding, and a good deal younger.

"It's simple, my love," Ritchie said. "You want the Dubriel collection for little Wili, you gotta pay for it. The old cow isn't gonna let it go for nothing. Know what she said? She said she'd rather burn it than let me have it for free."

"But this transfer is for one hundred and fifty thousand dollars. It is all that we have, every last sou. How will we operate, how will we survive without money?"

"Come off it, Maddy. For the outlay we get twenty-six masterpieces. No fakes. No doubtful junk. Work it out, and you'll discover it comes out at about six thousand bucks each piece. Even the Perugino, the *Hanging of the Cross*, is worth three or four times what we're paying for it, sold under the hammer in the States. You didn't imagine we'd get the Dubriel collection for fifty francs a frame, did you?"

"No. Now that you explain it—"

"So sign the bank transfer, okay? Since you control the account, I need your signature."

"But to have no working capital, no security, Ritchie?"

"For Gawd's sake!" Ritchie exploded. "Little Wili's gonna be here in a week. We're not gonna starve in a goddamned week. Little Wili'll shell out half a million dollars, or the equal rate in some other hard currency. Minimum. I figure we might squeeze him up to six hundred thousand if he likes the unlisted canvases I creamed from the Dubriels' front gallery."

"You forget, I have never seen the Dubriel collection."

"Which is why you need me, right? In case the old bird palms you off with fakes," said Ritchie. "Anyhow, I've done what you asked. I talked her out of the paintings. So why are you whining at having to shell out a few lousy bucks?"

"Where are the paintings now?"

"Still in the gallery, in the Comtesse's house in the Boulevard de Sebastopol. Did you expect me to lug them home in a bleedin' basket? Tomorrow I'll crate them and get them safe to the shop."

"The shop? What if there is bombing?"

"I'm not gonna stick them in the window, Maddy. They'll be well strawed and padded and safe enough in the cellar. Anyhow, according to your 'inside' information, the krauts won't bomb Paris. Too civilised to shell the good old City of Light, right?"

Madelaine breathed through her nose, trying to calm herself. She was beginning to regret having employed her husband in this transaction. But there had been no help for it. It was true; he had done a fine job. Six thousand American dollars was a piffling sum to pay for such fine works. She would probably be able to sell the collection intact to Wili Oberisch within a few days of his arrival in Paris. She might even persuade him to act as agent and also sell some of the other quality paintings which she had acquired in the past month. Madelaine had no reason to be unsettled and apprehensive. But she had grown used to the security offered by the Swiss account, by the knowledge that there were so many, many dollars salted away in her name in Zurich. She could have "retired" immediately to live like a royal princess on the interest, in Switzerland or some other neutral country.

Ritchie's fingers brought her back to reality.

It was too late to contemplate "retirement". Besides, it wasn't in her character to turn her back on another fortune, three or four times as large, in promise, as the one she had already amassed.

She scanned the document before her on the desk once more. It was part letter, part form. If she had been obliged to commit such a massive sum of money to her husband, she would have baulked. But the document transferred the capital to a numbered account in the name of the Comtesse Katerina Dubriel, and Madelaine could not fathom how Ritchie could possibly get his hands on it.

The Dubriel woman had already penned her signature, a crabbed scribble impressed over with a family stamp. M. Lenormant and M.

de Rais had acted as witnesses and their names were on the form too. No notarisation by a public official was required; the Swiss were all for simplicity and ease of manipulation when it came to capital. Even so, Madelaine hesitated.

Ritchie said, "Are you gonna sit there staring at the goddamned thing until the Gestapo kick the door in, and Wili hoves round here with his bully boys?"

It had not occurred to Madelaine before that Wili Oberisch might actually use his connections with the official Gestapo to gain his ends. He was, after all, an official employee of the Reich, as well as an independent agent.

Madelaine said, "Tell me again."

Barely restraining his temper at her obtuseness, Ritchie said, "I give the signed document to the old bird. Her legal eagle checks it out, gives her the nod. De Rais and me and a couple of lads pack up and crate the goods. We stash them in this van de Rais's picked up for the day and haul them round to our *galerie*, stack them in the cellar. Comtesse has her loot. We have twenty-six paintings. Then we put our feet up and keep our heads down and wait for little Wili to roll into town."

Madelaine glanced round at her husband.

"Kiddo, sign the bloody thing," he said wearily. "Sign it or tear it up and forget the whole thing. I don't really give a monkey's."

He released her, walked away to the cabinet and poured himself a glass of white wine, leaving her alone at the escritoire in the corner of the room.

Madelaine blinked, then signed.

In a trice, Ritchie was across the room. He whipped the document away from her, flapping it to dry the ink, then, folding it expertly, tucked it into his waistcoat pocket.

"Great!" he said. "At goddamned last."

He hurried into the bedroom and reappeared in his light-weight topcoat.

Madelaine shot to her feet. "Are you going out?"

"Got to see de Rais about the packers and make sure the van's okay for early tomorrow morning. We don't want any slip-ups at this stage, do we?"

Madelaine, more bewildered than ever, shook her head.

"See you tomorrow, then," said Ritchie.

"You will not be home all night?"

"I doubt it." Ritchie kissed her, *en passant*, and strode to the door of the apartment. "Miss me, won't you?"

Madelaine gave no answer.

The door closed.

She seated herself at the escritoire once more, slender hands resting on the polished wood and leather top, stared at the calendar pinned to the wall, and wished, in a way, that Wili Oberisch would arrive that night.

She was worried about Ritchie, very, very worried.

Somehow she suspected that she had been taken for a ride.

But she didn't—yet—know how.

4 Falling Leaf

Now that Italy had entered the war, it would only be a matter of time until the ports of the Mediterranean would be closed to Allied shipping. The phase of "the long haul" had begun for the seamen of Great Britain. The fall of France had increased the problems for navy planners. The backroom boys of the Admiralty who balanced logistics against economy, in close liaison with masters, defence officers and a multitude of other departments, were preparing for the worst.

David's days were filled with rendezvous, with routing officers, with debriefing couriers from Africa and other lands of the East, in consoling exiled owners of Dutch liner fleets and in helping to develop the 12,000 mile sea route to the Middle East. This route, which hooked far from its eventual destination, via the Cape of Good Hope, Mombasa and the Red Sea, was the back door entrance to be used if and when Suez was cut off.

In his capacity as an RN Intelligence Officer, David's daily duties often seemed utterly futile, planning for contingencies that might never arise, "floating" ideas that never reached the surface, and attending countless meetings as an Admiralty observer in the midst of situations where everybody else seemed to know what they were doing and only he had no positive task to perform. He was, however, expected to be familiar with the organisation and functions of the Ministry of War Transport Department, the high command, where the movements of all British merchant ships were plotted and recorded, to read every report that issued from the Commodore of Convoys and to cultivate, as best he could, his own circle of chums among the masters.

David had no leisure, no time left for himself—or for Holly. He was often out of London for days on end, and Holly, knowing nothing of the demands of the job, had no means of squaring David's "interest" with his absences. She assumed, quite muddleheadedly, that David was in cahoots with Andrea, was visiting his sister with unfailing regularity and that once more she was threatened by the Aspinalls.

She had telephoned Maury at his office but had been unable to track him down and, so far, her brother had not returned her call. In Applehurst, Ruth was too fully occupied with the children to pay much attention to Holly's conversation, though she invited Holly down for the weekend.

It was three days after her talk with Steve before Holly was able to meet her son. He called her and asked if she would have dinner with him at the Ritz. Unable to bring herself to interrupt the hasty young voice, Holly meekly agreed.

Chris was waiting for her in the foyer. He was dressed in service uniform and looked, she thought, haggard.

Pressed, as always, for time, Chris led his mother at once into the dining-room and, in that charmingly casual manner he had, persuaded the waiter to serve the meal as rapidly as possible.

"We could have eaten at home, you know," Holly said.

"No, I wanted to make it a bit of an occasion—even if I do only have a couple of hours to spare."

"What occasion?"

"Steve and I—we're engaged."

"Oh!"

"Aren't you surprised?"

"Not particularly."

"Annoyed?"

"Not in the least."

"I—well, I didn't know that Steve was so keen. It wasn't at my instigation that she came to see you "

"So I gathered."

"But it *is* a jolly good idea, Mother."

"A quick marriage, do you mean?"

"Coming to live with you."

"Yes," said Holly.

"I can tell that you don't approve of any of this."

"It isn't that I don't approve. I just wish you would wait. You don't know your own mind, either of you. Steve, perhaps, is being carried away by—by 'freedom', I suppose."

"None of us are as free as we'd wish to be."

"Don't pamper me, Chris, with platitudes."

"We've put things in hand."

"Will it be difficult?"

"Not really," said Chris. "The only difficulty will be in arranging time off for the actual wedding."

"Has Stephanie told her mother yet?"

"No, not yet. Tonight. She's gone home tonight. I gave her an engagement ring, just an hour ago. It wasn't terribly romantic. I just sort of thrust it at her, said 'Here', and ran. Perhaps, when Steve and I are old and grey, we will look back on all this and see it through a golden haze of nostalgia and think how charming and romantic it was. But right now it's all rather a cheat."

Yes, thought Holly, that described the process of growing, of satisfying need and necessity: all a bit of a cheat. She, for instance, had never managed to adjust the timing of her life, never had anything she wanted in the proper sequence. Even marriage to Kennedy, which had turned out on the whole to be exceedingly happy, had been foisted upon her by expediency. To Holly, in her forties, the love of four men and the fact that she had been the architect of a business which in its hey-day had netted thirty thousand a year in profits, came to very little balanced against the sacrifices which she had had to make, the things she had had to deny herself to make Chris happy.

Now Chris was a grown man, about to be married. She ought to be glad for him, relieved. But the war had come along and cheated her once more of even the smallest, the most humble of pleasures.

Unlike Andrea, who would rail heatedly against fate in the form of her husband and children, Holly had no fight left in her.

She said, "Whatever you want, Chris."

"Ah, Mother, that's always been your motto. But do you really mean it?"

"Steve's a very nice girl."

"Damned by faint praise."

"No," said Holly, "I do mean it. She is a very nice girl."

"Not losing a son and all that."

"Gaining a daughter, yes."

"And Steve likes you—even if she is an Aspinall."

"What on earth is that supposed to mean?" said Holly.

"You had an affair with her Uncle David, didn't you?"

"Chris, really!"

"But you did, didn't you? It wasn't a girlish infatuation at all, or if it was it got—got—serious. Aren't I right?"

"Surely you don't expect me to tell you?"

"A nod would do," the young man said.

Holly said, "It's none of your business, Chris. It's—it all happened so very long ago."

"But it did happen, didn't it?"

His persistence was cloaked by a kind of ruefulness, an amusement, as if he found the whole idea of his mother's relationship with the bearded, middle-aged naval officer faintly ridiculous.

Nonetheless, he was persistent.

For twenty years Holly had kept the secret, had made the keeping of it into a major issue in her heart. Now that the source, the essence of her bargain with Christopher Deems had challenged her to tell the truth, she felt no panic, only a bizarre sense of relief.

She said, "Who's been spreading silly stories? Have you been talking to Uncle Maury?"

Chris said, "I've been talking to David Aspinall."

"David is a pleasant chap," said Holly, "but not trustworthy. I wouldn't take his word on anything. What did he tell you?"

"Absolutely nothing. But he thinks he's my father."

Holly put aside a half-eaten crème caramel and helped herself to the champagne which Chris had insisted on buying in spite of its exorbitant price tag. Celebrations were in order? Was this why

Chris had brought her here, stolen a few precious hours from his fiancée, from his beloved aeroplanes, from his duty to the country at large? To find out that she had obliged him to live a lie?

Chris did not appear particularly perturbed. But then he had the knack of hiding his feelings, the gift of inscrutability which was well cultivated at public schools. If he had been dragged up in Lambeth, he would have been leaping about like a chimpanzee and demanding to know who he was, upon whom he must wreak revenge for the deception, for the raw deal he'd been given as his birthright.

"Did David tell you this?" she said.

"Of course not. He's a gentleman."

"I think you've got it wrong, Chris."

"No, I haven't. Steve and I worked it out."

"Oh, you did, did you?"

"Just for fun, sort of thing."

"A queer idea of fun," said Holly.

"Perhaps," said Chris, "he'd like to be my father."

"Don't flatter yourself."

"It was a compliment to you, Mother."

"And don't try to charm me."

"Is he?" said Chris.

"This whole conversation," said Holly, "is becoming farcical and slightly unsavoury."

"Unsavoury?" said Chris.

"I'm not, and never was, Lady bloody Cunard, you know," said Holly, with a trace of South London accent.

"So he isn't?" said Chris.

"Why are you badgering me, especially now?"

"Mother, you can't blame me for being curious."

"No, I suppose I can't."

"You haven't answered my question."

At last, he had put her on the spot. She could no longer evade it. She was faced with the choice of telling him a lie or of revealing her secret. He might appear to be treating the matter as a joke, but she sensed that beneath his light-heartedness there was tension.

"I don't know how to answer your question," said Holly.

"But—but you, you of all people, Mother. You must know "

"I don't."

"So." Chris's smile had stiffened. "So you—and I—don't know who—"

"I had an affair with David Aspinall." Holly delivered the statement in a measured tone. "Is that what you want to hear? I slept with him. He married, ran off with another girl. She was— neurotic. He felt sorry for her, I think. In any case, he married her on the spur of the moment."

"Leaving you pregnant?"

Now she told the lie. She wrapped it and presented it neatly in an odd-shaped package but it was, nonetheless, a lie.

She said, "I don't know."

"Oh, Mother. I can't believe it. You must have known."

"I married Christopher Deems on what used to be known as the rebound. I hadn't—well, I hadn't slept with Christopher. But all of it took place within a handful of weeks. Days, really."

"You married—married Christopher Deems out of *pique*."

She preferred that he think ill of her rather than of the memory of the dark, tormented man who had taken her in and given her not only shelter and a home but love too.

She answered, "Yes."

"Good God!"

"I didn't discover that I was pregnant until six weeks later. To save you wasting more time on the arithmetic," Holly went on, quite glibly now, "I may tell you that I don't *know* whether you were fathered by Christopher or by David."

"How could—could you—live without knowing?"

"I had you, and that was all that mattered."

"And poor old Deems?"

"He gave his life for you, Chris."

"Did he know about Aspinall?"

"Yes. I had no secrets from your—from Christopher."

"Good God!" the young man repeated. He leaned forward. "It's incredible. Really and truly incredible. He married you—knowing—"

"He was that kind of man, Chris. But none of this counts, does it? Really, does it? Kennedy raised you, and he raised you well."

"Is Steve my cousin?"

"I don't know. I don't think so."

Chris's eyes were round, boyish again. It was as if he had discovered a starfish in a stale rock pool, something unusual and alive in the scummed water. "I wondered why we were so attracted, why there was that immediate, instantaneous affinity between us. If we were cousins, that would explain it."

"Part of it, perhaps," said Holly. "If you are cousins."

"What do I put down on the form, the marriage application?"

"Don't be ridiculous! Do you want to make things even more difficult for the pair of you? Put down that you are Christopher Deems, bachelor, and she Stephanie Walshott, spinster, and let it go at that. It's not the business of the authorities. It's not illegal," said Holly, recalling the emphatic Maury, "and it's not immoral. If you love Stephanie, marry her and let it go. Please."

"Do you really not know?"

"Really and truly," Holly lied.

Unsure, embarrassed, Chris laughed. "It seems that I'm a chap without a father."

"Does it make any real difference?"

"I wish you'd told me the truth before now."

"To all intents and purposes, Kennedy was your father. How— why—would I tell you? And tell you what? That there was doubt? That's all. Doubt. Kennedy and Christopher are both dead. You've no memory of one and only happy memories of the other. Please let it go at that."

Chris sighed. "You're probably right."

"Right or wrong, it's all you can do."

"I could speak to David."

"Never! Absolutely not! What purpose would it serve?"

"None, I suppose. Be interesting, though, to find out what he thinks."

"I always believed," said Holly, lying again, "that Chris Deems was your father. Right from the first."

"Because it was convenient and comforting, somehow correct?"

"Probably," said Holly.

"Well," Chris lifted his champagne glass, "here's to the three of them."

"Don't be sarcastic," said Holly, sharply.

"Sorry, Mother," said Chris.

*

Unlike his sister, Ritchie Beckman's métier was the present not the past. The advent of the Nazis had exorcised from his sub-conscious all the troubling little torments of guilt and shame. He no longer felt weakened by his own wickednesses and, in treachery and deception, found himself restored, flushed with the energy and assurance of youth. De Rais had always maintained perspective, had revelled in his roguery. But it came as a surprise to Ritchie to see how the deal and the doing of it affected the pallid and undemonstrative Auguste Lenormant who—having damn all else to do—turned up to see the paintings packed.

As promised, Ritchie hustled the servant—who was, he reckoned, quite liable to spill the beans to the first kraut to walk down the boulevard—and the Comtesse into the bedroom and locked them in.

With the documents already in her possession, tucked away safe among family albums in a hat-box in the bottom of her wardrobe, the Comtesse played along with the game by making a great song-and-dance. Spitting out invective, she called the three dealers every bad name she could think of, including *socialiste*—until she wearied.

There was silence from the chamber while the scraping and hammering went on, echoing in the long gallery, punctuated by the guttural cries of the three *apaches* whom de Rais had dug up, men who would vanish again into the netherworld and would die before they would squeal to the Gestapo about what had gone on that day, tough young Jews from the Rue des Rosiers.

The dismantling of the Dubriel collection was done in double-quick time. The three workmen had had experience in this sort of thing and had come equipped with padded crates, slip-frames and cloths. The paintings were removed bodily from the walls, ornate gilded frames and all, leaving bare white patches on the dusty paintwork. The crates were manhandled down into the cobbled yard by the side entrance and ramped up into a large, box-roofed van which de Rais had purchased from a publisher who had gone bust, and whose sides still bore the legend *Librarie Altenbach* in large letters.

To Ritchie's surprise, Madame Sempach, de Rais' elderly housekeeper from his home in Marseilles, was seated stolidly in the passenger seat, with her old-fashioned cloche plonked on her head and a huge, stuffed carpet-bag on her knee. She looked more like a walrus than ever and glared at Ritchie without a word, as if he, and not Hitler, was responsible for this upheaval in the surly tenor of her life.

Ritchie drew de Rais to one side.

"What's she doing here?"

"I could not bring myself to leave her behind," said Hugues de Rais.

"She'd have been safe enough in Marseilles."

"For a little while," said de Rais, "perhaps. But not for long, Ricardo. I could not leave Madame to the tender mercies of lustful German sailors or sex-crazed Panzers, could I?"

"So you're not coming back?"

"Not until the tricolour flies over all of France."

"Horse manure!" said Ritchie. "You just want to be comfortable."

"That is the truth," said de Rais, without a sign of contrition.

"You wouldn't cheat me, would you?"

De Rais drew a circle in the air over his black hat. "In this matter, Ricardo, I am a saint." More seriously, he added, "I'm getting out, yes. I will spend the war years, long or short, in a pension in Berne, the Madame and I. She will knit and nag me; and I will sit by the log stove and dream up ways to make us all a fortune when the Germans are defeated and everything gets back to normal. What dreams I will have, Ricardo, what plans."

"Sure." Ritchie smiled wistfully and patted the old rogue on the shoulder. "Just so long as the Dubriel collection is intact when I want it."

"Will you give it back to her?"

"Yeah," said Ritchie. "Maybe I'll steal it again, though, but not until it's hanging on those walls."

"Why?" said de Rais. "I do not quite understand this sudden fit of honesty."

"Listen," said Ritchie.

The *pap-pap-pap* of machine-guns and the high, whining crack of snipers' rifles had become as commonplace and unremarkable in the past three days as the trilling of linnets or the crooning of pigeons.

"Is it just to spite the Germans?" said de Rais.

"You've got it," said Ritchie.

"Not to make amends for past misdeeds?"

"What past misdeeds?" said Ritchie, and Hugues de Rais laughed.

When the van was ready to roll, the crates stacked into the back, the ramp up and the tailgate pinned and the three *apaches* leaning over it, leering, and de Rais and M. Lenormant in the cabin beside the whiskery old housekeeper, then Ritchie went back into the mansion and unlocked the bedroom door.

The servant, her face contorted with a shifty sort of malice, swaggered out first, cursing him in gutter language. She was followed by the Comtesse.

Ritchie put the envelope containing the second payment— twenty thousand American dollars—into Kati Dubriel's hand, holding her shoulder to keep her from taking a swipe at him.

Both Ritchie and Kati Dubriel were aware that the servant's shrewd, calculating eyes were upon them.

Ritchie said, "You got a bargain, Comtesse."

"Thief," she spat at him. "Robber of the poor. Exploiter."

She tossed the envelope of money at his feet.

Ritchie left it lying.

He peered into her contused, owl-like face once more, in search of a sign that she understood his motives and believed that he would keep his word. There was nothing, however, to indicate that they were conspirators, no softening, only a genuine, uncontrived hatred.

"Suit yourself," Ritchie said and, turning, walked out of the empty, echoing gallery without another word.

Madelaine was hovering nervously by the boarded front window of the *galerie* in the Boulevard St. Germain when the van drew up at the kerb. Ritchie had travelled in the back with the *apaches*. He hopped out and banged away the pins that held the tailgate, then crossed the pavement and hurried into the shop.

"Do you have them?" asked Madelaine.

"Sure," said Ritchie.

"Who is that in the front seat?"

"Lenormant and de Rais."

"Who is the old man with them?"

"It's an old woman," said Ritchie. "De Rais' ex-mistress. He's giving her a ride out of Paris, back to Marseilles, when he's through here."

"Is that the truth?"

"Bloody hell!" said Ritchie, in English. "What's wrong with you, kiddo? You got ants in your pants, or something?"

"Did you get all—"

"Everything on the goddamned list," said Ritchie. "Now get on down to the basement and see to it that these guys stow the crates properly."

"I would prefer it if you—"

"I have to square Lenormant and de Rais," said Ritchie, who wanted his wife out of the way of the van for reasons of his own.

It was still very early and the Paris streets were calm, except for the sounds of battle, sporadic but loud, twanging the nerve-strings and making one glance up at the spires of Saint Sulpice or spin towards the trim bulk of the Institut at the head of Rue Mazarine, expecting to see the black smoke or the bearded flames of destruction.

Oddly, though, there was no smoke, no flames. But the populous corners were skinned of drifters. Philosophers and artists and would-be writers had vanished into their burrows like rabbits, while the Luftwaffe's advance guard of spotter planes and Stukas droned and buzzed, unhurried, in the blue sky over the *coupoles*.

Whatever defences the city of Paris intended to offer against the Hun they were not in evidence in Montparnasse or Saint-Germain. Ritchie had a sudden, fanciful vision of the Panzer tanks riding on muffled tracks towards the Panthéon, like Trojan horses drawn through the walls by superstition and a naïve sort of greed. Close behind the armour, in his smoked-glass Mannheim, would be Wili Oberisch, sly as a jackal.

"Maddy," Ritchie rapped, "get downstairs."

She obeyed him out of nervousness.

Signalling from the doorway, Ritchie ordered the three young men to unload the crates, those clearly marked with the big black letters MC on the raw plyboard, and bring them into the shop and down into the cellar.

He counted them, checked the black marks on each, since an error would be fatal in more ways than one, and when all were safe below the floor he paid the *apaches* in cash and saw them dart out into the streets and disappear. Before Madelaine could come up from below, Ritchie walked to the back of the van and closed up the tailgate.

M. Lenormant had got down from the cab.

"Is that it?" he asked.

"That's it—except for getting the stuff away, and that's de Rais' job, not ours."

"Very good," said Lenormant.

He offered his hand; the gesture was unexpected.

Ritchie said, "What'll you do? Have you time to get out?"

Lenormant shook his head. "I will watch the parades, I think."

"Be careful, old man," said Ritchie.

"I have less to fear—much less—than you do, my friend."

"Me? The Germans don't scare me."

"After the war," said Lenormant, and shook Ritchie's hand once more. "Take care, Beckman."

"Sure," said Ritchie.

The stately Frenchman walked off down the Rue Mazarine towards the Seine and did not look back.

In the cabin of the van, Hugues de Rais was impatiently awaiting the final *au revoir*, his arms resting on the spokes of the wheel and his black hat pushed back from his brow, his sleek white hair, for once, tousled. Beside him, Madame Sempach worked a fat red finger over a road map clipped to a breadboard; the navigator, who had never before been out of Marseilles in her life.

"How will you go?" said Ritchie, standing on the van's running board.

"Like lightning," de Rais answered.

In her guttural quayside accent, Madame Sempach declared, "Now that the French boys are withdrawing, your town will soon be in German hands. I think we will go through Troyes to Dijon and by Dole, Poligny and Morez to Geneva."

"I've a supply of petrol waiting with a friend at Troyes," said de

Rais. "Also we have food and drink in madame's basket. It will be a fine run, slow perhaps, but interesting. We will reach safety with the cargo, never fear, Ricardo."

"On your way, then," said Ritchie, and banged the panel with his fist. "And thanks."

"Thank me next time we meet," said de Rais.

The van lurched into gear and set off along the boulevard, heading south-east.

Madelaine ran from the door of the gallery and stood by her husband, staring after the vehicle. For an instant Ritchie wondered if she had tumbled, had prised open one of the crates in the basement, maybe. But no, her attitude was one of relief, almost of gaiety.

"Got what you wanted, love?" he asked.

She put her arm through his and rubbed herself against him.

"Yes, *chéri*, yes."

"Now you'll be safe, huh?"

"When Wili gets here, we'll both be safe—and rich."

"Sure we will," said Ritchie.

It was strictly a family affair and the bride did not wear white. The young man and the young woman were in uniform. They stood side by side not before God but before a representative of the Registrar, who wore a brown wool pullover under the waistcoat of his morning suit. Service hats lay on the chairs and the posy of summer flowers which Steve had carried in from the taxi-cab seemed incongruously colourful. It was held by ATS Sergeant Audrey Manners who was also in uniform. The sergeant had agreed to act as Steve's witness at very short notice, though she did not entirely approve of wartime marriages between members of the armed forces. Chris was supported by Pilot Officer Bob Crawford, a fellow-member of West Horsfall's fighter squadron, and not a very close friend. Crawford happened to be free that Saturday, having been relieved temporarily of flying duties after a bout of 'flu which had adversely affected his sinuses. Standing at the desk in front of the family, the four young people looked more like a guard detail than a wedding party.

The sight of the warriors made Andrea weep. The service itself was fairly perfunctory and Andrea, beset by the realisation that her one and only daughter would never now glide down the aisle of St. Benet Hampstead in swirls of white lace and get her picture in the *Tatler*, wept more loudly—so much so that at one point, David nudged her and whispered, "For God's sake, turn off the water-works, woman," a plea that Andrea, of course, ignored.

It was all over by twenty minutes past ten.

The party repaired to the Walshotts' house, a mile away, for the wedding breakfast.

Maury and Ruth had come up from Kent. David had wangled free of a duty in Hull. But nobody, least of all the bride and groom, seemed keen to linger, and the whole show was over by midday when Chris and Steve clattered away in the Railton for an eighteen-hour honeymoon. Endeavouring to whip up a little traditional cheer, Miles had tied cocoa tins to the back of the sports car. Sergeant Manners had brought a big bag of "office confetti" to scatter on the happy couple as they went down the garden path, a gesture she shared with Bob Crawford before she allowed herself to be persuaded to go off with him for luncheon *à deux*.

Three of the Beckmans' evacuees were down with chickenpox and Maury had an afternoon appointment in Whitehall. Anxious about her charges, Ruth also hastened away, leaving Holly and David alone with Miles and Andrea.

The four wandered into the dining-room where day maids were clearing the remains of the meal.

Andrea's face was puffy, her colour high. Miles was being particularly attentive to her.

"I didn't think it would be like this," said Andrea.

Miles gave her a squeeze. "All mothers feel sad when their nestlings leave."

"If only Mark had been here."

"Where is Mark, by the way?" asked Holly.

"Some silly camp. Said he couldn't get out of it."

"Officer training," said Miles. "A school venture; his last. He leaves school in ten days."

"He'll be next," said Andrea, dolefully.

"Well, can't have our son showing the white feather, Mother," put in Miles.

"I don't care about 'white feathers'. And don't call me 'Mother'."
Andrea seated herself at the dining-table, elbows between the
champagne glasses. "It was all so—so vulgar."

"Hardly that." Miles went to her but she brushed him away.
"Perhaps a tiny bit make-do-and-mend. But that's the way of it
these days."

"Why did you have to bring him here?" Andrea turned her
hostility upon David. "It's all your fault."

"Come on, old girl," Miles murmured.

"If you hadn't brought him here, none of this would have
happened."

"God, Andrea, you really take the bloody biscuit," said David.
"Do you honestly believe that this war is directed at making *you* feel
uncomfortable?"

"I'm not talking about the war. I'm talking about Stephanie and
that—that—"

"I don't like the marriage any more than you do, Andrea," said
Holly, "if it's any consolation."

"It isn't." Andrea raised her head from her hands. "What's
wrong with Stephanie, may I ask?"

"Stephanie's a charming girl," said Holly. "But it isn't the way
I'd pictured my son's wedding."

"Precisely," said David.

"No help for it," said Miles. "No help at all."

"At least you'll still have them," said Andrea. "They could have
come here, couldn't they? You would think a daughter would want
to be with her mother."

"Depends on the daughter," said David. "And on the mother."

"What on earth do you—"

Miles intervened. A quarter of a century hadn't quite killed the
animosity that had always existed between the Aspinall children.

"Tell me, Holly, you don't mind being landed with the couple?"
said Miles loudly.

"Of course not."

"Chris tells me you've renovated the first floor of your house,"
Miles went on.

"Maury managed to find a couple of decorators," said Holly. "I
didn't do much."

In fact she had spent an entire weekend, with Norma Butterfield's help, in selecting items of furniture from the attic and basement of the Tite Street house. She had washed curtains, shampooed rugs and carpets, brushed and polished the items personally and arranged them. Every trace of Chris's old room had gone, including his collection of model aeroplanes. Whether Chris liked it or not, the suite of rooms which Holly prepared was feminine, especially the bedroom. There was a simple Victorian brass half tester bed with a floral spread, its stuffy canopy removed. The bed went well with two late Georgian wardrobes and a nice clean reproduction dressing-table which she had discovered in a saleroom quite by chance. On a small Sutherland table, Holly had arranged a moss-rose sprigged china dressing set which almost matched the drapes which covered the windows on the inside of the heavy-lined velvet blackout curtains. In addition, there was a large sitting-room, comfortable if old-fashioned, and a small breakfast-room. Bathroom and w.c. and an "upstairs" cloakroom completed the suite. Holly was sure that Steve would like it.

Chris had popped in to inspect the work the previous afternoon and had declared it "enchanting", which was not the sort of word that Holly would have expected from her son. Love had altered him a great deal, had made him even more disingenuous than before, even more vulnerable. She was glad now that the couple would be living under her roof where, not to put too fine a point on it, she could "keep an eye" on the progress of the marriage.

It would be at least a week before Steve and Chris were together in Tite Street. The acceleration of Hitler's invasion plans had Britain's armed forces on their toes, and Steve, whether she liked it or not, was obliged to billet in a dormitory above the Thames Central Transport Depot garage in Shoreway Road. Though he kept the reason from his mother, Chris would be given no town passes at that time, newly married or not. Pilot Officer Deems was part of the RAF fighter screen, England's main defence against the Luftwaffe.

And, thought Holly, here we sit bickering like elderly relatives at a wake, instead of the parents of a young married couple.

"Well!" David broke into the lapsed silence. "Now you're one of the family, Holly. My father would be delighted."

"Yes, I'm sure he would," said Holly.

"Perhaps it was destined," said David. "If you believe in that sort of nonsense. We've know each other for such a long time, haven't we, Holly?"

"And too well, perhaps," said Holly.

Andrea snorted and pushed herself from the dining-table.

"What's wrong, dear?" Miles asked.

"I have a headache," the woman said.

"Wine before noon," said Miles, "always brings on your migraine."

He accompanied Andrea out of the room, leaving David and Holly alone.

David lifted a cheese vol-au-vent from a remaining plate and popped it into his mouth. He fished out his handkerchief and dabbed his lips. He seemed, Holly thought, edgy—which, perhaps, was not surprising after the strain of the past months. She hoped he would talk about the war, not the events of the day, of Andrea and Steve, of Chris.

David said, "They make a perfect couple, say what you like."

"Yes."

"Ideally suited. Made for each other."

"Yes."

"They might, you know, have been brother and sister—though that wouldn't have suited them at all."

"It's an awkward thought, especially today."

"Even cousins," said David.

"They aren't cousins," said Holly.

"Oh, I know that," said David. "He's Deems' boy. Deems' boy through and through. Even so—"

"What are you trying to say?"

"Will you marry again, Holly?"

"No."

"That's very categoric. Why not?"

"I've no need to marry."

"Need's an odd word to use. Materially you may be secure, but—"

Holly gathered her handbag and gloves from the side table where she had left them before the wedding breakfast. "David, I don't want to discuss it."

"If ever you *do* feel a need to marry—"

"I shan't."

"But if you do—"

"I hope this isn't a proposal, David."

"Certainly not," the man answered. "As every old sea-dog knows, you never propose to a woman or make promises you can't keep."

"I wish you'd followed that advice all those years ago."

"Ah, but I wasn't an old sea-dog then. I was a cocky young army officer. Quite a different breed."

Holly faced him. "Have you asked your question?"

"Practically."

"Have I given you an answer?"

"Unfortunately, yes."

"Then please take me home."

"Don't you want to wait to say goodbye to Miles and Andrea?"

"I'm sure they'll understand. I just want to go home."

"To Tite Street or the shop?"

Holly paused. "The shop."

David went out into the hall to fetch his hat.

With the coming of the month of July, eccentrics in the south coast's smaller hotels blossomed like flowers. They had, it seemed, developed a fine sense of what Hitler was about and their speculations, delivered to the dining-room at large, included many hair-raising predictions. Living within sight of the English Channel apparently entitled the terrier-types to express defiance openly and, as Chris put it, it looked as if the happy couple were doomed to pass their nuptials in a nuthouse.

The Grand Hotel, Sandsend, was the only hostelry within reasonable distance of the station in which Chris could obtain a room with bath at exceedingly short notice. The dumpy building set back off an apron lawn was like an ice-cream kiosk, fronted with a pale, mock-marble stone which had been all the rage in Twenties architecture. It was defended like a fortress, the lawn strewn with wooden posts and fencing wire, the gravel drive flanked with oil-drums full of sand, the windows boarded, sandbags mounded against the walls. Chris doubted if the Cabinet bunker in Westminster was as thoroughly impregnable.

All the old ladies and old men wore steel helmets and gas masks and one eighty-year-old—the owner's father—carried an antique pistol in a canvas holster strapped to his waist.

Arriving in time for afternoon tea, Chris and Steve were greeted with the sort of welcome usually reserved for heroes.

Unsuspectingly, they walked into this nest of patriots and found no privacy, spent the evening walking the streets of Sandsend, hand in hand, simply to avoid the aged civilians.

Everywhere on the coast there was evidence of war, the beach closed, the promenade an obstacle course of concrete anti-tank piles, the gardens turned into training grounds for Civil Defence volunteers. But it was the sky that truly told the couple what was on hand: swarming planes, distant tracers and, on the far horizon, dogfights over Channel shipping. Even on that very special night there was nowhere to hide from the war.

"We should have stayed in London," said Steve.

"Not at all. This is fine."

"Oh, Chris!"

The young man shrugged and let his smile fade. "Yes. It is rather—rather—I don't know—noisy."

"Let's go back to the hotel."

"We'll have to put up with the flag-wavers, you know."

"Perhaps," said Steve, "they'll go to bed early."

"Not them. They'll crowd around the wireless set waiting for the last drop of the day's news."

"Do you think they know?" the girl said.

"About us, about our being on honeymoon? I doubt it."

"Oh, théy must," said Steve. "They aren't blind."

"Well, it's back to the Grand for dinner, or it's stay out here like two lost sheep. Unless you want to head down the coast in search of a more secluded billet?"

"One day, one evening," said Steve. "That's all we've got."

"And the rest of our lives, darling."

"I wanted to remember this."

"We will. Well, sort of!"

"Perhaps we should have slept together, not got married."

"Regretting it already?" said Chris. "It isn't like you to be morbid."

"I'm not morbid, I just wish—"

"Back," said Chris, firmly, "to the dear old Sandsend Grand."

"All right."

Dinner over, Chris and Steve found refuge in the bar. They drank moderately, talked in low, guilty voices, flinched when one of the old gentlemen insisted on buying them beer, when one of the old ladies scuttled through from the lounge bearing titbits of news; a convoy attacked south of Portland, an Italian raid on Alexandria, Kiel bombed, and so on. Why, Chris wondered, did the patriots imagine that *they* were committed to the gossip of the war? It was *their* war, after all, and they *had* to be interested. For the old folk there was nothing else. Had they forgotten how monotonous, how deadening details of battles can be? If he had told them of the German parachutist decapitated by the wing of his plane, of the sickening jolt of flesh against metal, they would have shunned him thereafter, not because he was a killer but because he had dared to expand war to a reality. If the Germans did come in force across the narrow strip of sea, there would be reality enough for all then. Let them have their fun, their eloquence, their illusions. He just wished they would all go to bed.

Digestive biscuits and cocoa were served in the lounge at ten-thirty. Blackout was checked and re-checked. Gas masks were uncased, sealings thumbed. One dame put hers on and waggled her jaw at the company, making them laugh. Mr. Sloan brought out the ambulance kit and showed the others where it would be stowed. Mr. Caulkins demonstrated the use of bucket and pump in case of incendiary attack. Miss Harbisher laid out emergency blankets in the downstairs hall. It was all very sensible, a wonderful ongoing diversion.

At a quarter past eleven, the thirteen residents and four summer guests, including Chris and Steve, gathered in the lounge. The wireless was switched off. In a broad Yorkshire accent, Mr. Yeoman offered a prayer of intercession for all at sea, in the air and on the land, and prayed to the Lord God to keep all safe until the breaking of the day.

After that, at last the occupants of the Grand Hotel, Sandsend, were ready to go to bed, to stand alone in darkness against the authenticity of harboured fears and the proximity of death.

"Goodnight," said Mrs. Lea, with a friendly wink. "God bless!"

Steve realised that she *knew*. Perhaps they *all* knew.

She felt embarrassed.

Chris was not so immature as to mistake the flush on Steve's cheek as a sign of desire, her silence as sexual longing. He let her go alone upstairs to the suite-with-bath and waited, alone, in the darkened lounge, eating a last digestive.

In the hotel all was quiet, the plumbing still, the carpeted boards still, with only the muffled sound of one resident coughing over a cigarette in a first-floor bedroom. Outside, too, over the lawn, promenade, defended beach, over the sea, there was a lull in the nocturnal activities of warring nations.

Chris let himself into the bedroom.

The darkness was like a velvet shroud.

"Where are you?" he whispered.

"In bed."

"Where is it?"

"Where are you?"

"By the door."

"Put on the bathroom light."

"How's the blackout?"

"It's fine."

"Where's the bathroom?"

"To your left."

"This," said Chris, "is becoming something of a farce."

"Wait."

He heard the click of a cigarette lighter, saw Steve's face swim out of the darkness, lit not like that of a madonna but wickedly. She was not smiling. She was embarrassed by her behaviour. Perhaps it had dawned on Steve how much dependence there was between them, that she was committed, in all senses, to a young man whom she loved but hardly knew.

She held the wavering light in her right hand, quilt pinned to her breast with her forearm. Now that he could take her, was legally entitled to do as he wished with her, she was robbed of the thin, strong power of capitulation. The blue silk nightdress would not be seen. He would feel it, caress it, peel it from her body as an encumbrance. She would be naked by him and there was nothing in that to appease, to defend.

"Got it," said Chris.

The pale glow of a shaded bulb in the bathroom showed him up. He seemed furtive, as if he had waited for this moment to reveal a cruel streak.

Where was the love in it, the need?

Steve slid down in the bed. The pillows were hard, the covers starched, smelling of lavender and mothballs. She felt cold, shivered, hugged her arms to her breasts. She wished now that she had never gone through with marriage.

She had no curiosity about his body, though she had never before seen a naked male. She thought of, and feared for, herself. A thready confusion of emotions bound her limbs and made tension palpable.

Water in the basin in the bathroom, click of a light switch; the bathroom light went off. She heard Chris moving, moving freely in the pitch darkness now, like a puma or a leopard, the padding sound of bare feet on the room's thin rug.

"Found a night-light, Steve. Do you mind if I put it on?"

The whispered question sounded like a shout.

She shook her head.

"Do you? If you do, I won't," he hissed.

"No. Put it on."

A match gave dimension to the darkness. Chris touched the flame to the wick of a wax light, transferred it. The night-light sat in a saucer of water. She could see the rim of the china dish very clearly, see Chris, bare-chested, by the mantel of the fireplace. He wore only pyjama bottoms, carried his uniform neatly over one arm. By the faint light of the wick, he groped his way to the wardrobe and hung up the suit, stowed shirt and underwear into his valise on the floor.

"Leave the light, the little light," Steve said.

She did not want to be alone with him in darkness. In darkness he was a stranger. When he moved towards the bed her fear increased. She wasn't ready yet for this, for marriage. In school she had giggled over, yet flinched away from a marriage manual which Amanda Keating had smuggled in, had peeped but not examined the graphic diagrams.

Chris paused by the curtained window, head raised, listening.

"Quiet tonight," he said. "Perhaps Jerry knows."

"What?"

"About us." He turned, smiling.

Steve held the edge of the sheet, gripping it tightly with both hands.

Chris said, "Perhaps we'll have peace."

He sat by her, as if she was an invalid. His weight pressed down the soft mattress and she slid involuntarily towards him.

"May I kiss you?" he asked.

"Yes."

Softly he kissed her mouth.

He kissed her again, touching her fingers.

And it came in her suddenly, awareness of the meaning of what she had done, what this man meant to her.

He loved her, yes, and he would care for her. Tonight. Tomorrow. For ever. The manner of the kiss, the undemanding touch of his hands opened in her heart a sure knowledge of his feelings for her and of her love for him.

Uncertainty and confusion fled.

"Aren't you cold out there?" she asked.

"A bit."

"Come in then."

"Into bed?"

Nervousness released, she giggled. "No, into the wardrobe, silly."

Chris chuckled too and Steve wriggled over, making room for him.

She patted the pillow. "Come on."

He drew back a corner of the covers and eased himself into bed beside her. Shoulders brushed, knees touched. He sought her hand. She squeezed it reassuringly and brought it to her breast.

Whatever reluctance had been in her, her body's response was natural and thorough. Arousal began with stiffening nipples, an unaccustomed heaviness, a peculiar sensation in her loins. Feelings of languor and of a wanton need for gratification, for closeness, lay at odds each with the other. No trepidation, no uncertainty, no hint that only minutes ago she had been as frightened as a victim of sacrifice. It was Chris, her Chris who held her in his arms, who stroked and fondled her, who asked her if she was ready and who, when she gasped "Yes," cautiously lifted himself across her waiting thighs and cautiously placed his flesh against her.

"Yes," she said again, knowing that the roughness and fullness, the split-second's elastic pain were necessary. "Please, yes."

And he was with her, his arms and stomach and chest crushed against her breasts and belly, lifting her a little to him, and she thrust against him, and the languor and the heaviness and need grew with the warmth, the wetness, sudden unencumbered pleasure, signal not only of their intimacy and love but of their youth.

It was some time after three a.m. when the pumping of ack-ack guns wakened the couple from sleep. They lay naked, limbs entwined, each sensing that the other was awake. Chris laid his palm upon her stomach, crouching in the bed by her side, mouth upon her breast. Guns drummed echoes from the concrete beach and shook the windows in their frames.

In the hotel's lower rooms, the old folk stirred, called out to each other apprehensively. Rational replies calmed the more nervous among them. No sirens, therefore no trouble. Tonight the noises were reassuringly British.

Chris, though, continued to listen for the threnody of enemy bombers for several long minutes before he relaxed. He snuggled closer to his wife. With Steve in his arms he felt safe, unpardonably safe.

In the morning, long before the patriots' day began, before the hotel, or Sandsend, wakened, Chris and Steve had gone, their honeymoon over, the memory of it sealed.

By midday, Steve was back in London and Chris was on station at West Horsfall, waiting for the enemy to come.

On Saturday, June 22nd, two-thirds of the land of France was signed away by the hand of General Huntziger in an Armistice with Germany. The following afternoon, the Führer made a sightseeing tour through Paris and received a flag-waving welcome from those Parisians who had already been converted to the idea of living and working under the "New Order". From the minute the German motorised units passed through the Porte de Pantin, watched from behind drawn blinds, the big question that hung over the sacred soil of the City of Light was, "What would the Germans do now?"

The answer was, "Feed the Hungry."

Big shiny soup kitchens rolled in the wake of the tanks, and the French population, appetite sharpened by three weeks of semi-starvation, did not reckon that scoffing the conqueror's soup would much compromise honour. Especially in the poorer quarters, they trooped out, bowls in hand, to sup from the steamy forty-gallon tureens.

Courtesy and consideration were the order of the day for the thousands of troopers billeted in the city, all handsome fellows, blond, robust and toothy, as if they had stepped down from the gaudy posters that plastered the city's walls, above the evocative legend, "*Put Your Trust in the German Soldier*".

Certainly, there appeared to be no reason why one should not. There was no rape, no looting, no hint of persecution or brutality, of pogroms or purges. Shops re-opened, offices and factories swung back into production, encouraged by the military authorities, backed by a sagacious administration which realised that the average Frenchman thrived best on labour and thrift.

Discipline was necessary and expected; the nightly curfew, the blackout, the censorship decree, dismemberment of Parliament and right of assembly, prohibition of trade unions and employer associations, and free travel out of the occupied zone. On the whole, however, it was business as usual, a regime which blinded citizens to the slow tragedy of occupation and the bitterness of defeat, the new realities of life under the jackboot.

Food was scarce, fuel even scarcer. Soldiers drank beer in the street cafés and the *Mädchen* shopped for fashion shoes in the Rue St. Honoré. But money still talked and there were certain persons who fended off even slight discomfort with a waft of banknotes or the clink of the pure silver dockets that had come, in some quarters, into circulation.

Ritchie Beckman didn't mind the krauts. He rather enjoyed the pedestrian bustle, the appearance of thousands of bicycles, the absence of the irksome undertone of motor-car horns and squealing tyres. He enjoyed even more the freedom that he had rediscovered and spent more time on the pavements—walking, just walking—than he had done in the previous three years. Maddy, on the other hand, had become a creature of highs and lows.

The Führer's visit greatly excited Madame Cazotte. She was one of the throng on the Champs-Élysées, positioned appropriately outside the requisitioned National City Bank, who waved and cheered and tried to catch the great man's eye as he rode past in the open landau with swastikas flapping crisply and its retinue of motor-cycle guards and policemen. She dreamed, mooned, moped over Hitler for a couple of days and speculated as to whether one or other of Wili Oberisch's "clients" might gain her some sort of meeting with this, the most powerful man in the world.

Ritchie remained stone-faced, hiding his glee, as he discussed the possibility that she might become one of the charmed inner circle of Franco-German society. Nothing to stop her, after all. She wasn't a Jew, didn't even look like a Jew, and the Canadian thing would be an asset, not a liability. But when he had slipped out of the apartment, off into the freedom of the streets, Ritchie would indulge himself in a good guffaw at the crazy notions his bitch-wife entertained, and head out at a steady rate for the Marais and Rue de Vallon.

Zack's, of course, had become a kind of office for the wealthy gentleman, he of so many different names and so many different sets of documents. Zack and his missus didn't give a damn. They did what they could for him, by way of putting him on to the "right sort of people", the blackmarketeers. Mr. Beckman/ Cazotte/Gozzoli had cash and his demands were modest enough, a few bits of fresh meat, cans of pilchards and herring, fruit and veg, the odd bottle of wine—easy enough—and Metabrix fuel tablets for cooking on. This last was available in some quantity for it was issue stock to the krauts, and thousands of boxes of the stuff had already "gone missing" from German stores.

Ritchie did business briskly, meeting at the zinc bar with an assortment of a type with whom he had been doing business for years. He haggled, bartered, cajoled and, if necessary, compromised. In this manner he kept himself well beefed in the early weeks of the occupation, and saw to it that Anna Kern and her two boys did not go hungry.

"Why do you bring food here, Mr. Beckman?" Anna asked him.

Ritchie shrugged. "I buy it. You cook it. We all eat it."

"Have you no relatives to give it to?"

"No, no relatives."

Late one evening, when the boys were asleep and Anna Kern and M. Beckman were sharing a small piece of good, tangy Brie and a glass of *vin rouge* by a tiny wood fire in the grate, the woman asked, "Have I nothing to offer you in return for your generosity, Monsieur Beckman?"

Ritchie, who had been enjoying the silence, glanced up at her without understanding. "What?"

"Is there anything you wish of me?" She did not blush, but she did not meet his eye. "In return for your many kindnesses."

Ritchie did not answer at once. She was young and sturdy and had large breasts, but she did not remind him of anyone and he had never thought of Anna in those terms. He was polite, tactful in reply.

"It is kind of you, too," he said. "But it would not be quite right, would it? And you with the boys in the house."

"They are asleep. If you wished it we could—could go to your rooms, across the landing."

"Wouldn't old big-ears downstairs love that?" said Ritchie, with a grin.

"She thinks that I am—am—already more than your friend."

"Bugger her, then," said Ritchie in English.

"Pardon?"

Ritchie studied Anna again, carefully, as if she was an item whose authenticity he doubted. It was not the Frenchwoman's offer of sex which made him hesitant, but the wistful realisation that he no longer desired any woman in that way. He had never been a womaniser, anyhow. In fact, he had only been to bed with a couple of girls in his life—Ruth and Madelaine—and they had both betrayed him. Now, to his surprise, Ritchie found that he was empty of all sexual desire. Anna was too much a victim, too easy to possess. Besides, he didn't need her between the sheets. He already had what he wanted from her, a kind of ready-made home, complete with kids—and all without responsibility.

"If you want to," said Ritchie, "you could give me a kiss."

She sighed, smiled, rose. She didn't really want him, but she was an honest woman and felt obliged to offer him all she had to give. Without guile, she pressed her breasts against him and kissed him on the mouth. Her lips were warm, wine-tasting, with an under-hint of onion from the soup.

She was altogether too real for Ritchie.

He accepted the kiss then drew himself from her and stood up. He gave a little bow. "Thanks."

"Will we go across the landing?"

"Not tonight, Anna. Maybe some other time, when things are settled." That was a nice thought; God, wasn't it?

He could have got her out on the Gozzoli passport, back to Italy and from there, somewhere along the route, on to the English passport into Spain, maybe, or to Lisbon, out of it all. She would pass for an Italian, provided she kept her mouth shut. He could get away with it. But not the kids; he had no papers for the two boys. There was no way he would leave them behind.

Fargeau? Maybe! But risky at this stage. He wondered if Maddy was still lifting her skirt for the little weasel. He wondered what his wife did these nights. Had she found herself a high-ranking German officer to pay her ticket in the cafés? Maybe not yet—but she would, she would.

"When things are settled," the Frenchwoman said.

For the first time in months, Ritchie lifted his sights and directed his thoughts to the days that lay beyond the day on which Wili Oberisch would show up at the gallery, and he would have his revenge. He didn't *need* to be there, to hang around. But he had no place else to go, except here in the Rue de Vallon.

Across the landing, in his apartment, there was his travelling kit, a leather duffle, envelopes of various currencies, silver "bits" and old clothes he had purchased in the Flea Market, documents, old and new. Even with all that going for him, all that preparation, Ritchie had an inexplicable feeling that he would not be leaving Paris after all.

Anna kissed him once more, but this time only on the brow.

"Listen," said Ritchie. "What's that noise?"

"It is only little Alois, snoring."

"Is he okay?"

Concerned, Ritchie went to the bedroom door and listened there, then, after seeking Anna's permission with a glance, he opened the door and went into the bedroom.

It was a narrow room, the two cots placed end to end, a plyboard tallboy and a pine "stander" crammed against the inner wall. One columnar window was draped with cotton blackout and there was no light in the room save that which came from the open door.

In the nearer bed Chaim lay on his side with the blanket drawn right around his head. Nothing showed but his nose.

Ritchie shook his head. "Some night he'll smother himself."

Little Alois, on his back, arms akimbo, was more restless. His lids flickered and fluttered and his fingers twitched. He snored gently through parted lips.

"You sure he's okay?" said Ritchie, bending to peer at the child.

"It is just his way," said Anna. "He tells me he has good dreams."

As if to confirm the statement, the child chuckled in his sleep and sighed, and then was still as Ritchie turned him on his right side and tucked the blanket around his shoulder.

"Lucky him," said Ritchie and, taking Anna's arm, went back into the kitchen to finish the *vin rouge*.

Each day throughout the month of July and into August, Holly continued to follow her routine. She kept the shop open and attended whatever small sales cropped up. She dusted stock, repaired china, served the handful of customers who came through the door. There was really no need for Norma Butterfield to come in at all. Trade was drying up. The eyes of the nation were not on shop windows but on the sky, for out of the sky would come damnation or deliverance. Each day the newspapers posted the numbers of aircraft shot down, like cricket scores. Each day Holly waited for the telephone call or the telegram that would tell her that her son had been killed. Each evening she returned to Chelsea, to face an empty house, a silence from the first floor which told her that Chris was still in danger, that Steve had gone off with a convoy of trucks, that the marriage which she had resented and for which she had feared had not even got off the ground.

On only five occasions were Chris and Steve "at home" together. The progress of the battle of the skies was written in the young man's face. If Holly had thought him drawn and weary, it was as nothing set against the utter exhaustion which bowed him down now.

Holly did not need to take herself early to bed to give the young couple an opportunity to be alone. Chris slept throughout twenty of every twenty-four hours while Steve prowled about or slept too, while Holly, in her own quarters on the ground floor, tried to hold her nerve, to keep back tears, to behave as if nothing was wrong. Once, and once only, did Holly see her son and his wife in a moment of natural communion, and was able to regard them objectively, almost as a stranger.

Chris and Steve, hand-in-hand, crossed the road from the direction of the Inverness Church, towards the shop. It was mid-morning. Holly learned that it was coincidence, a fortuitous accident, that they had met on the way to Chelsea and, the day being fine, had put fatigue aside and come to take "Mother" to lunch.

They went to the little restaurant next door to the shop. The coffee house had taken over the premises of Fracelli's Fine Foods, and dished up luncheons between noon and two o'clock, odd but tasty concoctions of root vegetables and British fruits, in pies and casseroles.

Chris said little. Steve spoke with a strange mixture of cynicism and innocence of her work as a driver, totting up the "fantastic mileages" that the girls of Thames Central had notched up during the past fortnight. She described the sights she had seen—air fighting mostly—on her trips through the southern counties as if they were pretty, original ballets at Covent Garden. She also prattled on about her co-drivers and ATS mechanics and their trivial domestic problems. By this constant schoolgirlish flood, she seemed to be protecting her husband from involvement in the conversation.

"Chris," Holly addressed him directly, "are you still at West Horsfall?"

"No, on the shuttle."

"What does that mean?"

"Here, there and everywhere."

"Why?"

"Air Ministry orders. Strategy," said Chris. "Casualties."

"Where are you exactly?" said Holly. "Can't you tell me?"

"Tiny place called Straighton."

"Near the Isle of Wight," put in Steve, nodding.

"What's it like?" asked Holly.

"Primitive," Steve answered, nodding again.

The changes that nervous strain had engendered in the young people appalled Holly. She remembered Maury, Sergeant Beckman, returned from the trenches with no visible wounds but with rancour and bitterness scored deep within. Would it be like that with Chris? Would he have the resilience to go forward, to pass through this hideous phase and not to be marked by it?

He had spoken of it to Steve, that much was apparent. He had unburdened himself to the girl, had trusted her.

Holly felt distanced from her son.

Steve said, "Straighton's just a hole-in-the-wall. No proper mess, no proper feeding. Sleep in the dispersal tent and cook on primus stoves."

"It's all right," said Chris, diffidently.

"It isn't all right," said Steve. "It's a bloody disgrace."

"It won't be for long," said Chris.

"A bloody, *bloody* disgrace."

He let her complain for him, abuse air-force authorities without retaliation. Steve's vociferousness was as distressing as Chris's numb silence.

Holly was relieved when the meal was finished. Though she felt awful about it, she could not bring herself to be an audience for much longer.

"Why don't you both go back to Tite Street and have a sleep?" she suggested. "You'll feel better."

"I feel fine," said Chris.

"We're going back, though," said Steve. "I have laundry to wash."

"In that case," said Holly, "I'll see you at dinner."

"We'll be gone by then," said Steve.

"So soon?"

"Night run to Portsmouth, third in eight days," the girl explained, cryptically.

"And you, Chris?"

"Flying," said Christopher Deems. "Yes. Flying."

On August 19th, secret orders were issued to group and sector controllers from the office of Air Vice-Marshal Balaam. The orders were designed to combat the Luftwaffe's latest change in strategy, a new phase of the air war and a switch in targets from coastal shipping and ports to inland aerodromes, particularly those of the fighter squadrons whose stubborn resistance was, it seemed, beginning to get on Jerry's wick.

Instructions as to the revision of patrol rosters and the use of Polish and Canadian squadrons were specific. But the disturbing hint that the RAF was running low in men and flying machines was contained in late paragraphs; controllers were ordered not to despatch fighters to engage the enemy over the sea or to encourage cross-Channel pursuits. Forced landings in the drink were deemed too costly to be worth the gain.

The theory was sound but it did not take account of the brash young bloods who flew the Spits and the Hurricanes and who, weariness notwithstanding, now regarded the bloody conflict as sport, a game between aces. They would not be stayed by strategists, old men in Air Ministry cellars. They had tasted victory in smoke and counted their tally of kills like toffs at a pigeon shoot and, on quiet, grey, dangerous days of low cloud and monotony, skimmed heedlessly across the Channel to scour the coastline for Jerry air bases and vulnerable formations caught just after take-off.

Chris was not one of the madmen, one of the nuts, but flew to orders, fought well, disengaged correctly and no longer counted his kills.

He no longer flew alone. On each and every flight, Steve was with him. His head was full of her, his thoughts dominated by her. The fear that he had disappointed her by his inadequacy plagued him. Steve had never once betrayed disappointment in his failure to maintain amorous "interest". For all that, Chris was obsessed with his wife in raw sexual terms which mellowed into discreet, husbandly love only when he was very, very tired indeed.

With the R/T switched off, he would talk to Steve, tell her to be patient, inform her what it would be like when the war was over and he was freed of the demon of flying, of the need to live with his nerves on his skin, and his head permanently in the clouds. He told her that he suspected he had inherited this streak from his father, Captain Deems, the poet. But he assured her that he was fighting against it, just as his father had done. He played question and answer with his English rose, tapping replies back rhetorically amid the din of the Merlins, the hot roar of the guns. He called her "my wife" and indulged in a degree of feyness which was not only at odds with but served as an antidote to the nightmare of aerial combat.

In occasional moments of rationality, Chris wondered if he was going crazy. He found that he did not really care much one way or the other, thought of himself now as engaged in a race between madness and death.

While all that was going on in the space between his ears, he performed admirably as a pilot officer. He even stopped griping about the bad food and filthy quarters at Straighton. He was known to make flip remarks about dying along with the hard-nosed bunch, so that nobody, nobody at all, guessed at the turmoil that was going on inside him.

Monday was a quiet, grey day, a dangerous day with mist in the morning, a proper Axminster rolled out across the sea all the way to the coast of France. Drizzles of rain fell in the afternoon.

Two brigands stole away to raid a little German aerodrome at Bovet. Chris patrolled, four and four in vee formation, twice between dawn and tiffin, flying low in the hope of picking up Stukas on a raiding strike.

The massed German Air Fleet of big bombers did not materialise as expected, and as far as the boys at Straighton were concerned the day was a dead loss.

The Bovet action, to which the controller turned a blind eye, yielded four kills, unconfirmed. According to Laddie McLean, it left the Germans "buzzing like bloody bumble bees". On their return, Laddie and his chum, Jack Gull, were jubilant and very obstreperous and Chris had a blazing row with Jack, in a stupid incident involving a pork pie, on the grass in front of the sandbag blast pen which, empty, gave shelter to the resting crews.

While the shouting-match went on, and the unchastened pair of self-styled "aces" stirred up more trouble, the Wing Commander brought out a *Scramble* order; a squadron of bombers accompanied by fighters had been marked, heading for the inland 'drome at Maltington, a station which had already taken a severe pounding.

Minutes later, the quarrel put aside, Chris was in the air.

Interception course, orders notwithstanding, was across the sea. Nobody on the ground, it transpired, had quite deduced the scope and scale of the raid, though other squadrons had been scrambled too and there were Spitfires as well as Hurricanes in the layer.

Chris put on his headphones.

He was thinking of Steve as he had last seen her, wearing only the heavy ATS-issue knickers, her stockings wrinkled on unbelted suspenders, the rest of her body nude. The line of her spine was perfect as she bent over the wash-basin, hair in wet licks and thick slap-curls, a froth of soap around her neck. Fine, blonde hairs prickled in the cool air of the bathroom. He could have made love to her then, for he was rested after a night's sleep. But there was no time, no time. He put his hands about her and stroked her breasts. She gave an amiable squeal and backed into him. Droplets of water shook from her hair across his cheeks. He embraced her, pressing himself against her buttocks. He kissed the nape of her neck. tasting soap.

"I have to go, darling."

"Not now. Wait a bit."

"I'm late as it is."

"Chris? When will I see you again?"

"I don't know."

"Chris. Wait."

"Darling, darling. I *have* to go."

She turned to embrace him, her soft breasts crushed against the uniform.

"Take care, Chris."

"You too, darling."

Great sheaves of cloud were stooked against the horizon, corn-yellow and rye-coloured in the sunlight that leaked below the thunderheads. Strewn above was a boiling blue-back weather front which a stiffening breeze from Wimereux and St. Martin trundled towards Kent. The Straits of Dover were like strip-steel, plated and ribbed with silver, wave crests static, ships static, seabirds like tiny, white stitches on the dark cloudscape.

"*Yellow two. Yellow two. Answer.*"

"Benjy, is that you?"

"*It's Reed, Yellow two.*"

"Sir."

"*Is all well?*"

"Fine, sir."

"*I've just been through to the Flight. Much company is expected.*"

"I read you, sir."

"*Bill, are you there?*"

"Port side, sir. Just picking up. Got a cough, I'm afraid."

"*Bad? Do you want to go home with it?*"

"Not necessary, so far."

"*Yellow four. Go out to full. With Laddie and Jack. The three of you.*"

"Check with me, sir."

"*Jack Gull. Yellow one. Checking. You, Laddie and Chris. Okay-dokay?*"

"Okay-dokay."

It was in Chris's mind to ask if they were committed to engage but Reed had said nothing, taking it for granted that the three pilots would understand. Reed should have known better than to give Jack and Laddie sniff of a Stuka, sniff of a hundred Stukas.

Following McLean's aeroplane, Chris climbed at full power.

The bombers were at 18,000 feet, flying out of the cornfield of cloud, above it, really. He had seen nothing like it before. Hundreds of the bastards, spread across the sky like black flies.

Laddie was gibbering on the headphones, doing his Scottish nut with excitement. Where there were bombers, there were Messerschmitts, and the wee laddie from Edinburgh just loved Messerschmitts, gobbled them up like sardines on toast.

The sight was breath-stopping, magnificent, that rank of black flies, even and steady and deadly against the lavender-blue sky above the thunderheads and rainbow cloud. The German fighters were 2,000 feet above. The three British pilots had come head on against the formation. But there were flank defences in advance of the massed attack, a sickle of Stukas, sixteen in all, staggered below. They came out of the cloud suddenly, swooping up at the three Hurricanes before the main formation came within range.

"*Hairy Mary, look at that!*"

"*I see it. I see it. On your left, Lad. On your—*"

Meeting one's match, what? thought Chris.

He swung the Hurricane abruptly across the Stukas' sweeping approach, opening up the Merlins to full pressure. Dancing, bobbing, Laddie McLean parted company. Jack Gull's Hurricane, squirting tracers, went into a withering dive, down and down through the ascending Messerschmitts, down and down until Chris could no longer follow the graph of its descent and jerked back into isolation. He felt quite comfortable, though, peering into the paintbox sky, seeking a Stuka upon which to fasten his gun-sight, some object upon which to concentrate his mind. Wonderfully. But he knew, even then, he was done for, a minnow among pike, too damned many pike.

All he could hope for now was to put up a good show.

Laddie's Hurricane came from behind and starboard, slithering through Chris's range of vision and crossing the arc of flight in a sudden, fearful deluge of noise. The body of Laddie's Hurricane was streaked with flames, but the Messerschmitt on its tail was unrelenting and merciless, as Laddie would have been too, had the situations been reversed. Even as Chris watched, the Hurricane broke into a vicious spinning dive. Smoke spumed from it. He nosed his aeroplane down and tailed the tailing Messerschmitt. He brought it into the sights and fired burst after burst, hardly looking at it but watching instead, in fascination, the burning RAF fighter as it plunged towards the sea. He waited for the 'chute, thistledown in the air. Good old Laddie McLean ransoming yet another 'plane to the enemy. Surviving. But Laddie did not emerge. No blossoming parachute. Long before the burning parts reached the surface of the Straits, the Hurricane disintegrated.

Kill assured, the pilot of the Messerschmitt turned his attention to evasion. It was one of the new Me110 jobs, lively as well as fast. Chris was not surprised when it got the drop on him. Bottoming out of a raked dive—at 7,000 feet—it climbed steeply away from him.

Chris turned his head this way and that. He picked up another 'schmitt and swept in to engage it.

He suspected that the first Me 110 would come at him in a classic thrust, from behind and above, stooping to rake him with shell-fire. He blanked out this probability and went in from the flank on his prey.

What he hit with the Brownings was a mystery. The Stuka nose-rolled, banked and went down into a falling-leaf pattern. Chris mistook the action for evasion. He traced a curve to cut across the Messerschmitt's spiral, waiting for it to plane out. Three hundred, two hundred yards; he saw how the thing had happened. The Jerry's cockpit was shattered. Jagged shards clung to the frame, glittering. A glossy black stain spread over the cockpit area. The rest of the Stuka appeared undamaged. Its spiral was tighter now, about that concentric moment when the 'plane would simply drop, nose foremost, straight into the drink. In the wrecked cockpit, he could make out the pilot. Lolling. Wisps of smoke purled around him, though there was no visible flame.

Chris rammed his thumb on the gun button and unleashed a stream of bullets into the defenceless Stuka. Still no fire. It flicked and twisted, though, seemed to hang for a split second then went straight down, dead-drop. Chris knew it was finished. Any more firing would be a waste of precious ammo. At 5,000 feet he pulled away and sought height.

The panoramic sky was revealed, a sky that belonged to the Germans. Far off to the south-east were dogfights, the genteel aerobatics of aircraft intent on destroying each other. Close to, all that he could see were Messerschmitts and the big bombers in uninterrupted and undeterred ranks.

Chris said, "Yellow three, Yellow three? Are you there, Jack?"

The radio headphones hissed.

"Yes, Yellow two. Jesus, what the hell's happening?"

Chris did not see the German 'plane.

There was a startling rocket-like swish. The instruments on the dashboard went wild. Shells punched into the length of the fuselage.

Caught napping, Steve, my love.

Chris nursed no discordant thoughts. He felt mildly peeved. Long ago he had accepted the inevitable, long before the onset of the air battles, before the coming of summer. Marriage had been an act of selfish indulgence, an ill-fated bid for a little light relief in a gloomy sort of world.

The Hurricane trembled into a flattish dive, out of Chris's control. Tongues of flames crept lazily along the metal around the air housing. Chris weaved the stick, seeking resistance, response. The dive was less flat now. He was heading downward towards cloud. Not cloud. Smoke. He was following the trail that Laddie had left for him.

Shells striking the back fins made an odd gobbling noise. Then there was silence. God, yes, how there was silence! His bloody engines had cut out. He was gliding. Not so bad. All in one piece and gliding down to the sea. He would have one last go at starting the damned thing, then he would bale out. No problem. The needles of the gauges, lying flat in the dials, looked as if they had died of fright. What had been hit? A bunch of cables? Oil pressure tank? God knows, old girl! Chris jiggled the controls. Fitful contact. A light flashed. Needles twitched tantalisingly. Now that's better. We'll make it yet, darling. Be home in time for supper, after all. But the Jerry had other ideas. God, there he is! Doing what I would do. Raking me with wing fire to make absolutely certain I'm a dead duck. Nazi bastard!

The dashboard disintegrated. Black flames jetted up from beneath it and scalded Chris's legs. He beat at them with his gloves, blinded. It didn't seem clean, like fire. More like boiling oil. He couldn't see a bloody damned thing. Pain was abrupt and fierce in his legs, like two great vices gripping his kneecaps, saw-edged and crushing. He shouted and tore at the harnesses, at the cockpit cover release, pawing and tearing, and shouting like a chicken. Black flames turned red. Vivid yellow.

His Hurricane was spinning, a falling leaf, just like the Stuka he had cooked a couple of minutes ago. He was locked into the same spiral. Exactly.

Help me! God and Jesus, help me! Steve. Steve. Please!

It was all dark flame and pain, the 'plane in a straight dive. Blood rushed into his ears and nose, flooded his brain. He tried to thrust-

himself out of the cockpit. His muscles wouldn't work. How high was he? Steve, Steve, Steve! The Hurricane flipped over, breaking in half. He fell. Fell out. Fell down. All in a tatter of burning stuff, dragging pain with him, leadenly. He cleared the aircraft and went down, falling down, without the jerk of the 'chute to check him. Then felt it. Not right. Snagged.

Sky and sea glazed, dark and light polished like veneer

The parachute did not open.

Hurtling like a streamer, Christopher Deems plunged into the sea.

On receipt of the news, Holly had the sense to call Ruth first. In turn, Ruth called Maury's office in town. By sheer chance, she caught her husband before he shot off on the business of the day.

It was just after ten when Maury parked his car by the kerb in Tite Street. Glancing at the other vehicles there, he opened the gate and walked towards the front door which already stood open. If he had expected to find his sister alone, then Maury was disappointed. But he had been around long enough to understand that bad news travels fast. He was not too dismayed to find an assortment of people already there and breakfast being served in the dining-room. In this sociable manner, Maury knew, some women sensibly protected themselves against the terrible isolation of sorrow. He had not, however, expected to be admitted to the house by a total stranger. The bluff, curly-haired young man in pilot officer's uniform introduced himself in hushed tones as John Gull.

From the dining-room adjoining the hall, Maury heard the murmur of voices, smelled the aroma of fried bacon, hot coffee and cigarette smoke. It was as if the house had come alive again, wakened from hibernation after Kennedy's death.

Gull said, "You must be Chris's uncle?"

"Maurice Beckman. How's my sister?"

"Remarkably calm," said Gull. "I'm just leaving, actually. I was waiting until you got here. I gather you'll be taking charge of things."

"Did you bring the news, Mr. Gull?"

"Unofficially. I gather there's been the usual notification from the Air Ministry or whatever, the telegram thing. Our Winco called on the telephone, though he knew I was coming up. I asked his permission."

"Are you a friend of Chris?"

"Yes. I—I saw his 'plane go down."

Maury's stomach contracted with fear. Until then he had nursed the silly hope that *Missing* meant just that. Maury cleared his throat. He glanced at the dining-room door, waiting for Holly to burst out, for the expected moment of passionate grief.

Maury said, "I think you'd better tell me what you saw, young man, if you don't mind."

"Three of us, over the Straits of Dover, about fifteen miles out. We engaged—"

"When was this?"

"Last night. Evening. About half past seven."

"Go on."

"Dogfight. We were outnumbered."

"Was this the big raid?"

"Rather! Advance party, you might say. We hadn't an earthly."

Again Maury glanced at the dining-room door. Who was in there? The young woman, Steve Walshott? She lived here, after all. He hadn't quite taken her into account. He had only considered Holly.

Gull said, "Two—two of the 'planes, our 'planes, were shot down. I saw them both go. They went straight into the drink. My chum—McLean—was the first. Chris went down minutes later. All shot to perdition, if you know what I mean."

"Didn't he jump?"

"Hadn't enough height."

"He went down, then," said Maury slowly, "with the 'plane?"

"The wreckage sank instantly."

"Are you sure?"

"As sure as I can be, sir. I wouldn't have come here otherwise. I came, actually, to see his wife. I didn't realise that his mother—" Gull was embarrassed. "I mean, if I'd known I'd be first with the news. I didn't know what to do. What I've told you, though, is the truth."

"Isn't Chris's wife here?"

"Apparently not."

"Thank you," said Maury. "What, by the way, did you tell my sister?"

"I didn't mention that the 'plane had sunk immediately. I thought—I left her—you know—some hope."

"You've been very kind."

"I've got a mother too. I'm an 'only' too. I thought—"

"I understand." Maury offered Gull his hand.

Sheepishly the young man held up the heavily-bandaged mitt. "Sorry."

"What happened?"

"Couple of fingers. The tops thereof. Very lucky. Very neat sort of job. Got off without a scratch, otherwise."

"Painful?"

"They adminstered a little something in the hospital. It really isn't bad, though I have to smoke with my left hand." Gull gave a cheerful smile, modified it. "I really should go now, Mr. Beckman."

"Yes, thank you."

"I'm sorry about Chris."

"Yes."

Maury saw the pilot officer out of the house.

He closed the front door. The dining-room was only a step away. He wondered where the housekeeper was. Downstairs making more food, he supposed. He tugged down the wings of his waistcoat and ran a hand over his thinning hair. He had never been more nervous in his life, afraid of what he would find.

After Kennedy's death, after his nephew's hasty marriage—now this. Though he had prepared himself for it, though the tragedy had been with him in imagination these past ten weeks, now that it had come he was shocked by it and desperately worried as to how Holly would survive the blow. Chris had been the substance of her life. Beneath the tough, self-sufficient attitudes that his sister displayed, there had been love, love for and devotion to her son. Now Chris was gone. Maury took a deep breath and opened the dining-room door.

Nothing was ever as expected. Somehow, when he had envisaged this scene he had imagined Holly all alone, standing by a darkened window, in a tragic, silent pose. But mourning and sorrow were, by the nature of things, gregarious activities, and the first sight of his sister took him aback. Holly was seated at the dining-table, a coffee in one hand and a cigarette in the other. Her eyes were puffy but she was smiling at the moment of his entry, nodding in response to something David Aspinall had said. She wore a new print summer dress with a primrose-coloured chiffon scarf about her throat. On the table before her was a bacon sandwich. At the table, too, were David, Miles Walshott and Mrs. Butterfield. None of the three had that watchfulness, that solemn caution which Maury, with his flair for correctness, expected from friends of the mother of a deceased airman. He felt, at once, unsure of himself.

"Holly?"

She got up, putting down cup and cigarette, and came to him. He clasped her in his arms. She was tense but dry-eyed, managed another smile.

"I came as soon as I could," he said lamely.

"I'm glad you're here."

"Any—any further news?"

"Not yet."

Aspinall and Walshott had risen too, and queued to shake his hand.

According to the young pilot, Gull, Chris had been shot down only fifteen or sixteen hours ago. There was something almost cruel in the RAF's efficiency, in the speed with which they had informed the boy's next of kin. How this was done, what form it took, Maury never did discover.

Oddly, he felt distanced from his sister, as if the presence of Aspinall and Norma Butterfield was something which she had deliberately contrived to flout her independence, to push him, her brother, away from her.

Such selfish feelings, uncharacteristic of Maury, were a method of protecting himself against the first blow that the war had inflicted upon him personally, against the realisation that he was vulnerable, along with every other Britisher, to terrible haphazard losses, and living into a future that could not be predicted let alone planned for. Insecurity was the only sure thing, uncertainty the only stable factor. When Norma Butterfield offered him breakfast, to his astonishment Maury heard himself accept. He was hungry; actually hungry. He had left Applehurst at seven that morning and wasn't at all sure when he would have time for another meal.

As he seated himself at the table, there was a tiny silence, and he realised that Aspinall and Walshott were deferring to him, handing over responsibility.

Maury said, "Now we don't know he's dead yet."

The forthright statement—the word "dead"—settled him, made him feel positive.

"A young man—a fellow flyer—" Walshott began.

Maury glanced at the stockbroker, a soft sort of chap. To his dismay he saw that Walshott's eyes were red-rimmed, that the man had obviously been weeping.

"Gull? Yes, I met him at the door," said Maury.

"He claims he saw the 'plane go down," said Aspinall.

"So what?" said Maury. "The bloke was in the middle of a bloody dogfight. Just because he didn't see it, doesn't mean to say that Chris didn't get clear."

"Where is he, then?" said Holly.

"On board a freighter or naval vessel perhaps," said Maury.

"I told Holly as much," said David Aspinall. "Air Sea Rescue Service has boats all over the Channel and the Dover Straits. Believe me, they know what they're doing, these chaps."

"It isn't as if it's winter," said Walshott. "I mean, there isn't a breath of wind this morning. It must be like a mill-pond."

"A slight sea mist," said Aspinall. "Once that lifts, the rescue boats will pick him up."

Holly said, "The 'plane went down immediately."

Maury sought for an angle. He listened to them, comforters doing their damnedest to vault the facts, Holly logically arguing them down.

Mrs. Butterfield brought a plate of fried eggs and meagrely sliced ham, a fresh pot of coffee, and toast in a silver rack. She had cleared the used dishes from the table and brushed up crumbs.

Maury ate quickly, listening.

The rest of the war news had been blotted out by personal tragedy. He found that he could not scratch up the slightest interest in bombing figures or news from the Front, wherever the Front happened to be. He had an angry buzzing in his head, the uncomfortable ache of frustration and helplessness which had been constant when he was a young man in the trenches of France and Belgium. He wanted to tell them all to go to hell. The truth was that Chris was bloody dead. And they'd better start deciding what they were going to do about it, and the business of surviving.

Maury felt hard, cynical, and without warmth. Guilty too. He wiped his mouth with a napkin and let the blonde woman pour coffee for him. He popped open his cigarette packet and handed it round. Everybody took one of the Churchman cigarettes. Tobacco was hard to come by and you couldn't let the chance go past. Death or no death, tragedy or no tragedy. He swallowed the scalding hot coffee, smoked, studied Holly carefully.

"You think Chris is dead, love, don't you?" he asked suddenly.

"I—I don't know."

"The odds are that he is," Maury went on, relentlessly. "Gull's no dope. He wouldn't have bothered to come here unless he had something to tell you."

"I don't agree, Maury," said David, in the sort of tone he probably used in departmental meetings with his chiefs. "I really don't think you can write—"

"All right," said Maury. "The point is—how long we wait, how long we keep hoping."

"He may have been picked up by a Nazi boat. Be interned," said Walshott. "Isn't that possible? One reads of such strange things."

"How will his wife be told?" said Maury.

"Yes," said Holly. "Stephanie will have to be told as soon as possible."

"Won't she be notified? Officially?" asked Miles.

"I'm not sure," said David. "If Chris registered this address as the home of his next of kin, then—"

"Do you know where the Thames Depot is?" Walshott interrupted.

"I've an idea," said David.

"We had best go down there," said Miles. "We can speak with Steve's superior officer who will presumably know what one does in such circumstances."

It occurred to Maury then that if Chris *had* gone down with the Hurricane his body might never be found. What would substitute for a funeral? How long would they have to wait before putting that final punctuation mark on the young man's life, the full stop after which Holly, and the girl too, would be able to begin a fresh sentence?

The girl was not his responsibility.

He said, "Yes, that's a good idea. In the meantime I'll take Holly down to Kent with me."

"I'd rather stay here. In case there's news."

"I don't want you being on your own, Holly."

"I can stay," said Norma Butterfield. "Put up here. If a telegram or a telephone call comes through, I'll get in touch with you immediately."

"But Steve—" said Holly. "Shouldn't I—"

Maury exchanged glances with David Aspinall.

"We'll take her home," Miles Walshott said.

"But this is her—" Holly began.

David interrupted. "To her mother."

An hour later, in Maury's motor car, Holly set out for Applehurst, leaving Tite Street and all its memories behind.

Jacques Fargeau was small in stature and alert in manner, with shiny black eyes and hair napped close to his skull. He met Madelaine in the Café d'Or, not far from his principal place of business in the Rue Leproust which was also conveniently situated for the Cazottes' gallery.

Having learned that the gallery might be confiscated if she refused to remain open and to serve officers of the Reich, Madelaine glanced nervously at her wrist-watch while Fargeau unwrapped salami and slices of white pork which he had brought with him, to manufacture lunch. Bread and red wine completed the feast.

Though it was a quarter after noon, and a beautiful early autumn day, the Café d'Or was almost deserted. The Germans' "buying *Blitzkrieg*" had not extended to this quiet street. There were few open shops here, only commercial offices and pillars of the professions.

It was Madelaine who had requested the meeting, Fargeau who had chosen the time and place. He handed her the bread and porkmeat sandwich. Madelaine, who had already removed her gloves, tore the thing apart and ate hungrily. Fargeau poured wine from the bottle.

Madelaine said, "Did you hear what happened at Paul Rosenberg's gallery?"

Fargeau simply crossed one knee over the other, and nibbled a round of salami.

"Nobody came forward to re-open the shop and, within forty-eight hours, three moving vans, with Cologne licence plates, drove up, and every single item of stock was packed and taken away."

"It is no more than the Rosenbergs deserve," said Fargeau.

"You knew of it?"

"Naturally. It's happened to the Edelsteins and to Blumberg."

"But Blumberg did not flee."

"He has gone now," said Fargeau. "What did you wish to see me about, Madelaine? Are you in need of still more papers—or is it that you find me irresistible?"

The woman did not have it in her to play up to him. She chewed and swallowed and applied herself to the red wine while Fargeau's dark dancing eyes studied her.

"It's Ritchie," Madelaine said. "He stays out all night. He will not tell me where he goes, what he does."

"Perhaps he's joined the *Front Jeune*."

"Pardon?"

"Forget it."

"I'm afraid, Jacques."

"For him or for yourself, sugar mouse?"

"For myself."

"He stays away all night, does he?"

"Two or three times in each week."

"What's his excuse?"

"He makes none. He shrugs, says he was 'walking'. I remind him there's a curfew. He laughs, tells me to mind my own business."

"And you, are you at home every night, tucked up safe in your own bed?"

"Of course I am."

"What a waste."

"Ritchie's up to something."

"He'll have found himself a woman, some easy bint."

"He has *me*," said Madelaine, as if that fact precluded any possibility of her husband seeking company elsewhere. "Jacques, you have people who do work for you. You can easily find out where Ritchie goes and what he does. Whom he sees."

"I don't like to risk my boys getting caught in the curfew. Most of them prefer to steer clear of the Nazis."

"I've nobody else to turn to."

"Touching!" said Fargeau. "Salami?"

"No. Will you help me? I can pay."

"How much?"

"Not much. Not until—"

Madelaine did not wish to be drawn into talking of Wili Obersich and the treasure in the basement of the gallery. It was bad enough wondering if German Labour inspectors would suddenly descend with papers of requisition and loot the stock—the basement included—without having to reveal its contents to Fargeau. She trusted the little forger not at all. She knew he was lying when he said he was afraid of the Nazis. More than half the "boys" he had working for him were members of the New Citizens' Party or the *Front Jeune*, registered Fascists. She could not be at all sure that Fargeau himself wasn't in the pay of the Germans.

Ritchie had so arranged it that she was virtually penniless. Everything was tied up in the chests in the basement. She had no power to protect herself until such time as Wili got here. She had written to Wili, several letters to several addresses, but had received no reply, not even an acknowledgment. She was frightened to be away too long from the gallery in case Wili turned up.

Fargeau chuckled. "Everything costs, these days, Madelaine."

"But we are such friends, Jacques."

"If I do find out what you want to know, what will you do for me in return? What favour?"

"Any favour."

Fargeau did not frighten her. She had already made love with him on many occasions. In spite of his reputation he was speedy and almost casual in bed.

"Would you break the curfew?" Fargeau asked.

"Stay with you overnight?"

Madelaine was surprised. Fargeau had a wife and two daughters and, however much he indulged his taste for variety, was always home by midnight.

"You'll be safe enough with my friend," Fargeau said.

"Friend?"

"A lonely soldier."

"German?"

"Not a ranker," said Fargeau. "I wouldn't do that to you, sugar mouse. He's an important man in the military administration. Very important. And a major."

"Wehrmacht?" Madelaine enquired.

"No. SS."

"If I—if I keep your friend company, will you find out where my husband goes and what he does?"

"Your wish," said Fargeau, "is my command."

"Is your friend, the major, is he handsome?"

"Handsome and strong."

"I will be honoured to meet him," said Madelaine Cazotte, grimly.

There was a side to her daughter that Andrea had never seen before, a sharpness and a strength which disconcerted the woman and made her feel old and foolish.

"If nobody objects, I'd prefer to eat supper in my room," Steve had said.

"Nonsense," said Andrea. "You must eat with the rest of us."

"There's no must about it, Mother."

"You need your family about you at a time like this."

"I would prefer to be alone, at least for this evening."

"You'll just sit there brooding."

"I'll eat my chicken salad, drink a glass of wine and smoke too much," said Steve. "But I won't throw myself out of the window."

"Let her go, Andrea," said Miles.

"At a time like this?"

"And a bath," said Steve. "I'd love a bath."

"I don't know if there's hot water."

"Boil a kettle," said Steve. "Sit down, Mother. I'll see to it myself."

"What wrong with the girl?"

"Good God, Andrea! Don't you know? She's just lost her husband and she's trying to behave 'decently'," David had said.

"Don't you have work to do at the Admiralty?"

"Not tonight."

"Can't you *do* something?" said Andrea. "I mean, you must have *friends*."

"I don't understand."

"Friends who can find out if Deems is alive or—"

"Not that sort of friend," said David. "There isn't any point in my phoning round. There just isn't, Andrea."

"Of course there isn't," said Miles. "We'll hear in due course, I expect."

"It's horrible just sitting here," Andrea had said. "One feels so useless, so impotent."

"Yes, and we don't have any happy memories of the poor chap, as Stephanie has," said Miles.

"Happy memories?" said Andrea. "She hardly knew him."

"That's the tragedy of it," said Miles. "The poor, poor girl."

Miles and David had been waiting at the Thames Depot, together with Steve's commanding officer, a rotund little woman with greying hair who managed to exude an air of disciplined affection for her young driver and who had insisted on being the one to break the news in the privacy of the office. Miles and David, feeling foolish and inept, waited outside amid the din and acridity, on a balcony which overlooked the dispersal garage.

When Steve came out she was calm and contained.

The officer saluted her and Steve returned the salute. She had joined her father and uncle without a word and had preceded them down the wooden steps to the waiting car.

"How long do you have?" David had asked.

"As long as I need, up to two weeks," Steve had answered.

"Will you take it?"

"That depends."

David had driven, while Miles sat in the back seat and did his best to break through the wall of containment which Steve appeared to have erected around herself. She permitted her father to hold her hand, as much for his comfort, Miles suspected, as for any soothing effect it had on Steve.

The afternoon, what was left of it, dragged past. Preparations for dinner went on at great length while the four people kept at arm's length from each other like some silly comedy of alienation, each asking permission of the other to perform the simplest acts.

"May I listen to the wireless, darling?"

"Of course, Daddy."

"You're sure you don't mind?"

"Don't be silly."

And: "I wonder if Steve would object if I had a sherry before dinner?"

"Ask her."

"It doesn't seem—well—quite right."

"Ask her, David. She might like one herself."

"Whisky for me."

"Before dinner, darling?"

"With soda, Mother, please."

What else do you do when the young man that your daughter has loved lies in limbo? Not, it seemed, in any known element, in air or water, but in the papery spheres of Air Ministry record offices.

"Why," Andrea hissed in a stage-whisper, "can't they tell us the whole truth?"

"Because, darling, they simply don't know it."

Brooding too, David imagined the drowned shell of the Hurricane resting on the sea-bed, in the cold, peaceful region which was the final resting-place of so many men. He saw Chris in his mind's eye, strapped into the shattered cockpit, hair like weed, eyes staring, head nodding gently, in the undersea currents. He tried to change the image to one of a floppy liferaft and Chris kneeling in it, waving happily to an English inshore boat. But he could not dislodge the vision of death, of a body in a wrecked 'plane or a corpse cast up on a shingle beach, without identity.

Steve ate supper in her room.

Only six months ago she had been without experience of life, apart from girlish pretendings. Now she was a creature with a mind and a will of her own, and courage to mend her broken heart.

"I think I'll just see if she—"

"Andrea, leave her alone. She doesn't want to be fussed over."

Andrea obeyed her brother. A quarter of an hour later, however, she slipped off to her daughter's room and spent some time with her.

When she returned, David and Miles were drinking whisky in the library.

Andrea said, "David, she wants to speak to you."

"How is she?"

"She seems—she seems—I don't understand it. She seems determined."

"Determined?"

"Not to shed a tear," said Andrea, beginning to cry.

Miles moved to comfort his wife, and David climbed the staircase to his niece's room on the first floor.

Steve was seated, tensely, in a large, chintz-covered armchair. The room was thick with cigarette smoke though the window, behind the blackout curtains, was open. The girl, or Andrea, had lighted a standard lamp by the little "study desk" above which, on the wall, were framed photographs, school groups. On the bed there was a battered teddy-bear and a china-headed doll, and on the dresser more soft trophies and gifts from the past. Yet, David felt, this was not Stephanie's room now but that of a child who had been stolen away and would never again be found here.

"Do *you* think Chris will come back?" Steve asked, the moment he entered the room.

David did not hesitate.

"No."

"No miracles?"

"No miracles," said David.

"In that case I'd like to be with his mother, with Holly."

"Now?"

"As soon as it's light." Steve had gained enough experience of night driving in wartime not to undertake a needless journey. "About six should do. Will you come with me?"

"Of course."

"I'd go on my own but I don't quite know where the Beckman place—"

"I'll take you," said David.

Steve nodded. "I'll try to catch some sleep."

"Good idea. I'll waken you at half past five."

"Yes," said Steve. "At a time like this I think I'd prefer to be with somebody who loved him too. Don't you think that's best, Uncle David?"

"I do, indeed," said David. "Will you sleep?"

"Probably," Steve answered.

Sleep would not come to Holly. She had lived through too many crises to expect it and she did not fret over it. Dressed, she sat by the bed in the room on the ground floor which was "her room" when she visited Applehurst.

Maury had given her sedatives, but she left them in the saucer by the glass of milk on the bedside table. She did not want to exhaust herself with enforced sleep. She wanted to taste every moment of the experience of grief, to do justice to it for her son's sake. She wondered about Stephànie, how she was, if youth and weariness had given her sleep or if she was lying awake in floods of lonely tears.

Holly's grieving was deep, not a thing of the heart only but of the memory for the infant she had carried in her body and the baby she had suckled and the boy she had guarded and for the man that he had become. She longed for the return of each of them, and now would have none again, ever again.

She knew and accepted that Chris was dead.

It was some time towards two o'clock in the morning when Holly heard a tentative knocking on the door of her room. She was seated in a rocking-chair with a blanket over her knees The room was lighted by a single table-lamp strong enough to show a band of light, perhaps, under the door.

Thinking it would be Ruth or Maury, Holly did not get up. "Come in."

The knocking continued, very soft and hesitant.

Rising, Holly went to the door and opened it.

She recognised the girl, eldest of the evacuees, Beryl Minns. The girl's hair was unbraided, her face pale. She wore an ankle-length nightdress in printed cotton, tight across her budding breasts.

"Please, miss, I saw yer light."

"What is it, Beryl? Is it one of the children?"

"No, miss."

"Are you feeling unwell?"

"Can't sleep neither, miss."

Though there had been hotter nights that summer, the air was still and breathless in the old house. Very, very distantly, Holly thought she could make out the mutter of thunder, or of shore batteries, perhaps.

"Did something waken you?" Holly asked.

"Bad dream, miss."

"Come on, Beryl," said Holly, taking the girl's hand. "What we both need is a cuppa."

"In the middle of the night, miss?"

"To help us clock over, Beryl."

It was a relief to see the young girl, to have company and a voice in that still and silent hour.

Together, the woman and the girl padded down the corridors and downstairs into the huge half-basement kitchen where, at the gas stove, Holly put on a small kettle and lit the cooking ring under it. There were two new strip lights over the baking table but Holly switched on only the old-fashioned bulb in its fluted mantle and by its light prepared two mugs of hot, sweet tea. She found biscuits in a cupboard and put out the tin. No plates were needed for a midnight snack.

The girl watched her, not drowsily but with a kind of wariness.

Beryl; the thought popped into Holly's head unbidden—there was an unusual type of crystal which was referred to in the trade as Berylware. She had seen a few pieces, tinted aquamarine with a subtle attraction. She thought of telling the girl, then lost the thought as the evacuee said, "Miss, could y'give's a gasper, d'yer think?"

"Aren't you a bit young to be smoking yet, Béryl?"

"Me bruvver got me started, miss. Mrs. Maury slips us a Woodbine now'n'again, like. She wouldn't mind."

"Well, just this once."

Holly laid her box of Du Mauriers and a petrol lighter on the table. She watched the girl's furtive expertise, the satisfaction of the first inhalation. Tea and a gasper, the insomniac's friends. Holly poured tea and seated herself opposite the little Londoner.

Beryl puffed and sipped. The child in her had been replaced by the old woman that she would, in time, become.

Holly, too, lit a cigarette.

Beryl said, "I know why Mr. Maury brought you 'ere, miss. Why you can't sleep neither, like."

"I suppose all the children know."

"They don't understand like me, miss."

The tea relaxed Holly, softened the hard knot of resentment that, she realised, had lain in her breast. She breathed deeply, sighing, her hands around the mug.

"They're too young," said Beryl. "Kid's all they are."

"I doubt if you really understand either, Beryl."

"'Course I do. Me bruvver, him what give me the gaspers, he bought it last February. I liked Bert. He liked me an' all. It's him I got the dreams about, miss. But they ain't all bad dreams. Think he's still comin' home, sometimes, like a kid would. But Bert ain't. He's drowned, in the navy. U-boat got 'im."

It was a long speech from the girl, delivered with stoicism. Holly was taken aback. Out of her loss the young girl had shaped sympathy, had made grief into experience. In the life of the streets there was this maturity, this self-sufficiency and natural outward warmth. There was no retreat for the likes of Beryl Minns. Had she ever been like that? Holly posed the question in her mind while the girl dabbed ash from the cigarette into the saucer ashtray.

"Poor old bleedin' Bert. Me mum took it real 'ard."

Tea and cigarettes were not enough after all. It was not the night's restlessness that had brought Beryl to her room, but the embarrassing need to find someone who might understand the sad lessons that she, a child, had learned.

Thickly Holly said, "Chris—my son—he's missing. But he may not be dead."

"Hope yer right, miss," said Beryl.

"Your brother, how did he—"

"Destroyer he was on. The *Daring*. In the 'lantic Ocean. Torpedo got the boat. But nobody found Bert like. Drowned, I suppose."

"My son's 'plane went down in the sea, too."

5 Desperate Women

Christopher Deems, her first husband, had once told Holly that she had no sense of wonder. He tempered his criticism by admitting that she had a natural appreciation of the beauty of artifacts, the craftsmanship and skill of painters and makers, but of life and its incredible shadings, Christopher claimed, she remained innocent. Holly accepted it, thought little of it. She knew that she could not see things as the poet did. There was too much ambition in her for sensitivity to survive. And yet on that August morning, she experienced a heightened moment, a still point, into which she moved vividly.

There had been rain, which had cleansed the trees of dustiness and drew from the shrubs a dark salty tang to temper the fragrance of grass and flowers. All was still. In the sky no aeroplanes scored the laths of pale blue between drifting clouds, no guns pounded the borders of audibility. It was as if the pulse of war had stopped in the night, leaving no withering or decay but a strange perfectibility and sureness of peace.

Between seven and eight o'clock, the children stirred in the dormitory and there was the rattle of crockery in the kitchen, the smell of burned toast in the air of the corridor. Sunk in the chair by the window, Holly felt leaden. Beryl had long since gone back to bed and Holly had found no solace in the hiss of the rain shower and the cessation of noises beyond Maury's trees.

Somewhat lost, David weaved the car uncertainly up the path through the shrubs.

Abruptly distracted, Holly rose and went out of the stuffy room on to the broad lawn. A large yellow rubber ball, washed clean, sat boldly on the green, a pair of skipping ropes with painted wooden handles, a battered tricycle with black rubber tyres and a limp cotton flag tied to its spar, a tin gun, a sand-pail, a length of glistening garden hose—childhood trophies, toys and diversions, each object seemed brilliant on the motionless emerald lawn. Holly felt as if she was floating towards the motor car, to David and Stephanie. The flagstones at the edge of the terrace were hard, the grass soft. The figures did not move. Side by side they waited at the car. Holly knew that they had come to tell her that Chris was dead. She could tell by their gravity that they did not bring hope. It didn't matter. The son she had protected with guile and ferocity was lost, gone with the litheness and optimism, the myriad opportunities of her youth. She would grow old alone. Was old now. Alone now. She walked slowly, her feet, in slippers, groping for the grass.

Trapped in the moment, everything seemed to happen in sequence, not at once, so that Holly could stand apart from herself, walk by herself, as a ghost might do, unseen, unable to participate in the realities of the world.

She heard the ringing of the telephone within the house.

She heard David calling out to her.

She heard the ringing of the telephone cease.

David calling out.

Stephanie began to run, running like a leggy young animal, awkward and gentle and graceful all in one, running not to Holly but past her.

Maury's voice, behind, boomed out a great shout.

It seemed that the telephone was still ringing, ringing in her head. She could not stop or turn aside but must continue to walk away from it, walk towards David, who alone now waited, his arms out to her. She heard Christopher shouting, Kennedy's patient enquiries. Quite definitely the voices of men who were dead. It was so consoling to have them near, walking unseen behind her as she walked with the self she had been before. The telephone stopped ringing. Steve went past her. And Maury was shouting but she did not turn round.

She reached David before Stephanie and Maury reached her. David's arms about her, the brush of his beard on her cheek wakened her from the timeless sleep of that long, long moment.

"He's alive. Chris is alive. In London. In hospital. Chris isn't dead, Holly. Chris is still with us."

She turned, David thrust her forward. Steve flung herself into Holly's arms, the girl with her future restored, the woman dispossessed of the past.

"Mrs. Butterfield called. The hospital called. It's Chris. All right. Alive."

For the first time, and the last, in her life, Holly King fainted.

*

Doped to the eyeballs, of course, no wonder he felt woozy. Quite natural, nothing to fret about. The quacks had told him to expect reaction and a degree of pain, to sing out if it got too bad to bear. No shame in that, no shortage of morphine. One nurse, a tall, blonde girl he had confused with Steve, he had tried to hug. Rather embarrassing. Clear-headed enough now, though. He had tendered his apologies. What had the nurse whispered? Wouldn't mind being married to a chap like you, and Steve was a lucky duck.

No bandages on his face. Eyesight okay-dokay.

Read the large headline, please, Pilot Officer.

SUPPLY MUDDLE: OFFICIAL.

PARACHUTES A VAIN NAZI RUSE.

TRAIN BOMBED: SEVERAL KILLED.

The headline, please, Pilot Officer.

144 DOWN OUT OF 1,000.

The quack had thanked him, smiling.

Figures, official figures. Propaganda. Surprisingly it had not been at all cold in the sea at first, not like water at all, more like aspic, a warmish sort of jelly. Cold later, though, damned cold. Pain was the only thing that kept him from dozing off, probably never to waken again. How vast the straits had looked from the base level. He had surfaced in a rush that nearly tore what was left of his leg away.

No idea how long he floated. Not too bad, really, all things considered. We'll make it, Steve, my love.

Splashed by salt waves and parched with thirst. Nor any drop to drink. Drop to drink. Drop to drink. He had wallowed on his back and deliberately kept his left side as inactive as possible while he paddled with his hands, like fins, and waggled his right leg from time to time and watched the sky and the fly-specks of aeroplanes and signatures of smoke. He suspected he was in for a long night of it. Convinced he would be picked up eventually if he just kept floating and did not panic at the fact that the pain had gone out of the nerves of the leg and there was an odd sort of rusty stain which trailed him hither and thither.

The damned coastal barge almost ran him over. How he shouted and splashed when that great wooden prow with its painted letters loomed over him. But the bow wave bobbed him away and they had come bodily into the water to fetch him, two sailors, crying cheerfully, asking him where the 'ell he thought he was and what had he done with his 'plane, careless monkey. But he wasn't in much of a mood to banter since the leg had started shooting pain like a frayed electrical cable. And it had become worse and worse as they guided him to the barge and manhandled him over the side on to the deck, until he felt as if he was a bee tearing out its sting. Passed out, swooned clean away. Very lucky, really, very, very lucky all round. Especially as the doctors had told him he wouldn't have survived the night with the leg all mangled and losing blood.

It had been dark when the barge docked at Deal and he had been carried up in a blanket like some strange fish and given into the care of the RAF again, taken to a hospital not far off and, on instructions of a doctor there, slid back into the ambulance and whisked away to the Cyrus Street Military Hospital in London. He wasn't terribly interested in the reasons at the time. Wanted only to sleep, to be free of the pain which gnawed at his left side. Though he did manage to call out to them to tell his wife he was still in the land of the living. He knew he wasn't going to die or anything like it. He thought a good night's shut-eye and a bandage or two would put him back with the squadron. Poised in a limbo between sleeping and waking, he composed in his head the exact phrases he would use in his report on the loss of the Hurricane.

Bit of a shambles really, sir. Caught me napping, rather, sir. Sorry, sir.

They gave him tea to drink, and examined the leg every so often, three doctors and a buxom nurse. Made him sleep on his back with a wicker cage like a lobster trap stuck over his knees under the blankets. They were much more interested in the leg than they were in him. If he hadn't slept so much during the first round of the clock he might have suspected that there had been a muddle and nobody really knew who he was. Just a poor pilot with a busted stick.

Long after dark—Chris thought—the doctor came to him. He had been dozing in the cot in a little ward, protected by screens. Without morphine for seven hours, when the big gruff doctor touched him he experienced all the agonies of hell, daggers of white hot steel in thigh and groin and belly. Clenched himself.

Suddenly slick and odorous with sweat, he struggled. The doctor put a hand on him, restrained his thrashing.

"Hold yourself still, lad."

"What—what's wrong?"

The doctor was a Scot. He had wiry eyebrows, and hair in his nostrils, hair on the backs of his hands. He looked untidy, white coat open, a blue shirt and string-like black tie beneath.

"My name's Walsh, lad. I'm a surgeon."

"A—a surgeon? What—what—?"

"You've done something very nasty t' that knee. D'you feel strong enough t' take a wee look?"

Chris steeled himself. He had thought little of his body until that moment, had not imagined that it would fail him. Time, he supposed, would heal whatever ailed him.

"Yes; go ahead."

The buxom nurse—not a young woman, very starched—uncovered the wicker cage and lifted it away.

The first thing Chris noticed was the huge pad of soft lint upon which his leg had been placed and how dirty it was. He was naked from the waist down. His privates lay curled between his thighs—yet he felt not one jot of embarrassment.

Walsh put a hand behind his shoulders and eased him into a sitting position. The pain was breathtakingly intense. Chris looked down the length of his torso at his limbs. The right leg was discoloured, ringed below and above the kneecap with purple and brown welts, the shin, scraped raw, varnished with a gentian solution. But it was, nonetheless, a leg. His leg. It had shape, was quite muscular, and served to contrast the thing lying left of it.

"Dear God!"

"See why it's hurtin' you?" said Walsh.

"Oh, my God!"

"Thank your stars, lad, the damage is where it is. Four or six inches higher and the femoral artery would have been severed and you wouldn't be here to tell the tale. What happened? Do y' remember?"

Chris closed his eyes. Concentrated. Tried to blot out the image of that ugly twisted remnant.

"It would be useful t' know," said Walsh.

Controlling his hysteria, Chris told the surgeon all he could remember of the last phase of the aerial combat, how the dashboard had spewed flames, how he had felt a vice-like bite on his knees and how he had fallen out of the cockpit only seconds before the Hurricane had broken up.

The doctor nodded and patted his shoulder in sympathy and encouragement.

"Am I—is it burned?" Chris asked.

"Only superficially."

"What then?"

"I'm guessin' that your suit took the flames." Walsh seated himself on the bed while the nurse replaced the cage and sheet. "I imagine you caught your legs under the metal edge of the dashboard."

"Just—just how bad is it?"

"Well, we'll need t' see," said Walsh. "Under anaesthetic. I'm not keen t'wait too long. I thought we'd have a wee chat about it first."

"Is this the wee chat, sir?"

"Aye, I suppose it is," Walsh said. "Have you no family?"

The question was unexpected.

"Of course. My wife and mother—"

"Bloody damned clerks!" growled Walsh.

"You mean they don't know where I am?"

"I'll see to it. We've got your identity marked. I suppose rushin' you up from Oswald hospital on a pint of blood got the bloody damned clerks confused."

"I want to see my wife."

"Aye."

"Before—before anything else happens, I want to talk to my wife."

"You're going into the theatre at eleven o'clock tomorrow morning. That's in ten hours. I'll do my very best t' see that your family's informed."

"I'm not going to die, surely?"

"Och, no, no! You'll live t' fight another day."

"Will I?" said Chris. "Will I be able to fly a 'plane again?"

"Is it very important t'you?"

"Very important."

Walsh, Chris realised, had already been through this conversation with other pilots. He understood now why he had been transferred to Cyrus Street Hospital without delay. Walsh was the great panjandrum, a surgeon-specialist, "leg man" for the RAF.

"Listen, lad," said Walsh. "I'll tell you the truth. Even without X-rays I'm sure the patella—the cap of bone that covers the knee—is shattered. We can't repair it. But we can maybe do something about a replacement. Muscle has been stripped away. Tendon and ligamental material is damaged, perhaps severed. It won't heal and we can't properly repair it."

"Are you telling me," said Chris, through bone-dry lips, "that I'd be better off without the leg?"

"Better off?" said Walsh. "No. No, I'm not sayin' that."

"What are my choices?"

"You're a strong lad. You weren't in the sea long. You didn't lose much blood and you're not shocked. I can begin dismantling your leg at once. But I don't know what I'll find until I have it apart. You'd be surprised what we *can* do with a machine like a human limb. But we *can't* work miracles."

"You want my permission to—to amputate, is that it?"

"It might be the best thing in the long run."

"Infection might set in?"

"Aye. Patched up, repaired and looked after," said Walsh, "you might get away with it. But there's a fair number of things you won't be able to do again—and you'll never win any beauty contests."

"What if you take it off?"

"We could fit an artifical limb."

"If this was your leg, sir, what would you do?"

"Have it off," said Walsh, without hesitation.

"Why?"

"Because it's going to be painful, very, very painful. It's going to require much surgery and, at the end of it all, you'll have no flexion in the joint. I told you, we can't work miracles."

"And I won't be able to fly?"

"I doubt it," Walsh answered. "With a neat mechanical job you'd have something close to normal mobility."

"Either way. I'm maimed."

"I fear so."

"Are you just being polite, Mr. Walsh," Chris asked, "or will my wishes affect what you do tomorrow in the operating room?"

"I can remove the lower part of the leg without danger. In two or three months, when healing is complete, you'll be fitted with a new leg and might even be flying again before the year's out."

"If not?"

"If not, I'll do what I can to restore what's left, to make sure it's not going to become infected and that the tissues will have a chance of restoring themselves. But I can do nothing about function. Without a knee joint it will be stiff for the rest of your natural days."

"May I think about it for a while?"

"I'd rather you slept."

"I can sleep all day tomorrow."

Walsh got to his feet. "I'll be back in an hour, lad. After that we'll both be needin' our shut-eye."

Chris clenched his fingers into fists as pain beat against him. Sweat ran freely down his cheeks and breastbone. He looked straight into the doctor's sad, experienced eyes.

"Thank you for being honest with me."

"Best policy," said Walsh. "See you in an hour."

When the doctor had gone, Chris put his arms above his head and gripped the iron rail of the cot, stretching his back as if to extend and thin the rods of pain which came from his legs. Morphine would take the edge off it. But he needed an unclouded mind.

Well, Steve, darling, what do you suggest I do?

An artificial limb; the concept appalled him. Metal and bakelite and buckles and straps, like something a worn-out old man might wear. He believed Walsh, believed that, indeed, he might have more freedom of movement with a limb that wasn't his own. But it would be horrible to look upon, an alien thing. He would never be able to show it to Steve, to let her look upon it, to lie by her side again.

But, Steve, I can't fly a 'plane with a gammy leg, a stick which won't bend. Miracles or not, I'll never be able to pilot an aircraft with what's left of this leg.

He would be whole, though. The ugly twisted thing could be kept hidden, never exposed. He would learn to cope gracefully with the limp, would ask Mother to find him a dashing cane which he

206

would use with élan, cavalier style, like Lord Byron. At least he would still be able to swim. What would the RAF do about it? Would they automatically discharge him? He had heard of chaps who had remained in the service after being wounded. The authorities would probably allocate him some sort of desk job. But not to fly again? Never to pilot a 'plane again? What a bloody choice! Experimentally he put one hand down beneath the sheets and gripped the thigh above the injury, pressing it, as if to strangle the pain. He must be prepared for this, for lots and lots and lots of pain. It would be demanding, warping. But he would put up with it. If only there was some way, some means of guaranteeing . . .

Where was Steve? Why hadn't they told her where he was? Why didn't she come? If he could have looked at her just once, he would have been able then to decide what to do for the best. But he was alone, had to make his own decision.

He thought of the red tile roofs of Blaze Cottage at West Horsfall fleeing beneath the fuselage, of the great welcoming panoply of the sky and the throbbing power of the engines, the glazed reflections in the gauges and the smell of the hot oil and the rubber. All the things he had dreamed about since he was old enough to dream. All given him like gifts showered on a spoiled child.

He thought of Stephanie, silken and soft and warm, her flanks against his thighs, her stomach under his caressing hand, her breasts.

Chris shouted aloud.

The nurse came, bearing a kidney dish and a hypodermic. Thrashing his head furiously to deny himself the relief of sedation, Chris shouted at the nurse to fetch Walsh.

The surgeon was with him almost immediately.

Once more Chris controlled himself, fought back the tears, the anguish. He locked his fists together under the coverlet.

"I've made up my mind, sir," he said.

Herr Oberisch came at last. He arrived, without announcement, late in the evening just as Madelaine was on the point of dragging out the shutters to secure the gallery for the night.

She had been depressed all day, after a night spent in the company of Fargeau's Nazi "friend", a certain Standartenführer

Heinz Butler, who had treated her with coldly insistent charm. He had dined her, wined her and conversed with her on matters of art and culture and had taken her to bed in the gilded splendour of the Hotel Saint Ambroise.

Butler was a lay-model for the new-image officer of the SS, with Prussian haircut and features as blunt and smooth as shell casing. In age, forty, as a lover he was ruthless but not cruel. The bizarre pleasure he gave her increased Madelaine's feelings of shame and guilt. She had an appointment to meet the colonel again in four days.

She had returned to the apartment soon after the lifting of the curfew, half expecting to find Ritchie and that she would have to invent a lie—though her husband would not be deluded. But Ritchie was not at home and did not return at all that day.

Tired and fretful, with a congested sort of hangover to add to her woes, Madelaine hung about the gallery and worried in case Ritchie had abandoned her. A check of the documents in the apartment indicated that he had not taken anything from the box.

Though she trusted nobody, not Ritchie, not Fargeau and certainly not her new protector, she was not unduly surprised when a young boy, already bearing the scraped, furtive look of a criminal, slipped into the gallery and without a word of greeting or explanation put a plain envelope upon her desk and departed again as stealthily as he had arrived.

She opened the letter and read the contents which were printed in execrable French in pencil on a leaf from a cheap notepad.

He has a room in No. 17 Rue de Vallon. He stays with a Jew named Anna Kern. She is a widow with two sons. He has done black market business. Mille Baises, J.

Fargeau had kept his end of the bargain.

Clearly she had satisfied the SS administrator who knew so much about art. She read the note several times, with peculiar diffidence.

A Jewess with two sons. Jewess. Sons. Widow. Room. So Ritchie had found another hole to hide in. Had settled for one of his own kind, some stinking fat Jewish Mama. With sons. He had bought himself a family for the price of a few horsemeat steaks.

Madelaine looked up the address in her Paris *Guide*. The Marais. Hard by the Jewish quarter, on the first level, a spit from the

Hebrew synagogue. Even Fargeau must have smirked when he received the news back from his boys. God, but she might be better off with Heinz Butler than with her Jew-peasant husband.

Rage replaced worry. She paced the boards of the gallery, forth and back, for most of the afternoon. She still nurtured a chilling suspicion that Ritchie was up to something which intimately concerned her future and safety, but she could not deduce from the scant evidence in her possession what it might be. If only Wili would turn up. She would feel much safer with Wili on the scene and the Italian paintings re-converted into cash. She would be out from under the yoke of debt then, able to put her relationship with Standartenführer Butler on a different basis, to make use of him without Fargeau's intervention, to become not his prostitute but his Parisian mistress, almost his equal.

Such fancies, mingled with anger at her husband and at the situation in which circumstances had placed her, occupied Madelaine Cazotte for the whole afternoon. It was almost evening— the dead hour between six and seven—before she thought at all about what she was going to say to Ritchie when next they met.

She would say nothing. She would hold her tongue, pretend that everything was sweet between them. Perhaps he would bring her a piece of meat or a bottle of good wine as a peace offering, a gesture which would be typical of the deceitful, two-faced English bastard, but one which she would accept without a murmur of protest.

Madelaine had gone into the rear of the gallery to haul out the heavy shutters when she heard the squeal of motor-car tyres outside. Nervously she darted back into the shop and peeped out of the window, keeping herself hidden. Her extreme agitation manifested itself in a tic at the corner of her mouth, and in an uncontrollable fluttering of her eyelid.

A uniformed chauffeur strode round to the passenger door of the gleaming Mercedes and opened it. She expected to see Butler or some other high-ranking officer step forth. Instead, there was Wili Oberisch, *sans* uniform, just the same plump moon-faced Wili in his soft-cut three-piece suit, with his polished shoes and his banded Fedora, looking for all the world like a Bohemian gangster.

Wili ignored the chauffeur, who closed the door of the Mercedes and stood by it at attention, while the little agent picked his way across the pavement and entered the gallery by the front door.

Madelaíne ran to him, her joy, for once, unfeigned.

"Wili, how good it is to see you. What took you so long to call on your old, your dear friend?"

"Madelaine." He did not kiss her hand, or her cheek. He had no need now to indulge in displays of affection. He glanced curiously around the bare-walled gallery. "Have you sold everything to my countrymen already?"

"Only the trash, Wili." She took his arm, not daunted by his manner. "The best, the very best, is safe and sound, reserved for you, *chéri*, just for you."

In French, Oberisch said, "Including the Dubriel collection of Italian masters?"

"Yes, yes. Did you not receive my letter?"

Wili did not answer her question. He disengaged his arm from her grasp and stripped off his soft, black leather gloves. Outside, the military driver stood to attention, staring straight in through the glass.

Madelaine said, "I will unpack the paintings tomorrow morning, let you see them in daylight. But tonight, Wili, tonight we have other things to do."

The faint suggestion of a smile crossed Oberisch's lips.

He said, "Standartenführer Butler would not approve."

"Butler?" Madelaine could not hide her dismay. "Do you know Herr Butler? Is he a—a friend of yours, Wili?"

"He is a friend of yours, Madelaine, and that is the only relationship which has any importance."

Contritely, Madelaine murmured, "But the Standartenführer told me nothing of this."

"No doubt he will instruct you in his own good time," said Wili Oberisch, "and in his own inimitable way."

Comprehension chilled Madelaine. Oberisch was Butler's servant too. Perhaps it was Oberisch who had "chosen" her for Butler, and Fargeau was no more than a convenient matchmaker. The deviousness and complexity of the German occupying force could not be underestimated. Suddenly Madelaine was on the defensive. She was being reduced to property, something of value, certainly, but something which had merit as a trading item and not a collector's piece to be kept and cherished.

She said, "What Herr Butler doesn't know—"

Oberisch cut in. "What the colonel doesn't know it will be my business to find out, Madelaine. However, I didn't come tonight to discuss *amour*. I came for the Dubriel collection."

"The collection?"

"It *is* ready for collection, is it not?"

"Packed and crated, but—"

"Let me see."

"Very well, Wili. But—but tonight?" Madelaine stammered. "So close to curfew?"

"I'll make sure you are escorted home."

"Do you intend to take the collection away? Tonight?"

"Of course."

"And—and—payment?"

"You will be recompensed, Madelaine, in due course."

"How soon, Wili?"

"As soon as my department processes the purchase invoices."

"Wili, it cost me a great amount of money, all I have, to acquire the Dubriel paintings. I can't survive without capital. I must be paid very soon."

"Do you want to be paid at all, Madelaine?"

"Yes, of course. But—"

"You are, like it or not, a humble citizen in an occupied country. You can't expect special treatment. German administrators have more to do with their time than pander to you."

"But—but you *will* pay me?"

"We are not thieves, Madelaine."

"There are other paintings and sculptures which I've been saving for you, Wili."

"One thing at a time," said Oberisch. "Show me the crates which contain the Italian works."

Meekly and obediently Madelaine took the German agent through the curtain at the rear of the gallery and led him down the broad wooden staircase into the basement. There was a wall of whitewashed brick and a stout wooden door through which, in a vault-like corridor, the crates which Ritchie had transported from the house of the Dubriels were stowed away.

Oberisch allowed himself a grunt of satisfaction at the sight of the crated treasures.

"Good," he said. "I'm glad you've been sensible, Madelaine. We'll make a German out of you yet."

"Now what?" said Madelaine.

"Now," Wili Oberisch glanced at his wristlet watch, "my transport will have arrived. Go upstairs, please, and show them the way."

Madelaine climbed the stairs again and, from the window, saw that a box-sided lorry bearing numerals and insignia which she could not interpret had drawn up at the pavement's edge directly behind the Mercedes. Four uniformed men of humble rank stood by the side of the lorry conversing with the chauffeur.

Madelaine opened the door of the gallery but had no need to instruct the soldiers. They filed smartly past her, and at her signal vanished downstairs.

Within minutes the crates had been taken out and hidden within the lorry, the manoeuvre accomplished with such rapidity and efficiency that Madelaine imagined that the Dubriel collection had simply vanished. It was possession, a smooth, clinical act of plunder which left her aghast.

Puffing slightly, Wili came upstairs.

"All is well," he said. "I will inspect the works at my office in due course and will call on you again."

"Wili, I need money."

"You need food and clothing and a warm place to sleep, Madelaine. That is all you need. Such luxuries will make you a queen in Paris, believe me."

"Wili, you promised me—"

"Ah!" Oberisch glanced again at his watch. "I see we have been so quick that you do not need an escort. Hurry, though, and don't get caught by the curfew patrol."

Without another word the fat little German rolled out of the gallery and ducked into the waiting Mercedes. The car prowled away from the kerb and, trailed by the lorry, vanished swiftly from sight.

Stunned, Madelaine stood on the step of the open door and stared after them, then, in a sudden outburst of anger, cried, "I *have* been caught, you Nazi pig. I have been caught already."

Wili Oberisch was far out of range and the Parisians on the Boulevard kept their heads down and ears closed to the stream of invective which poured from the distraught woman by the door of the gallery, even to the tears and sobbing which followed. Everybody had problems of their own and those souls who knew the Cazottes at all felt, cynically, that Madelaine would not weep for long.

The smell of frying garlic sausage permeated the stairs of the apartment. In total control of herself again, Madelaine sniffed the air hungrily and, knowing that Ritchie had come home, rapped on the door until he admitted her.

Her husband looked comfortable and at ease. He had put on a dressing-robe over his shirt and trousers, was shaven and perfumed, and gave her a grin by way of welcome.

He said not a word to her about the "business" which had kept him away all night. He waved a skillet cheerfully and asked, "Are you hungry, kid?"

Madelaine managed her brightest smile. "Ravenous."

"Glad to hear it." Ritchie returned to the kitchen and she heard the splutter of oil and the unmistakable hiss of eggs sliding into a pan.

In spite of herself, Madelaine felt momentary affection for her English husband, saw him as a provider, a satisfier of her appetites.

On the kitchen table there was a bottle of red wine, a new loaf of bread and a gigantic cream meringue, just like the kind they used to sell in Robert's before it closed. He'd even stuck a candle in a bottle and folded the table napkins into little tricorns, as she liked. Suspicion, of course, lurked under Madelaine's hunger but she was learning to live for the moment and, shucking off her coat, seated herself without further ado at the table.

"Got two polonies," said Ritchie, over his shoulder. "I stuck 'em in the ice-box; is that right?"

"It will do them no harm. Where did you buy them?"

"Place I know. Cost me a bleedin' fortune."

"Everything does."

Could Fargeau have been wrong? Perhaps the Jewish woman wasn't her husband's mistress but only a black market dealer with whom he was obliged to curry favour.

No. Fargeau was never wrong.

Madelaine was enveloped in the aroma of sausage and egg. Young enough to respond to such stimuli and put from her mind the terrible anxieties which tormented her, she lifted her fork and set to immediately while her husband uncorked and poured wine. Neither the woman nor the man, though, saw fit to light the candle and they ate by the blue glow of the low-pressure gas ring.

Ritchie said, "I got coffee too. Brazilian coffee. None of your kraut muck."

"You are so clever, *chéri*."

The hot food filled her mouth, increased her hunger even as it assuaged it. It tasted better than the veal she had enjoyed with Heinz Butler twenty-four hours ago in the splendour of the dining-room of the Saint Ambroise.

"More?"

"If you please."

Was he being nice to her to pacify his guilty conscience?

Did he want to go to bed with her? She would not object to that. On the contrary. It would be a suitable sort of thing to do, to lie with her undemanding husband on the moth-eaten fur, smoking a cigarette and sipping the last of the wine until he felt like making love to her—if that was on his mind. Had he tired already of the woman in the Marais, in the hole-in-the-wall in the Rue de Vallon? The woman was probably passive and unimaginative, blotchy and fat and coarse. It would be ironic, though, the pair of them making love after each of them had been with another partner; she with an officer of the infamous SS and Ritchie with a Jewess.

Ritchie filtered coffee through a muslin bag into the slender china pot. Madelaine mopped up the last of the savoury oil with a chunk of bread.

Should she tell him now or later?

Ritchie pushed the plate with the cream-dripping meringue upon it towards her. She sucked her fork and broke the confection and ate it, delaying decision a minute or two longer.

Finally it was all gone, the last sugary crumb. She drank the strong black coffee and took the cigarette Ritchie had lighted for her.

Outside it was almost dark. The curfew would be in force for French citizens. She asked her husband to light the candle, which he did. It was too late for him to leave now. Obviously he intended to spend the night at home.

Madelaine said, "Wili Oberisch finally turned up."

The pause was almost undetectable. "When?"

"This afternoon."

"Early or late?"

"Late."

"About time," said Ritchie, casually.

"He took away the Italian paintings."

Another pause. "What did he think of them?"

"He didn't bother to open the crates. He had a lorry and soldiers. I think Oberisch is on the staff of a military group."

"Perhaps," said Ritchie. "Didn't he want to look at any of the paintings?"

"He could not whisk them away from the gallery fast enough," said Madelaine. "He stole them."

"He hasn't stolen them," said Ritche. "He'll pay."

"A few hundred francs per painting, perhaps," said Madelaine.

"Then he won't get any more," said Ritchie.

"He has what he wants from us."

"Did he *tell* you he wasn't going to meet the price?"

"He implied it."

"You don't seem upset, kid. Don't tell me you expected it?"

"No, no, I did not expect Wili Oberisch to let me down."

"Because you slept with him?"

She was too relaxed to be angry. She darted a glance at her husband. A cigarette was dangling from his lips and he held a bowl of coffee in both hands, leaning against the dressing board by the stove.

"I thought Germans were honest."

"Sure, they are," said Ritchie. "Keep faith with them and they'll keep faith with you."

Puzzled, Madelaine said, "What do you mean?"

"I mean, Wili and his pals won't let you down, Maddy."

"Ritchie—"

"Listen, we'll jaw about it later. Right now I just want to get to bed."

"Yes. I want to, also."

'Right. Why don't you go and get ready?"

"And you?"

"I'll check the blackout and the locks. Be with you in a brace of shakes," Ritchie said, speaking English. "Go on, love."

Madelaine hesitated, then, taking the wine bottle and two glasses, she went into the bedroom through the long lounge.

She took off her shoes and dress and lay on the beaver-skin quilt. Its faint musky odour seemed comforting tonight. She needed Ritchie by her, the consolation that he would offer her and the assurance that while he was still her husband everything would somehow be made to come right. Ritchie's cunning would provide for them. She had been wrong to try to shake him off, to deceive him. Deliverance did not lie with strangers and enemies but with the old English "shoe" she had married.

She moistened her lips with wine, then, with the glass still in her hand, put her head on the pillow. She could hear Ritchie moving about in the room next door.

He came to her after three or four minutes. He had taken off the dressing-robe and wore a shirt and the trousers of his suit, his waistcoat still unbuttoned. Sleepily, she looked up at him and smiled with a warmth that she had not bestowed upon him for several years.

Gently Ritchie took the wine glass from her fingers and put it on the bedside table. He touched her brow and she felt the caress of his knuckles as he brushed a straggle of hair from her cheek. The food and wine and the long day's tension had made her so sleepy. He did not kiss her—later she would remember that—but whispered, "Hang on, kid. Hang on."

Madelaine blinked and struggled to keep awake, sitting up for a moment to watch her husband go out of the bedroom again and into the living-room. There was no light and she could not deduce from the sounds he made what he was doing so she sighed and called out his name.

He murmured an answer, and she caught a glimpse of the white shirt moving through the gloom before she sank back in the bed, closed her eyes and, within seconds, fell asleep.

She never saw Ritchie again.

It was the longest day of young Stephanie Walshott's life, the uncertain wait between arrival at the Cyrus Street Hospital and the moment, very late in the afternoon, when she was permitted to see her husband.

Chris could not "see" her, of course, for—as the doctors explained—he was still "out for the count", recovering from the anaesthetic and it would be very unwise to endeavour to rouse him.

Even so, Steve's relief at looking on her husband's face for the two or three minutes allotted her was intense, and removed the doubt which had darkened the day and made it such an agony of uncertainty.

He was pale and hollow-eyed but peaceful in sleep, his breathing rhythmic. He looked more boyish than she remembered him. She could not associate him with the man who had made love to her with such ardour, almost as if she had rediscovered him at an earlier age in his life.

The astringent odours of the hospital, shiny linoleum floors, cheesecloth screens on squeaky wheels, the glimpses of other men, bandaged and sullen and in pain, alienated Chris from her but, paradoxically, increased her longing for him. She wanted only to have him back, to redeem him from this sterile place and nurse him back to health and strength.

There was a doctor named Perkins, a chirpy little man with gold-framed spectacles and a bald pate rimmed with golden hair; and a surgeon named Walsh, a Scotsman, who was as hairy as a sheepdog and gruff.

Perkins spoke to them—Holly and Uncle David and herself—before she was permitted to see Chris; Walsh afterwards. Inconsequentially, Steve wished that she had put on her ATS uniform. These doctors were ranking officers and she might, somehow, have gained more from them if she had been in a service uniform.

The day was punctuated by three conversations.

Perkins: "Pilot Officer Deems is remarkably strong. There is no need to fear for his life. He'll make a full recovery from his wounds, I'm sure. He'll soon be out and about again."

Steve: "His wounds?"

Perkins: "The bones of his left leg have been crushed. My colleague, Mr. Walsh, will be conducting exploratory surgery on the limb in an hour or so. Your husband, Mrs. Deems, is in pre-op at this minute—which is, alas, why I can't offer to let you see him."

Holly: "How badly crushed?"

Perkins: "Rather severely, I'm afraid."

Steve: "Will he—will he lose the leg?"

Perkins: "I really can't say. That's a matter for Mr. Walsh to decide."

There was nothing to be gained by staying in the smoke-reeking waiting-room of the Cyrus Street Hospital. David took the woman and the girl out for lunch, though they ate very little and were back at the hospital by two o'clock in the afternoon.

Perkins: "I'm pleased to inform you that Pilot Officer Deems underwent a successful operation and is now out of theatre and in the recovery room."

Steve: "What do you mean by a 'successful' operation?"

Perkins: "Well, that's for Mr. Walsh to say. He will be out of the theatre in a couple of hours. You had better talk with him. Shall we say five o'clock?"

Steve: "How serious is my husband's injury? Why won't you tell us?"

Perkins: "Because, Mrs. Deems, I really don't know."

Another interlude: Holly called Maury, Steve telephoned her mother and David took them out again for tea in a nearby café. Bomb rubble and an unusual view of Highgate, carved out of the side of Cyrus Street, reminded Steve that the war was still at hand, close at hand. The café was squalid but the tea was strong. They hardly spoke of Chris, hardly spoke at all. They were back within the hospital by half-past four.

It was six before Perkins reappeared.

"Mrs. Deems, you may see your husband now."

"Where's Mr. Walsh?"

"He'll talk with you afterwards."

Steve allowed herself to be ushered along a broad corridor and into a closet-like ward which contained two beds divided by a plyboard partition at head height. There were sundry tubes and bottles, a porcelain sink surmounted by glass shelves. The room had no windows and a fan on the ceiling stirred the chemical air listlessly. A nurse, hardly older than she was, stood in discreet attendance while Steve lingered by Chris's bed.

It was Walsh who came to escort her away. He took her into his office, more "army" than the rest of the hospital, bearing a quantity of printed regulations on the walls and rows of filing cabinets behind the desk.

Walsh settled into a wooden chair behind the desk and lifted a tarry briar pipe from a tin ashtray. "Do you mind if I puff?"

"No."

Walsh lit the pipe.

"You're very young, Mrs. Deems. How long have you been married?"

"Not long."

"You're a lucky lass. You near lost your man, y'know."

"What do you mean?"

"His 'plane went up in smoke and he went into the drink wi'out a parachute. In my book that makes him a survivor who's lucky t'be alive."

Steve sensed that Walsh was preparing her for grim news.

"What do y'know about anatomy, Mrs. Deems?"

"I've had basic first aid training, with the ATS."

"Och, so you're an Auxiliary, are you?"

"Yes."

"All right then." Walsh put down the pipe. "Your husband's left leg is seriously damaged. Crushed bone and stripped muscle, severing of the tendons. The kneecap is gone, shattered by impact. The head of the two big bones—the femur and the tibia—have been broken. Fortunately they're not fragmented, just snapped across the head." Walsh held up his fist and tapped it with a forefinger "Across there. The blood vessels below and above the knee joint are bruised but intact and the arterial system which keeps the lower limb in trim should heal near perfect."

"Can you repair the bones?"

"Aye. But it'll require two operations at least and a month or six weeks in hospital. I'll wire the heads of the bones together and try to insert a wee metal pin to make the joint rigid. Provided the blood supply system resumes its function, there should be no infection."

Steve said, "You've saved the leg. I mean—"

Walsh shrugged. "It's a hell of a mess, lass. It would have been better to be rid of the damned sorry thing. But he—your husband—he'd have none of it. He might regret it later, because he'll have a lot of pain and awkwardness."

"A permanently stiffened kneecap?"

"He'll have to learn t' walk again. But he's young enough t' adjust."

"He's—Chris is a pilot."

"Flying an aeroplane? Not a hope. He'll not even be able t' drive a motor car, I doubt," said Walsh. "What did he do, his job, before the war?"

"He went directly from school to Cranwell. He's never done anything except fly aeroplanes."

Walsh frowned. "He'll have t' learn then. But I'm puzzled, Mrs. Deems, puzzled as t' why he didn't grab at the chance to have a new limb fitted, one that might allow him enough knee movement to carry on as a pilot."

"He did it for me," said Steve.

"Then," Walsh got to his feet, "you'd better deserve it, lass. He'll need care, attention and understanding. The next few months won't be easy for your man. Will you love him as before, in spite of what's happened?"

"I'll love him more," Steve promised. "When may I see him again?"

"Tomorrow. After doctors' rounds. Eleven o'clock."

"Thank you, Mr. Walsh."

"I've done you no favour, lass," Walsh said, as he showed her out into the corridor. "Just remember what I've told you in the difficult days ahead."

Steve promised, "I will."

Anna Kern wore a cotton nightdress which clung to her full figure and which, in her haste and fright, she had neglected to cover with a gown. From behind the closed door, trembling, she said, "Who is it? What do you want?"

"It's Ritchie Beckman."

Bolt and catch were released and the door opened an inch. The wan beam of a pocket torch shone into Ritchie's eyes.

"Come in, come in quickly."

Ritchie went into the apartment, which was exceedingly dark. The woman put her hand on his shoulder.

"I'm so glad to see you. I've been really worried."

"Worried? About what?"

"The Germans have been in the district."

"The Germans are everywhere," said Ritchie.

"I mean, searching."

"Searching?"

"Come in. Sit down. I wasn't asleep. Do you want coffee?"

"No. Tell me about the Germans."

"Soldiers. And Gestapo. They have been in the streets. Not just here but in the—" Anna paused, touched him again. "How did you arrive here? Did you break the curfew? It's after eleven."

"Never mind that," said Ritchie. "Tell me what the bastards have been up to. Did they come here, to this building?"

"No, not to this building. In the Rue de Rosiers. Madame Tutois told me. She's worried because of what I am."

"Uh?"

"Because she thinks it's Jews they are hunting. The Madame's frightened that they will come here and make trouble for her."

"Has she told you to get out?"

"She can't."

"Who's the owner of the building?"

"I don't know."

"Maybe he's Jewish too," said Ritchie.

They were standing in the pitch dark, close to each other, the woman's hand still on his arm. She had switched off the torch to preserve the battery.

"I saw them. They came along the Rue de Vallon in two cars."

"Tonight?"

"Yesterday morning, and again in the evening."

Ritchie gave a little sigh of relief. "Did they find what they were looking for?"

"The Madame says they took away three men and two women from the building next to the garage. Do you know the place?"

"Yeah," said Ritchie.

"Is it the beginning?"

"The beginning of what?"

"The sort of thing I have heard of in other countries, in Poland, in Germany itself."

"France signed a peace, Anna. The krauts can't be obvious about exercising their racial policies. I'm not saying they won't. I'm not saying they won't get help from 'loyal' Frenchmen. . .they certainly won't be hindered by the gang in Vichy—but, no, it won't be like it was in Poland."

"Why, then? Why did they take these people away?"

"Because they'd done something wrong, I reckon."

"I'm glad you came. I feel—I feel safe when you are here. Madame Tutois says they were Jewish criminals. Saboteurs."

"Could be," said Ritchie.

"Monsieur Beckman—pardon—but I thought, when I heard, I thought that they were searching for you."

"Why the hell should you think that?"

"Because you are—are mysterious."

Ritchie chuckled. "Me? Mysterious?"

"You hide here, don't you?"

"Yeah," Ritchie admitted. "I hide here. I hide from my wife, if you must know."

"Your *wife*?"

"Disappointed, Anna? It's nothing more sensational than that."

"Your wife?" Anna said again. Her hand had not left him. "Why? Are you afraid of her?"

"Not afraid," said Ritchie. "I just can't stand the cow. I like it better here, with you and the boys."

"But you are rich."

"Wish I was."

"I don't understand."

"Anyhow," said Ritchie, "I'm not hiding any more. I'm on the move. I'm going to get out of France, first thing tomorrow morning. Whiz. I'm off, Anna."

"Oh!"

"Want to come with me?"

Anna did not ask him where, did not require a reason for his sudden departure.

She simply said, "I have no papers to take me out of France. They won't let me go."

"I've got papers."

"You?"

"Sure. Italian passports and travel visas."

"For all of us?"

"Not for the boys."

"I can't leave Chaim and Alois."

"I know that," said Ritchie.

"How can I go with you, in that case?"

"I reckon I can get papers for the boys too."

"Why are you doing this for us?"

"God knows!" said Ritchie in English. In French he said, "Because it's best if we all stick together."

"Your wife—"

"She has papers of her own, Anna. Anyhow, she wants to stay in Paris. She *likes* the Germans."

"Oh!"

"Are you on?" Ritchie asked.

"Monsieur Beckman, are you a spy?"

"Bloody hell! No, I'm not a goddamned spy. I'm Jewish. I'm an English Jew. You're right, Anna. What you saw in the street yesterday, what the Madame told you, yeah, it'll spread like wildfire. It isn't going to be safe for us in Paris. Hitler isn't going to slack off until every one of our kind is dead."

"But we have done nothing."

"So what?" said Ritchie. "Will you come with me? Trust me?"

"To England?"

"Yeah, to England, if we can make it."

"But how will we—"

"Through Spain, I think."

"The papers—"

"I told you, I'll fix up papers for the boys. First thing in the morning."

"Do you want—do you want to sleep with me tonight?"

"Anna, Anna, for God's sake!" said Ritchie, softly. "No, not tonight."

"When we are out of France? When we are free?"

"How do I know? If you want me to, yeah, sure."

She would not take something for nothing. She was proud and independent in that way—but stupid. It was a fine kind of stupidity, though, one that Ritchie had not encountered too much. He didn't know *what* he wanted from her. Marriage? Her sons? Maybe that more than making love. He still had his coolness and his bold brass bleedin' neck and his experience to help him across occupied France and into some neutral country. Maybe not back to England at all but with caution and foresight, to the good old USA, to a new life in New York.

He wasn't fooled when Anna put her arms about him and hugged him, her head upon his chest. She needed him only because she needed somebody, and he was the best bargain in these circumstances.

He said, "Is that your answer, Anna?"

"Please take us. My boys too."

"All right," said Ritchie. "Pack."

"Tonight?"

"As soon as it's light. Pack and get ready to travel. I'll make a couple of phone calls, see if I can scrape up documents for the boys double-quick."

"How much can I take?"

"Hand luggage only."

"Are we running away?"

"You've got it," said Ritchie.

The first Madelaine knew of Ritchie's duplicity was when the crash of a hand-axe sounded upon the door of the apartment. Sick and groggy, she was jolted instantly out of a deep sleep. Still in her underclothes, lying on top of the quilt, cold, trembling and deathly afraid, she called out Ritchie's name. But her cry was drowned by the splintering of wood and the clash of jackboot heels on the flooring as the four-man squad of SS troopers burst in on her.

Bolt upright, she screamed at the sight of the menacing uniforms and snub-snouted machine-guns, at the image of the soldier with the axe in his fist. The Germans pounded, searching, though the apartment's rooms and down into the deserted studio by the wooden stairs.

The troopers shouted in guttural response to the high snapping voice of a lieutenant, an Obersturmführer. He was tall and young, as gaunt as a timberwolf. Behind him, Madelaine saw another man, in a short shiny leather coat and pork-pie hat, no longer elegant and faintly Bohemian but as cruel and ugly as a Grosz drawing. Recognition came slowly—and with it relief.

She reached out her hands. "Wili? Wili?"

Oberisch strutted towards the bed. The moon face was twisted, the blue eyes glassy with fury. He caught her by the arm and flung her backwards, twisting her elbow and wrist so that pain changed her cry from one of relief into a shriek of pure terror. One leather-gloved hand closed on her throat, the other tangled in her hair, dragging her body into a bow. Scrambling, Oberisch planted his knee against her breasts.

"Where is he?"

Madelaine gagged.

The knee bored into her breasts and she tried to scream again, but the gloved fingers strangled the noise.

"Did you suppose you could trick me?" Wili Oberisch hissed "I'm not one of your simple-minded clients, my little whore. The German government does not like to be tricked by greedy whores like you. You knew there was nothing in those crates, didn't you?"

Madelaine's fear changed into horror.

She choked, striving to utter denials, then thrashed her head wildly against the restraining forearm and biting fingers.

Oberisch released his grip on her throat, curled his hand thickly into her hair and hoisted her head up, his face close to hers, his slit-like mouth, pouting, displaying the fine white line of his teeth.

"Sweetheart, you had better come clean with your dear Wili. For your own good, I warn you. I want the whole truth. Instantly."

"He—he was here. I fell—he was here when I fell asleep. Ritchie was here, Wili. He was standing there, in the—the last time—last night—about eleven o'clock. Wine, drinking, I fell—I must have fallen—"

"What have you done with the Italian paintings?"

"You—you took them—you—"

"Listen." His fingers pinched her earlobes. He hoisted himself over her, straddling her breasts with his knees, the leather coat crackling. All she could smell was the new leather and the odour of his sweat. His face was sleek as basted pork. "Listen carefully; there were no paintings in the crates, only dummy frames, make-weight frames of plain wood. Not one goddamned painting. Did you intend to take payment from the Germans, the stupid krauts, and run away? Was that the plan?"

"Wili, Wili, believe me, I did not know."

"You must have known."

"*No, no, no, noooooo.*" Madelaine closed her eyes and shrieked out the denial. "*I swear before God. No.*"

Oberisch slid from the bed. He brushed his gloved hands over each other then balled them into fists and cracked his knuckles. "I believe you, Madelaine. Oh, you are so pretty, and so lucky. It would be a shame to take away your pretty face, piece by piece. But not difficult. In five minutes not even my ugliest Schutze would look at you, never mind your friend Heinz Butler. For the Standartenführer's sake, I will spare you for the time being. Now, if you do not know where the paintings are, you can tell me at least where your husband has gone."

Madelaine had no hesitation.

"He is with a Jewish woman, in the Marais. Number 17, in the Rue de Vallon."

"What does he do there?"

"It's where he hides," said Madelaine. "He doesn't know that I know of it."

"Who told you?"

"A—a friend."

"Jacques Fargeau?"

"Yes."

"Will the Italian paintings be there?"

"I don't know, Wili, I swear to God, I don't know."

Wili Oberisch nodded curtly, turned and stepped away from the bed.

Sensibly Madelaine remained rooted, watching. She saw how Oberisch talked with the vulpine lieutenant. She thought that her protestations of innocence had been believed. Nobody who was not completely mad would cheat the Germans and not try to escape. The fact that she had been here, asleep, would surely convince Wili of her innocence.

The troopers who had crashed through the apartment and the studio had been ordered outside again, the search having yielded nothing. Madelaine felt no fear now, only a molten hatred of her husband.

When the lieutenant and Wili Oberisch moved towards the door, about to leave, she called out.

Oberisch turned.

"Wili," said Madelaine, "I ask one last favour of you."

"What?"

"When you find my husband," Madelaine said hoarsely, "kill him."

Wili Oberisch, Gestapo agent, showed his teeth in a smile and delivered a formal bow. "For you, sweetheart, it will be a pleasure."

A minute later the Germans were gone, heading for the Rue de Vallon.

Ritchie had not expected the Germans quite so soon. Having got off with it on the previous evening, he did not feel hounded. He had last met Oberisch three years ago, just before he handed over the Zurich trip to Madelaine. He had marked the dealer as a stickler for detail and correctness. Whatever office Wili worked for, Ritchie convinced himself that it would not open until eight-thirty a.m. He would take no chances, however. If Fargeau couldn't give him an iron-clad guarantee to deliver a couple of viable passes to help them get the kids across the border—any bleedin' border—and have them in his hands by nine o'clock, then he would spin a lie to Anna, pack up the lot of them and take the risk of sweet-talk and fat bribes to get them, at worst, into Vichy territory.

He wasn't dealing with just any old gangsters now, though. He had to bear in mind just what sort of organisation fat Wili Oberisch might have behind him, and not dawdle around. He had already settled a deal with Zack to drive them out to Rambouillet in the rattle-trap old van which was laid up in the yard behind the *bistro* and which he had paid Zack to keep in fuel. From Rambouillet they would catch a train going south or south-west, or he might be able to buy himself wheels and petrol, if it could be done without arousing suspicion. Once clear of Paris, travelling as a family and with several sets of *cartes* and a stack of francs, Ritchie was confident that he could get out of the occupied zone.

But he didn't have much time.

Chaim and Alois were wakened at six. Anna had already packed a suitcase each, and Ritchie had taken a change of clothing from his room across the landing. Chaim seemed to understand what the fuss was about, to sense that they were fleeing from the Nazis because they were Jews. But Alois remained innocently excited at the prospect of a trip in a motor car. At seven, Ritchie took the younger boy with him for the short walk down to the *bistro*, mainly because Alois wanted to accompany him and would give him some kind of protective guard.

When Ritchie left Number 17 to walk the short distance to the corner, Anna, aided by Chaim, was cutting sandwiches of bread and meat to pack into a container to sustain them on their journey. She asked Ritchie to bring back some fruit, if Zack had any to sell or if he could find a convenient market open at such an hour. Alois was ready for the journey, dressed in a comfortable tweed jacket and with a cap on his head. His knees looked like little spindles under the top weight, his polished brown shoes clicking on the cobbles as he matched Ritchie's step.

There was some movement in the Rue de Vallon; there always was in the Marais. Workmen were out and about, and shawl-wrapped anonymous Mamas with straw shopping baskets. But there was no sign of a German presence in the short street, and Ritchie did not hurry. Alois, excited, held Ritchie's hand and chattered away about where they would go and what they would see and do. He had been on vacation once with his mother and father, to Honfleur, where an old friend of his father had a shoemaker's shop, where he had bathed in the sea which was very cold, and Chaim had cried it was so cold but he hadn't; he had been very brave. '

Ritchie listened to the child's prattle, but kept his eyes peeled and senses alert for Nazis. He too was excited but with Alois Kern's tiny hand in his, Ritchie felt a degree of shame at his past, at the selfish recklessness, at the deceit and episodes of violence; yet it was the experience gained then that would save the Kern family now. He would 'make sure that Anna and the boys never learned the truth about him. With them he intended to make a fresh start, clean as a whistle.

It was chance, coincidence, that Ritchie was not in the house when the Germans arrived. If they had come stealthily, they would have had him for sure. But they came with a noisy show of force, at speed.

Ritchie and Alois did not even reach the *bistro*. It would have been the same sort of story even if they had. If he had called Fargeau and Fargeau had told him to wait and the krauts had arrived . . . Goddamned slimy Jacques! Nobody else could have traced him to the Rue de Vallon. The troopers in the back of the big-wheeled truck and the guy in the black Mercedes, they hadn't come for anybody else. In his gut, Ritchie felt it. He had no doubt about their purpose. He didn't even have to see Oberisch to know what had happened.

The Mercedes came around the corner from the Rue Antonini, leaping on the kerbstone, the uncovered army truck hard behind. Gently but firmly Ritchie drew Alois from off the pavement into the doorway of a shop that had, until recently, sold second-hand carpets and rugs. He stood there, hand on the boy's shoulder, while the Mercedes and the truck shot past.

"Monsieur Beckman—"

"*Ssshh*," said Ritchie softly.

"Monsieur Beckman, they are stopping at our house."

"So I see, Alois."

"Are they looking for us?"

"It is possible, Now, please be quiet."

Glancing down, Ritchie saw that the child's pale face had become even paler, the dark eyes quite round.

He slipped to the side of the doorway, pressed against the old boards of the window, the boy before him.

"Alois, whatever happens, please hold still."

"Yes. Monsieur Beckman."

Monsieur Beckman: what in God's name had possessed him to

reveal his true identity to these people? Hell, it would have made no difference, might have bought a few minutes' delay. Might have got poor Anna and her elder son out of trouble. Too late for regrets, though.

The doors of the Mercedes were flung open.

Oberisch. Bleedin' little Wili, all decked out in Gestapo "uniform", all that leather. He watched the dealer strut into Number 17. An instant later Madame Tutois emerged. In agitation, she pointed upward. Two troopers with sub-machine guns in their mitts horsed from the lorry and into the building, Oberisch and an officer after them. Two more troopers flanked the doorway. In the car and the truck were drivers, probably also armed.

It was no great mystery. Madelaine had seen Fargeau, and some of Fargeau's bully-boys had trailed him here. He had underestimated Maddy. He should have been more careful.

"Monsieur Beckman—" Alois whispered.

"Quiet, kid."

"Mama and Chaim—"

"Quiet!"

He needed a few seconds to think it through. One rash move at this stage would cost him his neck. It might already be too late for Anna. When Oberisch got through the door into the apartment and found the packed cases and the documents and Anna and the kid making ready for the road, there would be no way by which Anna could convincingly deny that she knew him and that he, Monsieur Beckman, was still in the vicinity.

Madame Tutois would already have blabbed, was blabbing, pointing down the street towards them.

Even when two armed troopers peered down the street at him, Ritchie didn't turn. He remained where he was, with Alois held tightly. He could still get himself out of it. No problem. He could vanish into the Marais, into the heart of the Hebrew quarter. Let the krauts tear the district apart, they wouldn't find him. He could leave the kid where he was. Not even the krauts were liable to put the screws on a kid as young as Alois. After all, he had paid his rent. He owed Anna Kern nothing. Wasn't he Ritchie Beckman, the arch scarperer, who'd sprinted out of umpteen scrapes in his prime? He could be in Zack's and out of the kitchen door and across the yard and through the lane by the Pironete picture-house and across the Rue Maillot—and away. Maybe the spring had gone out of his knees but he wasn't yet a decrepit old codger and was sure he would find speed with the Gestapo barking at his tail.

Alois stiffened against his grasp, like a little whippet.

And it was too late.

Anna's screams rang from the echoing stairwell. A second later the woman was pitched into the street and sprawled on the pavement. Oberisch followed. There was no wheedling or threatening. He exercised immediate and direct force, a raw and brutal action like that of a petulant schoolboy possessed by impatience. He drew back his foot and kicked the woman in the ribs. Anna did not scream now. She reached out her hand to draw her elder son to her as if, even in the ultimate moment of helplessness, she might still, somehow, protect him from harm.

Pinned by one of the troopers, Chaim was suddenly a pinwheel of fury. He spun on his heel and kicked the soldier, wrenched himself from the man's grasp and flung himself like a monkey on Oberisch. He tore off the pork-pie hat and dug his fingernails into Oberisch's ears. The Gestapo agent cried out and beat at the boy and a soldier stepped from his post and smote Chaim across the small of the back with the muzzle of a sub-machine gun. Though obviously hurt, the boy did not release his biting hold at once and Oberisch danced and pranced, until Chaim let go and dropped to his feet.

So far the whole incident had lasted only a couple of minutes. Ritchie watched in amazement. He had not expected Oberisch to be so gross and so stupid. The second phase was even more rapid, over almost before it had begun. It was all Alois' fault.

The little boy broke from the doorway before Ritchie could prevent it. He ran, shouting for his Mama, towards the group outside Number 7 Anna stumbled to her feet and ran too towards her younger son, followed by Chaim. The soldiers lifted their guns and the officer was snapping at them, and Oberisch, with blood streaming down the sides of his face, was jabbering shrilly, and the Kerns were running like crazy.

Ritchie tugged the Star from his pocket.

He shouted, "Anna. Here, Anna."

He began to run too, not away from but towards Oberisch.

Used to acting on orders, the troopers did little for an instant, except cover the escapers. Ritchie stopped, braced himself and met Oberisch's eye; one hundred metres separated them. Anna and Chaim had almost reached Alois when one of the soldiers fired. It was a short, guttural burst and it cut Anna Kern across the shoulders. She tripped and dived, stomach down. Chaim fell over her, shot too. Alois stopped in his tracks.

Ritchie fired four shots. He saw one of the soldiers fall. The other Germans, including Oberisch, did not return his fire but dived for cover

Bewildered, Alois spun round.

"Here, son. Come here." Ritchie sensed that the boy would not, could not, obey. Not with his Mama lying dead only yards away and his brother, the brave Chaim, crouched bleeding over her body. "Come here!"

Ritchie fired again. He darted forward and caught the child in the crook of his arm. Now he was stuck with him. Burdened. Claimed at long, long last.

Alois kicked and struggled. Ritchie dragged him, swinging his matchstick legs in an arc so that his back was to the guns, the child protected. And he ran as he had never run before, even back in the dark streets of Lambeth when he fled from a crime. He remembered the old Jew, Steiner, whom he had coshed in a house off the Shadwell Road, years and years ago, remembered the horror of it, and the satisfaction, and the sinister glass eye, the eye of the Almighty, inset into the lintel above Steiner's door. How that eye—*Shaddai*—had haunted him. How his mind threw it up now. *Shaddai*. With the little Jewish boy kicking and struggling and flailing. And all he had to do was drop the kid and he could still get away.

A burst of gunfire: Ritchie waited for pain.

He heard the whine and jibbering of bullets on the walls.

He ran on.

Zack's was open, the shutter of the *bistro* door half up.

Inside was the bulky Frenchman and his buffalo-sized wife. Ritchie threw the child inside and dived after him. Zack was shouting at him and pointing and, scooping Alois up again, Ritchie went through the back door, past the greasy bead curtain, into the

232

kitchen. The wife was bellowing and pointing. He ducked by the sinks and there was the back door open to the yard and out he went, still carrying Alois Kern before him. He felt rather than saw the door slam behind him, and was alone with the child in the yard.

The lorry was there but Ritchie didn't even contemplate using it. There were no means by which he could get the vehicle out of the yard and away from the high-powered Mercedes. He had one thing going for him: Oberisch hadn't much of a squad with him. Five men, plus the drivers. By the time they raked up a search-party, he would be well away.

"Alois, Alois, I can't carry you. Run. Hold my hand. Run."

"*Mama, Mama. Mama is sick.*"

"Mama wants you to be safe."

He stopped, holding the kid in his arms, nose to nose, as he might have held a toy dog. Alois had given up struggling. In the little boy's eyes was puzzlement. He had clutched at the silly explanation. He worked on it, chewing it over.

"Mama sent you out with me to be safe. We'll find Mama later."

"What did the soldiers do to Mama and Chaim?"

"Listen," said Ritchie, "we won't find Mama and Chaim ever again unless we run away from the soldiers."

"Is it because of Papa that the German soldiers want us?"

"Yeah," said Ritchie, thankfully. "That's it, yes."

Alois nodded solemnly.

"Hold tight to my hand and don't let go," said Ritchie.

"Yes, Monsieur Beckman."

There were still no sounds of pursuit from the front of the *bistro*. Zack, perhaps, would have run down the metal shutter.

Ritchie went out of the yard, with a last regretful glance at the van. He led the child at a brisk walking pace across a narrow street and down a lane by the side of the picture-house. Barely had they entered the lane before the German army lorry roared past. Listening for the squeal of brakes, Ritchie hesitated, but the vehicle went on and he started off again, walking at a right-angle to the Rue de Vallon into the hinterland of the Marais, towards no particular destination.

Fifteen minutes later, Ritchie stopped again.

He reckoned they had covered the equivalent of five city blocks through the tortuous byways of the district. He had seen no further sign of Oberisch or the SS troopers. By sheer good fortune, it seemed he had chosen a route that the krauts hadn't figured out. Maybe bleedin' Wili had sent for reinforcements. The request wouldn't be denied. It didn't matter what sort of caper the dealer was engaged in, the military authorities would be only too pleased to have an excuse for a man-hunt.

Ritchie did not doubt that Anna and Chaim were dead.

He said nothing to Alois Kern during the flight, and could read nothing in the tight, solemn little face, no clue as to what the child was feeling.

Ritchie still had no notion what he could do to evade the Germans' net. He did not dare go to Fargeau for help, or back to Madelaine. He had papers and money, plenty of money. And the Star pistol with ten bullets left. Perhaps he could have disguised himself and tried to find transport out of Paris. But not with Alois in tow. It did not occur to Ritchie to ditch the boy. The hand in his was the strongest bond imaginable, symbol of a trust which Ritchie Beckman had never experienced before. He had to find refuge, somebody who would give him shelter and, if it came to it, look out for the boy. But where?

If this had been London he could have called in old debts, gone to Stan Nuttal, even to Holly or the old man, to Maury. They wouldn't have turned him away. But it wasn't England, it was Paris, and he was a stranger here, exiled in every sense of the word.

Ritchie stopped at a bakery and bought a pastry for the boy to eat.

Wili Oberisch and his Nazis, Ritchie realised, could not be far away.

The streets were no longer quiet. The French were going about their business. Shops were opening, factories. German soldiers were strolling the thoroughfares, even in the Marais. Ritchie kept to the lanes and back streets, still with no positive sense of direction, just moving, moving away from the Rue de Vallon, shepherding the little boy in front of him or drawing him along by the hand at his side.

It was a little after nine o'clock when Ritchie Beckman reached the place to which, inexorably, he had been drifting without conscious motive and, taking Alois Kern into his arms, beat his fist upon the dooor until, reluctantly, someone came to open it.

The rift between Steve and her mother was as sudden and dramatic as it was inevitable. In due course there would be a truce, for Miles' sake, but on the day following Christopher's first operation at the Cyrus Street Hospital, Andrea alienated her daughter completely.

The crisis came to a head after mother and daughter had visited Chris together and had returned, by bus, through the rubble of bombed buildings, on a stifling day of oppressive cloud.

Steve was withdrawn, revealing nothing of her feelings, a fact which irritated Andrea beyond reason.

As the pair walked through Hampstead, Andrea could contain herself no longer.

"What are you thinking, Stephanie?"

"I'll have to go back soon."

"Back?"

"To work. To the depot. I can visit Chris in the evening."

"I didn't mean that," said Andrea. "I meant, what do you think of him, of your husband?"

"I'm very, very sorry for him."

"Being sorry isn't enough."

"Oh, I know that, Mother."

"It would be a kindness to leave him to his mother, to Holly Beckman."

"Leave him to Holly? What in God's name are you driving at now?"

"Surely you won't stay married to a cripple."

Steve drew up. "Chris needs me more than ever."

"That isn't the point. The point is, he isn't going to be much use to you, is he? I mean, with that—that leg."

"I love Chris, Mother."

"He isn't the man you married. It's all changed. You must realise it. I mean, really, what can you do for him now? Hideously scarred."

"There are many worse than Chris."

"Not in our family."

"My God! I can't believe my ears!"

235

"No need to raise your voice."

"What a bitch you are, Mother."

"I've more experience of—of these matters than you have, dear."

"You've *no* experience, Mother. No experience of anything. Life? You barely know the meaning of the word. If you suppose for one moment that what's happened to Chris makes one jot of difference to what I feel for him, you're wrong. Utterly, totally and completely *wrong*."

"Perhaps when you've had time to consider . . ."

"A cripple? Chris isn't the cripple. You're the cripple. You and your hunger for having everything 'just so', all smooth and planned. It doesn't matter to me that Chris will limp, will have to use a stick."

Andrea shuddered. "So—so ugly."

"Mother, you've a genius for making people dislike you."

"Dislike . . .?"

"I don't know how Father has put up with you. It's no wonder Mark never comes home. Well, listen to me, I will not leave Chris. Not ever. We're two of a kind, and what's happened to him makes me love him all the more. If it had happened to me—"

"You're far too sensible ever to put yourself in a position to—"

"It can happen to *any* of us. Don't you realise that this isn't a war for young men to die in? Didn't you see the bomb craters and the broken buildings? People died in them too. People were injured, maimed for life. Ordinary people, people who didn't ask for it. Do you understand me? No, I don't suppose you do. To you, it's always been cause and effect. You've always blamed others for their misfortunes."

"I only thought I'd mention it, darling," said Andrea. It had dawned on her that, finally, she had overstepped the mark and would not this time be excused. "I didn't really expect you to listen to my advice."

"It isn't advice; it's demand."

"Stephanie, really!"

"Really, Mother, you can go to hell."

"Now, now!"

"As for me, I'm going home."

"We're almost there. I'll have Mrs. Watson make us a nice cup of—"

"*Home.*"

"Surely you don't mean . . .?"

"To my husband's house, to Chelsea. What's more, I won't be back."

"And how will I explain that to your father? He'll be most upset."

"Not half so upset as he will be when I tell him the reason why I'm leaving."

"I think we should both calm down."

"I'm perfectly calm. It's high time I was back where I belong."

"With Holly Beckman?"

"With my husband."

"Your husband is—is—"

"Say it, Mother. Go on, say it just once more."

"Stephanie, I don't want you to go."

"Too damned bad."

They had reached the gate of the Walshott residence and Steve angrily stalked up the path. She did not even pause to ring the doorbell or fumble with her key but hurried round the side of the house and entered it by the kitchen door. She went past Mrs. Watson without replying to the woman's greeting, and headed directly upstairs.

Before Andrea had time to do more than enter the front hall and take off her hat and gloves, Steve had returned. She carried an army service bag of brown canvas, and her ATS uniform on a hanger.

"You can't go like that."

"I would have gone anyway, Mother. It was only a matter of weeks."

"It's dangerous in London," said Andrea, reaching for her daughter's arm. "Bombs . . ."

"It isn't bombs I have to be afraid of," said Steve. "It's old-fashioned prejudice."

Without another word Steve went out of the house and, bag slung over her shoulder and uniform folded across her arm, set off along Laurel Avenue in search of a taxi-cab.

"You'll regret this. Mark my words, you'll regret this as long as you live," Andrea called from the door.

But Andrea, as usual, was wrong.

*

The door of the house of Dubriel opened cautiously and Ritchie looked into the suspicious eyes of the servant, Peta Brichard.

"I've come to see the Comtesse."

"The Comtesse is not to be disturbed."

"Open the bloody door," Ritchie snarled. "The krauts are right behind me."

"Who is that child?"

"Mine," said Ritchie.

Peta Brichard studied Alois Kern who, with candour and no calculation, smiled at her.

Peta Brichard removed the stout chain from the back of the door and let Ritchie and his companion into the hall. It was not a moment too soon.

Roaring up the Boulevard de Sebastopol came the black Mercedes.

Ritchie closed the door with his shoulder and put Alois down.

"Where is she?" he demanded.

"In her sewin' room," Peta Brichard answered.

"Come on, Alois. We're going to meet a lady."

She looked smaller than ever, the Comtesse Kati Dubriel, more like an owl, a very old and shabby owl shedding its feathers. The housecoat increased the impression. It was brown with faded gold threads and a moulting collar of knitted amber silk.

The Comtesse had been wrapped in a sour day-dream, seated in an *Egyptienne* chair which, like the throne of an emtombed queen, stood on a little dais with an Armenian rug upon it. No books, no wool or cloth or thread, no newspapers gave the impression that the Comtesse had been busy trying to occupy the remaining hours of her life. She rose with, at first, the air of a woman who had been interrupted in the solemn business of dying. The opening of the door stirred dust motes about the old and weary woman, as she came out of her reverie.

"He says there are Germans after him," Peta Brichard explained. "It's the one who locked us in the cupboard and stole the paintings."

Kati Dubriel blinked. "Pardon?"

Alois Kern kept himself half hidden by Ritchie's thigh.

Taking the child by the hand, Ritchie led him across the echoing room towards the dais.

From below came the thunder of fists upon the house's main door.

Kati Dubriel's eyes lost their glaucous quality, gained a lustre of interest. She sensed, perhaps, that she was about to witness an act of vengeance against a man she detested, the English thief. It would have been splendid in its circumstance and she would have relished it greatly if it had not been for the presence of the child, the little, sallow-skinned, dark-eyed, apprehensive boy. He was an anomaly with which the Comtesse could not immediately come to terms.

"That's them," said Ritchie. "The Nazis, the Bosche."

"What do they want here?" snapped Kati Dubriel.

"Your paintings."

"But you, you have my paintings."

"Too bloody true," said Ritchie in English.

"Peta, let the Germans in."

"Wait," said Ritchie.

"It is you they want, is it not?" the Comtesse asked.

"Yeah."

"And this . . . person?" The Comtesse nodded her head at Alois.

"An orphan, only he doesn't know it." Ritchie switched to English, hoping that the old woman would understand. "They shot his mother an hour ago, and his brother."

"His mother, your wife?"

"No, hell no! He isn't mine."

"In that case, what's he doing with you?"

Ritchie sighed. "God knows."

"Why have you come here?"

The drumming on the door had become massive; machine-gun butts. It would be axes soon, a full-scale assault on the old oak. Ritchie had no time left for sweet-talk, for persuasion and cunning and threat.

"I had no place else to go."

"You knew the Bosche would follow?"

"Take him. Look after him."

"He *is* yours?"

"No."

"But he is a Jew?"

"Yes." Ritchie turned and jerked his thumb. "You, go let them in."

Peta Brichard glanced at her mistress who, scowling, nodded.

"Tell them I took the paintings. Tell them anything you like. But keep the kid out of their hands."

"Why should I do this?"

Ritchie did not answer the Comtesse Dubriel. He stooped and spoke instead to Alois Kern. "Do what she tells you. Don't say anything."

"Where are you going, Monsieur Beckman?"

"Out for a while. Be good, Alois."

The boy nodded. Ritchie noticed that there were huge tears in his eyes.

"Don't be afraid."

"No, Monsieur Beckman."

"What do you intend to do?" the Comtesse asked.

"Go and face the music," said Ritchie, and went out of the sewing room.

The last he saw of Alois Kern, the boy had taken the old woman's hand and had buried his face in the folds of the musty housecoat.

From below came the servant's excited shouts.

"*He's here. He's here. He came to rob us again.*"

Perfect, thought Ritchie and, closing the end door of the gallery, settled himself on one knee and took out the pistol.

It would not have done for him to die sensibly, not after all that he'd been through. He wished he was more nimble, less weary, that the young wolf he had once been would come again and inhabit the aging body. He felt calm as he listened to the servant's shouts of encouragement and the stamping of the jackboots.

The door at the end of the long gallery, close to where a Botticelli and a Caravaggio had faced each other across the corner, burst open. The krauts poured through. Not so many of them, though, only three troopers, the lieutenant, and fat Wili Oberisch.

"Hey, Wili," Ritchie cried.

The Gestapo agent came, innocently, through the door between the tall uniforms, his eyes automatically lifting to the bare and unencumbered walls, until Ritchie's shout snatched his attention.

Ritchie put four bullets from the Star into Wili Oberisch's chest before he was mown down by the troopers' guns.

The Obersturmführer was confused for a moment. He stepped

over Herr Oberisch's lifeless body, standing on the pork-pie hat, and walked down the length of the gallery, service revolver unholstered and in his hand. Cautiously, the troopers followed, until they came to the door at the gallery's end against which, sprawled in pools of blood, lay the fugitive.

The Obersturmführer had never really discovered what Oberisch's deal was all about or how the English Jew had tricked him.

The servant was still shouting.

"Good, you have killed him. You have killed the thief."

The Obersturmführer went down on one knee and made sure that the victim was dead. He was still stooping there when the door to the sewing room opened and a tiny, owl-like woman stepped forth.

"So you have killed the pig, have you?" she said, without a trace of emotion. "It is what he deserved."

"Why did he come here?"

"To force me to give him more money."

"At gun point," put in the servant.

"Was there a child, a boy, with him?"

The Comtesse raised her eyebrows. "There was no child when he reached here."

"I must look," said the SS officer. "It is regrettable, Madame, but it is my duty."

"Of course." The Comtesse Dubriel opened the door into the sewing room with her forearm. "You will find no stranger hiding, I assure you. Only my grandson."

The Obersturmführer stepped into the sewing room.

There was a boy, a child, sallow and solemn, dressed in a style that had gone out of fashion thirty years ago; a pair of velvet pantaloons and a white brocade shirt, like something from one of the paintings that these aristocrats collected. The boy was standing by an ornate chair. Small and upright, he looked exceedingly aristocratic, the lieutenant thought, and quite uncowed by the gunfire. He also seemed faintly familiar.

The Obersturmführer might have grasped the truth by further questions. But he had no heart for it. He had never respected Herr Oberisch or liked the assignment. After all, what if the old woman was lying? What was the life of one Jewish child? He had the corpse of the fugitive to justify his actions and more than enough paperwork as it was.

"Your grandson, Madame?"

"My grandson," said the old woman.

The Obersturmführer let it go at that and returned, without further enquiry, to clean up the mess in the gallery and get back to the business of war.

6 Calling the Roll

Cream-coloured puffballs of smoke from anti-aircraft batteries on the south Thames shore marked the beginning of the raids on London. Originally the raids were reprisals for the British bombing of Berlin but with the Luftwaffe's failure to destroy the RAF and make sea-passage invasion safe, mass air attacks, a war of attrition, became Nazi policy.

Day and night during the late summer and autumn, a chorus of sirens rang throughout London. Aerial dogfights took place above the towers and office blocks. Each and every morning the face of the capital was changed. Familiar landmarks were replaced by smoking heaps of debris and snug-walled streets became serrated and gap-toothed. It was impossible to live in the city and not be somehow engaged with winning the war, defeating the German terror machine.

Holly Beckman King did not wish to remain uninvolved. A quickened sense of purpose came to her with the first sight of her son with sticks.

Cut and stitched, wired, pinned and stitched again, Chris's leg was as scarred and emaciated as a piece of driftwood. The limb appeared to have no real connection with Chris, who dragged it along with agonising patience and concentration, re-learning the instinctive art of balance and upright motion. He endured pain with stoicism but, at first, no humour. Not Maury, not even crass old Leo, who made a special trip from Hastings to visit his grandson, made jokes about the crippled limb or jockeyed the young man along with false encouragement. Friends and acquaintances, including old mates from the squadron, were grim about it, reflecting Chris's attitude. The more understanding among them asked their questions and got their answers with down-to-earth directness.

Officers called at Cyrus Street for discreet "out of visiting hours" conversations. It was a relief to Chris to be finally informed that, as soon as he was fit, he would be retrained as a Special Duties officer in Intelligence or Control. Chris had no wish to take the soft option, a discharge from the service he loved. To be with pilots would be difficult for him, but better than to be cast aside.

He talked only to Steve of his difficulties but it was consoling to the young couple to know that they could still fight hard and well against the enemies of freedom, that though they might struggle desperately there would be no despair. Despair was a cousin of defeatism and had no part in the British character in the year of 1940.

Steve had returned to duty with the ATS. She was driving again, mainly "short-run" deliveries of petrol and oil from the big underground dumps at Within and Lockston. On rotation shifts her days and nights were so full that she had no time to brood about her husband. In turn, Chris gained strength from Steve's commitment. He shared the stresses and adventures of her job, putting his own condition on a lower plane.

The house in Tite Street became a place to sleep, and a focus of dreams of peace. It hardly seemed to exist for either Chris or Steve, though they referred to it, casually, as home. Together the young couple adjusted to the priorities of their time, sacrificed their youth to the cause of the nation, without one whisper of regret that it had fallen to them to bear the brunt of ill circumstance.

Only the very old and the very young were victims of German war lust. Others, all others, soon became participants, milkmen and postmen, fire-fighters and munitions workers; everyone worked to lick Hitler. Holly was no longer exempt, no longer cared to bide her time, regarding the conflict as if it was an unjust sentence passed on her by blind fate.

"Come down to Applehurst," Maury suggested. "It's bedlam down there now. We've twenty-three kids on the property and it's more than we can cope with. You'd be a big asset."

"I'd rather stay where I am," said Holly.

"Can't say I like the idea of you stuck in Chelsea when the Jerry bombers are after the docks and the railway stations. The river's their line of approach, you know."

"Maury, I'm staying put."

"There can't be much doing at the shop."

"It's like the grave."

"So close up. Bring the best of the stock down here . . ."

"I can't."

"Keep the home fires burning an' all that?"

"For a while at any rate."

"I still don't like the idea of you being alone."

"I'm not alone. I have Steve, and soon I'll have Chris, though the doctors want him to go off to a convalescent home for two or three weeks. He's resisting, but thinks the RAF may insist on it. After all, they're still paying his salary, or whatever it is. He still belongs to them."

"Do you see David?"

"Regularly. Life's very hectic for him," said Holly. "But I often have Norma round to stay. She's almost as much in need of company as I am. She's a bit concerned about Les. Apparently he's 'somewhere east of Suez'."

"All right," said Maury. "You've convinced me. But if things get too hot in old London town, or if—Heaven forbid—your house gets damaged, you're coming down to Applehurst with me whether you like it or not."

"Bully."

"I allers was," Maury said.

Holly had bought six bunk beds for the cellar of her house. She had transferred many of her nicer antiques, strawed and boxed, to the brick-lined chamber. Paraffin heaters, ambulance kit, tinned food and buckets of water, even a chemical lavatory, had been installed in the "shelter" below the old Chelsea mansion. The whine of sirens sent Holly and whoever happened to be spending the night post-haste to the door below the stairs, down into the musty but comfortable refuge.

Holly did not go out of her way to watch the incredible spectacles that the blitz of London presented. Now and again, though, she would be confronted by awesome sights as the winds swept the river and the day's dawn became a chiaroscuro of black smoke and limewash cloud, pricked by fire on the south bank shore. Once, Norma, returning at five a.m. from an all-night shift at the station, roused Holly from her bunk and dragged her out on to the embankment, littered with flakes of burned wood and the corkscrew remains of an ornamental lamp-post uprooted by a half-pounder.

Transfixed, Holly stared at the Thames under a gigantic canopy of flushed cloud. Cut from wharves by Lots Road and Cremorne, blazing timber barges swarm with the ebb-tide, driven swiftly on by hot winds from Clapham which had taken a pasting soon after midnight. Tailed by fire-boats and drenched by arched columns of water from the tilted hoses, the barges burned sullenly until, with the waft of the wind, they flared and blazed once more—a river pageant more grand than any ever seen, and more terrible.

The reek of tarred timbers made the women choke as the craft waltzed on, nudged the pillars of Cadogan Pier and spun out again, gaining speed, on down towards Battersea and the piles of Chelsea Bridge. Riveted by the spectacle, Holly and Norma stood for an hour and watched the harried fire-boats contain the dangerous wrecks and, almost lost in acrid mists of steam and smoke, finally beach them on a sand-bar far beyond the embankment.

Eyes streaming and throats raw, the women went back into the shaken old house to brew tea, toast a slice or two of bread and marvel at the sight they had seen.

"It's alive, you see," Norma explained. "Fire's alive. So's water, like, but it ain't the same. Fire never lies down flat. Know what they'll do? They'll put them barges out, then call in an expert to blow them sky-high, to keep the channel clear. Tons and tons of good timber. Bang. All gone."

"Fire killed my grandfather, my husband, and it almost killed Chris too, when he was only months old."

"The old shop in Pimlico?"

"I'm still afraid of it, of fire."

"No bleedin' wonder," said Norma Butterfield.

"I sometimes think it's still waiting for me. That I'll die by fire too."

"You ain't going to die."

"But when I do," said Holly, "it'll be by fire."

"Don't be so morbid."

"Not morbid," said Holly. "It's what I feel. Conditioned response, I suppose."

"Just so long as it isn't a premonition."

"Whatever do you mean, Norma?"

"I've had enough of mystic gubbins without you starting. Went into a street shelter the other night and found one old duchess with the cards spread out. Telling everybody's fortune, she was. Know what she was telling them? All the same thing: they'd never see the dawn. One black card after another was turnin' up. It was a trick, of course, but, God strewth, I ask you! What a dirty trick to play. More scared of them spades and clubs the poor folk were than of Jerry bombs. If me and Mrs. Simpson hadn't turned up when we did, half the silly twerps would have been runnin' into the road."

"That's awful."

"Ain't it? So, Hol, no more premonitions."

"All right," said Holly. "No talk of fate or destiny."

"Take each night as it comes."

"And what's coming now?"

"For me," said Norma, yawning, "shut-eye."

"Aren't you going to bunk in the shelter?"

"Too stuffy. Besides, the All Clear's gone and the Jerry pilots'll be havin' breakfast. I'll use the guest room, if you don't mind. See you later, at the shop."

"Of course," said Holly. "If it's still there."

"It's still there." Norma yawned again. "I took a look-see on the way here."

After Norma had gone upstairs, Holly sat by the window looking out at the garden which, through neglect, had grown weedy and lush. She supposed she should turn it into a vegetable patch but she had no knowledge of or interest in gardening. Perhaps she might be able to employ somebody. Kennedy had always claimed that the soil was alluvial and quite fertile. It would be strange to see turnip tops, carrots and potatoes sprouting where once there had been grass and border flowers. When he returned home again, perhaps Chris would feel like planting and tending a vegetable plot.

Holly mulled over the recreative project then, with a wry chuckle, dismissed it. Chris wasn't that sort either. Besides, though he would no longer be flying fighter aeroplanes, he would still be an RAF officer and no doubt fully occupied with his duties.

Finishing the tea in her cup, she wrapped her dressing-gown around her once more.

Though it was well into September, the air was still warm when the dawn breeze dropped away. She went out by the kitchen door. The housekeeper wouldn't arrive until eight and it was not yet seven o'clock. Behind a high brick wall lay the Gyll residence, a larger and more ostentatious house than the Kings'. It had lain dormant for months; the Gylls had departed for their country place, leaving only an old couple to act as caretakers. Although she had lived in Tite Street for almost two decades, Holly had no association with her neighbours. It was very different from Lambeth where everybody would have known her business and she theirs. Holly preferred privacy. She had inherited the house from Kennedy, knew its history and felt comfortable there. But she did not expect it to stand strong and snug for another century, perhaps not even for another month. Chris would not inherit it from her; there would be nothing left to inherit. Norma would not approve of such sentiments, of course, but Holly was possessed by the feeling that all the grand old houses that lay along the Chelsea reaches would go up in smoke, that all of London, in the course of time, might be laid waste. But not the people, never the people. Londoners were indefatigable and indomitable, more enduring than the old cobbles and stones. Dressed like a rag-picker, Holly went out by the wooden gates and on to the embankment for a view of the river.

Heat was palpable. The sun lay under a smeared blue fog of smoke, through which, like the towers of a castle, loomed the Battersea power station. Upriver, the atmosphere was clearer and she could see traffic rolling patiently over the bridges. But far across the river reach there was fire, the vermilion scribble of houses or stores burning still.

Holly shivered. She wished that David was with her. David was the only one of her friends and relatives who would best understand and sympathise. After all, he was Mr. Aspinall's son, and they had loved each other once. David, perhaps, needed her in a way that

247

Chris did not. She watched the fire blossom and abruptly quiet again, a licking dragon's tongue of flame, felt anxiety in her heart turn, like a compass needle, towards her future and her self.

Shivering uncontrollably, Holly hurried back across the street to seek refuge in the kitchen, telling herself as she fled that her fears were foolish and that Norma Butterfield was right: each night must be taken as it came.

Thirty-eight hours later, on Friday night, the first of the massive German air attacks on London began and three hundred Luftwaffe fighter-bombers brought fire down from the skies.

Holly and Steve met in the now-familiar waiting-room on the first floor of the Cyrus Street Hospital. They were greeted pleasantly by the staff but, with Chris on the mend at last, were given no special treatment. Awkwardly, they sat amid distraught and weeping relatives whose husbands and sons had been recently admitted or were dying somewhere within the white-tiled corridors and little green wards, quiet behind cheesecloth screens.

Strangely, Holly felt something like guilt at the fact that her son was recovering. Touched by the suffering all around, she smothered her pleasure at seeing him again. Not only airmen were brought to Cyrus Street now, but victims of air raids, civilians whose wounds demanded the immediate attention of experts like Walsh; much of the red-tape had been hacked away by the sheer pressure of need.

Though Chris had been out of bed and on his feet for ten days, they had always visited him in the long ward, sat by his bed with its locker and water-jug and strategically-placed rail on the wall by means of which a patient could haul himself upright without putting too much strain on damaged limbs. But that Friday night things were different. Holly and Steve were instructed by a nurse to wait in the waiting-room after the visitors' bell for admission to the wards sounded. Glancing apprehensively at each other, the women remained seated.

Steve lit another cigarette. She had been driving all day and her body ached and her eyes were gritty with dust and smoke and her uniform was no longer fresh, though she had used the "depot brush", and had combed her hair and touched up her make-up in the hospital toilet. She had brought Chris a bag of apples and a packet of State Express. Holly had brought books and two new magazines but the gifts seemed immaterial after the nurse's message and the women waited with increasing concern.

"Perhaps," said Steve, at length, "they've taken him away."

"But why?"

"I don't know," said Steve. "Out of London, to be safe."

"They'd have notified us, wouldn't they?"

"I don't know."

Holly and Steve did not have long to stew, however. A few minutes later they heard a peculiar bumping, scraping noise in the corridor outside and the door of the room slowly opened: no nurse, but Chris. He was dressed in flannels and shirt with a cardigan across his shoulders. He was no longer supported by crutches. In his left hand was a heavy ash-wood stick with a rubber knob on the end. He balanced himself, shoulder against the door-jamb then, with caution, levered himself upright, weight pressing on the knee joint, stick lifted, and stood unaided before them.

"How's that?" he said.

"Oh Chris!" Steve dashed towards him, ready to take him in her arms, but the grimace of alarm that crossed her husband's face checked her.

"Steady on, darling. I may be vertical but I'm not the Rock of Gibraltar."

"But . . . but you're walking."

"Sort of," said the young man. "Demo run coming up."

Chris put the stick down to the floor and hobbled towards Holly. Steve offered no assistance, letting him labour painfully into the waiting-room and across it. The motion was grotesque, almost crab-like for the initial two or three paces until he discovered how to do it again, with his right knee taking the weight of his body and a little rolling swing of the left leg. It looked exhausting, awkward but also triumphant.

"Good evening, Mother." Chris stood before her without the stick.

In spite of herself, Holly began to cry.

"Come on, it's not that bad, is it?"

"It's wonderful," said Holly.

Chris put his arm out and she took it, supporting him while he kissed her.

"Hardly wonderful." Chris eased himself on to the wooden bench, the leg stuck out before him. "But it's progress. I'll be doing ten miles a day before you know it."

"What did Walsh say?"

"He's done about all he can," Chris answered. "I'm being shipped off tomorrow, like it or not, to a convalescent place in Hulke in Shropshire. It won't be all lying in the sun and barley water, though. They have trained nurses and doctors there who'll help me with special exercises to build up the muscles that are left."

"How long will you be gone?" asked Steve.

"Three weeks to a month."

"Will I be able to visit?"

"Of course, darling. It's not a prison."

"And after?" said Holly.

"Oh another couple of weeks at home," Chris answered, "and I'll be fit for duty again."

Holly said, "Not flying?"

Chris stared down at the rigid limb. He patted the thigh lightly. "No, Mother, not flying. I wouldn't be much use in a cockpit, anywhere in a 'plane, with this pin."

"What'll you do, Chris?"

"What they tell me to do. Desk job, I expect. Instructing, or map-reading, perhaps. I don't actually know. And I don't actually care."

"And afterwards?" said Holly.

"Afterwards?" Her son seemed surprised at the question.

"After the war, I mean?"

"We'll face that when we come to it," Chris replied. "Steve and I, we'll find something to do. Something utterly useless. Perhaps I might learn the antique trade, become a shopkeeper and follow in your footsteps."

"If there is an antique trade," said Holly.

"If there is an end to the war," said Chris.

Holly and Steve drove away from Cyrus Street in Holly's little Sunbeam motor car, using almost the last drop of her petrol ration.

On Wednesday night an HE bomb had fallen on the corner of Briggs Road and the façade of the North Western Marine Insurance office block was shored up by crude scaffolding. At the mouth of Scrutton Street a couple of shops and three terrace houses had been gutted by fire from an exploding gas main. Barricades closed off the thoroughfare and gangs of workmen toiled in and out of the gigantic hole in the roadway. Brandishing an ancient, hooded bull's-eye lantern, a PC was on duty at the junction. Politely, he redirected the women by an open route back to Groves Square.

The darkness was not complete. Torchlight and the wan beams of lorries and cars seemed like gelid reflections of the searchlights which swept the sky. On rooftops, fire-watchers had already taken their posts. Wardens and other voluntary workers were making their way from their homes to their stations and a column of Volunteer Pioneers, "amateur navvies", were marching down Oakhampton Road, chins in and chests out like a platoon of guards, shovels and pickaxes hoisted over their shoulders. They were the local "dig out" squad, and would work in liaison with police and fire services. A new emergency water tank, bolted up in haste and filled too full, had sprung a leak and the road was awash for a quarter of a mile. A gang of small boys, who should have been long in bed and would no doubt cop it from their worried Mas, were unhelpfully building dams in the gutter with sand from a builder's barrow while two AFS women wrestled with a mounted hand-pump to empty out the tons of water before real damage could be done.

It was squalid and exciting too, all this purposeful activity countersunk into the business of the evening, absorbing everyone, Holly and Steve included, as they navigated the maze of steeets back towards the Fulham Road where, by arrangement, Holly had agreed to pick up Norma who had been on day-shift and was due a night off.

"Good to see Chris on his feet." Holly raised her voice to make it heard over the sluggish growl of the Sunbeam's decrepit engine.

"He seemed depressed," said Steve. "I suppose he'll get over it."

"Did he mean it, do you think, about going into the antique trade? I could give him such a start."

"He said it without meaning it," Steve answered. "You heard him. He really doesn't know what he intends to do. He wants to go back into the RAF. I expect there will be lots of chaps like him, unable to fly."

"Too many, perhaps," said Holly, thinking of the jobless ex-service men who had limped round Lambeth in the aftermath of the Great War.

"If it comes to it," said Steve, "I can work; after the war, I mean."

"You? But won't you be looking after the home and having babies?"

"One doesn't preclude the other," said Steve. "There's no law saying that I can't have a career and a home. You did, didn't you?"

"I suppose I did." Holly was tempted to add, "And see where it got me." But she did not yet share enough intimacy with her daughter-in-law. "Anyhow, Chris is probably right. It *will* be a long war and it may not really be up to us what we do afterwards."

"I hope you don't mean you think Hitler will win."

"Lord, no!" said Holly. "I mean that there will be so many pieces to pick up, none of us might have much say in what we are obliged to do."

Steve nodded and craned forward in the passenger seat to peer into the darkened roadway. "Where are we?"

"I'm not positive," said Holly. "In Blackward Street, I think."

"We seem to be driving round in circles."

"True," said Holly. "Is that a convoy just ahead?"

"Looks like it. What a hold-up!"

"We'll be here for hours. I hope Norma waits."

Canvas-hooded and securely roped, carrying supplies, not personnel, the army trucks looked mysterious. Even their motor-cycle escorts had a sinister appearance in helmets, goggles and silk face-masks.

It was now completely dark.

Holly switched off the Sunbeam's engine. She would have reversed and sought out a suitable detour but three more cars had piled into the narrow back street, blocking escape. Factory and warehouse walls soared on either side of the car and the convoy trucks—a dozen or more, it seemed—nosed and jockeyed for position through a corridor of rubble, defined by·the blackened skeleton of a London bus drawn up as a marker. The air smelled bad.

"Sewer," said Steve, matter-of-factly. "Put up the window."

Holly did so and the two women, having run out of conversation, waited while an excitable subaltern and a phlegmatic police constable redirected the heavy traffic.

The Sunbeam jerked, crawled forward five or six yards, halted again.

Holly and Steve were still sitting in Blackward Street when the siren sang out and, instantly, the shuddering pump of anti-aircraft guns began. The siren was close, up on the roof of one of the warehouses, and its wail was deafening. The women could hardly hear the guns, only feel them, the sensory impression of approach distorted by the walls and the elephant-herd of army trucks.

"Oh-oh!" said Steve. "I don't like the sound of it."

Holly did not hear the bombs at first; the girl's ears were sharper than her own and attuned to differentiate sounds.

"That's a biggie," said Steve.

"I didn't—" Holly's words were blotted out by yells from the excitable subaltern who had run up alongside the Sunbeam.

"Get out of here. Get out. Take shelter. Take shelter."

"Where, for God's sake?" Holly cried. But the subaltern had gone off again, running, crouched, up the line of cars into the darkness. To Steve she said, "Shall we get out?"

"Stick with the car," said Steve. "We don't know where we are or where the shelters are situated. With bombs falling, this convoy will shift itself quickly enough, you watch."

The girl's experience with the ATS had taught her well. Indeed, the big army trucks sorted out their confusion very quickly under the whip of the sirens, and, roaring, slid away down the length of Blackward Street towards the lattice of searchlights which fanfared the night sky above the buildings.

From here, oddly angled, the women could discern the spire of the Inverness Church, as the car weaved past the waving policeman and turned right into a residential zone east of Fulham.

"Keep driving," said Steve. "Do you want me to take the wheel?"

"No, I'm quite all right."

"Then put your foot down."

"What about the people?"

"They're all making for the shelters. Flick the headlights."

"I'll be arrested."

"No, you won't. Go on."

Holly did as she was told, knuckling the long switch on the dashboard. The lights were hardly piercing and would not be seen from above by the pilots of the Dorniers, as the car sped between streams of folk seeking refuge in the communal shelters which had been allocated to them.

"How far away is the fire station?" asked Steve.

"Three or four blocks."

"Go there. It's probably as safe a place as any," said Steve. "Besides, you never know, we might be able to help."

Above and ahead, the terraces steepened into office accommodation; not unduly tall, though, and laid out under an increasingly visible sky filled with feathers of ack-ack and the sweep of searchlights.

"Keep going, Holly."

Suddenly, swooping towards them, only a few hundred feet above the road, was a huge bat-like shape. The howl of wind and the tear of propellers was deafening as it drove along the length of the street like a monstrous owl hunting a country lane. Involuntarily, Steve covered her face with her arms.

"German. A Jerry dive-bomber. Look out!"

The package of fire bombs darted over the top of the Sunbeam and exploded on the pavements and rooftops of the terrace, spraying small debris outwards in all directions and bringing instant light, flashes and radiant smoke and blushes of yellow fire.

"Drive, drive, Holly. Don't stop now."

Mouth set and fists rigid on the wheel, Holly glued her eyes to the road ahead and did not turn around, as Steve had done, to view the havoc behind. Another shape shot over the car but instinct told Holly this 'plane was British, a hunter, and Steve confirmed her guess by shouting, "Spitfire. Get him. Bring the devil down."

To Holly's right, in the direction of Sloane Square and the Pimlico Road, the darkness blazed already, while distant sirens howled.

Along the Fulham Road fire tenders and other emergency service vehicles were in full flight, bells clanging, tyres shrieking. Pavements under the shop-fronts were thick with scurrying pedestrians, most clutching clothing bundles or blankets, or young children wrapped snug in shawls and quilts.

There was no need for lights now. The sky was brighter than moonlight and definition at street level was almost perfect. Holly nosed the Sunbeam into the main thoroughfare and, crawling by the kerbside, kept out of the way of clanging tenders.

They were close to Murray Grove, where the auxiliary fire station was situated in a requisitioned Ford garage and showroom, when the first HE bombs sprinkled the area.

The wall of Litchfield & Locke's department store, a splendid building designed and built in 1937, buckled outwards and, without apparent cause, broke and fell forward in a cascade of glass and mock marble slabs, followed by a torrent of plaster and brick.

Holly heard screams shrill above the rumble and the dull, oppressive thunder of the explosion itself. She heeled the Sunbeam to the left into the mouth of Murray Grove, while Steve, slewed round in the passenger seat, murmured, "Oh, my God! Oh, dear God!"

Murray Grove had drawn itself in tightly. Apart from a trio of wardens gathered round an elderly woman who had stumbled and hurt herself, there was nobody in sight.

The emptiness seemed more frightening than the crowds. No lights in any of the houses. No glimmer from the street lamps—yet the Grove had not been bombed or damaged. It was a backwater, passive and calm, lying long and straight between the fires. It might have been the wee small hours and not half-past nine of a Friday evening. Even the Grove's one public house, a straight, plain place with only a lacquered sign to give it identity, had closed up at the first chirrup of the siren, decanting its clients out of the back door into the lane between the gardens where earthbanks or hummocky iron shelters would protect them as they scurried home to attend their various duties.

The Ford garage—Vernon Bros.—had a mock-Tudor frontage and a wide forecourt where, in happier days, the pride of the Ford Motor Company's products had been displayed. Two tall petrol pumps had been removed to give faster access to the doors of the repair shop. Fuel tanks remained below the flagstones, however, and the pumps were indoors now, close to the red-painted brass-bound fire engines. But the interior of the repair shop was deserted. Lit by two dim blue bulbs, the floor showed slicks of oil but not another sign of its function, and not a single piece of litter. Acrid exhaust fumes lingered in the atmosphere.

Holly parked the Sunbeam against the far wall, out of the way of any possible activity in the garage, and sat back.

"What a ride!" she said. "I hope there's some place we can shelter here."

"There's bound to be." Steve seemed completely composed. "The engines have gone but there should be female auxiliaries on the premises. Telephonists and fire plotters, I expect."

Tentatively, Holly sounded the Sunbeam's horn which echoed mournfully in the space—and elicited no response.

Steve got out of the car, followed by Holly.

Bombs were falling close by, along the line of the Fulham and Kings Roads, by the sound of it. The drone of aeroplanes fluctuated, punctuated by guns from the battery. There were no "whistlers", however, only the thud and blast of the bombs and a crackle of the air.

Looking up, Holly saw that the thick sea-green glass roof of the garage had been sandbagged, and was glad of it. She felt unpardonably secure in this shelter and might have stayed there, in the car, if Steve had not sensibly led her by the hand across the garage to a door in the side wall. A short corridor and another narrow door admitted the women to the office where Norma and a Mrs. Grindlay were doing their best to cope with a state of emergency bordering on chaos.

The office was dominated by a large-scale map of North and West London, marked by coloured inks and pricked with ball-headed pins. Sub-station or not, auxiliaries or not, Murray Grove was run as part and parcel of the vast organisation of emergency services which had been created and which, in this past week, had found itself tested to the limit.

The room had once been the office of Messrs. Tom and Cyril Vernon. Ford dealers for Fulham and Chelsea, but the gigantic plate-glass window which had overlooked the forecourt had been replaced by layers of plywood slatted with pine against which, externally, a baffle of sandbags had been erected. The office was stuffy but had a closeted feeling that made one feel it would stand against blast, vulnerable only to a direct hit. Unlike the yard and tender area, it was littered with soft-drinks bottles, tea-cups and saucers, brimming ashtrays and assorted equipment, including wicked-looking axes and big rubber gasmasks like tribal adornments.

In addition to the map there was a Mobilising Board and District Deployment chart which Norma, with a phone in one hand, was trying to keep up-to-the-minute.

"Mr. Dunn needs a portable dam," Norma was saying, her voice several degrees louder than usual. "Did you get that message direct? Well, *did you*? Find out if it's on its way, will you? Mr. Dunn's hanging on in a call-box for an answer. *Dam*, I said. A portable dam. I *tried* Morton Street. They say *you* have it. He didn't phone you direct because he couldn't get through. *Fetch the bleedin' officer then, double-damn-quick*."

"Steady, Norma," said Mrs. Grindlay, a handsome, curly-haired woman in her late thirties whose husband and elder son were both in the regular London Fire Brigade. "It'll be some poor, bewildered little girl on the other end. I don't suppose things are any easier at the district office or Pikeman Place."

"Yer, but that's not going to help Jimmie Dunn if the paint store blows up."

She put down one telephone and lifted another which had been lying off its cradle on a table close at hand.

"Seems they've lost the rubber dam, Jim. Jim? Are you still there? Jim?" Norma's pretty features contorted with worry. "Jim? What's happened to the man?"

"Keep jogging them at Pikeman Place," suggested Mrs. Grindlay. She noticed Holly and Steve for the first time and managed a friendly smile. "Good evening, ladies. Come for the show, have you?"

Norma spun round, one hand on her breast as if temper had made her breathless. "Hol. Sorry, love, but I'm stuck here. Reasons are obvious. It's blue murder out there. Did you run through any of it?"

"Yes, the beginning," said Holly.

"How bad is it?" asked Steve.

"The biggest raid yet," said Norma. "Dive-bombers by the score. Bit too fast, in the mass, for our lads to keep away from the city. Reports say there's a huge wave of heavy bombers coming over the Channel. If they strike, I don't know what we'll do."

"Are there only two of you?" asked Holly.

"There should be five girls on duty, but none of the others have turned up," said Mrs. Grindlay. "They were due half an hour ago."

"Many streets are closed," said Steve.

"If it's humanly possible to make it, they will, I'll nob," said Norma. She spoke into the phone again, less stridently now. "Right, so the dam has gone out to Cheshire Street with the three DPs from your station. Right, thanks, love, that's all I wanted to know."

She hung up.

Immediately the telephone rang again.

Norma shrugged at Holly and Steve and snatched up the receiver. "Murray Grove Sub-station." She listened, frowning. She said, "Sorry, sir, we haven't a tender left in the place. Auxiliary Butterfield speaking, sir. Sorry, sir. You'll just have to take my word for it. To the paint store fire in Cheshire Street, sir. It was Officer Kelly's decision, sir. Big blaze in danger of spreading. He has both DP appliances and a Heavy Unit from here, with full crews. He was meeting up with the Water Unit from Oxborrow. Can't say, sir. Will I let you know if the gen comes our way?"

Norma nodded and, shaking the receiver violently, cried into it, "Sir? Sir? I've lost you, sir."

"That's the new wire gone," said Mrs. Grindlay. "Is it dead?"

"Stone dead."

"A paint store?" said Holly. "Is that the huge warehouse, Loboda's, that you pass on the way in from Lots Road Power Station?"

"That's the one. Perhaps the Jerrys were after the electricity supply. I dunno. But if they were, they missed it by a couple of miles and got poor old Loboda's instead. Filthy stuff, paint. The big tins explode like bleedin' bombs when they get hot enough, and spew all over. Cause a mist so thick you can't breathe. Clogs and mucks up the pumps so you can't get them to work properly."

"However, I think," put in Mrs. Grindlay, "that it's what's stil to come that might make it terribly hard for our chaps."

"More bombs," said Steve. "Yes, and if the wind blows up, as the forecasters predicted, then it could be an inferno."

"Well, I'm stuck here for the night," said Norma Butterfield. "What d'you two want to do? Stay put or risk making for Tite Street?"

"They must stay here," said Mrs. Grindlay. "No question of going out in this barrage. It would be quite suicidal. I'm afraid you'll just have to make the best of it, Mrs. King."

"There's a sort of shelter, through there and downstairs," said Norma, pointing with the telephone receiver. "Dozen cots. Clean enough."

"Are we in your way?" asked Steve.

"Not in the least."

"I'd prefer to stay here. I've gone off deep shelters, to tell you the truth."

"In that case," said Mrs. Grindlay "perhaps you'd be good enough to make us all some tea. There's fresh water in the milk churn under the table; one never knows what's going to come out of the tap after bombs start falling!"

"Tea coming up," said Steve, who, in the environment of the fire station, seemed to have shed her fatigue.

In the course of the next hour, in the company of the AFS women, Holly learned what war work really meant. Norma and Mrs. Grindlay, who had been on duty all day long, had no moment to rest. Telephones jangled constantly while the raid continued outside. A warden called in, uniform coated with dust, face blackened. He drank a cup of tea, imparted information about the scale of the raid, and left again. So far, it seemed, the bombs had missed Murray Grove and the long street remained intact. To the west of the sub-station, however, buildings were blazing and the whole area around Cheshire Street and Anchor Road, where the unit was, had become an infernal bazaar. Fumes made life even more difficult for fire-fighters and breathing apparatus was being sought all round the district. If Norma and Mrs. Grindlay feared for the safety of their colleagues, they hid it beneath feeble jokes and in activity. They knew only too well that the majority of volunteer firemen had not fought a major fire before and that the raid by the German Stukas had now given way to a full-scale blitz by heavy bombers.

The sounds from outside were continuous, blasts and barrages and the crash of falling buildings muffled by the suspiration of fires from all of two miles away, frightening in their magnitude. Holly felt scorched by the sounds and smells. Deep-rooted panic grew in her, an inescapable sensation that, by staying here, she would become a victim of fire, stalked and trapped by it. It was not, however, as she had ever imagined it in her nightmares; not personal, intimate and murderous as the fire in Pimlico had been.

Restlessly, she waited in the cluttered office for something to happen, some deepening strain to sound in the symphony. There was nothing supernatural in her response, no element of fatalism. But she knew that if she remained here, she would become a part of it whether she wished it or not.

It was half past ten when the call came through.

Norma responded. She listened gravely, shaking her head. "You'll have to try somewhere else, sir. Sorry."

She listened again.

Mrs. Grindlay had raised her head from her own conversation, detecting a note of shock in Norma's voice. Mrs. Grindlay covered the receiver with her hand. "What is it, Norma?"

Norma Butterfield continued to shake her head. "Yer, we've got the tank but we haven't got a lorry to haul it, nor drivers."

"Petrol," said Mrs. Grindlay. "We've a single spare fuel carrier round the back of the repair shop. It's strictly for emergencies."

"Isn't this an emergency?" said Steve quietly.

"Can't you send somebody round to fetch it, sir?" said Norma into the telephone; then, in amazement, "Nobody? Nobody at all?"

"Ask if the police can't help," Mrs. Grindlay suggested.

"Police," said Norma. "Oh, yer, I see."

Steve moved from her chair by the tea-table and came to stand by Holly. "I can drive," she said.

Mrs. Grindlay said, "There's no available lorry to connect to the fuel tank. It isn't all that large, really, but it's got no engine of its own."

"Hang on, sir." Norma Butterfield laid the instrument on the desk and turned towards the map. "They're only a mile or a mile and a half from here. Can't we find somebody, Mary?"

"Are the tenders grounded?" Mary Grindlay asked.

"Stuck in Cheshire Street," said Norma. "Seems we're the last chance."

"Last chance?" said Holly. "What do you mean?"

"The fire's closed off the perimeter. We have to haul fuel to the tenders within ten minutes or a quarter of an hour to get them out." She flicked at the ball-headed pins with her fingernail. "There's nobody I can contact with a haulage vehicle in time."

"There's my car," said Holly. "It's small but—"

"Could it pull, say, a caravan?" Mrs. Grindlay leaned her hands on the desk and addressed the question with some severity.

"I imagine so," said Holly.

"I'll drive," said Steve.

"Do you know where you're going with it?" said Norma.

"Cheshire Street," said Steve, doubtfully.

Holly got to her feet. "I know where it is. Which it is. Which roads are open?"

Norma picked up the telephone again and relayed Holly's question to the district officer.

"Only one route open. Down High Well Road into Anchor Road. Do you think you can find it?"

"Of course," said Holly.

"Listen," said Steve, "I don't like you being involved. I can go on my own. I'm experienced in this sort of thing and it's what I do."

Holly said, "It's my Sunbeam, and it's my neighbourhood— well, almost—and I want to go."

"But the whole area's on fire," said Norma. "Hol, you don't have to do this."

"Yes, I do," said Holly. "Of course I do."

It was but the work of a minute to steer the Sunbeam out of the repair shop and around the broad side of the garage building. The petrol tank was much smaller than Holly had imagined it would be. A primitive iron cylinder on a bolted trolley with two fat rubber tyres, it was tucked away in a brick shed. Norma unlocked the metal doors of the shed while Steve, at the wheel, reversed the Sunbeam into position. The girl got out and inspected the link rod and rear of the little motor car by the light of a pocket torch.

"I'm going to rope the tow-bar to the sub-frame," said Steve, dropping to her knees and peering under the car. "I just hope to heaven that it takes the strain. Once we're running, it should be all right."

"There's a rope in the boot," said Holly.

Steve found the length of thick hemp rope which Holly carried about, at Maury's insistence, against the possibility of breakdown. The old-fashioned Sunbeam had never broken down on her, however, and remained steadfast and reliable. Holly did not offer to drive. Small though the fuel tank was, it weighed a great deal and, on its long vee bar, would not be easy to handle. It took Steve no more than two minutes to secure the bar to the Sunbeam's frame and climb back into the driving seat.

"Norma, to whom do we report?" asked Steve.

Norma laughed. "Anybody in a fireman's uniform. I reckon they'll be on the lookout for you."

"Hold tight," said Steve. ·

She slid the car out of neutral gear.

The engine thrashed and whined furiously, the entire car vibrating as strain snapped through it; then Holly heard Norma cheer as the petrol float rolled from its rest and meekly followed the car into the yard.

Mrs. Grindlay had supplied Holly with a steel helmet and the elder woman sat with it in her lap, together with a pair of gas-mask cases, as the car and float negotiated the exit from the forecourt. Once in Murray Grove, they headed towards the frieze of fire that hung like garish tapestry over the rooftops. Suddenly Holly put the helmet on, settling tapes and little chunks of sponge rubber and the webbing strap so that it fitted snug and square on her head.

Steve glanced at her mother-in-law. "Eee, yer don't arf look a treat, Ma," she said in an applied accent. "Chris wouldn't 'ardly know yer."

Holly was no longer tired, no longer diffident. She shared fully in Steve's rekindled energy, the assertive vitality of youth. But she feared the fire, even as she was driven towards it. Through the rear window she could make out the high-riding tank on its stout tyres, feel its thumps as it ran over debris, the transmitted liveliness of it coming through the pull-bar. She noticed that Steve had a very upright driving stance, helmet jammed hard against the inside of the roof. The girl's face was flushed and pretty, her eyes large and luminous as she concentrated on the way ahead.

They drove along the Fulham Road for two hundred yards. It was clearly not open to any kind of traffic, however "official", blocked by a shambles of fire tenders and hoses. Fires sprouted up where once there had been stores and houses.

Holly said, "Turn right at High Wells Road."

Steve directed the Sunbeam and its trailer across the street. She found space between an abandoned bus and a lake-like sheet of shattered glass which had been blown out of the windows of Wyatt's Bridal Specialist. Together with ghostly veils and gowns, one rather horrible dummy, bald and twisted, in white lace and tulle, lay sprawled across the kerb. Traffic lights weren't functioning and the Sunbeam travelled unimpeded into the side street, heading towards a swollen cloud of lime-white and yellow flame which, obviously, hung above Loboda's.

"Now," said Steve, "the going gets tough."

The first sign of disaster came seconds later when a crowd of twenty or thirty civilians, led by three wardens and a couple of policemen, swarmed out of the back-lit fog. Distorted by the hideous light, they appeared like alien creatures. They were running frantically, terror evident in every step—men, women and children. Bricks and loose slates covered the street. A tree had smashed over a hedge, scattered leaves like cornflakes over which the Sunbeam crackled. Steve slowed the car to walking pace, cursing under her breath. The crowd flooded around the car without pause, children crying. A couple of the women and one hobbling old man were weeping. Wardens urged them along with great scooping motions of their arms.

It was a warden—a woman—who stopped the car. She stood in its path, arms raised, a torch and red flag in her fists.

"Hell! Hell and damnation!" Steve braked to a halt.

The warden came to the window. Steve opened it. The woman was young, early twenties, fat-cheeked like a country lass and out of breath.

"Where d'yer think ye're goin'?" she demanded.

"Fire Service," said Steve, coolly. "Cheshire Street."

"Not this way, you ain't."

"Is it closed?"

"Rupt'ed gas main on Anchor Street. Could blow us all sky-high, any minute."

"But is the street open?"

"Gotter get the people out."

"All right," said Steve. "But is the street open?"

"Can't go through. I say you can't go through."

Steve's mouth compressed and she divorced the fat-cheeked warden from her attention, completely ignoring her. She revved the engine and, with considerable expertise, coaxed a flying start from the laden motor car, shooting it forward away from the warden who, thwarted, shook her fists and shouted like a madwoman.

"What if it is closed off?" asked Holly.

"It isn't. She didn't say it was. She's only doing her job but she's a bully and very frightened. If the street had been blitzed she would have said so."

"The gas main, though?"

"Well, yes, there is that," said Steve with a strange little shrug. "But if there is a ruptured gas main, then the police will have cleared the area and we should be able to drive unimpeded into Cheshire Street."

"Unless we're blown up."

"Do you want me to stop?"

"Under no circumstances," said Holly.

Steve laughed. "Good! Look at it this way. Things aren't as bad as they might be."

"Aren't they?"

"Uncle David might be driving."

Holly giggled as the car nosed on down the empty street into the brilliant haze of light which was Cheshire Street.

The gas main was hard by the corner, by the first of the tall buildings. Beside the block huddled two small cottage-style dwellings, nineteenth-century relics, one of which had lost its roof. The main lay at the bottom of a hole. The HE bomb had torn up a privet hedge and flung it, like a feather boa, around telephone wires strung from the office block which had lost more than half its windows. There was glass everywhere, and rough turfs and cobbles suppurating from the road surface. Three men in overalls and tin hats peered curiously down into the fresh crater.

"Smell it?" asked Steve.

"Yes. But it isn't all that strong."

"A leak, perhaps," said Steve.

Two of the workmen turned and watched the Sunbeam and its trailer jolt past, but they made no sign or gesture and did not try to prevent its progress.

"False alarm?" said Holly.

"It hardly matters," said Steve. "Look."

The cottage garden with the hole in it had at least been recognisable; the length of Cheshire Street, east and west, was not. It had been transformed into a gigantic Wagnerian stage-set; a ring of fire. Sheets of flame, showing through the flats, dwarfed the engines and firemen, all but erasing them in the furnace-like glow. Curled back on the wind, the stench was foul, not so much an odour as a presence, a thick, clotting sensation in throat and lungs.

Holly began coughing at once and Steve, hanging on to the wheel, gagged. Across the windscreen of the car a milky substance blurred vision and the wipers served only to smear it further.

"Oh, God!" said Holly.

She spoke calmly, with apparent resignation, but, enclosed in acrid fumes in the blind interior of the car, her fear of fire welled up once more. She clutched the gas-mask boxes and closed her eyes. Even against the lids the livid glow of the flames pressed upon her vision.

Peering through the smeared windshield Steve drove on. Fifty yards or so into Cheshire Street, however, the glass clouded over completely. Tugging off her helmet, the girl punched it against the shield. The glass cracked and shattered and she scooped away the jagged fragments with the rim of the helmet to give her an unimpeded view of the road ahead.

At the sound of breaking glass Holly's eyes jerked open.

She felt suffocated by the intensity of the heat. The car was almost enshrouded in flames. There were no ambulances, no rescue squads in the street, only straggling hoses, withering where they lay, and the roofless shell of the paint store vaulting up like a huge luminous cathedral. On the left, Holly saw small buildings spattered with flames, etched by dense smoke against the reflection of the warehouse blaze. Behind and beyond the corner was another untended fire, an ill-kempt, ragged paling of flame which blocked off escape by that route.

The Sunbeam lurched and the petrol tank yawed. Steve slowed the car to a crawl. The girl was afraid too, but her determination was unwavering. Two hundred yards ahead of them were fire engines and pump units, though not many of them, seeming not just vulnerable but already defeated by the scale of the fire. On a spidery ladder clung the fly-shape of a man. Even as the women saw it, the ladder buckled and toppled inwards. Pencilled delicately against the yellows and pale reds, the ladder hung poised for an instant, then, with its fly-shape still intact, vanished into the inferno. A spray of sparks was the only indication that a human life had been lost but, seconds later, like a dirge, came the sonorous hiss of molten paint bursting and cascading from a wound in the blackened brickwork.

Holly shouted, "Won't the petrol tank explode in this heat?"

"It might."

"Can't we leave it here, let them come for it?"

"How can they?"

"Yes, you're right. Go on, drive on."

Suddenly the car was rocked by blast. Bombs had tumbled silently out of the sky beyond the junction of Anchor and High Well Road. The plane, a heavy bomber, droned on, its underbelly lit by the glow from below. The explosion overturned the petrol tank, up-ending it against the tow-bar and dragging the Sunbeam to a gradual halt. Steve flung herself on her mother-in-law. The women crouched, cowering in the well of the car, not a moment too soon. A prolonged subterranean rumble was followed by a crack of sound like tearing buckram, but louder than thunder. It seemed to peel the skin from the surface of Holly's face and detonate in her eardrums, deafening her. The gas main had exploded. Strong white light, like noonday, filled the car which was lifted in a piece from the cobbles and dumped on its off-side.

Thrown together, Holly and Steve were jammed between the seats' edge and the steering column. For a minute or so they hunched motionless, while broken stones and gouts of earth rained upon the car. Then the massive noises died and there was again only the roaring of fires and the casual crash of timbers within the paint store and its neighbouring blocks.

Painfully, Holly braced herself while Steve struggled over her and groped for the doorhandle which was now where the roof should be.

"My God, there's petrol everywhere."

So this was it, thought Holly.

She lay absolutely still while the younger woman clambered on her bent back. The stench of the spilled fuel was sickening. Pierced by shrapnel the tank rivered petrol all around them. One spark, one flake of burning paint and the Sunbeam would become a pyre. Holly, however, did not think of herself. She mourned for Chris's loss, thinking how awful it would be if he were to lose his young wife in such manner, to be left crippled and alone. She cried out for help. Foolishly. There was nobody to help them now; no Christopher, no Maury, no David, not even little Miles Walshott. She was responsible for herself and her own destiny.

The car door sprang open. Steve straddled Holly's legs and hoisted herself upward, emerging into the scalding air. One foot on the seat, a knee in the small of Holly's back, a thrust, and Steve at least was out of the car. "*Now, you. Now, you.*"

Steve lay on her tummy across the car's wing and stretched her hands inside the vehicle, clasping Holly by the wrists. She had surprising strength and dragged the woman bodily out of the crushed wreckage.

Holly looked round. There was precious little left of Cheshire Street. Where familiar buildings had once been was only fire, rufflets of flames wavering against the night sky, crimson and vermilion splashed with gold. It was—almost—magnificent. Puddles of petrol reflected the flames. The reek of leaking fuel was choking, like a gas.

"*We must run. Quick.*"

Steve's cry was piercing.

Holly stumbled from the car, fell against Steve and the pair staggered drunkenly away from the Sunbeam, heads bowed. The street was sprinkled with burning embers. The wall of Loboda's had the fragility of burned paper. The heat was overpowering, all-consuming, the one and only reality which had to be coped with and surmounted. A strong streaming wind gusted around the women, half blinding them as they ran, arms entwined, towards the tenders.

The lake of petrol ignited. The Sunbeam vanished in a sheet of cornflower flame. Ten seconds later the tank ripped open. Neither Holly nor Steve paused to glance back. They ran on under the downpour of fluid sparks, down the left-hand edge of Cheshire Street, in search of help. But there were no firemen. None of the pumps were working. The units had been abandoned. Holly's nightmares were coming true. Buckled walls, held stickily together by paint, would cave inward at any second. It was all fire and flame. Every hue and subtle shade of flame that the human mind could imagine. No exit, no darkness showed. Where were the firemen? Had they been swallowed up by the flames too? Had they found a way out, an avenue of escape?

Painted a beautiful red by the glow, a single engine stood across the width of Cheshire Street. Here, spillage from the fallen gable of Loboda's had formed mounds of incandescent debris. The engine stood defiantly against it. Left, incongruously, was a London bus, tail in the air, smoke belching from its gutted interior. A huge pit had been hewn from the fallen façade of a once-trim office block. Holly and Steve focused on the engine, headed directly for it, their final hope. But the tender was useless, tyres ripped, glass smashed and the body holed by flying bricks.

"Where are they? Where are the men?" Holly cried.

"They've gone. Oh, God. They've all gone."

"No, we ain't," said a cheerful voice. "Wouldn't leave a coupler lovely ladies behind, not us."

"Did you hear—?" Holly asked.

"Yes, but—where. Where are you?"

"Down 'ere, love."

Stained and sooty as an imp of hell, the fire officer leaned his forearms on the pavement just below the edge of the engine. For a bizarre moment it seemed as if nothing remained of the man except head and arms. Hysteria welled in Holly.

"Best be quick, ladies," said the head. "The whole shebang's a-gonna fall down in a minute."

"How?"

"Sewers." The fireman raised himself from the rectangular hole in the surface of the road. "Sorry it ain't nicer. But any port in a fire-storm, like."

"Go on, Holly," Steve urged. "Go on."

Holly allowed the fire officer to assist her as she slid under the engine. She felt space, feet and legs enveloped in a cool, dank emptiness. Hands grasped her ankles, turning her so that she was tummy to the edge of the manhole, and gently guided her feet to the rungs of an iron ladder against the side of the shaft. The officer crouched by her, giving her support. Though he had spoken with cheeky assurance, Holly saw dread in his face now.

"Best be quick," he said again, through his teeth. "Bleedin' bloomin' quick."

Holly let herself go, almost falling into the shaft, and Steve and the fire officer tumbled in on top of her.

The side of Loboda's crumbled and fell outwards across Cheshire Street. The ground shook and Holly clung to the iron ladder for dear life. Only the position of the engine saved the three from serious injury. The unit bore the brunt of the weight of the falling wall. Past Steve's hips and the fireman's silhouette Holly glimpsed the last collapse of the paint store.

"Mary, Mother of God," intoned a voice from below. "What was that now?"

"Store's gone," called the fire officer.

"Everybody safe?" came the grave voice.

"Everybody safe."

"Step down, missus, if you please."

Holly picked her way down the ladder and joined the group of two dozen firemen who gathered on the stone pavement at the bottom of the shaft. Steve and the fire officer followed her. Nobody offered them a welcome or a greeting. Lit by a circle of pocket torches, the group were staring upward at the shaft, at the aperture through which they had escaped, which was lit now by a haunting rosy glow. The rumbling faded slowly, and the crackle of fire dwindled. In the dank odorous sewer it was as still and hushed as a chapel.

"Close, very close."

"Too bleedin' close."

"How many are injured?"

"Hawkins got a broken leg, and your Georgie's burned.

"How bad?"

"Not so bad," said the man named Georgie. "It's the 'ands, like."

"Who else?"

"Nothin' serious, Len."

"All right. I don't want us strayin' all over them tunnels. Might never be seen again, some of you idiots. Tell you what, you four take the ladies and head north. I'll take you three with me and we'll go east. Right away from that there gas main. The rest of you—stay put. And I mean *put*. We'll get a rescue party to you somehow, by the tunnels or by the manhole if we can. Hawkins?"

"Sir?"

"You in pain?"

"It's not too bad, sir, when I keep still."

"Right, Georgie, keep your hands covered and tucked away. Don't want to risk infection in this place, like."

"Put them up me jumper."

"Right. Ladies, are you fit for a bit of a stroll?"

"Yes."

"Mr. Godwin, which way's north, sir?"

"That way."

"How d'yer know, Len?"

" 'Cause I'm a bleedin' officer, that's how I know."

Led by a subordinate officer to Len Godwin, Steve and Holly followed the torches down the slippery pavement above the sewage channel. They held each other's hand. The tunnel was arched, high enough for the men and women to walk upright. Fine old brick-work, Holly thought, product of the finest in Victorian engineering with, here and there, a grille or grating of wrought-iron, ornate enough to be in a museum of art. She tried not to look at the river of black water. It gave up a thick effluvia and was occasionally swamped by a foaming flood as water from fire hoses above drained away down the kerb gratings. There were rats, but not many, and the creatures scampered away before the advancing firemen as they trudged along the pavement which they hoped would lead them to an exit north of the blitzed area. This netherworld was not at all frightening to Holly, less to be feared than the fiery streets above ground. She felt safe with the firemen, all regular employees of the London Brigade, seasoned and pragmatic and cautious.

Several possible exits were inspected and rejected before the young fire officer declared himself satisfied that Fulham Road and Chelsea must be far behind them. Finally he climbed one of the inspection ladders while the rest of the group waited below. Minutes later he climbed down again and gave a thumbs-up sign.

"All clear."

"But where the 'ell are we?"

"Right outside St. Stephen's Hospital, the Werner Street corner."

"Just round from our station."

"Any sign of bombs fallin'?"

"Nope. It's quiet as the grave up there."

"Must be a lull."

"Hup we go then. Ladies first."

Ten minutes later, dazed by the sweet night air and the delayed effect of their ordeal, Holly and Steve stood on the corner by the hospital wall, watching the last of the firemen draw himself from the manhole. To south and east fires blazed but this neighbourhood was untouched by bombing.

"Now what?" asked Steve.

The young officer shrugged. "Can't rightly say what the proper procedure is. We'd better get back to our stations quick as we can. Where are you from?"

"We're not AFS girls. We're volunteer civilian drivers," said Steve. "We were bringing you extra petrol, but didn't make it in time."

"Brave of you to try," said the officer. "Listen, best find a shelter until mornin'. Don't know when Jerry might come back."

The rest of the firemen had taken bearings. One had hurried up the avenue to the hospital to search for a phone. Another two had headed off towards the Cleary Street sub-station to swallow a cup of tea and, if needed, to plunge back into action immediately.

"You be all right?" asked the young officer.

"Perfectly," said Steve.

"Know where you are?"

"Yes. Not too far from home."

The officer shook their hands and, no doubt regarding them as responsible citizens, left them there.

To Holly the events of the night had been unique; to the men of the fire service they were part and parcel of the job, worse than usual but not rare.

"Steve, what shall we do?"

"It seems quiet enough," the girl answered. "Let's head for Tite Street."

"Are you sure?"

"Positive. Where else can we be certain of finding a whole, unopened bottle of gin?"

Stepping lightly, quickly, the woman and the girl set out for home.

The windows on the Thames side of the house had been shattered by blast and the taping had not contained the shards. Glittering fragments sprinkled the carpet of the dining-room. The polished surface of the Regency dining-table, an heirloom and Kennedy's pride, was coated with plaster crumbs and wood splinters. On the mantel one of the clocks had copped a single stone chip which had been driven through the glass and face and deep into the works like a tiny bullet. Its companion had stopped in sympathy, observing a seven-hour silence in honour of the deceased. The dining-room, though, was the only part of the house which had sustained any real damage; it wasn't too bad, all things considered.

Cleaning, tidying and boarding up would soon set things in order again and Holly, dressed in a loose gown and with her hair uncombed, inspected the damage unperturbed.

David said, "When I heard what a beating Chelsea had taken, and when I saw the devastation this morning, I really imagined—"

"The very worst?" said Holly.

"Last night was beyond belief."

"I think we had better get used to it."

"Where's Stephanie?" David asked.

"She rose early and went back on duty."

"God, what it is to be young."

"And tough," said Holly.

"Were we like that?"

"Not quite like that," said Holly. "I admire them, don't you?"

"Who?"

"The young people, like Chris and Steve."

"They don't admire us much."

"Can you blame them? Still, there's life in the old dog yet, as they say."

"You sound pleased with yourself."

"I am. Last night I discovered that I haven't lost the knack of meeting a crisis. What's more, I survived."

David had been trailing Holly from room to room. He had arrived directly from the Admirality building at nine o'clock, utterly convinced that he would find Tite Street in ruins and Holly buried under them. His relief at discovering that the old mansion had withstood the bombing had turned to surprise and uncertainty at Holly's attitude. She seemed ridiculously gay. Perhaps it was the after-effects of the gin; the bottle and glasses were still on the table in the basement shelter. Without make-up, ungroomed, Holly looked close to her age at last. For all that, she seemed—what?—satisfied. It was a most peculiar reaction to what must have been a dreadful experience. But David thought that he understood.

He followed her into the kitchen.

"Are you really all right?"

"Hungry, that's all," Holly replied. "Have you tried the new dried egg powder. It isn't bad."

"Holly, you can't stay here."

"Why ever not? I'll board up the windows at the front, and bed in the basement. In all probability the Germans will leave Chelsea alone for a while."

"That's nonsense, and you know it."

Humming a waltz tune. Holly busied herself with baking bowl and spoon, measuring out a heap of the yellow egg powder according to a chart on the packet. It looked so damned frugal; one pint of milk, a minute knob of butter on a knife, four slices of stale bread. The long marble counter of the kitchen dresser had been designed to cater for feasts, not such lean pickings.

"I've enough for two, David. If you're very hungry I can make some Quaker oats."

"No. No thanks. Holly, what's come over you?"

She splashed milk into the bowl and whisked briskly. "I told you. This morning I feel decidedly favoured, smiled upon by fortune."

"Because of what happened last night?"

"That's it."

"Is there something you haven't told me, Holly?"

"Lots of things."

"For instance?"

"I'm not sure what they add up to, David. But I don't feel defeated any longer. I'm a Beckman, you see."

"You always were."

"Perhaps I needed reminding. It seems that we're a hardy little family after all. It may be an illusion, but I think we're going to come out of this all right."

"Am I included?"

"If you want to be. Two slices?"

"Please."

"Adolf isn't going to get us, darling."

All the statistics, the logistics, the plain run of sense, said otherwise. But David was sincere when he answered. "I agree. Have you any coffee?"

"Only tea."

"Tea will do. Listen, you're not serious about seeing it through right here in London?"

"Perfectly serious. Country living may suit Ruth, but not me. Besides, there's lots I can do in town, apart from keeping my tin hat and gas-mask handy."

"The shop, do you mean?"

"The shop's nothing. I'll put up the shutters for the duration."

"And Chris?"

"What about Chris?"

"His—his leg?"

"He'll learn to live with it. He hasn't much choice. Sorry, I don't mean to sound callous but he has Stephanie to look after and to look after him. Perhaps he's flown enough to be happy without wings now."

"Don't lie to me, Holly. You're doing it for him, aren't you?

You're determined to put yourself in danger by staying here for his sake."

"Not true."

"He's always come first."

"In the past, yes. But not now."

"God, but you're stubborn, Holly Beckman."

"Allers was," said Holly, in a Lambeth accent.

She slid the egg mix into a greased frying pan. The liquid hissed and congealed.

"But," she went on, glancing round at David, "I'm *not* doing it for Chris. I'm doing it for me. I'm damned if I'm going to run. That's the long and the short of it. I will not be bullied. I will not give in."

David snorted. "Independent to the bitter end."

"I don't see why the end should be bitter."

"You don't need anything or anyone, do you?"

"Only you."

"Oh, no," said David. "No, no, no. You can't get away with that one. I'm not going to be your excuse."

"What are you going to be?"

"I—what *do* you mean?"

Holly flipped experimentally at the thickening pancake.

"Candidly, I don't need you at all, David. Not your manly protection or your financial support. I do not need one damned thing from you any more."

"But you said—"

"I said I needed *you*, not what you can give me."

"Once before, Holly, a long time ago, you needed me."

"But you weren't there."

"And now?"

"Now it's different. We're different people, in a different world."

"But I—I—look here, I love you. That isn't different."

"Perhaps not."

"I still do love you, Holly."

"I know. I think I might learn to accept love without promises."

"Marriage?" said David.

"I accepted that long ago."

"It would have to be marriage?"

"Having second thoughts?"

"No, no second thoughts. I'm puzzled, though."

"Good," said Holly. "That's as it should be. I've no mystery left. But, being a woman of character, perhaps I can still bewilder you from time to time."

David laughed. "Are you teasing me?"

"Of course I am."

"About marrying me?"

"Not that. About everything else," said Holly.

"But you *will* marry me?"

"Yes."

"When?"

"On the first day of October."

"Why the first day of October?"

"Autumn is such a pretty time," said Holly Beckman King.

7 Postscript: 1947

It was wickedly cold in London at the beginning of the year. Paris was no less bitter. The glow of victory had waned, the nations of Europe were left with ruins and austerity and the urgent need to shape a future which would be more equitable and enduring than the past. Modernisation was the watchword in France. The plans of the new wave of politicians had not yet been implemented, however, and the flight from Gatwick to Orly was marked by delays and an interminable amount of fussing with baggage and customs.

The Aspinalls had booked a room in the Alsina in the Avenue Junot but there was a misunderstanding about the exact date and more delay at reception while Holly exercised her rusty French in sorting out the confusion. As they were now late for their appointment, lunch had to go by the board. Holly began to regret that she hadn't made a reservation in one of the de-luxe hotels, the Ambassador or the Moderne, for instance. But Mr. and Mrs. Aspinall, though well-to-do, had become used to doing things with a certain comfortable frugality. Holly had had her fur coat remodelled and was very glad of it in the cold grey city with hints of fog along the Seine and a fretwork of snow visible in parks and on the domes of tall buildings. Though the weather stole away much of the thrill of being back in the City of Light, it did not diminish Holly's curiosity or lessen the mystery which had brought her, with her husband, to Paris in the depth of winter.

Back in London, the "new" business was beginning to take root in a large shop in the Kings Road area. Much to David's relief, the process of acquiring a basis of quality stock had almost ended. He had forgotten what a demanding vocation that of the antique dealer can be. His part in it, a part he accepted without complaint, was that of general dogsbody and accountant. The hard labour of attending house sales and auctions he left to Chris and Steve guided by Holly's vast experience.

Strictly a family concern, the name of the new company had given them all much thought. He had been all for retaining the old name, trading on King's reputation, but Holly had wanted a fresh start and had finally persuaded the others to accept the rather grandiose label of *Aspinall, Beckman & Deems*. Where the Beckman came in now was anybody's guess, but David was flattered which, he suspected, was part of Holly's intention in including his name on the letter-head and on the gilded sign above the doors.

David did not resent his wife's return to business. It was, after all, mostly her capital which she chose to invest. Almost every item in their life together belonged to Holly, including the refurbished house in Tite Street which was their home. Ten years ago David's pride would have caused him to demand more than her love and a fair share of her time and interest. But no longer. The war had taught him too many hard lessons. Active again, doing the job she loved, Holly appeared to be happy. He was content to be part of it, along with Chris and Steve. He had been accorded an exact twenty-five per cent share in the company, and couldn't grumble about being left out of things. He did what was asked of him, whether it was driving the Bedford van out to a country house or totting up accounts or calling on lawyers. Naturally Chris, Steve and Holly attended the major sales together, which was all part of the young folks' training.

Life was very comfortable, almost cosy. Parted from her

husband, who had run off with another, younger, woman, Norma Butterfield was employed as an assistant. Ex-corporal Wilf Ackers, a boyish forty-five, was in charge of packing and storing. In spite of these connections with the pre-war world, though, David did not dwell on the past. It seemed to have happened to other people, such a very long time ago. That particular show was over, the passion and demands of youth passed on like stage props to the younger troupers.

They saw very little of Holly's father and step-mother who never left Hastings now, rather more of Maury and Ruth who were back in residence in Richmond, but nothing at all of Andrea. The rift between mother and daughter had never healed and David's loyalty lay with his niece in preference to his sister. Miles Walshott dropped in at Tite Street from time to time, for there was a bond of affection between the little stockbroker and his daughter. But there were no "state occasions", no family dinners; David did not regret it. Andrea was suffering from her own ill-humour, and deserved it. Even Mark had abandoned Hampstead. He was now a commercial airline pilot based in New York. Each of the Aspinalls, each of the Beckmans, was settled at last, engaged in various programmes of rebuilding, of making the country, if not the world, a fit place for their children and grandchildren to inhabit. All of that tribe from Pimlico and Lambeth were pinned down—except one.

Maury had made enquiries about his brother, mainly at Leo's cantankerous urging, but Ritchie Beckman had vanished, leaving no trace at all. It occurred to David, as it undoubtedly did to Maury, that Ritchie might have been one of the countless victims of the Nazis who had died in concentration camps. But that was a trail too fraught with pain and horror for Maury to pursue and old Leo was palmed off with the tale that Ritchie was believed to be in America, a lie that left the elder Beckman with hope. After a year or so, Maury stopped thinking about Ritchie and concentrated on business, on building homes for the homeless at prices they could afford, and in raising his own children as decently as possible.

It was the end of the first week in January in the year of 1947 when the letter from Paris arrived at Tite Street, addressed to Mrs. Kennedy King.

Mr. and Mrs. David Aspinall were breakfasting in the kitchen. It was a freezing day and the house was chill in spite of a new oil-fired stove in the kitchen, which was supposed to filter warm air into all the rooms.

Holly placed the letter against the marmalade pot and, with her tongue literally in her cheek, frowned at the postmark.

"Paris," said David. "Who do we know in Paris?"

"Not a soul now."

"Open it."

"I suppose it could be from Monsieur Lenormant or Hugues de Rais or one of the other dealers I used to know before the war. I haven't heard a word about any of them since the German invasion."

"One way to find out: open it."

Still Holly hesitated.

"What's wrong, darling?" said David.

"It could be from my brother."

"Ritchie?"

"If it is, it probably means trouble of one sort or another."

"Oh, for Heaven's sake, open it. Here, I'll do it."

"No, no." Holly slit open the heavy embossed envelope with a butter knife and unfolded a single sheet of thick pale-blue paper marked with an ornamental family crest. "My God. It's from Kati Dubriel. How astonishing. I thought she must be dead."

"The *Comtesse* Dubriel." David peered over his wife's shoulder. "Going up in the world, aren't we?" He read the French, typewritten and terse and simple. "She wants you to call on her. What on earth for?"

"Possibly she has something to sell."

"Really? Anything worth crossing the Channel for?"

"Dearest," said Holly. "If it's what I think it might be, it's worth walking to Tibet to acquire. A collection of fine Italian paintings."

"Can we shift them?"

"We can shift these all right."

"Why do you look so concerned then?"

"I just hope this isn't the beginning of another of Ritchie's tricks, that's all."

"Come off it, Holly. You haven't heard a word from Ritchie in centuries. Why should it be from him?"

"A bad penny always turns up, you know."

"Absolute rubbish. Have you actually seen this collection?"

"Enough of it."

"What's it worth at today's rates?"

"More than we can afford, without a hefty bank loan."

"I think we can swing that," said David. "I gather we're talking big art, and big money?"

"A hundred thousand pounds, or more."

David shrugged. "So?"

"It doesn't scare you, spending that much?"

"Why should it? I'm a dealer and the son of a dealer, and I used to be a gambler until I saw sense. I can feel the old stirring in the blood again when you trot out sums like that."

"Are you serious?"

"Only slightly. We will go to see this old bird, I take it?"

"Who could resist?" said Holly.

Four days later, optimistically armed with a letter of credit from the Westminster Bank, and bundled up like Latvians against the icy winds, Mr. and Mrs. David Aspinall set out for Paris and an appointed meeting with the Comtesse Dubriel.

In the ten years since Holly had last met the Comtesse Dubriel the woman had grown very old indeed. Her flesh was wrinkled, her movements painfully slow. Only her brown eyes seemed alive. She made her entrance leaning on a stout stick. Involuntarily David and Holly rose as the old woman came into the room and waited, in silence, as she shuffled to a gilded chair by the fire and lowered herself into it.

Spartan though the furnishing of the room was, the fire was large and a huge log box by the grate was piled with cordwood and knobs of coal, expensive luxuries. A sinuous Charpentier reading stand by the side of the chair held English magazines. A neo-classical divan completed the décor.

The Comtesse scooped a tiny velvet footstool from under her chair and planted her feet upon it.

She stumped her stick upon the floor.

"Peta, bring tea now."

The voice was not so much peevish as assertive and determined.

The servant departed, and the old woman turned her alert brown gaze upon the English couple.

"Sit."

David and Holly sat.

In English the Comtesse asked, "Who is this gentleman?"

"My husband."

"He is not your husband. Your husband is old."

"You refer, Comtesse, to my late husband. Kennedy died many years ago."

"Killed?"

"Of natural causes," said Holly. "Mr. David Aspinall and I have been married for almost seven years."

The Comtesse studied David intently.

"What do you do?" she demanded. "Your profession?"

"I'm in the antique furniture business."

"I might have expected it. In the war, what did you do in the war?"

"I served with the Royal Navy."

"How could it be? You are too old."

"I am not as old as I look, Comtesse," said David soberly.

"What age do you have?"

"I am fifty years old."

"I am eighty years old."

"I hope to be eighty years old too some day," said David.

The Comtesse was unable to decide if it was a compliment or a clever piece of English insolence.

She said, "A sailor, eh?"

David did not correct her.

Transferring her attention to Holly, the old woman enquired, "Is your business good?"

"On the whole, yes," said Holly.

"In France it is terrible. There is no money to spare. It has been a struggle these last years."

"I am sorry to hear that, Comtesse."

It had to be the Italian collection, Holly thought. Obviously the old girl had managed to hide her treasures from the Germans, to keep the paintings safe during the occupation. Now she needed to sell all or part of it. Holly thought of the seventeen canvases which had hung in the long gallery, each a masterpiece. Which would be on offer? The Canaletto, the Giotto, the Botticelli, perhaps? Any one of the works appearing on a drab London market would create a stir and help put the name of Aspinall, Beckman & Deems on the map again.

Ambition flared in Holly once more. If the Comtesse was selling the whole collection intact, Holly decided that she would sell them privately out of a special gallery she would have built in the Kings Road property. Chris and Steve would enjoy the excitement of preparing a handsome catalogue, of having American buyers dropping in, of the fuss that would surround the sales. Apart from anything else, it would make them all a very great deal of money.

"I ask a favour of you," said Kati Dubriel.

"I'm sure," said Holly, "we will help you in any way we can."

At that moment the door opened and a boy brought in a wheeled tea-trolley. The Comtesse watched the boy fondly as he steered the trolley across the room and placed it with great care by her chair.

The boy was about twelve years old, handsome, with a clear sallow complexion and jet black hair. He was dressed, Holly noticed, in a neat, hand-cut suit with long trousers, and wore black outdoor shoes. He was well-mannered and careful but, as he manipulated the trolley past the divan, darted a quick apprehensive glance at David and Holly.

Speaking English, the boy said, "Shall I pour tea for you and your friends, Grandmama?"

"No thank you, Alois. I will call for you when you are needed."

The boy kissed his grandmother on the cheek. It was not, Holly reckoned, a duty but a genuine sign of affection. He acknowledged the presence of the visitors with a little bow and left the room without another word. Smiling, the Comtesse watched him go.

"I did not know that you had a grandchild, Comtesse," said Holly.

"As you see:"

Assisted by Holly, tea was dispensed. There was a plate of hard rye biscuits smeared with margarine. The ceremony was all terribly un-French. Holly wondered why the Comtesse had gone to such trouble. Either Kati Dubriel was making a very special effort to be friendly or attitudes had changed here in the Rue de Sebastopol too.

There was no small talk while tea was drunk.

The Comtesse's withered hand trembled as she put down her cup. She fumbled for, found and leaned upon her walking stick.

"Come," she said. "I have something to show you."

She got to her feet and made her way towards a rear door, a door which, if Holly's memory served her correctly, led into the long gallery where the Italian collection had hung in the years before the war.

Holly nodded to David as if to say, "This is it."

"Open the door, if you please."

David obeyed the old woman, and stood to one side to allow her to precede him into the gallery. Holly followed. Holly held her breath. She stepped nervously into the echoing gallery. Gelid reflections of tall windows slotted the parquet flooring. Holly blinked, turned her gaze to the walls. Yes. Caravaggio looked across at Botticelli, Perugino at Raphael.

Holly sighed: the collection was intact.

"I am delighted, Comtesse, that your family paintings did not fall into the hands of the enemy."

Leaning on the stick, the Comtesse said, "I have your brother to thank for that."

"My brother? Do you mean—you can't mean Ritchie?"

"But yes." The Comtesse then proceeded to tell Holly and David exactly what had occurred. In conclusion she pointed with her stick, swaying slightly. "He died there, by the door. I saw it with my own eyes."

"My God." David took Holly's arm. "Are you all right, darling?"

"I'm fine," said Holly, softly. "Comtesse, are you telling me that my brother was shot by the Gestapo."

"He died bravely. He brought the child here, knowing, I think, that he could not hope to escape."

Holly said, "Comtesse, is the child my brother's child?"

"No. Of that, Madame, you can be sure. He is the son of a Jew, a shoemaker, I believe. It is as I told you. There is no mystery."

"But you called him your grandson?"

"I have made him, by French law, my heir by adoption. I have given him a new name, our family's name. In time, when I am gone, Alois will be the head of the house of Dubriel. I have your brother to thank for that. It seemed fitting that you should carry a little part of the responsibility too."

"I—I don't understand what you mean."

"I will explain."

Holly stared at the corner of the gallery, at the spot where the Comtesse claimed Ritchie had died.

It was difficult to accept the fact that she would never see him again, never again be troubled by him. She felt sorrow, yes, but it was overwhelmed by relief.

What Holly had no difficulty in accepting was the truth of the old woman's account. It was typical of Ritchie; not so much the act of self-sacrifice as the gesture of defiance. When cunning ran out, all that would be left for him would be a raw sort of courage. What had driven him to it, though, was something she would probably never discover.

The Comtesse continued. "My paintings were returned, as promised. The one named de Rais brought them back from Switzerland in person. I gather that he had prospered there, war or not. By transfer, as agreed, I returned his share of the loan-fee. But he could not advise me what to do with the lion's share, the portion put up by Beckman, your brother."

"What about Monsieur Lenormant?" asked Holly.

"Lenormant died three years ago. My solicitor sent his share to his widow and children."

"Before you go on, Comtesse, tell me what happened to Hugues de Rais?" Holly had always liked the old rogue, *le Fantôme*. "Where is he?"

"He told me to tell you that he had grown tired of living inside a cuckoo-clock. He told me to tell you that he was going to America, to Los Angeles, to make one last and final fortune."

Holly smiled; that too had the ring of truth to it.

David said, "Such money as Ritchie left should, by rights, go to his wife. He did have a wife, I believe."

"His wife cannot be traced. I have made every effort. Here, in Madrid, in Zurich, in Hamburg and Berlin. She has vanished. If you choose, you may make further enquiries."

"She may not wish to be found," said Holly.

"That had also occurred to me," said Kati Dubriel.

"Ritchie's legacy? How much is involved?" David said.

"Over one hundred and sixty thousand dollars, American."

"*What?*"

"It is correct. I have a statement of credit, with accrued interest, from the Bank of Zurich," said the Comtesse. "The fifty thousand dollar payment which was made to me is gone. I have used it to keep myself and Alois alive. I have sold many things, too, including some paintings, to keep a household for the boy and for myself."

"And now?"

"Now I am too old to have long to live. I wish Alois to be educated in England. You may select a suitable school for him. I know little of these matters and, having no other kin, I am obliged to trust you. I wish you to be his guardians during the period of his adolescence. For this I will pay you, of course."

"But—but, Comtesse, why do you come to us? You don't even like the English."

"Perhaps not. But I admire them, in some ways. Besides, it is as Beckman would have wished it."

"It isn't what Ritchie would have done, believe me."

"It is, then, what he *should* have done."

"Comtesse, you love the little boy. Any fool can see that," said Holly. "How can you bear to give him up?"

"It is for his good. He has been shut away with this foolish old woman for too long. Besides, he must have a good education if he is to return to France in time and re-establish the name of the house of Dubriel, is that not so?"

"Comtesse, I cannot take the responsibility," said Holly.

"Wait," said David. "Tell me, what does the boy feel about being sent abroad, to live with strangers?"

"Alois has known for two years what my plans were. He is a sensible child. He knows that it is for the best. He has been anxious to meet Monsieur Beckman's family."

"Does he recall what happened to his brother and mother, and to Ritchie?" asked David.

"Naturally, he remembers. He will always remember."

"Is Ritchie Beckman a hero to him?" said David.

Holly realised that her husband was thinking of Chris, making a parallel with Chris and Christopher Deems. She felt frightened of the child, of his intrusion into her comfortable world. And yet around her the paintings seemed dim in the wintry light, their richness faded somehow. In time the little boy would inherit them. Perhaps she should take on the mantle that Ritchie had unwittingly left her, make sure that Alois knew what those masterpieces meant and how beautiful they were, how to cherish them for the future. Holly's soft dread melted. She felt proud that this cantankerous old woman saw fit to trust her with things of such high value, not paintings, not money, but a legacy of honour and integrity.

"Yes," the Comtesse answered David's question.

"Well, we won't deny him that," said David.

"Will you take him, guard him?" said the Comtesse Dubriel.

Holly did not answer. She had no need. The man to whom she had denied a son answered for her. "Of course we will," said David Aspinall.

"When do you wish him to come to England?" Holly asked.

The old woman stumped her stick upon the parquet.

The rear door of the long gallery opened and an excited Peta Brichard escorted Alois into the room.

The child was apprehensive but controlled. He had been well prepared for this moment of meeting and parting.

"Alois is ready to go with you now," said Kati Dubriel, "if it is suitable."

"Quite suitable," said David.

He wore the dark blue suit, a woollen overcoat and red scarf, ready for his journey to England, to his new home. Holly marvelled at the boy's calmness, his apparent maturity.

"Alois, this is Mr. and Mrs. Aspinall. They have kindly agreed to look after you, until you go to an English school. It is as we talked about."

"And will I return at holiday time, Grandmama?"

"Of course, my child. Peta will keep your room aired and all your books dusted."

"You will not forget me?"

"Never, never. How could we forget you when we love you so?"

Peta Brichard gave the boy a gentle nudge. He nodded, his faith confirmed, the contract sealed.

He came forward and politely offered Holly his hand.

"My name," he said, "is Alois Beckman Dubriel."

And Holly, breaking and unstinting at last, took the young stranger into her arms.